[JYZEMELT]

Annals of The Jyze Age

Jyzeburst

Jyzemelt

Jyze and Jyze Alone

Jyze in Love

Deep Jyze

The Jyze Millennium

Jyze of the Heavenly Year

Scat Jyze

Jyzemelt

G.P. Sandefjord

Annal Two of The Jyze Age

Cover art by GPS
Published by House of Jyze
ISBN 978-0-9964173-2-7
Library of Congress CIP pending
www.HouseOfJyze.com

Special thanks to Buddy Guy for
the lyrics to "Damn Right, I've
Got the Blues" (1991) quoted in
Chapter 29.

For V.M.C.M.S.

All that is solid melts into jyze.

-- Karl Marx (apologies to)

BOOK I

[Real Jyze]

1

    Which vessel is this? At the outset the usual
struggle for bearings. What's the name of this thing?
Rectify the names! (If only in your own mind.) -- It's
one of the two small foot ferries, this much I can say.
The ones that ply the mile-wide waters between the home
port and the transit port, back and forth all day and
well into the night, each round trip half an hour --
rinky-dink little covered wooden tubs painted black with
white trim, low-riders of the inlet -- a big wave comes
along (wake of a large navy ship or state auto ferry)
and they all but vanish in the trough.
    Idling in place -- or no, now about to cast off and
back out. Skimpy passenger count, a dozen or so. But
before we boarded, an unloading like a trick car at the
circus spewing bedraggled clowns: looked like sixty,
seventy riders, most of them homewardbound shipyard
workers as almost always at this hour.
    Another cruel week. We took two new hits, but more
on those later. (I'm sitting on a wooden bench at the
back of the cabin; stencil-painted in white on the
powder blue of the bench is "10 Adult Life Preservers."
Oddly enough one of my missions tonight is to research a
dubious "miracle" life-preserving cancer treatment, the
kind the tabloids are always hyping -- cynically
arousing desperate flailing last hopes -- but no, things
aren't flying out of control, we all recognize the
quixotic nature of this quest.)
    Putt-putting along now in the middle of the inlet.
Transparent plastic stern tarp lets me observe our wake.
(wake, another death word. They're swarming me these

days.) -- But it's too inky black to see much else
out there except the receding lights strung along the
shore and some scattered twinkling reflections of same
on the water.

At night I usually sit back here so I can read.
This rear portion of the cabin is raised about a foot
above the central part, putting you that much closer to
the wall-mounted lamp. Like all the other lamps on
board, this one's feeble, about twenty watts I'd guess,
and a shaky, flickering twenty, but up close it
suffices. And a few steps forward in the middle of the
cabin the engine pounds away inside its blue coffinlike
(see?) cover, on which feet rest, legs stretched out as
on a big hassock (swing-shifters going in, again mostly
shipyard workers, all dressed alike: jeans, flannel
workshirts, sweatshirts, hooded jackets -- but a wide
variety of well-worn footware: boots, tennies, oxfords,
military hightops, classic clodhoppers).

We've arrived.

*   *

I get my wish. Now aboard the big, fast oceangoing
auto ferry that substitutes on this run while the
regular boats undergo off-season overhauls.

It's rarely a problem claiming a booth on this one.
Up here in the forward cluster they're eight rows across
and six or seven deep. Except for a few low partitional
screens they all offer a panoramic view ahead, as do the
hundred or so deck chairs arrayed in front. And another
passenger deck sits above ours, its cabin not quite as
wide but you can walk outside. Promenade deck that is,
also called canteen deck. The regular ferries on this
run have only one passenger deck.

"Blue-collar boat." This time I counted as the
throng thundered down the ramp right in front of me: of
the seven or eight hundred debarkees from the city,
exactly five wore suits and ties. Scruffy, grim-faced
crowd. The suburban commuter-train bunch of my early
Gatewood days this was not. Nor was it a student group.
Unionized manual laborers for the most part, swing-
shifters at the shipyard, most dressed just like the

ones on the foot ferry (and like me, the nightscoper).

Departure's so smooth on this thing. No roar of massive motors. Suddenly you notice the lights outside appear to be moving, that's all. Only now as we get up to speed (before slowing for the narrows with their twisty passage shaped like a sideways Z) -- only now, I say, do you hear a few creaks and rattles. Also thumps and bumps of kids cavorting overhead.

Seven parallel banks of inset fluorescents above, continuous, running along the aisles between booths, here and there a dead or fluttering bulb, the operating ones ranging in color from frosty white through gray and cream to yellow, like rows of teeth in varying degrees going bad. And in the windows on both sides hang curtains of compacted reflections of these same fluorescents like shimmering Northern Lights, and if you look hard at those windows you can see more such reflections mirrored in the windows on the opposite side of the boat like distant strung-out galaxies and so on in infinite regression, in theory at least, back and forth across the cabin, although of course only the first few stages are visible without some sort of optical help (not that I'm sure that would work either).

-- Did I say took two new hits? Yup. First and worst, reporter Naomi goes and gets herself pregnant (presumably with husband Larry's aid). My last lifeline at the office. If I'm reading her note rightly the kid's due in June and so sometime shortly before then I'll be out of my last vestiges of a job, since Naomi's the only one at the office Jyzer Ink (that's me too!) is doing any work for.

Second and almost as bad, my home computer bites the dust. Apparently a power surge got it, possibly earthquake related -- all power's out at the shed since last week's tremor -- but also human error related, because I'd forgotten to buy a new surge protector for it (we'd shifted the old one over to guarding the microwave last month after several fuses blew in the house). The computer was on its last legs anyway, but still, its loss could hardly have come at a worse time.

[Jyzemelt]

    In clumps and bunches the bad news notoriously (not
to say nefariously) hits. Now all I can do is see
whether I can turn any of it to my and/or our advantage.
    At least I didn't lose any files. Everything was
backed up and all the backup diskettes are good; I've
already tested them on the office machines.
    (Probably Naomi will return to work after six
months or a year, would be my guess, but whether she'd
want me back or circumstances would allow me to go back
is something else again.)
    Hum of the engines. Rattles and creaks. Quiet
voices. A mop falls on the deck somewhere with a sharp
whap. Middle-school kids whomp by -- "No running!"
barks a deckhand in blue uniform and orange fluorescent
vest, and the kids slow to a fast walk until they round
the corner and then with exuberant whoops take off
again. Meanwhile a sleeper snores softly two booths
over, invisible from here except for a bony denim-clad
knee poking up above the backrest and an impressively
scuffed-up ankle-buckled black engineer boot sticking
out a good foot -- a big foot! -- into the aisle.
    -- And Mother. Finally I talked with her again
last night. Her spirits seemed good, but then, as she
pointed out, and I well know anyway, she much prefers to
be upbeat when she talks with me. This is true for her
with everyone but probably more so with me because I
refuse to let her mope around in endless rehashings of
her medical travails. A certain amount of it is fine
and she needs to do it and I need to hear it, but beyond
that it's wasteful and counterproductive for everyone,
not least herself. -- Not that I'm a hard dude about
this. I try to kid her out of it. Gentle little
satirical jolts that throw her monologues out of kilter
if she's gone off on one. So she rarely does it with me
nowadays and as a result we have some very good talks
that are true dialogues and we're both happy about this.
    And her breathing didn't seem any worse than
before, though she says it sometimes is. Two nodules
eating up space in one lung, one in the other. "All the
slow-growing type." The cancer hasn't entered her

bloodstream yet. "These foreign objects growing in me."
(But they're not really that, I'd say; they're intimate
personal objects, one's own flesh that is also one's own
ultimate comeuppance.) At night she sometimes wakes up
with the frights but takes a tab or two of acetaminophen
and she's all right. (Sounds miraculous almost.)

*

   -- On this boat you've got about a hundred-foot
hike to the head. Now I'm back for the stretch run.
   So. Her trip home took three days and two nights
and the car was "packed to the gills" but they made it
without incident. Jim Q. (that's what she usually calls
him, with his middle initial Q. included) -- Jim Q. is
rising to the occasion and it now appears he'll be
seeing things through to the bitter end. For the next
month or so he must be elsewhere tending to family
business but he'll be back -- doubtless conflicting with
sister Barb, though, who also intends to shepherd Mother
all the way to that same end.
   Planning the end-time is what it's mostly about
these days. Mother always was a take-charge, highly
organized kind of person and she appears to be
sublimating a lot of her fears into this role now,
talking about various aspects of what lies ahead with
the same sort of breathless (and I regret the unintended
pun) urgency and even excitement she might have devoted
in the past to a family reunion or a big anniversary
party. "I've always preferred to be in control," she
acknowledged. "Sometimes it's good and sometimes it's
bad, but it's just the way I am. I never liked to get
drunk or to lose my bearings -- you know me."
   The main question now is how to schedule the visits
of the three sons. Because space in her apartment is so
limited and the logistics would be so difficult and
angst-ridden (she couldn't prevent herself), she'd like
to have each of us visit separately rather than all
show up at once. A full reunion would be wonderful,
everyone agrees, and she'd love to be able to host one,
but the strain would be too great. Therefore we'll be
showing up one at a time as our schedules permit -- "I

won't be forgetting for a moment you all must be getting
on with your lives" -- and since at this point I can be
the most flexible, even though I'll be rolling the dice
on unemployment and any remaining contract work through
the office, she'll set things up with Jeff and Rob first
and then see where she can fit me in.

Probably I'll make the journey by train. Have I
mentioned this already? (More forgetful and therefore
more repetitious than ever is what I'll be now, it's
virtually guaranteed.) And one of the errands I'll be
running on the way to the office tonight calls for a
stop at the depot to check out timetables and prices.

-- A slight bump, delicate almost. We're in.

*   *

At the depot about half past eight, the usual
somnolent scene, close to desolate, a dozen folks
hanging about well scattered in the large main waiting
room that seats hundreds. Bulletins taped to the glass
case of the arrivals/departures board announce new
service cutbacks, and with the former congressional out-
party storming the capital -- we're about fifteen days
into the hundred-day period in which they've vowed to
implement their draconian party platform -- far more
severe cutbacks undoubtedly lie just ahead. In the
former-out-party view this national rail passenger
operation is a socialistic outrage, pork-barreling down
the tracks out of control.

As always the board classifies the trains by three
types: local, regional, continental. The continental
I'm here to check on leaves, the board says, at nine-ten
every morning. It'll put me within walking distance of
Mother's place in just under twenty-four hours. By my
reckoning that's an average of about thirty-three miles
an hour. (Can there be any question why intercity
rail's not much use as transportation in this country
anymore? Of course it might do a lot better if the feds
weren't already buckling to the highway lobby and the
freight railroads and starving it of funds.)

-- I did manage to find out something about
hydrazine sulfate, the "miracle cure" Jim Q.'s been

touting to Mother. Just one reputable study's been done
on it in the twenty years it's been on the (black)
market. That study found that when used in conjunction
with chemotherapy it increases life expectancy for
Mother's type of cancer by 99 days, from 209 to 308.
Its effect when used in isolation is not mentioned.

(Here comes my continental now -- same one that'll
be heading out in the opposite direction in the morning.
A guard unlocks Door 3 and cold air sweeps in and all
but flash-freezes me in place twenty feet from the door:
after six weeks of balmy temperatures a nasty cold front
was supposed to be rolling in tonight, and now I can say
it's here. -- And so's the train. Unexpectedly high
and close, the cars gliding in right outside the door,
the horizontal red-white-and-blue stripe squiggling a
bit from car to car with ridged silver side panels
holding steady above and below except for the occasional
blank lower-level window. Squeal of brakes. Sniff of
ozone and diesel smoke. -- And quickly the entering
mob. As with the ferry, it's mostly just folks, but in
general not the kind who look to live around here. But
then also not the kind who look to have much clout
wherever they may live. Luxury private executive jet
service this is not. Which to be sure is one of the
things that's most likable about it.)

Three hundred and eight days. That lays it out
with dramatic specificity. And that's with chemo. Does
she have even half that long without chemo? And how
many days have already gone by? The diagnosis came down
in late December but it was based on x-rays taken in mid
November (as I understand anyway) so the probable end
may be much nearer than any of us had been thinking.

Or it may not. This is all about as iffy as it
gets, at least in the short run. Today or early next
week she'll be seeing her regular doctor, the very one
who missed the diagnosis on the November pictures. (The
radiologist said it was cancer but the doctor overruled
him and said it was arthritis invading the lungs. The
radiologist's opinion wasn't mentioned to Mother until
much later.) Then we may get a better picture of the

way things really are. -- Or may not. And the range of
possibilities is so narrow not much can realistically be
hoped for. -- But you hope anyway. Even more now after
talking so recently with the condemned soul herself who
sounds so full of life -- so normal!

The crowd still waiting for the baggage carousel to
start up. But I'd better move on so I can be at the
office in case anyone tries to reach me at the newly
appointed hour for family calls: nine-thirty p.m.

*   *

Back aboard the splendid substitute ferry and this
time at nine a.m. or a few minutes before, and as usual
I find myself occupying the exact same seat as the
previous night except at the other end of this double-
headed, bisymmetrical craft. It never turns around
(unless it happens to feel like it, I suppose) but the
captain switches from the wheelhouse at one end to the
wheelhouse at the other end, and two or maybe it's three
decks down I do much the same thing with booths.

In the past few days I've come across new essays
written by three of my favorite "public intellectuals."
All of them terrific. And again I have to wonder: why
aren't more people paying attention to these worthies?
Why are so many listening to the right-wing crazies
instead? What the hell is going on? -- Not that this
is a new kind of feeling. But it does seem to keep
intensifying. For decades now it's been doing so.

As for what the hell's going on to cause this
rightward slide, this isn't the time or the place to
start laying out my personal theories, for what they're
worth. Maybe such a time and place will never present
itself. Probably I'm better off, and certainly the
world is no worse off, if I devote my jyzing energies to
things other than politics and social issues. Not
always, of course, but when I can help myself.

You wonder: did the creator of Huck Finn have the
same sort of feeling? The creator of Prince Myshkin?
Such enormous talent and energy those two great
fictionizers possessed to be able to keep plugging away
at politics "on the side" the way they did while also

12

churning out their masterpieces. But would they and/or
the world have been better off if they'd directed more
of that talent and energy into their fiction?

I'm not saying I know. I'm saying I don't know.

Gray, cold, misty morning. Plowing along.

Before leaving the office I wrote what I expect
will be my last Valentine's card ever for Mom. Or maybe
by extreme good fortune there will be occasion for one
more next year, though I don't believe there will be;
I'd just like to. And I hesitate before admitting such
a thing because I hate to come off all smarmy like this.
As I said in my card to her, it can't be helped. Things
start flying out of control and I'm not any happier
about it than she is. -- Although immediately I regret
saying this too, because I don't like retaining too much
control either, and I often do like -- and as a jyzer
find essential -- a kind of semi-guided "loose reins"
loss of control.

Dispense with that unpromising line of thought.
(Sound of a deck of cards rippling a few booths aft
reminds me of how she's always enjoyed playing
solitaire, just as I did as a kid. Later on I talked
myself out of doing stuff like that -- card and board
games in particular, but also gambling of all kinds,
electronic games, pinball -- because I wanted more time
for other things, "serious" things, "more important"
things. -- But best not to wander off on that tangent
either. -- Just a whole lot of foolish tangents are
beckoning these days. Keeping focused is tough.)

(The narrows turn, the big sideways Z again but of
course this time going at it from the opposite end.
Pretty much the same hard right, though, then hard left,
the engines grinding just as mightily as last night --
because in twelve-plus hours the tide, like the boat,
has reversed direction and the current runs so fast and
strong through this perilously narrow passage.)

This weekend Barb's helping Mother go through her
things and decide what to throw out. All weekend.
(Thursday night before her call to me Jim Q. took her
and Barb out for dinner and they had, in Mother's words,

"a gay old time.") Years ago she started figuring out
who would get what, often driving the designated
recipients, myself included to be sure, to distraction
(not to say catatonia) with long lists of questions
about how much this or that would mean to us -- "Would
you rather have the painting of your great-great-great-
grandfather Jonah or your father's rosewood desk?" And
you don't really care much about any of the specified
items except in a general mildly sentimental way, but
you can't say so for fear it would hurt her too much.

    As she told me Thursday night, she doesn't want us
around at the end -- us boys -- because she'd prefer we
not see her "that way." Barb, however, insists on being
there, and this is acceptable to Mother. Probably Rob's
or Jeff's or my presence would be acceptable too if we
pressed her on it, but she's trying to give us an out.
It's like Barb to insist on doing the right thing, the
high ethical thing, no matter what the cost to herself
or others. -- I just know it will be unbearable with
Barb. Makes my head spin to think about it. The hyper-
good and yet also hyper-rebellious sister. Her lifelong
sense of high moral rectitude (however flip-floppy when
looked at year by year). Righteousness over solidarity
and loyalty at all times. The martyr. The fierce
crusader. The indignado. Until the end!

    A hospice will be hired. A registered nurse will
come by every other day. Beyond that I know few details
at this point.

    -- And then there's my own work. This was a
crucial week. I nearly abandoned the whole damn Mentoka
project. I just can't have at it right now, so in a way
I'm fortunate Naomi's pregnancy has come along and given
me an excuse to focus on other things for a while.

    More on all that another time when I have the heart
for it.

    -- And the final turn. Am I facing months and
months of such lugubrosity? -- But strangely enough I'm
also grateful to be able to immerse myself in it, almost
as if it's an unexpected way of returning home one last
time. (Turn, turn. Turn, turn, turn.)

2

     Some jyzercise. Jeez I'd like to be jaunty for a
while. I really really would.
     This is not back where jyze began but right above.
Just for variety's sake the radio's tuned to a new
station. I don't know what it is. Nouveau punk stuff
so far, lots of rundowns on upcoming performances and DJ
yakkety-yak for one o'clock in the morning. It may soon
prove unendurable.
     What news? Long phone talk with Barb, possibly
disastrous. I'll admit I'd sometimes like to wring my
own sister's neck. However, in the end, after thrashing
things out, we agreed to start afresh. But then Mother
didn't call me in the designated period as she'd
promised she would, and now three days later she still
hasn't. I'm afraid Barb's regressed to mean, I'll say,
and gone running to her with a complaint about me, and
Mother's playing along with her on it or maybe even
believing her.
     The hard times ahead. I groan. Can't resist
feeling sorry for myself. In some inexplicable way I
must've deserved an outcome like this.
     (Lady U and I talk it over for a couple of hours
while pacing the kitchen and parlor. Her view of Barb
is even worse than mine -- overlooks most of the good
traits and the rareness of her sensibility (and I know
it must sound like I do that too, but at least I try to
stand up for her a bit with D) -- and she, D, Dani,
Mel, Lady U, can't see any way out either. Or any way
through, I should say. We both agree: I'll just have to
suck it up and do the best I can. In the end that's

all we can come up with.)

And this when Mother's dying. Just as it was with Barb and me when Dad was dying. The unbearable sadness of it. (I should try to be accurate and say not when Dad was dying; when Dad had just died. His death was sudden and wholly unexpected, a very different kind of situation from what we're facing now.)

And a note from the office saying dayscoper Doris's husband Ralph has gone in for heart-bypass surgery and this may mean they'll have more work for Jyzer Ink "if you're still interested." Things look manageable for the moment, they say, but could change quickly.

This should be good news for me (and never mind how terrible for Doris and Ralph -- him I scarcely know) but the timing is very bad. It'll make my trip or trips to see Mother even riskier and far more difficult. If I tell the office Jyzer Ink's not interested in the work I'll have to answer to Employment Security, and I might, in fact probably would, lose my only chance to regain full-time or significant part-time contract scoping at the office or anywhere else.

Oh well. At this point I still don't know when Mother wants me to visit her. Or for that matter if she still wants me to.

-- So far, contrary to expectations, my life's been going on in just about the same way it was before word of the diagnosis came down. But any day now a big change. Just how big I can't tell yet. The old way of life -- mine and D's as well -- may not survive it.

Barb and I talked about Mother's plans to have her ashes strewn in the ocean. A certain national funeral-home chain which specializes in this sort of thing would handle the arrangements. We'd all ride out in a boat they provide, complete with individual life-preserver vests and personalized mementos of the voyage. Sounds pretty tacky to me, but then what do I know? Barb thinks Mother would prefer to be buried in Kaskieki if her kids weren't all living so far from there. Barb "would like to have her nearby." So maybe we should strew the ashes in a place of natural beauty as we did with Dad's?

Maybe a certain secluded countryside grove Barb knows
about within easy driving distance for her (though she
doesn't drive)? Maybe an isolated corner of a park
within walking distance of her apartment? (I didn't
think to ask if Turtle Rapids would be a possibility,
the same "bucolic Mentoka hillside" at Buena Vista with
Dad. I guess not; for everyone but Jeff it's almost as
distant as Kaskieki. But I'd vote for it myself.)
     -- One way life hasn't been going on as before is
the Mentoka project. "Jyzer" is back on the shelf. Or
maybe in the ditch. Meanwhile I'm focusing on other
stuff I'd like to revise and reprint during the
downtime, and it's not hard work; it's relatively rote,
just time-consuming, which may be exactly what I need
right now and in any case it seems to be all I'm capable
of. Also I'm about to start putting together a booklet
of protojyze excerpts and a somewhat expurgated full-
length version of "Jyzeburst" to take down when I see
Mother, in lieu of any presentable Mentoka-trilogy
material.
     (The radio station, it bills itself as a rock venue
and it's coming out of a local community college;
alternative or indie rock I guess it is. "Indie rock
for an indie contractor!" All pretty dull and/or
annoying stuff so far. But it's harder to hear now that
the heater's switched back on and so I'm no longer
feeling as cranky about it.)
     Lady U on codeine the past four days with severe
migraines. Her parents will be arriving in five weeks
for another visit, this one also, like the one last
August, penciled in for just under a full month. Papa
U's got a whole new list of upgrades he wants to make on
the place before putting it on the market. The stress
caused by learning of this visit, on top of everything
else, brought on the migraines, D thinks. Sounds
plausible to me. It's certainly happened before.
     Black windows. Just for the jolt of it I'm jyzing
here. Everything's stacked so high and so hopefully.
The gang of miniature ceramic otters. The flock of
colorful wooden hummingbirds with movable white

whirligig wings. The lineup of black-and-silver J-
sticks, with old No. 3 standing proudly upright on its
makeshift pedestal at the center of the memorabilia
shelf. The rows and rows of reference books off to the
side. -- And rain tapping all this time. (Earlier ten
inches of snow, for three days the usual colossal
traffic snarls and unending emergencies. Luckily I
wasn't trapped in the city or caught en route.)

What am I doing otherwise? Reading the Mentoka
newspapers that arrive by mail and no others. Eating
mostly standing up in the kitchen. Napping on the couch
here in the study from half past two until half past
four a.m., an odd assortment of towels and jackets and a
single thin blanket pulled over me (head above chin
excepted). Nerfing in the utility room at least thirty
minutes a day. Traipsing up to the shed with a
flashlight at all hours when I need to fetch something
because the power remains out up there and will stay out
at least until Papa U's visit. Reading several books
I've been wanting to get to for years, and going at them
more or less simultaneously: one before naps, one after
breakfast, one on the throne (but of course) -- and with
ever-more-towering stacks of must-reads waiting to move
up into those three coveted slots.

And (more daily regimen!) waking up at three-fifty
p.m. so as to be ready to take calls from the office
from four to five. Again hanging around the phone from
nine-twenty to nine-forty p.m. for family calls.
Camping out in the library/guest room ("where jyze burst
into being") from five-thirty to two a.m., the writing-
related work. Eating breakfast and working through the
bottomless stack of magazines and quarterlies from four
to five-thirty p.m. Again camping out in the library
from four-thirty to eight-thirty a.m., more writing-
related time. Eating dinner and tending to chores and
business from eight-thirty to ten a.m., and again
chipping away at the mag/quarterly stack during that
period if time's available.

-- Where's the excitement? The adventure? The
wild love? -- Hey, they're all in there!

[Real Jyze]

     The red desk lamp with the telescoping elbowed arm
and the iron-heavy black circular base, it's right here,
shedding light. Spread beneath this J-book as
cushioning is the big softcover atlas/gazetteer for the
Mentoka zone with the detailed county maps which I've
spent so many hours studying (and in which like a
schoolboy I marked each day's progress and side trips
during the Mentoka research visit almost a year and a
half ago now). And here's the self-inking rubber stamp
that says "NOTE:" with a horizontal arrow following the
colon and pointing to the right when it's stamped, all
in bright red: what's this doing here? (I used to
employ it to mark the relevant parts of clipped articles
but haven't done too much of that lately.)
     A colossal mess this room is in. I suppose I'll
have to tidy it up some before the U's arrive, this and
a few other rooms, closets, hallways, sheds, storage
areas, and more. -- But certainly none of that right
now. Right now it's time to burrow under the towels and
jackets and one thin blanket for some serious (though
nowhere near extended enough) shut-eye.

                         3

     Hundreds of bicyclists down there. They're filling
up most of the parking area and also a full block of the
strip across the street. They've even hired their own
large auto ferry, coming in now, on which no other
vehicles or passengers will be allowed -- "Entrants in
the X Only," as the sign says, where X is the name of a
bicycle tour in which the words "hilly" and "chilly"
feature prominently.
     Just heard an attendant asking the captain of the

incoming boat over the radio, "You want all these folks to walk their bicycles on or does it matter?"

And the captain: "Walk them on most definitely!"

"Roger!"

Guess this is just about the first sign of spring. And it's coming on a gorgeous Sunday morning not likely to be chilly at all by the time the riders get over to the hills. (All that fancy gear. Very colorful Lycra. A good number of tandem bikes. Kids lashed into little two-wheel trailers. Couples. Gays and lesbians, all races and creeds, scarcely anyone who's obese and this makes it a truly unusual scene for these porky times.)

Our boat's not even in sight yet. Maybe I didn't cut it as fine as I thought in making my dash from the office. Could've scoped another five or ten pages.

As expected this has turned out to be a tough week with dayscoper Doris out on personal leave. I've come in four nights in a row and after taking tonight off I'll be coming in at least two more. Scoped over seven hundred pages on which I'll net seventy cents a page, but of course the state will get most of it (three-quarters) under the current Employment Security formula. Nonetheless this is my first taste of what life might be like were Jyzer Ink to pick up fairly regular contract work at the office. And I like it. I put in only about five hours a night and clear well over twenty dollars an hour and during the off-hours can tend to my own stuff, sometimes using the office computers and printers if necessary. But of course it's unlikely weeks like this will ever be the norm. This may be as good as it gets in the Jyzer Ink era. And after reporter Naomi goes on leave to give birth I may have no scoping work at all. (More than six hundred of this week's pages were hers.)

-- And I'm jyzing now rather than at home tonight because I'll be needing every minute there for revising the story of another birth of sorts -- of jyze. Still a long way to go on the extra-expurgated version of the already expurgated version I gave Lady U for Christmas, but with some of those earlier expurgations restored for ol' Mom's delectation (and some not).

[Real Jyze]

     Probably I'll also try to call her tonight --
brother Jeff's visiting her this week and her birthday's
coming up and by the time I get to the office Tuesday
night (when they'll be celebrating it) it'll be too late
to call and catch Jeff because he'll already have gone
off to bed at Barb's, most likely. As a homebuilder (or
freelance carpenter may be a more accurate term for him
now) he can't handle the late hours, and especially not
my own Nightscoper Upside-down Time (NUT) version.
     Mother finally did call on Monday, five days late.
She said she tried to get me Wednesday night but not too
strenuously because she doesn't like to disturb me when
I'm working -- so the three and a half rings I heard,
that was her. I still think my earlier talk with Barb
had something to do with the delay, but she, Mother,
didn't bring it up and so it doesn't really matter -- if
Barb did complain to her, they evidently decided, or
Mother did by herself, that it would be wiser to keep
quiet about it. And if that's what happened -- either
one of those -- I think the decision was a good one.
     Mother still seems her normal self on the phone.
Once in a while she drifts off into a strained self-
pitying tone (and who can blame her?) but for the most
part she's cheerful and focused and all wrapped up in an
enthusiastic way (her way!) in orchestrating her own
end-of-days scenario. Sometimes she sounds a little (or
a lot) frenzied and self-involved but again this is far
preferable to the other ways you might expect her or
anyone to be under the circumstances. And despite the
occasional grim moments I find these calls quite
enjoyable. On both sides the incentive is strong to
avoid the kind of petty squabbles we've fallen into at
times in the past (fairly frequent times -- though only
rarely, and mostly in earlier years, did those escalate
into anything of urgent concern).
     -- A moment ago it was announced our boat will be
running twenty to thirty minutes late. We're eleven
minutes past departure time right now. Forty or fifty
people in here, mostly navy sailors returning from
overnight leave, many sprawled out on benches catching

up on their zees. -- And I see it out there. Way out.
But I wolfed down my dinner at the office instead of
waiting to eat on the boat as I usually do and for the
first time in months I drove to the home port last night
and parked up by the courthouse, so the late departure
should have no adverse effects on me; I don't have to
worry about missing a bus. (Even less am I hungry,
because Naomi kindly left me a four-inch square of
freshly baked brownies, foil wrapped, still warm,
resting atop the corrected grand-jury rough draft
inside the safe when I first arrived at the office.)

     Mother's dropped the nautical funeral plan and now
wants her ashes to be scattered in the iconic hilltop
park with the renowned view near her apartment. It
would be illegal and we'd probably have to do it under
cover of darkness but I still think it's a good idea.
These past seventeen years of living in that area have
meant a lot to her. And she'd "be right there for
Barbara," whereas the rural grove or another potential
spot we all like up in the mountains would be almost as
inaccessible for Barb as Kaskieki or Turtle Rapids.
     -- But it's time.

*

     On. Happily it's still the replacement boat and
I've got a good booth, though it's not my preferred one.
The regular boat will be back on March 1.
     I learned something new about this vessel. When it
first came into service twenty-eight years ago (along
with three sister ships) it was the largest double-ended
ferry in the world (it's longer than a football field,
both end zones included). In a coastal indigenous
language its name means "swift" or "fleet."
     -- Now a toot on its foghorn (as the boat tied up
a few yards to the north in Slip 2 is still loading
those bicycles) and here we go. (Bicyclists waving
through their windows -- most wearing helmets and pin-on
numbers -- but not too many of us over here on the
"blue-collar boat" wave back.) (Do I? No. A nod only,
but a kind of skeptical smiling nod. Straddle the
differences if you can.)

-- She talked at length about the old church graveyard in Kaskieki where her parents are buried. Yes, she'd like to "be there with Mother and Daddy, but I'm afraid there just isn't room." As for Turtle Rapids, perish the thought -- "There's no place I've ever felt less wanted and more uncomfortable!" Much more emphatically than in the past she's also saying Dad wouldn't have wanted his ashes scattered there either. "Gatewood was his home. That's where he wanted to be. But you kids had your own ideas." I bridle a little at this because I was the one pushing hardest for Turtle Rapids and at the time everyone seemed to think it was a good idea, Mother included. And I haven't changed my mind about that. But last week a long pause preceded Barb's reply when I asked if she thought it had been the right choice -- and then she said, well, she guessed so in light of subsequent developments, meaning the heightened interest Rob and I have taken in the area and its history, including family history -- but the clear implication was she herself felt otherwise. So my guess is she and Mother, on this as on many other matters, have gradually nudged each other out of their widely differing views of twenty years ago (and even more so earlier) and converged on common ground, something they could agree on as opposed to "the boys' view," Barb no doubt being the main instigator and Mother mostly going along to get along. -- Which again, even though I don't much like the result in this case, is fine, acceptable to me, if it leads to something meaningful for them and not to greater friction with everyone else. And so far, at least, it seems to be working out all right.

It appears Barb will be moving into Mother's apartment when Mother's gone. The rent's a steal at $450 a month. Most of the furniture will also go to Barb, as it should, and Mother speaks hopefully of Barb's relationship with Keith -- they're thinking of living (eventually) in a house he'll build himself somewhere out in the suburbs. Everyone's worried about Barb being left alone in the world with Mother gone (Mother quoted Jeff on this) and I suspect Barb's trying

to ease Mother's concern by playing up the chances of
her getting serious with Keith. But I hope I'm wrong.
He sounds like a pretty good guy -- kept a travel
journal in Portugal after Barb's early departure (when
Mother's diagnosis came down) so she could read it upon
his return (a week after hers). He's an editor at the
same medical academy where she does clerical work and is
trying to steer her into editing by way of proofreading.
Mother talked of Barb becoming a critic and/or editor
like the chichi wife of a certain assassinated USAn
president but that sounded pretty dubious to me. She
also mentioned in passing that Barb's been working on a
"writing project" for years. This too is news to me.
What could it be? She hits the cafe circuit on weekend
mornings and tries to have at it. But recently she
confessed she's been encountering writer's block.
-- Hey, I can relate to that!
     -- Rounding the bend. Or the bends rather, the
same pair, the right and the left, a-one and a-two.
Jyze wends the bends in polk-polka time....
     And this: at last I saw the whole raccoon family
whose antics D's been telling me about. Three of the
portly little masked thieves out there looking like the
"Goldilocks" characters in miniature -- Papa, Mama,
Baby (or better, Junior; almost as big as Mama) --
right outside the parlor window, actually inside the
carport, snacking on cat food and virtuously washing
their paws afterwards in the cat water, even in the
absence of a sign saying they must. Not at all spooked
by the sight of a giant Goldilocks in male drag in the
window going wide-eyed at the sight of them: the jyzer.
     My visit with Mother, by the way, is now
tentatively set to begin the 18th of March and to last a
week. It'll be dicey leaving the area even for such a
short period. The crunch at the office should be over
by then, but Employment Security will surely stir up
another crisis for me by that time if not before.
     -- Last turn. How'd I do? Squeezed out a little
over eight quick ones. Jyze is all. Or jyze is all I
could do today anyway. Or no, call it subjyze. But it

ain't just nuttin'. (And there goes my foot ferry.
Means I'll have another wait here, half an hour this
time, so jyze will likely be back after all.)
*

     And is. Goddamn uncomfortable thin-slat hard-edge
wooden benches of the transit terminal. At one time a
few years ago I had to sit on them for twenty minutes
twice a day, and sometimes longer, and once in a while
(usually on an exceptionally foggy day) lots longer.
Got bruises on my flanks. Finally figured out a better
way, a different set of ferries I could ride and
significantly pare back the waiting time.
     Low ceiling. Ferry posters. Not too many nasties
around, but then it is Sunday morning. That funny
janitor with the high-pitched whiny voice, Elijah, he's
still working here, I know. Old Paul retired a few
months back. Fine fellow -- greeted most of the
regulars by name, and there must've been several
thousand of us (still are -- just I'm no longer one
myself). None of the other ferry personnel I know of do
anything remotely like it.
     Directly to the left, visible between two of the
saloons, rises the gray superstructure of the chief
local tourist attraction, flags and pennants flapping, a
kind of floating Fort Sumter for our times. "Commies
attacked it and that's how the Vietnam War started!" --
except the attack story is a total fraud. And yet they,
story and warship both, somehow still manage to stay
afloat.
     Over to the right a black squad car noses around
sullenly just inside the high fence of the naval
shipyard. -- And there goes the boat I was on,
returning to the city. Swiftly and fleetly zips along
almost yachtlike, so sprightly for its size and basic
ferryboat nature. As gulls wheel overhead, eager to see
what kind of breakfast those big ferry screws are
chopping up for them today. And right here just outside
the window a gull perches on one leg on the top rail of
the fence, an archetypal sight for the whole region,
irresistible to Sunday painters and photographers not to

mention hungry bald eagles. And now a jyzer.
     -- The gull's-eye view of the world. While
waiting for ferries I've put in lots of hours
(cumulatively) pondering that view and trying to stare
it down when it was aimed at me (it's red-eyed; and
that's probably just what it notes about me, especially
when I'm on the way home after a long night at the
screens) -- and also watching the gulls tangling with
each other and with pigeons for crumbs, some tossed by
me (though you really shouldn't do that, folks; there
are even signs saying so).
     Over here on this side of the drink we've got low
gray clouds with a few scattered and ever-shifting
patches of blue, like jigsaw pieces auditioning for
roles in upcoming celestial puzzles. The changing light
(though far from Sandover) makes for tremulous silver
glints on the water.
     -- Writing exercises. Jyzercise! For the first
lifetime it's all practice.
     Don't want to miss this foot ferry too so I'll
mosey on out.

*

     And aboard. Why not one more quick one. Until the
ink runs dry. -- Again atop "10 Adult Life Preservers."
     Hurried past the six concrete picnic tables, the
four working fishermen (saw a guy haul in a big toxic
silver flopper there just last night), down the long
floating ramp, sailboats and yachts and commercial
fishing boats bobbing on one side, though just a few of
each scattered among the many empty slips, and my ferry
already in on the other side, also bobbing on caroms of
its own bow waves and wake, the pilot out accepting
fares. "The muttonchop sideburn guy" as I thought of
him for the first couple of years until I overheard his
name: "Rolf," as I thought. (As we pull out now by the
great circle route since no auto ferry blocks the way.)
-- Ever since then Ralf (as I've recently learned he
spells it) has called me "Cousin" because I told him I
have a cousin who goes by the same name as his, Rolf, as
I thought. This Ralf here is probably in his sixties,

an old salt quick with a quip. He's been at the helm of
these wooden boats off and on for decades and swears he
can pilot the cross-inlet route blindfolded and often
does so just for fun, "especially if I know you're back
there." Always wears hickory-stripe work shirts and
black denim pants, sometimes with snazzy red suspenders.
     The wake behind, I can almost dip my hand in it.
It suddenly stirred up bottom-dwelling memories of the
island at Loon Lake during my teen years, the motorboat
rides out and back -- a nice little Marcelian burst.
     Long row of docked navy ships, many mothballed,
taking on collective definition as we get farther out.
Behind them, jagged snowcapped peaks today wreathed in
gray clouds. A pelican flapping along. Just four
people aboard the foot ferry this run, and one's a
traffic counter for the county transit system, of which
these foot ferries are now a part. (Noticed a stack of
sections from local papers and went over to check them
out but none were the right one, the want ads.)
     Ralf cuts the engine. Gliding in.

4

     Jyze central. The real place. Where it's
happening. As no place else.
     What to say now? After a long sleepless afternoon
in bed (or the first half sleepless anyway) I'm thinking
I just want to keep pushing it. Break into the zone and
ride, Daddy, ride; hie that dy-no-saur. Because, as it
turns out, nothing else works. Not the way I'd like.
Not right now. This jyze is it, the one thing.
     -- Meanwhile Mother's still dying, or so I have to
assume, and next week's my time for paying final

respects. (Of course I'll be paying more final, and more-final as well, respects later on, but these coming up are likely the only ones for which she'll be healthy enough to register them fully.) I've made my train reservation for a week from tomorrow.

The birthday call didn't go very well. Jeff, Barb, and Keith were there and they'd all been out for dinner somewhere and Mother was still in her hyped-up partying mode. I talked briefly with Jeff and he said he thought she didn't have much time left. I didn't ask why he thought this; I knew she was hovering nearby and figured it would've been too awkward for him to answer. I also said I hoped we'd all be making an effort to keep in touch when she's gone, and I must say his reply put me off a bit: something about, well, he's not good at communications, his tone shading toward the cavalier, or so it seemed to me.

I'd been holding out some hope for Jeff. Now it begins to appear not much will be left in the way of family ties. Rob and I will likely remain close, having a great deal in common and living only an hour's drive apart as we do, but if I want things to hang together with the others I'll probably have to be the one to make it happen. Even assuming I'm capable of playing that kind of role -- and I'm not at all sure I am -- do I want to do it? I'm not so sure about that either. It's something I'll be mulling during the grim months ahead.

-- And it's been a hellacious couple of weeks at work. Last week I went in six days straight and cranked out over eight hundred pages, with many at a high degree of difficulty. Hopefully the crunch will be easing later this week with dayscoper Doris scheduled to return from leave (though it's not yet certain she'll be doing so). I've also had to juggle the books to keep Employment Security from cutting me loose simply because Jyzer Ink is suddenly raking in the dough. By spreading the two weeks' contract-work windfall over a full month (during the first week of which Jyzer Ink earned nothing and for the last week of which I'll be with Mother) I'll fall just short of the cutoff, at least as I understand

the way it operates. The risk is that ES will try to
contact me while I'm out of town, but then there's no
requirement that I be in town while looking for a new
job (in theory, that is, I could just as easily be
making my "inquiries" in person down there).

*

That was the couch and this is the "Mowjo Queen"
director's chair. Upstairs I grabbed a few scoops of
stuffing from the pan on the stove and a few spoonfuls
of cranberry sauce from the dish in the fridge. Roast
chicken's all gone and so's just about everything else.
Stuffing without the fixings is it, plus cranberry
sauce, yes. Yet an undeniable taste treat.

Vinnie the near-feral black cat snoozes on his
white pillow in the next room. The pillow rests on the
loveseat where I would normally hunker down if I were
watching TV, which I almost never do. These days if I
go in that room and D's in there, Vinnie's likely to be
curled up on her lap. "Woman and cat." Between the
two of us (woman and jyzer) we've just about
domesticated old tough-guy Vinnie.

And here on the jazz station we've got a new
weeknight lineup, the DJs for the graveyard and late
swing shifts having swapped gigs. I'm still trying to
adjust to the reversed cues and rhythms.

A big mess in this room, the great bulk of it
consisting of my binders and assorted research
materials. I'm seated at my little table in the middle
of the room with mounds of this stuff entirely
surrounding me on the floor, except for a narrow access
pathway.

-- And ten straight days of bad migraines for D.
Not even the codeine which she saves for the worst
episodes has helped much. If it continues like this for
a few more days it'll be her most debilitating spate
since we moved over here.

So sure, we both have plenty to worry about. She
still has no job and may not be able to take one at all
if her health is worsening again, and I'll still be
losing what remains of my own job come the end of May or

29

so. -- But right now none of this is what I'm
personally worrying about most. Rather it's the Mentoka
momentum. Can't bear to lose that. Also fear losing
command of the research material. Desperately don't
want all that work to go for naught.

But I know I won't get very far on any of this as
long as Mother's plight is hanging over us. Mostly I'll
just be mulling and brooding.

-- Tonight I'm fried. Brain-fried. Tomorrow it's
back to the office, a long spell of punching in
corrections; then in the morning, after the government
offices open, I'll launch a hunt for tax information.
Taxes, that's another big headache (sorry, Lady U).
I'll be owing a bundle. Hopefully I've got it covered,
the quarterly filing as well as the annual, both due
April 15. But now that I'm technically self-employed
the annual will be much more complex than I'm used to.
Each of the filings will be the first of its kind in
which Jyzer Ink has figured; as of today I have no
solid idea what this will entail.

Squirming. Maybe those cranberries ain't settin'
so good. And this chair never was very comfortable.
-- Oh, I was starting to say this room must be spic and
span before I leave town because the U's will be staying
here during their visit. Nor is it a surprise that
they'll be doing so: this after all was the very purpose
for which they had the basement remodeled (along with
fixer-upper value enhancement, of course). -- And it
appears the chair is gouging a hole in the rug. I just
noticed this right now. The expensive new rug Papa U
installed himself just last August!

Oh well. -- And I'm cutting this entry short to
save space for travel jyze. When next I appear I'll be
aboard the death train carrying me back to ole G.A.-
Georgie-Georgianna-Mom. "G.A. on My Mind." Maybe call
the scratchings for the visit, if they turn out to be
worthy, "A Jyze Tribute to Mom."

[Real Jyze]

5

    Well no, not a train. Instead it's the oldest of
the wooden foot ferries, the Dad's-birth-year boat, the
small upper-deck passenger cabin. Brown wooden benches
built into the side walls here, rectangular portholes
looking out in all directions except straight ahead
where the pilot's cabin stands, so about 320 degrees.
It's shortly before sunset; late rays are flashing off
the windows of the state ferry halfway across the inlet
as it makes its wide turn into the dock. In a few
minutes a mad dash -- by me -- to catch it.
    Won't be a train ride this time. Not on the way
there. A series of vicious storms has washed out the
tracks in numerous places and all passenger service has
been canceled until Thursday at the earliest. We
learned this only a few hours ago just as I was putting
what I thought were the finishing touches on my
preparations for the trip. And therefore I'm not
carrying a suitcase now as otherwise I would've been.
    The new plan? Fly out Thursday morning. On such
short notice the only flight I could get will take me
into a regional airport -- should be interesting. (This
airport's reputation is so bad they dangle a fifty-
dollar discount for choosing it even when no flights are
available into the international airport. And it's
closer to the city than the international is!)
    -- Now we hit the shore ricochets of the big
ferry's waves -- we're almost in.
                            *
    Aboard. It's one of the regular vessels, yup, and
seemingly unchanged by its three-week overhaul. The

31

replacement ferry is now subbing for the other regular
boat on this run.

   And the same booth I always go for. At this hour
it's usually free, except for the days when a certain
other guy who favors it, a shipyard worker who's about
six-five and three hundred pounds of sheer ornery, works
late or for some other reason misses the five-twenty
sailing. He likes to hit the passenger ramp early and
grab first place in line no matter how bad the weather
(the ramp is partially open to the elements) so he'll
always beat any competitor, including me, to this booth.
If someone does edge him out somehow, he's been known to
plop massively down on the booth bench opposite and
glare until the interloper gets the message and leaves.
(But he's never tried that with me. Because if I see
him coming I immediately give way under the regulars'
seniority rule; that is, he's been claiming this booth
longer than I have.)

   -- Although I won't be taking much down with me (a
single small suitcase plus my rucksack and shoulderbag)
packing was still a chore owing to the washings and
dryings and previsit cleanups (for the U's) that were an
integral part of it. With a few hours of last-minute
proofing of "Burst" and the protojyze excerpts mixed in,
the chore as a whole took me two full days. (And now
I'll be able to print up clean copies of both offerings,
I'll call 'em, since I won't be so rushed at the office.
Around 225 pages in all, roughly 100K words.) ---
                         *

(Old buddy Tom T. suddenly showed up right there.
Catchup time. Jyze had to give way. -- And the word is
he may soon be transferred to the new company
headquarters fifteen hundred miles southeast in cowboy
country. The only guy I can really talk with on the
boats, or off the boats for that matter. Which means
I'll miss him even more than I already do, since he's
been working swing for most of the past year and we
rarely run into each other.)
             *   *

   The good old federal cafeteria now, second floor of

the highrise federal building (named after our premier
local warhawk of the past half century). I got here
just as the place opened at half past six a.m. and
grabbed a window seat overlooking the street
intersection (with its entrance on the far side to the
footbridge leading to the ferry terminal) but I have to
sit with my back to the lively scene out there so I can
keep an eye on the clock in here (which because of the
way the overhead lights reflect off its glass face I
have to stand up to read anyway, it turns out).
     (Pause to peel a federal banana.)
     So later last night I called Mother to inform her
of the change in plans (calling collect on the office
phone) (collect is the only option now that I'm not an
employee and of course continue to lack a charge card --
in fact I've never had one).
     She was not in good shape. She and Barb had gone
to see an oncologist in the afternoon and most of the
news he had for them was very bad. He had examined the
x-rays from November and agreed they show no sign of
cancer, supporting the interpretation of her regular
physician. But the reason the signs are so prominent in
the December series is that, contrary to what her winter
doctor told her, the cancer is a fast-growing, virulent
type.
     (Life goes on if it can. With my left hand I'm
spooning applesauce from a plastic container as I jyze
away with my right about this truly dire matter.)
     How far gone is she? No specifics on this, but far
enough, the doc said, that the hospice could be called
in right now. And the cancer's entered her bloodstream.
     She could die in a variety of ways; it mostly
depends on which crucial organ the metastasizing cells
happen to attack first. Or I suppose she could
suffocate since the disease is already well advanced in
her lungs. -- But for some reason she doesn't think
this is likely.
     The doc also held out a sprig of hope.
Chemotherapy these days isn't nearly so bad as it used
to be because now a battery of drugs exists to

counteract the malign side effects. She might as well
give chemo a try, he advised, because they'll know after
a single session (not three as the winter doc said)
whether it will shrink the main tumors in her lungs. If
it does she'll have an extra six months to a year.

     Not surprisingly to me (but quite so to Barb),
Mother's reversed herself on the chemo, at least to the
extent of being willing to try it. She'll go in for the
first treatment Friday and I'll be the one who takes
her. Barb's a total wreck at this point and by the
usual kind of nasty coincidence she's also being hit
with lots of work at the academy and suffering from a
virus (as Mother is too). And I'll probably be sleeping
at her place, Mother's, rather than at Barb's. I didn't
ask why but I can guess.

     (-- Damn it's hard to read that clock! why so
much glare? Gonna hafta move, get a better angle on it.)

                              *

     (Just 7:11. I'd thought it might be 7:21.)
     She broke down a little telling me all this.
"You'll have to give me a moment now to compose myself
so I can get back to a cheery phone voice -- you caught
me unexpectedly, you know."
     We did talk last Wednesday for more than two hours.
That was grim at times because, among other reasons, she
was on my case to treat my sister better. Just as I
feared, Barb had gone to her after our earlier phone
call and painted me as the villain for "starting" the
fight we got into that night (and this after she'd
promised a fresh start herself during that same call!).
And so I must ask myself: has anything at all changed
between me and Barb since we were grade-schoolers? But
to hell with it -- insofar as that's possible -- or
then again hell might not want to put up with it either.
     (Time to deliver the tray with all the trash to the
conveyor belt on the far side of the room and pack up my
lunchbox, saddle up my various bags. with any luck at
all I'll arrive at the terminal in time for a quick
restroom stop before the gate opens for the seven-forty.
If unlucky I'll have to swim upstream against the

debarking day-worker throngs on the narrow footbridge.)

*   *

    -- And I was lucky, by a whisker, meeting the first outrunners of the swarm from my boat just as I stepped off the footbridge. I skipped the restroom stop and hit the gate seconds after Lenny shoved it open and by the law of momentum I was the first one aboard by several steps, just the way I like it. -- And took a whiz here instead, and we're still loading now -- well no, here we go. A deep blast on the horn and the rumble-roar of the engines, and it's loud because the door just around the corner is still open as a long line of vehicle occupants files up from below.

    Out with plastic snackpack and cola of the caffeine-free type so I can sleep when I get home (ha).

    -- There is one other bit of news, and this is (gasp!) positive. For it to be properly appreciated I should mention that during the call last Wednesday I learned Jim Q. had purportedly suffered a heart attack the night before as he drove back to rejoin Mother (though not to resume living with her; she wouldn't have any more of that, given the nasty temperament his new medication, or lack of it or faulty administration of it, causes) (Wednesday she finally explained all this to me and in excruciating detail).

    The purported heart attack hit, Mother told me, as he was driving on the freeway only a few miles short of the city. Somehow he managed to stay in control of the car and to get off at the next exit and pull up at a motel where an ambulance was called and thus his life was saved. It wasn't a mild purported heart attack either; it was major, and Mother knew this because the doctor himself told her so on the phone when she tracked him down at the hospital.

    -- Except it wasn't. It wasn't even a heart attack. It was just a "stress swoon" of sorts. But Jim Q. didn't find this out until the tests came back yesterday. So this means the card I sent him joking morbidly (as he likes) about "wisdom of the heart" and "you gotta have heart" -- this was back when I thought

it really was a heart attack -- is now a dead letter as
it were and I'll be seeing him in a few days after all
and he'll probably be his same old genial good-guy self
as always, that is, hearty as ever (with me anyway).

    -- And Mother's already lost so much weight her
pants are sagging on the floor, and even under current
circumstances she was crowing about this: about having
"slimmed down" (not that she was ever much over 130
pounds that I know of). And she was disappointed to
hear I don't own a suit or "slacks and a sports jacket"
(I'd almost forgotten the phrase existed) I can wear to
a fancy restaurant. She's determined we're going to eat
out somewhere -- says they've planned a big surprise for
me -- almost gave it away!

    -- And as it happens reporter Verna is sick this
week and Naomi's taking her two days of grand jury and
wants me to scope them. Thanks to the flood-caused
delay in my departure I'll be able to stop off at the
office again tonight to do one of those GJ days before
shuttling out to the airport from downtown for the
morning flight. The other GJ day I'll have to leave for
Doris to scope. Yeek. Maybe she'll put in extra time
on it and do a great job and Naomi won't see my work as
being special anymore. Oh well. (I'm just thinking of
the long run; I'm still hoping if Naomi decides to
return to the reporting wars next year she'll call on
me. And even if I have another job by then, I'll answer
any call from Naomi for sure. The chances are minuscule
that the other job -- any other job -- would be even
half as good for my purposes as this nightscoper gig.)

    -- And when I get back home this morning I'll find
all in readiness for my departure -- as with a hold in a
space-voyage countdown to blastoff, say -- but then I'll
have to take another pretravel shower and deal with a
couple of new bills that arrived yesterday (including
the near-calamitous biggest electric bill of the year)
and come up with some different clothes to wear, maybe
even wash and dry them -- and all that. And all that!
And more! Because that's how it is!

    -- Next setting for jyze I expect to be just short

of eight hundred miles due south of here and I'm afraid
things at that point will be pretty grim -- but this
jyze vessel is a dread-not, didn't I say?

6

      Jyzin' at the alley. That's the alley of the
clowns where many a riff I've protojyzed before. Tucked
in at the base of a grove of celebrated skybusters and
facing northwest where a necklace of orange suns once
slowly unstrung itself down to the horizon -- the
hilltop horizon, that is, meaning way up there -- and by
the time it finished doing so the era of Lady S and Lady
V had itself come irreparably undone -- if I can just
pull myself together here.
      The in-person deathwatch is four days on and
counting. But the old lady is still spunky and full of
life, charging around like a maniac -- don't tell her I
said that! -- but schmoozing with full emotional
intensity coast-to-coast on the phone with friend after
friend, relative after relative, for hours every day,
arguing, pushing, cajoling, flattering, sputtering --
working just as hard as she can to get ready for what
everyone knows will soon be coming down.
      But maybe not so soon as we'd all been thinking.
She took the chemo well, "sailed right through it," not
a trace of side effect (she insists, and I sure haven't
seen any) -- but it'll be three weeks before we know the
results that count, that is, does it shrink the tumors
or does it not? A "before" x-ray was taken when we went
in on Friday; the "after" version is set for April 7th.
So that's the next crucial date.
      A big blowy stormy rain is -- what? -- (long pause)

is raging. That's what. Out there. Yeah. ("Raging," I
can't retrieve "raging"? Is it because my inner rage
mechanism has burned out under the tough conditions down
here? Or what?) -- And on to the next conundrum.
Umbrellas. A much higher percentage of umbrellas is
deployed against this storm here in my old hometown than
would be mustered against a similar tempest in my current
one, while the percentage of attached hoods ("hoodies")
is far lower. And yet the ratio of black umbrellas to
umbrellas of color, so to speak, is higher here than it
is there, which is the opposite of what I'd expect. Is
it that people down here don't feel as strong a need to
counter the effects of wintertime gloom? We up there
need all the help we can get?
     -- And here in the alley the clown faces mounted
high on the walls are offering the usual full spectrum of
responses to all that transpires below: from absurd to
hilarious to quizzical to mock tragic. And the live
quasi-clowns seated more or less permanently at the
counter are arguing is this or is this not the official
first day of spring, and they're saying either way they
sure do hope the new season won't be as wet all the way
to the end as it is out there right now, and especially
not after the city's winter of gargantuan storms. (I'm
still hoping myself to take the train back on Wednesday
night but if this keeps up the newly repaired tracks
might wash out again.)
     The morning slow period. Glistening black tiles in
the little triangular patio just outside: the rain makes
them seem to wink like little square eyes. And an arc of
white bulbs is winking in more mechanical fashion a few
feet above the gated entrance to the patio, with the
juicy-red burger-joint sign hanging up there meanwhile
glowing steadily; and old Victorian spires and cornices a
few stories up across the street are pitching in to make
a handsomely contrasting wide-screen backdrop. This
alley's been here long enough now or been franchised out
enough that its "Original" status is trumpeted as part of
the sign. -- Fine with me, because I'd picked up the
rumor somewhere that the whole chain had gone out of

business. Obviously false. Great news.

    None of the above is to suggest that the proceedings down here have been friction-free. One brief battle with sister Barb and one much longer one with the mother of us all and the still-living, still-breathing center of the universe as we sibs know it -- and this second battle was enough to sicken me and I won't deny I was thinking about hopping the next plane ouddaheah. But doggedly, grimly, obstinately, perversely I persevered -- and now all's fine or anyway seems fine. Fights are probably over. I argued only for conciliation, only for them to admit the possibility that the categorical judgments they were handing down on this, that, and everything but especially on me and my ways -- and even more especially on my views regarding the Lady S/Elgie conundrum and Lady U's part in it -- could be mistaken. The mere shred of a possibility that those ways and views of mine might be right -- at the very least be right for me or for Lady U and me taken together -- and they can't be certain theirs are and they might even be committing a kind of category error in applying theirs to me and/or us. "Conflict resolution." And to my utter surprise it worked. I'm pleased.

    The first morning I get up (I'm sleeping on an air mattress in an open space at the center of the small living room in which I fit perfectly, tight as the tail of a dove -- a jyze peacekeeper!) and I go out and I'm walking along just three blocks away -- past the hotel where I stayed for six weeks after my return to the States shortly before Dad's death -- and past all else still remaining from that era (which appears to be just about everything) -- and who do I bump into moseying along on her way to work after picking up coffee-to-go at a nearby cafe? It's my sister! My only sister in the world! And so I walk her five or six blocks to the academy where she works, the side entrance thereof. And then on the phone with brother Jeff yesterday I learned that he had the same kind of chance street encounter with Barb during his stay here. (A happier talk with

Jeff this time because the news of the chemo's lack of
side effects has opened a window of hope for us all.
-- Lots of joshing with him about what he "can just
imagine" I'm going through now. During his visit he
slept on the couch in the living room rather than on
the floor. Otherwise a lot of the same, except the
categorical judgments that went down on his life from
these two formidably opinionated women were probably
even more brutal than the ones they've been laying on
mine. But then again he seems to know how to shrug
them off better than I do.)

Hours and hours of talk with Mother about which of
her possessions will become whose -- because this is all
too often her topic of choice -- and do we really want
them or should they be shifted to someone else, swapped
for this or that -- and the stories behind every last
item, some going back two centuries or more. Info
overload. Tabletops crowded with bowls, flatware,
photos, linen, glassware, antique silver, each object
with its tale to tell. Whole bookcases of mostly
heirloom volumes to go through. (Check, it's done.)
-- And the funny thing is I'm enjoying it all. It sure
does beat pounding on the scope-office computers. But
no, I mean it. But seriously, folks (fellow clowns).

(That's my city No. 2 out there and also No. 7,
speaking lifetime and chronologically and leaving out
stays of less than three months. No. 2/7, waddaya know.
I figured this out during the flight down. It's also
the one I once thought would be my last city lifetime.
But that was before the consequences of the Lady V/Lady
S/Elgie imbroglio had become clear to me.)

-- And last night a really good talk with Mother
about my new life as a jyzer in which she was fully
supportive, admiring, understanding -- much of it long
after we'd already decided she must get to bed (several
bad coughing spells had erupted) but in the hall outside
her room we couldn't stop, we were on a roll of high
rapport. Lovely. She's hoping my share of the estate
she's gone to such great lengths to conserve for her
kids will enable me either to buy a few years of

unimpeded fictojyzing (a/k/a JIFT, still), which she
understands I need badly -- or even better, if I can
get those years some other way, then to somehow assure
publication of the Mentoka trilogy (which of course
can't be assured, or at least not in the only way
publication matters, at least to me; but certainly
private "vanity" or self-publication would always remain
a last-resort possibility).

For much of the afternoon yesterday we went over
the protojyze excerpts and the doubly expurgated version
of "Jyzeburst" I brought down for her, which she's been
reading in bed at night. At her request I showed her
exactly how I edit and proofread these days, my last-
minute interlineations done on the plane coming down
being right there for her to see; and this demo brought
tears to her eyes "because it reminds me so much of
Daddy" (meaning hers). -- And she chuckled aloud quite
often as she read some of her favorite parts of "Burst"
aloud to me -- even guffawed several times. Of course I
do wish she'd done that more, say at least as often as I
guffawed silently while listening. But I'll admit
that's asking a bit much. -- Still and all she seemed
to get a big kick out of our "story conference" (which
is what I told her it reminded me of).

The Friday visit to the clinic for the first chemo
treatment also had its good moments. As we listened to
Doc B. explain the odds and what she could expect --
none of which was really new -- I flashed back to my
visits at ages five through seven or eight to the
Gatewood Road office of the ominously named Dr.
Frownburger (invoking a jyze-rules exception here on
citing nonfamily surnames). I couldn't really remember
in any detailed way what Mother was like back then but
somehow it seemed she hadn't changed at all; the
perspective I was seeing her from was just a couple of
feet higher in the chair. Then during administration
of the chemo by intravenous drip in a small darkened
room we talked long and intimately, mostly about my
love life over the years but also about hers. She
professed shock over a few X-rated revelations

regarding my high-school romances -- "What, Cindy let you do that right in our rec room?" -- but then my jaw dropped an inch or two over her own revelations about her thirty-years-younger boyfriend of a decade or so back.

This apartment of hers is not at all the shameful little dump she described it as (and wept in humiliation over) when she first moved in six or seven years ago. It's not huge but it's a fine place -- high ceilings, splendid paneling, bay windows with a pleasing view that includes a short stretch of the bay itself and about two-thirds of the iconic bridge way off in the distance -- and she confirmed she still pays just $450. People would kill for such a place at twice or even three times the price. She realizes this now.

Do I want to try to describe the relationship that's developed between Barb and Mother? Will I let myself fall into that trap right here and now when instead I could be up poking around on my old turf (any of maybe a dozen prime patches of same in this city) and I probably won't have another chance -- well, to do either? Certainly they're an odd pair, this mother and daughter, so strikingly unalike in most ways other than being formidably opinionated. But I'm feeling better about them now. So drop it for the time being.

I will say this, though. Barb is still the master of the subtle little "unintentional" inflammatory remark. By which I mean they're her master as well. All in the name of "spontaneity" and "honesty," I guess. I try to ignore them or laugh them off. Among her new ones, delivered with nostrils flaring: "You certainly are a challenging man!" (This is supposed to be a compliment, Mother tells me, covering for her.) The main impetus behind this particular one was her purported surprise over my support, which of course is longstanding though she insists she's never known this, of various feminist ideals and causes. But going further, a number of brotherly dimensions, of which that's just one example, fit together oddly to her way of thinking, I'm sure. The philosophy talker, the

scribbler, editor of newspapers, political activist,
teacher of adult literacy classes, noble martyr of
dedication to a semi-handicapped wife (zen type), steady
clerical worker for an all-female court-reporting firm
yet also a former jock and still a macho-man type
sometimes in her view I guess. I guess! (She says she
thinks all the "drive" went to me when the character
traits were handed out -- as if there can be nothing
intentional about "drive." But I'll grant that at some
level it should be seen as a gift and a talent, in its
own way as valuable as perfect pitch, say, or quick
reflexes. Or more so. Of course it can also be an
onerous cross to bear, to use Barb's kind of language --
and she talked that way long before she officially went
religious last year. -- And I shouldn't fail to mention
she thinks all the "spiritual" qualities went to --
herself! Actually says this!)
     -- Reminding me. In the message appended to a
Christmas card sent several months ago, I've learned for
the first time as of this visit, Mama U suggested to my
mother, or hinted unsubtly, that it was her, my
mother's, duty to help with my support now that I've
become an unemployed or partially employed ne'er-do-well
largely dependent on the dole. It must've been pretty
bad because Barb's new boyfriend Keith (whom I'm to meet
tonight) suggested Mother should tape a couple of
pennies to the reply she was working on, a scathing one
which she later toned down. But Mother couldn't bear to
tell me about all this before now. Barb too was
enraged, supposedly on my behalf. Don't those U's
realize I've been slaving away to support their daughter
for all these years, practically wearing my keyboarding
fingers down to nubbins? Either they get their daughter
out there pitching in (this is not Japan and it's not
the 1950s!) or how about if they sell some of their
property and assume her part of the burden since they're
so wealthy (though they're really not) and she's their
only child?
     Just an adumbration here, a quiver of things ahead.
     -- But Mother does see how much I love my life and

knows I'm aware what an immense debt I owe her for my
being able to live it and appreciate it. The zest
probably more than anything. This quality of hers I'm
in awe of but also think I can come close to matching.
Except in the social sphere, that is, where she has
friends galore and maintains intense and loving or at
least vibrant relations with them all (not to mention
with family near and far, extended over several
generations and degrees of relation), and she's done so
all her life. -- Bits and pieces of my childhood flash
into the present (again and again) as I sit in her
apartment trying not to eavesdrop on her phone
conversations, yet because of the emotional intensity on
display being utterly unable to do otherwise -- the full
range, the laughter, the shock, the tears, the
enthusiasm, the intrigue. It's such an old, old story
for me with her I can scarcely wrench it far enough out
of the everyday to get a grasp on it so I can jyze a few
lines about it.

    -- I probably won't see her like this again. I
want to remember her this way. (Makes my eyes mist over
yet again to write this.) -- I ought to tell her all
these things because I know she'd like to hear them.
"I'll have so many good memories from this week -- and
especially from last night, our 'story conference.'"

    But it's almost certain I'll be coming back down
when her condition begins to worsen. Even with the
hospice handling many of the basics, she'll still need a
great deal of help and the load will be too heavy for
Barb to carry by herself while she's also working a
full-time job which itself is highly stressful for her.
Of the three brothers I'd be the logical one to supply
backup relief because of my employment situation. And
oddly enough I'm now looking forward to doing so. Just
wish I were handier in the kitchen. But so it goes.

    -- And here I come. Or there I go. Can all but
see myself. Slouching up the hill over there toward my
former favorite bookstore of them all. The jyzer: the
new guy, but also the old ghost, in town.

[Real Jyze]

7

    This'll be jouncy.
    At last aboard and we're rolling northward. I'd
say it's about eleven p.m. and though neither coast nor
starlight is anywhere in sight (not that I'm doubting
they're out there) it doesn't matter, it's still fine to
be right here. -- Where? I don't even know and I've
lived around here for roughly a sixth of my life. But I
do know we're only just getting started.
    This is the club car and it closes at midnight. Or
the concession stand on the lower level does. Up here
in the view lounge we may be allowed to stay on
indefinitely; I'm not sure. And if all turns out truly
well they'll shut down the horrible movie playing
raucously right now on screens at both ends of the car
along with the one downstairs. Here in the middle
portion of the lounge all the other seats are empty.
    -- The usual night train internal window
reflections shimmering almost motionlessly on both sides
of the car against deep black backdrops which you feel
are flowing slowly rearward like a river -- but only
because at most times at least a few surface lights are
in sight out there and they appear to be moving that way
also. (And now lots and lots of them -- chemical plants
and a sulfuric smell too -- so we're just about to roll
into a town where I used to do some reporting of the
newspaper kind. Soon, though, we'll be moving beyond
the outer bounds of my old regional turf and I won't
even be able to guess where we are, or at least not in a
way I can pin proper names to. Not that I'd want to do
that anyway. This is jyze!)

45

[Jyzemelt]

    Jim Q. ran me over to the terminal in his little
black "heart attack" sports car. It was a fine thing to
do -- but it turned out to be the wrong place to go.
The bus which connects with the train station now leaves
from the ferry terminal. A clerk at the first terminal
steered me that way (Jim had already left) but time was
short and taxis were scarce. It seemed unlikely I could
make it by foot unless I ran, so that's what I was
doing, suitcase and all (and that suitcase loaded with
heavy stuff including several thousand bucks' worth of
certifiably heirloom silverware) (which of course I've
sworn never, ever, ever to sell). And then a taxi came
along so I made it with five minutes to spare.
    I do love to hear steel wheels clattering over
junction boxes. The diesel whistle sounding way too far
ahead to be related to this train but also sounding,
yes, unmistakably related to this train. The squeaks
and wheezes. Even the steady low roar of the air
conditioning.
    -- And here's a station stop. Hard to read the
sign from this angle. As we came in, streetlights were
shining a few feet away almost directly overhead as seen
through the handy view-section skylight windows.
    From the movie a gaggingly phony southern accent.
(I know it's attempting to be southern because the Cawk
narrator's saying that's where he's been "brung up awl
mah lahf" -- just like a whole bunch of my ancestors on
Mother's side were, as of course I've been hearing about
all week; but I strongly suspect none of them, or any
other true southerner, ever sounded quite so moronically
cornpone, or maybe I should say 'baccypone, as this.)
    -- Lights reflecting on what appears to be real
water down below as with a new kind of clatter we head
out onto a big bridge of rushing black diamond-shaped
struts. And the dim overhead lamp by which I jyze.
-- And now that's abruptly it for the bridge, the new
clatter, the struts, and probably also the salt water,
if that's what it was, or is, as we angle inland,
heading toward the mountains -- that much I know.
    It just feels right to be riding a train at night

after a week like this.

Like what? Grim yet loving. Intense yet numbing.
Unreal yet achingly moving. -- Rolling along almost
entirely in the dark. A few scattered interior lamps
still shining, including the one casting its soft yellow
cone down upon what's just gotta be the first jyzebook
ever to appear in a club car on this or any other train
(though of protojyzebooks there have of course been
many, including, on other trains, several of my own).

-- Last night Barb and I went out for dinner while
Mother entertained Jim Q. A chance for both pairs to be
alone together. And I'm pleased to report that, though
awkwardness won't go away, we two sibs do seem to be
doing better. I'm encouraged enough to keep trying.
Mostly we talked books. Carefully steered clear of all
contentious matters, including, but of course, politics
and religion. I did get to hear quite a lot about the
sights of Portugal. Ate at a joint whose name
translated from the Italian, I assume, means "The
Chicken." While there we saw two local celebrities I
once knew slightly: Herb G. the novelist charged in to
pick up a takeout box and Larry F. the poet and
bookstore owner wandered moonily by outside. Both
nodded to Barb and both know Mother now but neither
seemed to recognize or even notice me -- which was just
as I would've preferred anyway. But if Steve V. the
class-action barrister had bounced up and started
jabbering nonsense as is his wont (rumor has it he's
squandered all his lawsuit winnings on cocaine and is
now living in the parks) -- if he'd appeared, the "The
Chicken" experience would've been, for me, complete.

Mom still in a hyper state these past few days.
The dynamo. Coughing some, breathless often (especially
if she bends over) but you just can't stop her. She's
going through papers, old photos, the lengthy list of
bequeathals (many typed pages long and bristling with
scratch-outs and scratch-ins) but mostly we're talking
about family relationships: her disappointments, her
hopes. And I'm reading old diaries I've never seen
before or known to exist, hers and Nana's also, and

finding them fascinating (indeed just as she says she
finds the excerpts from my old journals -- a/k/a
protojyze, of course -- and the bowdlerized "Burst").

(The movie's over, the crowd's cleared out, the
cleanup's completed. Now in this whole long car only
one other occupant and she's at the forward end, a book
held open with one hand but she's staring out into the
black just as I'm often doing, and she's also wearing
ratty jeans, like me, and her rucksack's at least as
beat-up as mine. Two lives for a few hours running
massively parallel though still wholly separate, I guess
I should note. "The lady in purple" -- the color of her
sweatshirt. She's maybe ten or twelve years my junior
and a pleasure to sneak looks at. Lord help us. In
another era something might've developed here.)

We're making good speed now -- an impressive pitch
and yaw to go with the intensified clickety-clack and
the isolated lights streaking by up close out the
windows like meteorites flying under the radar.

-- I really lost it just once and that was shortly
after I walked back to Mother's place after writing the
"clowns" entry and tried to tell her what that entry
said I would try to tell her. Every time I started to
say how much the previous night's talk about jyze had
meant to me I started tearing up and then goofing to
mask the tears so I wouldn't look so much the goddamn
blubbering fool but of course succeeding only in looking
even more that way. (But I enjoyed it too. I enjoyed
the whole trip. It's lots of fun being so close with
ol' Mom even though in brutal truth at this stage in our
lives it's mostly the imminence of her death that makes
it possible. -- I'm even hoping I'll be able to come
down and do it all over again in a couple of months if
luck is with us and modern medicine extends her life by
the six months to a year it's saying it can do (though
after the conference with Doc B. the chances as I make
them out that it'll go the full year or more are no
better than one in four or five).)

But so many good talks at her kitchen table! Mom
sneaking potato chips she shouldn't be eating and coffee

she shouldn't be drinking. Barb dropping by at five or
so each evening after work. -- And the "dinner party"
with the three of us and Barb's friend Rikki from
downstairs and Jim Q. and Keith: finding Keith to be a
quirky and intelligent fellow, little bit of a geek,
little bit of a goof, little bit of a moralizer (and
even though half-bald and blond, reminiscent of my
college roommate Albert E. with his oddball antics and
unexpectedly high-pitched squeaky voice), and best of
all a fellow journalizer (I won't say protojyzer since
that didn't come up) and animated, lively, possessed of
a delightful dry wit (and also, reputedly, a hair-
trigger temper, just like Jim Q.) -- and eleven years
younger than Barb, or maybe it's thirteen, I forget.
     -- But pull the table out into the middle of the
kitchen and swing up the side leaves so everyone can
gather round. A pork-chop main dish and for dessert a
homemade spice layer cake ala mode. Jim Q. looking
tired and pale but compared to what I was expecting a
week earlier (a corpse) looking great. A handsome
small-bearded man of medium height who might be taken to
be the off-duty captain of a cruise ship or, better yet,
a ferryboat; in fact I'm thinking of one such pilothouse
personage I know who looks even more like him than
brother Rob looks like me (which is to say: a lot).
     -- Of course always I'm wondering can it be true
this will be the last time I'll be able to do something
like this -- or this or this -- with my one and only
mother in the world. And not believing it can be, yes,
and quite possibly will be. I do have this -- and this
and this -- indestructible (it seems) hope.
     -- And after rolling along all these miles we've
now wheezed to a stop out in the middle of a big black
mysterium in the middle of the night, this train has.
After all we're national rail in an era of rampant
privatization. A speed freight or time freight owned by
some megacorporation (who else?) will rumble by sooner
or later and then we'll be allowed to swing our sorry
socialistic selves out onto the mainline again -- unless
another private freight's coming along. (And if a

corporation is a person in the eyes of our country's legal system, is a megacorporation a megaperson? Just asking.)

I ate too much garbage and drank too much bourbon on this trip. Let my hair down quite a bit. Had Mother feeling pretty good most of the time, I think, and did it without abandoning any major principles or conceding any truly important points (important to my future ability to live with myself, that is). So I can say: just about an unmitigated success. For sure I'm happy about it. And I'm still trying to dread not. And I'd say she's going out with admirable style. Sometimes that style is a bit too Auntie Mame for me (her namesake niece Georgie even calls her Auntie Mame) but only sometimes and even then I can take it all right and on occasion toss something similarly high-spirited right back at her to keep the party rolling.

She knows I love her a lot and I know the feeling's mutual.

Gush gush gush.

-- Now the freight's gone by and we've pulled into a station built in Spanish-mission style and clearly it's serving a fairly large city even though no passengers are out there on the platform (but several motorized baggage carts are, and one's in operation hauling a full load of luggage at surprising speed). I could even hazard a guess what the city is (and probably be right!) but won't. Jyze rules rule.

For a seatmate back in the coach I've drawn a short rotund lady of an age close to Mother's who's not at all pleased to have to make room for one of my lengthy and scruffy ilk. She and her husband wanted to drive wherever it is they're headed to see the grandkids, I learned, but the storms kept the freeway closed even longer than the railway. The husband stayed behind a day for some reason, perhaps so that the whole grandparental unit wouldn't perish in one fell swoop if our train should plunge into an abyss somewhere. And this is about all I know so far.

(Rolling again. Feels good even though I'm about

to keel over. I'm way behind on sleep. And two full
nights of scoping work await me back home -- one of them
before I even get to go to the real home.)
     I like to imagine traveling around the country and
the world just like this. Rail jyze. Short stays in
city after city and everything totally unknown to me.
But I know it'll never happen.
     -- All the new information, it's overwhelming. I
used up almost twenty pages of this J-book for notes
(starting at the back and working forward in traditional
protojyze fashion). Nothing momentous; just lots and
lots of tidbits. Gossip. Family history. Here's a
batch of letters Lady S wrote to Mother a whole passel
of years back and I've never seen most of them before
(they must've been misplaced when I went through a
similar but even bigger trove of Lady S letters after
Dad's death). Here's -- but I'd better stop. System
crash imminent: my own.

*   *

     Easing upgrade. It's eight in the morning now and
we're running two and a half hours late and traveling on
the shirttails of a major storm that's coated everything
with perhaps a foot of fresh snow and isn't done yet.
Spectacular scenery here: mountains, cliffs, canyons,
giant boulders, a rushing green trout stream paralleling
the tracks forty or fifty feet down. And every branch
of every tree picturesquely frosted (and that's a lot of
trees and a helluva lot of frosting).
     (A series of switchback loops now materializing and
the front and the back of the train are simultaneously
visible through the same window from right here -- same
club-car seat where I was going at this same touristic
yet undeniably jyzey pastime last night. Cameras
clicking hectically away like mini castanets. Snow
swirling blizzardishly beyond and against glass on both
sides of the car. Every seat taken as folks wait to be
called for the diner one car back. Lots of loud talk,
led by strong-voiced members of a touring adult choir
from a farm state half a continent thataway, many
clasping bibles like tightly folded security blankets

51

as they declaim to each other and anyone else who'll
listen and some who'd clearly rather not. Of whom I'll
admit I'm one, though I've kept silent about it so far.)

     I did get a few hours' sleep. -- "Like throwing a
big white sheet over it, innit?" That's someone talking
about the snow out there, but he could be referring to
the way I slept too (don't I wish). Visibility now is
no more than a hundred feet and snow accumulation looks
more like two feet. We're peering down a steep drop-off
almost from trackside, near vertical. Hundreds, maybe
thousands of feet -- plenty of visibility down that way.
Evergreens galore! Wow! Iz all I can say!

     At the moment we've got several bona-fide diarists
in here, I see. -- Or a couple anyway, and that's not
including Janell Y., last night's lady in purple with
whom I did wind up talking for a few minutes despite
being in system crash (and she's quite charming but
nothing would come of it even if I weren't a confirmed
fidelitarian). And next to me now a gray-haired
Canadian lady and her USAn grandkid, pretending to be
blase' about all this scenic grandiosity, he in gray
sweats and a "Crusaders" ball cap. (A little tacky,
innit? Why not just come right out and say "Murdering
Religious Fanatics"? But that's a little wordy, true,
for the space allotted on the cap.)

     -- Audible oohs and ahs: as if bursting into a
canyon we hit a sudden and wholly unexpected majestic
mountain panorama and patches of blue sky -- even though
out the windows on the other side of the train it's
still snowing. Just one mile, a sign says, to the
famous volcano named after a soft drink (or am I turning
that around?). Cozy little cabins about the size of my
shed back home half-buried in snow over there, smoke
curling up from stovepipe chimneys. We're riding right
along the fringe of the storm -- a few hundred yards to
the left it's a whole different world, almost snowless.
How bizarre this is! -- And to the right, as the P.A.
is now explaining, the famous volcano itself would be
looming were it not completely obscured by clouds. I
myself have awe-filled memories of this volcano's beauty

from the time D and I drove down. (Well, but now I see
the bottom half isn't obscured and it's plenty
impressive all by itself. -- So when it comes to
volcanos maybe I'm a skirt chaser? -- Scratch that.)

   It seems at this point I'm wholly incapable of
serious thought. Could be I'm emotionally exhausted.
(Could it be otherwise?) -- But here's a string of
boxcars. How fine the sight of rusty old boxcars
sitting on a spur out in the middle of nowhere!
Railroad logos exotic and half worn away, each one
different, some from an earlier historical era for
sure. Better yet, rusty old boxcars topped and bearded
and webbed, as here, with snow. (Now I see a logo from
the line that, before it went defunct, was the mainline
of my childhood: it ran from Centropolis through
Gatewood, through Lahontan, on up through Mentoka Falls,
and then all the way out to my city No. 12 which, from a
different direction, we're rolling toward now.)

   -- Talking with D by phone Sunday night I learned
Employment Security hadn't called and neither had anyone
else. Up until that point at least we were in the
clear. My hope right now is to be able to squeeze out a
couple more months of unemployment benefits. Probably
in late May or early June I'll pay Mother a return visit
regardless of the state of her health, or go sooner if
an alarming deterioration sets in. In any case the
dole's end is in sight -- and hooray for that. Even
though it follows that I'll soon be totally without
financial means.

   (Wow again -- we round a bend and another big
mountain/valley extravaganza presents itself from a very
high perspective. Must be fifty or sixty miles across
in places!)

   -- I suppose I could go on all day making these
feeble golly-gee swipes at describing scenery. Or I
could read for a while.

*   *

   A kwikjyze postscript as we cross into my home
state of the current era. Last I heard we were running
five and a half hours late. Not that it really matters

53

a whole lot for me or that it's unusual for these trains, as everyone knows. It's been a spectacular trip because of the snowstorm we've been plowing through for the past twenty hours or so and maybe still are -- and this on the third or fourth day of spring!

Why are we so late? Four or five separate incidents, including a burned-out cable and two sizable bridges which, prior to the train's crossing, crew members had to "walk" for a safety check owing to swollen rivers and fear of hidden structural damage from last week's floods. And up in the high country we stood motionless for over an hour in the blizzard while waiting for a time freight to clear a series of twenty-two tunnels and innumerable permanent snowsheds. During that hour-plus alone it appeared another six inches of snow fell -- yet that same creek was rushing blithely and greenly and sinuously and splashily through it all just outside (I easily could've looped a fishing line into it from my window if the window had been the kind that opens and if I still remembered how to loop a fishing line -- which I'm all but certain I don't).

This going down in my familiar club-car seat. Tonight's movie stars a certain puzzlingly mediagenic Hollywood collie, and it's in its roaringly (not to say woofingly) melodramatic final reel. (I don't know if movies shown on trains still have reels, actually, but surely this one's old enough for me to hazard using the term.)

My coach seatmate and I worked things out pretty well, alternating shifts there except for a few hours late at night when we squeezed in together. (Also the woman in purple I was talking with last night, Janell, has returned, and she's still in purple but with a nifty little sequined silver vest covering much of it.)

-- It's over. Soaring violins, heartrending barks, the lounge clears out fast. And Janell just gave me a smile and a little wave. And I nodded in gruff but I hope not totally unkind acknowledgment. -- But I do wonder once in a while (just as always) what would happen if I were suddenly thrust back into the bazaar.

No doubt I'd be lucky to find a woman like her:
midlifedly attractive, trim, warm, well-spoken,
friendly, openly yearning to have a man around -- she
actually said this -- who in "cultural" realms could do
something more than grunt on cue. On the other hand
she's a single mom with two daughters, ages ten and
thirteen. A path I've been down before and quickly fell
off, or more accurately was shoved off, and that
involved just one daughter, age eleven. (But it won't
be all that long before the prospects start looking much
better for me, should the need arise, with women this
Janell's age and older, as the kids grow up and the male
competition starts dropping off like flies -- unless, of
course, I first drop off that way myself. -- Well, DUH,
I'll dare to say. And in undeniably age-eleven style.)
     Here's our next-to-last stop before I have to morph
back into my nightscoper persona.
     One other thing this trip was good for was biting
off a hefty chunk of a book on neoprag aesthetics. I'm
not saying I necessarily understand every last word of
it but it certainly evokes memories of college days --
of sitting up overnight in a club car much like this
one, for example, while grinding away at required
reading for Metaphysics 101 or maybe Transcendentalism
299 finals after having failed to crack open a book
over Christmas vacation at home. ---

8

     It's not the day of the fool. Not quite. A few
hours short of that. (Nor is it the day of the feast of
the fools, though while browsing upstairs a bit earlier
I came across a new novel built around that very topic

-- work of the same fellow whose previous novel, set in Japan, presents that country much as I saw it myself in roughly the same era he was writing about. -- But it is a feast of the fool, singular, right here, I can say, since I just polished off a chunk of apple crumb cake weighing in, including the ala mode bonus, at about five thousand calories, just as a guess.)

A new sizzle because today for the first time in a while "Mentoka Dreams" seems to be taking off. This is only in my head, true, but at the rate it's gaining speed it may wind up getting airborne ahead of "Jyzer." (Is it still "Mentoka Dreams"? Or should I try to come up with something more directly jyze-related for the title? Might it even be "The Return of Jyzemaster G"?)

(In the reading room meanwhile a female chanter is whacking on bongos -- don't know if it's a women's equivalent of those recently fashionable iron (but no way ironic) johns or maybe the equally hokey business about running with wolves -- in any case it's definitely not yet mainstream stuff -- the audience maybe a dozen or so but only if all the clapping is one-handed. But wait a minute, even as a potential Zen koan that makes no sense -- or I guess I should say no (un)sense.)

What's this now? Sober up!

I've sent Mother several cards but have received no news from her or Barb, by mail or phone, except indirectly through Lady U. I spilled the news to her, D, about her own mother's Christmas-card note to my mother and then had to work hard to keep her from freaking. For a full day and part of the next we thrashed out the matter and eventually she decided to call Mother (mine) herself and apologize on Mama U's behalf. D's odd yet typically facesaving way of dealing with the situation was simply to tell my mother that Mama U is going senile. While perhaps not quite totally untrue, it's still far from a full and accurate description of Mama U's mental state as I've observed it firsthand since my return. -- But never mind, Mother seemed to buy it all right, at least according to D. Any straw to grasp was probably straw enough for old Mom

in her current condition. Mainly I'm sure she
appreciated D's caring enough to make the effort.

     So now brother Rob and his kids should be nearing
the end of their visit down there and the U's are at
mid-visit up here. Mid-visit and counting. For twenty-
seven days running poor D can do little else but
entertain them and serve as Papa U's second assistant
(or phony up excuses to avoid doing so) as he goes about
his many self-appointed tasks in boosting the value of
the property that is, after all, theirs, that is, the
U's'. Yes, he's still the same "Beaver" he always was,
as indeed everyone calls him, after the mascot of his
undergrad university but equally as much for his truly
castorian energy levels and work ethic.

     Today he was also "hammering man": keeping me awake
most of the afternoon, even while trying not to do so,
but unable to desist from pounding away because various
"emergencies" arose as he laid ceramic tile around the
woodstove in the new basement pantry, so-called. Nor
does it help that his hearing has deteriorated further
(as a result of all those years working near massively
noisy electric generators) and everyone has to talk very
loud in his presence, as he himself almost always does
without necessarily realizing it. And now that I'm on
the dole my intra-family prestige, never too high to
begin with, has slipped further and therefore the U's
seem to feel less need to worry about how much sleep I'm
getting while pursuing my eccentric and utterly
unproductive, in their view, lifestyle -- though to be
sure none of this is ever made explicit. On the
contrary, form is followed at all times, but just not
too diligently except when face is directly involved
(that again! -- but I'm grateful for it and of course
try to exploit it to the max just like everyone else).

     And there's this: right at the start D and I took
advantage of our own diverse plights, including the
state of my mother's health, and also a bit of good news
regarding a rising market in this area for properties
like ours -- that is, theirs -- to convince Papa U (he's
the boss) to let us stay on in the same caretaker role

at our current place for another year -- in fact for
eighteen months, as it's now turned out, until September
of next year. And therefore the house can wait until
next spring or summer to be painted. Nothing is so
urgent as it seemed. (Except the project of finding D a
job, upon which she's once again made no further
progress by herself -- and my unemployment benefits may
run out in four to six weeks or possibly less.)

And this: the computer system at the office has
been upgraded and now that I'm self-employed my
training on it will have to be accomplished on my own
dime. I don't know much yet about what's involved but
it can't be too elaborate; most likely the biggest time-
consumer will be backing up all my personal files
(again!) onto storage diskettes which will work with the
newly enhanced system. At present I have no way to read
these diskettes at home, but Papa U tells me he's pretty
sure his machine can handle them and what's more he'll
be glad to let us have it after he moves up to the
latest model this fall. (In past years he's donated his
old machines to the local high school.) And thus it
would appear my long-range computer problem is solved
(D and I will share the computer; for the first time
she's expressed interest in learning how to use one).
Now the only computer problem I face at home is the
short-term matter of getting through the summer while
having access solely to my ancient backup "insurance"
machine.

But tonight I'm planning to sneak into the office
with a bag of diskettes. I'm hoping I can learn the new
upgrades in eight hours or less and at least get started
on the downloading.

-- That has to be it if I'm to make it up there in
time to receive a family phone call (just in case one
comes in, though it's unlikely). And besides: I don't
want to write too much this round. With all the notes
at the back of the volume I'm well ahead on my jyze
schedule. Next entry I may have more need for the space
with the chemo results due.

*   *

[Real Jyze]

     -- Except I should mention the main topical local
news item of the week. I stepped outside the bookstore
tonight and there it was -- it bopped me pretty good.
Boy am I the absentminded jyzer type these days. It's
Final Four weekend! The games for the college hoops
national championship are being played right here in
Jyze City, a few blocks down the street from where I was
standing. If Papa U hadn't dinged his back we probably
would've been attending one of these games ourselves,
all four of us. Maybe even right at this moment.
     (And I'm sweat-shellacked from the swift uphill
walk to the office -- but at least I'm in now and no
one's here but me. And outside the windows,
searchlights are pivoting and narrow beams of green and
red seem to be slicing and dicing the upper reaches of
nearby highrises while transforming tonight's typically
drab and drizzly mist into shafts of mizzly dazzle --
it's the big Final Four laser light show.)
     The sidewalks and streets were clogged most of the
way as I hurried up -- horns blaring and fans screaming,
peddlers camped every five feet hawking Final Four
knickknacks and geegaws and gear, gear, gear. And the
dome was all lit up and laser-lined like a giant
butcher's diagram (three-dimensional!) of an upside-down
pork belly, and a carnival complete with merry-go-round
and ferris wheel was rollicking away in a nearby park
and you could hear maybe a dozen different bands at once
blasting at top volume in the clubs in the area and
roving gangs of students everywhere were checking out
the nightlife scene, cutting up as only students can do
(oh yeah, them were the days!) -- there being Bruins and
Tarheels, Cowboys and -- what was the fourth? Not
Otters anyway, and not Zorilles either, although I'm
thinking Otters and Zorilles at all times regardless, as
in Mentoka State Silver Otters and U of Mentoka Zorilles
squaring off at the big game in "Jyzer." (But when the
crunch comes I'll probably have to drop the name
Zorilles, even though I've got a dynamite backstory for
it tying in with the French Voyageurs/Lahontan/"Longue
River" scheme, because it's all just too damn obscure.

[Jyzemelt]

So go with Gophers and Badgers then and to hell with the
fictive? Or Holsteins and Muskies maybe?)   -- But did
enjoy this walk, yes. And now at 9:53 it appears the
phone won't be ringing tonight.

9

     The J-stick felt light. Therefore I ran hot water
on the lid of the ink bottle before pulling on my knee-
high rubber "barn boots" and trudging up here through
the wet grass (freshly cut and thus even more vividly
green than usual) -- to the barn. The old blackened
sagging cedar barn. Where I hardly ever venture
anymore. -- And along the way seeing yellow flowers
popping out on the fringes of the wooded wetland lot:
not daffodils but maybe jonquils. As if I could tell
the difference anyway. But Mama U says jonquils.
     It's a little chillier than expected up here. Hard
to keep a firm grip on the J-stick. Ripper the cat
followed me up and is pestering for attention -- here's
a paw poking over the top edge of the J-book, a sooty
calico bewhiskered muzzle and pleading eyes and some
powerful anticipatory purring. This barn is where
Ripper spent her first six weeks of life; during that
time I slept up here for a couple of weeks to avoid
noisy daytime construction work at the house and she and
I did the proverbial bonding bit (makes our whole world
hang together, it does, the bonding bit, but of course
also makes it fall apart) (to venture a rather grand and
useless generalization) -- but sorry, Ripper, not this
time. A few scratches and that's it.
     -- And this: the news about Mother is good. She
beat the odds. The chemo is doing what it's supposed to

do. The main "cancerous mass" has stopped growing and
the two smaller ones have actually shrunk. And her
blood looks "surprisingly clean," the doc says.

Yet she hasn't immediately decided to continue the
treatment. Why not? Evidently it's Barb's doing again.
In Barb's view Mother has become "more irritable" since
undergoing that first treatment. Mother's afraid she'll
increase Barb's burden and their relationship will
deteriorate at the end. And, although everyone else is
in favor of Mother's continuing with the chemo, Barb is
refusing to take a stance on it, saying, as Mother
explained to me, she "doesn't want to be blamed."

Trying to be as diplomatic as possible I sez this
is sheer rot. The gall of this sister of mine! As if
her stance isn't clear anyway! -- But then she's on the
firing line and will indeed have to bear up under the
burden for a longer period now because the chemo's
working. But then again to bear up under the burden is
supposedly what she's been angling to do all along.
It's the role she wanted to play, and this by her own
frequent and insistent proclamation. -- And now she's
saying, without actually putting it into words, that
Mother should decline this new lease on life? (The doc
estimates she'll gain six to eight months' worth.) And
Mother is suffering none of the usual chemo side
effects? And the results are so good the dosage can be
kept at the same reduced level (two-thirds), meaning the
treatments can be stretched out fifty percent longer
than usual?

Hard to believe. But so it is. And so now
Mother's deciding. Said she'll let me know by tonight
but also said she wanted to let the doc know by Monday
(which is today) and promised to contact me before
talking with him -- and promised too, should she choose
not to continue the treatments, to let me have a chance
to talk her out of that decision before making it final.

So things are a bit fraught, yes. But I'm
confident she'll make the right decision. Even if it
means bucking Barb's insidious (though nonetheless
loving, to be sure, in her strange way) -- influence.

[Jyzemelt]

    So we'll see.
    -- Ripper's exploring her old nursery grounds.
Bounding around. Papa U, in one of his most spectacular
beaverish bursts, cleaned this place out last summer and
so there's not much up here now: mostly my old boxes of
clips and stacks of various Mentoka newspapers. Also a
rolled-up rug, some light fixtures, a few handmade storm
windows, now warped beyond any possibility of redemption
(just as we warned him, Papa U, would happen back before
he made them). And a couple of huge ungainly wicker
chairs our neighbors Ben and Beryl unloaded on us, in
one of which I'm sitting. The black one. Near one of
the large south windows previous owner Andy installed
shortly before we moved in -- in fact the spindly wooden
scaffolding he jerry-rigged for the installation is
still standing outside these windows (he was planning to
apply some finishing touches to the small garret window
above them) and at this point the scaffolding has been
standing there so long (at least six years) and has
weathered so handsomely it seems like part of the
building and we couldn't bear to tear it down.
    But the two big windows sit fairly high up and this
bizarre chair rides low in the middle (toward which all
things tend to slide, my rump included, if I try to inch
outward and upward or shift my position in any other
way) and therefore the only things I can see out the
windows are tree limbs and sky. Gray sky, in which the
sun is visible only as a faintly glowing silver wafer.
And budding limbs, or in many cases early-leafed limbs.
Oh yes, and some power lines looping along. (What,
power lines marring our Walden? We'd never allow it to
happen! -- As if we could do anything about it, except
maybe move to a more pristine place. Besides, those
lines have hung there sixty years plus, or so Andy told
us, and he should know since his father was living here
and working for the electric utility at the time they
went in, which is why they wound up where they did --
meaning he wanted, and got, easy (free) access to them.)
    And birdsong, several varieties, for none of which
I have a specific name. And birds in flight -- mostly

crows so far but also a soaring hawk.

   (And of course we wouldn't dream of moving to a
purer place -- and regardless of that we wouldn't do it.
Granting rural living all its undeniable charms, we'll
still be hightailing it back to the city as soon as we
can, given our penurious circumstances -- that is, we'll
hang on here as long as we can because it's rent-free to
us -- and for now that means eighteen more months.)

*

   Oy but this miserable chair is bad for jyzing. I
just stood and stretched and peered out one of the small
west windows at our house -- down the hill. Way down,
and it is all downhill though the slope's gentle for the
most part and it's all green, a huge green yard, a one-
story (as seen from this side) tan house with gable-end
roof and flat-roof carport and a gray cedar deck jutting
out to the north (my right) above the small fenced
corral, so-called; and also halfway down the hill a bit
farther to the right, standing in its own little
clearing that reaches about thirty feet back into the
wetland woods, is the shed -- my shed, the only thing
around here I can rightfully call my own -- a room of my
own, as it were, built and paid for by me -- and near
the shed, some ten feet uphill from it, the creaky old
grape arbor hailing from Andy's father's era, with the
vines still nearly as gray as the weathered wood of the
arbor itself and just barely starting to bud.
-- Wherever we do go, and whenever, I wish we could take
that shed with us. But it won't be happening this time.
(Last time I dismantled the innards of my previous shed
in the city and brought them down here and eventually
rebuilt them to fit inside the larger dimensions of the
new shed here, meaning I effectively have a shed within
a shed, almost as if I were seeking double protection to
achieve true reclusion. -- But it's too damn much work
to try anything like that again.) (And the shed still
lacks power. Papa U's as mystified as I am about what
might've gone wrong with the underground wires.)

   Oy oy oy. (Not a word I'm used to writing, oy. A
"foreign" word. A word Lady K uttered quite often and

63

that therefore appears quite often in the chronbooks
from our time together but rarely after that. It never
worked very well for me in real life, that word, perhaps
because to my provincial Mentoka-zone unconscious it
resembled a sound that might be made by one of Old
McDonald's critters. And just maybe it was because I
had such an unconscious that Lady K didn't want to head
out to Mentoka with me after college in the first place.
And for that reason and a few others much like it I now
have the makings of a good core story for "Jyzer" if I
could only get the damn thing off the ground.)
     -- Just about five hours ago we delivered the U's
to the pickup spot for the airport shuttle over by the
supermarket some eight miles north of here (the very
place where we do most of our grocery shopping and where
I finally opened a local bank account last year). It
was still dark then -- my assigned task being to roust
everyone out of bed at four a.m. At last they had hit
on something a howler operating on NUT time might be
good for! And I did it too -- except they were all up
already, with one exception. Mel Bear. (That's been
one of D's nicknames ever since the infamous incident,
described in last year's jyze, in which she scared the
stuffing out of me by popping up outside the shed window
wearing Ben and Beryl's bearskin rug, head and eyes and
fangs included, as a Halloween gag.) (Of course Mel
Bear! With Meleinani as a middle name -- one of her two
-- you could almost say it's a natural.)
     This visit produced no new confrontations. Lots of
petty annoyances on all sides but nothing too serious.
For me sleeping was unusually tough ---
                        *

     Poor Richard would be proud of me. What foresight!
Not only did I remember to bring the ink up here but as
a precaution, as noted before, I ran hot water on the
cap to loosen it up. And right there above the single
star the ink ran out. (Of course it was predictable,
almost to the page, but the feat of foresight on the
ink bottle still ought to count for something.)
     And continuing with small annoyances: for everyone

else Papa U's failing hearing was hard to take (the need
to repeat things for him and always speak clearly and
loudly and facing toward him, and having to listen to
everyone else do this) and so was his propensity to tell
the same story over and over, and hardest of all was his
tendency to become a tinhorn dictator (however endearing
otherwise) with his wife and daughter, at least one of
whom was required to be at his side and at his beck and
call at all times, acting the Girl Friday role, as he
went about his self-appointed task of adding value to
his investment property (also known as "U Acres," yes,
still, and to everyone). -- The many gambits employed
by the two women to avoid falling into his clutches
always an amusement to behold, even for him, though he'd
laugh and joke about the gambits for a moment or two at
most and then turn tyrannical again.

    -- Dogs barking. Motors starting up. A chain saw
shrieking somewhere not too far away. Twittering.
Chirring. -- But no Ripper, she's given up on me and
bounded off to the carport for the morning chow-down.

    Meanwhile I'm loving a Russian poet's
autobiographical essays to the point where I'm strongly
tempted to mention her name. And I ask myself: why is
it so hard to restrain myself? But I must, yes. Jyze
rules. Sacrosanct. For after all, without jyze rules,
no jyze. No this. Q.E.D.

    And I'm also making my way through a Chinese-
Canadian woman's very lively street diary. And
revisiting a USAn Beat icon in a newly issued reader
which offers a number of short pieces I've never seen
before. And each night taking up one more in a
collection of modern Japanese literary diarists,
"modern" meaning those who came after my namesake's (my
middle name is his last name) dastardly "opening" of the
country in the 1850s. And gearing up to try out a hot
new USAn novelist -- one who dares to acknowledge in
print for the mass market his stylistic debt to certain
USAn urjyzers of the nineteenth century and their two
heroic twentieth-century successors (both of whom have
been short-listed for a Jyzemaster Lifetime Award).

[Jyzemelt]

*

    Had to stretch again and stumble out to take a whiz
in the weeds. Stumble and stagger because this farcical
chair had caused both of my legs to numb out on me.
    Am composed again. Pleased to announce the latest
backup of my every salvageable written word is faring
well now that I've finally hit on the secret of how to do
it. On her written directions prepared for office-wide
use dayscoper Amy made one tiny but crucial mistake which
cost me about six hours of cold sweat: she sloppily wrote
what looks like ".WP" where she should've written ".W1"
-- and I commend myself for hanging in there and turning
the thing every which way until I could figure this out.
Now Papa U is taking a test diskette back home in his
suitcase to make sure his machine can handle it.
Assuming it can, I'm all set for the next round of the
never-ending cycle (which however of course will have to
end someday, damn it anyway, even if -- and yet also in a
sense because -- the computer upgrades don't).
    And I'm moving ahead on "Mentoka Dreams" or "Jyze
Dreams" (for now I'll just go back to the brief and call
it "Dreams"). The raw material is there and it's great
stuff -- of course it is! -- but my god is it ever in
bad shape, meaning raw -- so what's to gripe about?
    -- As now blue breaks through gray and on the
barn's wooden floor parallelograms of yellow are fading
in and out and back in -- very slowly pulsating --
pulsating -- pulsating -- and I decide I've had it with
this highly awkward sitting. Rather than maniacally
push on with the jyze I'll retreat to the house and try
a comeback later in a different -- setting. Probably
sitting too, but not here. Never again here.

*   *

    The triumphant return to the room where jyze began!
-- well all right, triumph doesn't really have a whole
lot to do with it. It's simply a matter of pleasure to
be back at it in the primal spot. And it's now all neat
and clean here after being so recently occupied for a
day short of four weeks by Papa and Mama U. And a new
four-by-eight sheet of three-eighths-inch plywood rests

66

underfoot so I, the bumbling howler, won't mar the rug any more than I already have (and unknowingly!).

Two lamps and the overhead fluorescent shining. Jazz station playing. Near-feral Vinnie skulking about just as before, his towel back in place on the far corner of the couch. Big wallful of Japan books, their order altered here and there, I notice, probably meaning Mama U was dipping into them. Floor-to-ceiling curtains (creamy tan with brown dapples) stirring slightly in front of the sliding glass door -- it's open a crack.

And here's my next card for Mother all set to seal. Its printed message is a quote from one of those USAn urjyzers mentioned earlier: "The earth laughs in flowers." It verges on sappiness but doesn't quite cross the line. The art saves it. "Original painting by Miga R. 1994."

Mom didn't call tonight. Clearly these days she's preferring to get ahold of me at the office. And she knows I'll be there tomorrow night. So I'll wait until then before I let myself worry about whether I should be calling her. (All the difficulties of someone who's dying and here she is your mother. What special things should you do, or should you not try to do anything special? Our time on the set comes to an end and we're no longer here and in an undeniably crucial not to say excruciating sense that's all there is to it.)

-- And down on the floor the five binders of material which I hope will provide most of the supporting details I'll need for "Dreams," with the opening thrust set for tonight.

(And a lost hour searching for an essay I meant to send Barb years ago on her favorite religious martyr of the past century or two -- who offed herself around the same time as the Russian poet I'm reading did likewise, and both deaths came a year or so after my birth and two years or so before Barb's -- and now I'm thinking maybe I did send the essay and Barb, possibly out of pique, just never acknowledged receiving it. Or maybe I misplaced it in my shabby filing system, and I'll concede "system" is a blatant misnomer.)

[Jyzemelt]

     -- And today D got a nibble on a want ad she
answered last week. It's an ophthalmology clinic a few
blocks from the transit ferry terminal -- a long commute
but I'm hoping she'll go for the job anyway. An
interview at one p.m. tomorrow. Also in play is a
minimum-wage opening on the swing shift at the market by
the bridge approach near the south-county bus stop. But
it's only part-time, and even at full-time we probably
couldn't get by on the income from that alone. Still,
I'd be willing to try if she would. And that market's
just a three-minute drive from the house (or a ten-
minute bike ride or a forty-minute walk). Meanwhile she
could pick up some skills and maybe use them to find a
better job later -- as a checkout clerk or barista, say.
     Help her get established on this course so we have
a basic income and then focus fiercely on the JIFT
(which if I haven't noted it before in this year's annal
is jyze in fictive time). That's the aim. It's now or
never for me as far as the Mentoka series goes -- and
who knows, maybe everything else as well -- so this is
exciting.
     I'll get it done or go down flailing wildly.
     -- And once every eight days I'll continue with the
JIRT (the real-time stuff) -- even when it deteriorates
into sheer pep-talky self-motivationalism, as above --
and that's a promise.

10

     A fine day for a jyze sail. Warm, sunny, the air
sweet with blossoms and -- earth. In fact this is Earth
Day, which for me does not easily register as a holiday
(because it became that kind of day too late for me, or

68

I materialized into Earth's realm too early -- and thus
too late also).

   On the way in (as the engines rev). Staying in
the city late this morning to pick up D's lens solution
shrank my dreamtime at home to under three hours. But
it was rich, perhaps because Josh, a kid from up on the
loop, came by selling his baseball-league candy bars for
a buck apiece -- his Rottweiler named Wolf snarling and
flexing at his side like a goon enforcer -- and D bit
("Suckah!"). (Last time the kid showed up on a white
horse which dropped a huge turd in the driveway and
that in turn drew a swarm of rats -- "Norski kind for
sure!" in D's view. And she's probably right.)

   In the dream I dashed off some watercolors, mostly
of cavorting lovers, and was widely praised for them.
Very gratifying. But that's the only remaining trace.

   -- So here's some news that fits this unseasonably
gorgeous day. I learned of it a full week ago and thus
I've digested it -- for just that long -- and it fills
me with relief. Yes, even though (like all relief) it's
only temporary, more or less. (Big arrogant blond dude
strolls by in studded black leather motorcycle chaps,
the kind that leave only the rump and the upper legs in
back exposed -- baboonlike, I've gotta say -- and at his
side a caramel-skinned beauty in a tropical sun dress,
mostly red, short-skirted, and matching red spike heels
-- some kind of flash and strut! -- And now, already,
these two members of a clearly superior species are
promenading about on the aft deck as a photographer
scurries in circles around them. They're models on a
shoot! And a rental cop is guarding the door to keep
the hoi polloi out! -- Or rather, inside.)

   But my news.

   -- Is reprieve the right term? Respite? New
lease on life? In any case Doc B. clarifies his earlier
pronouncements and declares the x-rays are even better
than they first appeared to be and so the death sentence
is -- not commuted, no. But the execution is postponed.
And for longer than I would've thought possible. She
may have, the doc says, as long as eighteen months.

(And could that maybe mean even two years if she's
lucky? Two and a half?) (My sad hunch is the blade
will fall in a January -- of next year, I was thinking,
but maybe the year after that? -- If, of course, some
sneak attack doesn't get her even before this coming
January.)
        The doc's clarification: at the rate she's taking
the chemo, it can continue for six to eight months
before her body becomes immune to it. After that,
thanks to its effects, she'll have another six months to
a year. (Gosh, sez the doc, I should've said it better
the first time. -- Or maybe he didn't even say this.
Being a supreme arbiter he can say just about whatever
he wants.)
        So yes, I'm feeling even more vindicated. (And has
Barb issued a mea culpa or a thank-you or even answered
my letter? No way.)
        Meanwhile: Beryl's dad drops dead at age seventy-
four. One day he's out bowling with Beryl and the rest
of the family and having a grand old time, two days
later he's gone. Bowel obstruction. (This is Beryl W.,
our next-door neighbor. Ben, her husband, knocks on our
kitchen door with the news, a strange nonplussed look
already saying a lot before he speaks.)
        And Hoppy the cat, the most intellectually
challenged cat of them all, disappears. He's been gone
a week now, so he too must've met up with the blade.
        (This going down beneath a blown-up and framed
photo of a convoy of early log trucks rolling out of a
nearby forest, each bearing a single log the diameter of
a grain silo -- old growth, this, and it too met the
blade, of course, and I'd say that was roughly sixty
years ago. Always draws lots of gapes, this photo.
-- And so much blue out there today when I look around
and also a picturesque foggy haze right at water level,
almost like an infinitely extended whipped-cream
topping. On an afternoon this fine who wants a fourth
hour of sleep, even one that might feature a dream of
myself blazing out more watercolors better by countless
orders of magnitude than any I'll ever do in real life.)

Now also a full week in our wake: Tax Day. Turned
out it wasn't that bad after all, neither the labor nor
the size of the bill. So -- another small windfall.
This time my share of it went to a massive hardback
volume of the works of -- the man who invented the
(Western) essay. I figure it's time. I didn't like him
too much in past samplings but then neither did I go for
either of my longstanding this-lifetime ficto-lit fave-
raves the first or even the second time around.
Seventy-five bucks (plus tax) for this one volume.

And almost a job for the jobless one -- the other
jobless one. (For this one here, the jyzer -- and he's
actually only two-thirds jobless -- the unemployment
checks keep merrily rolling in, though he fears each one
might be the last.) The eye clinic by the state ferry
dock, that was the near miss. A state-of-the-art
operation, family run, they wanted our "so cute" and
"vivacious" D to "join the team"; but they said so only
after a couple of unseemly flip-flops and also after
revealing they're health freaks to what seems a highly
unhealthy degree and, worst of all, after clarifying
that the job would be for just twenty-nine hours a week
at six dollars an hour and would include no benefits,
which by state law must kick in at thirty hours a week.
Much anguish -- and then the lady decided no. On top of
everything else she would've been required to keep a
daily nutrition diary open at all times to the owners'
inspection. And besides: the commute (forty miles round
trip) is just too long for such meager wages.

The next hope is a funky little camera factory deep
in the woods to the west. Five bucks an hour rehabbing
throwaway cameras, both day and swing shift available --
maybe. D likes the idea of being a camera "shucker," as
they're called, jargon for the one who strips down used
cameras. We've already driven out there twice -- twenty
miles round trip, not bad at all for these parts. The
boondocks in that area make ours look almost civilized,
but then this is not necessarily a drawback. However,
it'll be a couple of weeks before we know their verdict
-- suddenly they tell us. It seems jobs are even harder

to come by in their neck of the woods than in ours.
     But...but...the sail is just about over. (Will we
smash into the dock? Can an ocean liner stop on a dime?
Can a jyzemaster? And why haven't the models swaggered
by the booth again? Did they jump overboard? -- More
on all this. Maybe. Or just leave it tantalizing.)
                        *   *
     What is jyze? Thinking about it again as I walked
over here. I won't say what I came up with, other than
to note I should try harder to abide by the precepts set
forth at the end of "Jyzeburst." And therefore perhaps
I should review them to make sure I know what they are.
"The Ten Arms of the Jyzopus." Trouble is, at the
moment I can think of only six or maybe seven.
     (Pause to pour root beer into a glass already
bearing ice cubes. A three-letter set of initials
appears on the bottle. What they stand for I have no
idea, but since it's probably a brand name, those same
jyze precepts bar mentioning them. "No product placement
-- ever." Then again the initials could signify some
generic chemical which, when it's not being used to
extend the shelf life of root beer, serves to, say,
clear acres of unsightly weeds to make room for massive
new malls. In which case it's fine for jyze. But play
it safe here, and yet optimistically too, and call this
the good stuff in the dark brown bottle with no label,
that is, no paper label, but all the words molded on the
glass itself and tough to read, especially when obscured
by condensation and glinty reflections, as now.)
     Back here a new batch of paintings on display.
Great stuff! Forget the praise in my dream -- obviously
the praisers hadn't seen these (though I had, last time
I was here -- which in fact may have triggered the dream
-- and was reminded then of the teeming "outsider"
drawings of Barb's half-mad but authentically talented
high-school friend Donald). -- Amid bricks and books
and blue tables. And pipes. And an open wooden
staircase in the middle of the room. And the clatter of
go pieces being poured out on a board right now. -- And
high heels sounding on the wooden stairs and a couple

coming down, quite possibly that same flashy pair from the ferry -- but no. For a fraction of a second, though, I thought yes, that's who they were. Seeking me out, like vengeful deities from the overworld.

Infatuated with the Russian poet/essayist I blow another thirty bucks. A second bio of her. I couldn't risk losing a shot at it -- just one copy on the shelf. And three items from the remainder table, all hardcovers, all the work of my contemporaries who just keep churning out book after book after book while my wheels spin helplessly in Mentoka mud.

"Bloodiest terrorist act in U.S. history" -- guess I ought to mention that too. A car-bomb blows apart a nine-story federal office building in a city about the size of the one in which I'm holding forth now but some fifteen hundred miles to the southeast. Well over a hundred dead. At first right-wingers scream foreign Islamic crazies must be behind it (this includes major media and the government itself saying so) but no, it turns out homegrown right-wingers themselves are the villains. Surprise! As the body count even now keeps mounting. Racist Cawk militia guys from nearby central states did it. Probably not a whole lot different from the ones infesting the woods out where we live, and lots of other woods around here and across the country.

"TERROR RIPS U.S. HEART" trumpets our newly sensationalistic morning paper. This is before realizing the perpetrators are from the newspaper editorial board's end of the USAn political spectrum but just a little further out on it. -- And when I drop by our own principal federal office building for a six a.m. dinner stop, a cop turns me away at the door for the first time ever: only employees may enter. "Hopefully we'll have this thing fixed in a few days." -- But, I want to tell him, the first cousins of these bombers are already running this place on the inside, don't you see? (Only a slight exaggeration.) -- And outside the flags flutter at half mast. Then and still today.

*

A pause. Only because I needed a break. Always I

have this problem that my brain isn't functioning as
well as it might be if only I'd been able to sleep a few
more hours, preferably consecutively.

Three or four conversations I can tune in on from
here. Someone just arriving, talk of the difficulty of
parking. "You too?" "Oh yeah, definitely. Parking's
the bane of my existence." To which talk I say, "Just
park it right now, both of you! All of you!"

The year of "Notes on False Dreams." I'm looking
into it again for its relevance to the Mentoka trilogy.
My god what a year it was. What tumult! If only I'd
done better at writing down my impressions at the time.
It regularly blew all my circuits. By the time I was up
and running again another week or two had gone by and
much that had happened in the meantime was lost. I just
didn't know how to find a slant on it. And the odd part
is this: I thought I wasn't good enough (as an urjyzer),
but no, now I'd say that really wasn't it. Rather I was
too self-critical to be able to hang on to a slant long
enough to learn how to work it. That's all it was! Or
better to say: without doubt that was a big part of it.

-- And wasn't it just about a year ago this week
that I restarted what I thought was the protojyze
(though I didn't call it that yet) and it turned out to
be jyze? The biggest breakthrough of them all! Or in
any case I'm certainly a believer. So far the only one,
true, except for Mom and zen wife D (in both cases with
what I regard as only minor qualifications), and maybe
we three will be the only ones in my lifetime. Or ever.
Who knows! And what's more it doesn't even matter!
-- And this may be the best thing of all jyze can do for
you. "The jyze slant on things." Relish it! Cherish
it! Don't ever let it slip away!

Meanwhile I'm on my usual sort of mission when I
come into the city on a Saturday night. Nefarious
doings. More copying of old files onto diskettes. The
first returns from Papa U are encouraging: his computer
will at least acknowledge that the trial diskette I gave
him contains some sort of digital information. But,
alas, at this point he hasn't found the particular word-

processing program he thought would reveal what the information is, even though that program is not the same one I used to put the info on the disk. -- Also I have a big batch of my own notes to type up and a letter I'd like to write.

On three hours' sleep I'll be doing all this? And how much dozing? How much magic-carpet riding?

-- Yeah, maybe I'd better be moving along. (I do aim to return.)

*   *

Terminal fast food. A dozen customers in here already, which isn't bad for a Sunday at six-forty a.m. -- the exact hour at which my boat pulls out on any other day of the week (unless I catch the seven-forty or some other run). But not Sundays, no. There is no six-forty on Sundays. I forgot.

A cup of softie vanilla. So exceptionally fine was yesterday's weather that this joint used up an entire week's supply of cones and not a single one remains, though an emergency shipment will be coming in, the counterlady told me, sometime later this morning. "So it's a cup or nothin'," she said. "So a cup then."

-- A little bit of a scare as I left the office in a rush to catch this nonexistent boat. I hit the hall just as the night patrol did. To him I probably looked like a criminal. I know I felt like one. Hell, let's face it, I was one, at least in terms of what my former employers expect from their vendors. And being startled like that, and being in a rush to begin with, I acted like one -- nervous, furtive. Couldn't help myself. Fortunately I think the guy had seen me once before. Either that or he didn't want to start anything -- I outweigh him by maybe seventy or eighty pounds. (How nervous was I? I left the office door wide open. He pointed this out and I had to hurry back from halfway down the hall to close it -- as he watched. Suspiciously. And then I had to ride down on the elevator with him. Neither of us said a word. Fortunately again, he got off on twelve. A few more floors and he might easily have changed his mind. A

75

call to headquarters, a heads-up to one of the partners
-- it wouldn't've looked good. And it still could
happen. "Vagrant seen leaving Suite XXX at 0615,
appeared highly agitated, left door wide open....")
    And in my bag: the swag. A box of perfectly
ordinary diskettes containing my backed-up files and a
binder holding nine perfectly ordinary single-spaced
pages of freshly typed notes. Why was I getting so
uptight about someone finding such items in my
possession? Even if one of the partners had come in
personally to examine this contraband, what could she
say? A nightscoper can't be carrying diskettes and a
few pages of typed notes in his bag? Sheesh!
    Here in the fast-food joint I don't feel out of
place at all. I'd even say that of the dozen or so
customers in here right now I'm not only one of the
least scruffy-looking but also one of the least
agitated. Could even be, I'm thinking, my street camo
needs some updating.
    Here's the question of the moment. Do I dare to
haul my lunchbox out of my bag and start chowing down
right here? On my own homemade grub? I mean, I did buy
something. Am I not entitled?
    Nobody's paying me much attention. Muzak's rolling
and all the workers are going about their appointed
tasks behind the counter (in their spiffy blue uniforms
including brand-new blue visored caps). Out here in
the main dining area the scruffiest and most highly
agitated customers have either moved on -- it's already
warm enough to sit outside and the sun's not even up
yet, or at least not down here on the waterfront with
the big hill to the east -- or they're sitting way over
by the sidewalk windows (which is why I'm sitting over
here by the exit to the ferry parking area).
    Oh why not. Dare to be bold. -- As if I haven't
already proven my mettle with that guard this morning.
    But the counterlady is now out cleaning tables.
And she's saying to her coworker that the most highly
agitated of all the customers left his bag behind when
he departed. She doesn't want to touch it. Greasy ugly

thing with a dirty green rolled-up sleeping bag attached
to it with gritty brown twine. They may, jokes the
coworker, have to call in the decontam unit. And I'm
thinking she soon might be saying to the decontam unit,
"While you're at it, spray that guy over there too, the
one who's pretending to be writing." (Because in truth
my street camo's not all that bad.)
     Here goes nothing. Out with the lunch.
                         *   *
     Now on the threshold. Of what? The shed! The one
with no power! (But with all the power.) -- Because
you just gotta say something about a day so splendid.
     Or rather -- morning. Sunday. Sun. Birds. Such
sweet air, just a slight breeze, cherry blossoms in it,
earth, the horse pasture next door (two horse pastures
in fact, two next doors, both to the south, one above
the other on the hillside). Trickle of the creek (or
actually, again, two creeks, literally one for each ear
-- the right ear tracking the little tumbling stream
back in the woods to the north, the left focusing on the
noisier one a little farther away in the opposite
direction, running down the south property line).
     Grass growing high again already, up to eighteen
inches in places, my shoes and pantlegs still wet from
walking in it. And lots of dandelions poking up, a
boisterous mix of short dazzling golden blonds, taller
puffy gray spike-hairs, and even taller baldies, almost
like a cartoon version of the recent evolution of
hairstyles -- or of punk, say, after the longhair era.
     Streaks of high clouds, cirrus I suppose. Caws and
twitters, snickers, nickers, neighs, barks, baa-baas,
quack-quacks -- a good sample of the usual motley array.
     -- Driving home from the foot-ferry dock an hour
ago (a stop along the way for pop on sale, three cases,
works out to fourteen cents a pop -- of pop -- and
poppety-pop goes the jyzersiccle hittin' on two) (and
now a honking horn, "We're late!" -- for church!) (not
us, but Ben and Beryl; for church D and I are not just
eternally late, we're off the chart and beyond all
redemption, never to be raptured up ever) -- and I'm

thinking how sweet it is, this day, this life, the
rustic setting, and someday I'll no doubt be sorry I
failed to jot down more details on this sweetness out
here -- how vividly green everything is, how woodsy and
pastoral -- the magnificent trees and farms along the
road coming home -- cows grazing by the creek down in
the glen, ducks and geese gliding on this pond and that
pond as ponies cavort nearby, kids frolicking rural
style with sprigs of weed hanging from their lips (just
what kind of weed I can't say for sure) -- and this
being Sunday it's wonderfully peaceful in this the least
churchgoing state of them all -- though of course you
still see plenty of churchbound folks anyway, often
dressed to the nines, and the particular one most of
them in nearby realms are bound for is the bible church
about a quarter mile away up around the loop where, from
what I've heard, the sermons sometimes call anathema
down on anyone who's not a militia member or at the very
least a prospective militia recruit. (Were my three
sibs and parents and I ever a family looking like the
one I saw on the road this morning with its brood of
four, three boys and a girl just like us, and all so
well-behaved?) ...And just a whole barrowful of idyllic
Sunday-morning-out-for-a-drive-in-the-country thoughts.

(Also noticing a strange soreness on the right side
of my tongue so far back I gag if I try to touch it with
a finger -- and what new failure of the flesh might this
portend or reveal?)

Refusing to take another step after getting off the
foot ferry -- stopping right there on the dock because I
burned to finish the Russian poet/essayist's marvelous
piece on her mother the musician -- laughing out loud
over it as oddly well-dressed skateboarders whizzed by.

The carts in the market. The checkout line. The
senior bagger trying so damn hard to be speedy as the
much-younger manager peered sternly out at him from her
bulletproof glass cage. The gray wagon parked somewhere
out in the lot -- where was it again? (Almost always at
least a few of them around, same year, same model, same
color as ours.) The awkwardly big ignition key. The

automatic shoulder harness whose abrupt way of collaring
you from behind -- just how building security might do
it back in the city -- I'm still not used to.

     Here on the interior shed wall a dozen of Lady U's
smaller paintings, among them my favorites from a decade
back, the matched set of Fauve/Cubist ukiyo-e dancers.
This gray cedar siding which truly is handsomely aging
now (except for the one peculiar sprung sliver about a
foot long and half an inch wide, right at eye level just
inches to my left as I sit on the doorsill with legs
sprawled in the grass -- a big old bumblebee nosing
about near my right foot, a couple of yellow moths
fluttering gaily a pace or two farther out). And in the
powerless dark shed inner sanctum where the breeze is
driving out the winter mustiness through opened windows
even as I push the J-stick ever onward out here I see
(and I mean right now peripherally) the glowing Mentoka
"45 x 90" bumper sticker ("exact center of the Western
Hemisphere, northern half") and another one for the
recently defunct Wachute Catbirds -- stacks of boards
tucked in and standing at an angle awaiting a return to
duty of the carpenter (who's been self-laid off now for
a couple of years -- and right here he sits) -- but oh
such a fine piece of work this shed is! (As a big
surprising whinny sounds in the upper pasture, and
another, and another -- maybe a stallion on the mount --
delivering its spunky sermon thereupon, so to speak.)
     Think how you can live for years in the city or
even the suburbs and never be surprised by such a sound.
Though best not to wax too rurally euphoric here.
Cities can surprise you in fine ways too and places like
this, well, they can sicken you, horrify you, bore you
to death. -- Well but of course. As what place can't?
     -- And I'm thinking if I break this off right now I
can likely still catch Lady U in bed for a fine Sunday-
morning mounting of my own (or her own -- either would
be fine with me and both still better). Because it's
been too long for sure. This old hoss here has his
sermon ready for the mounting: a major, major jizzburst. (What's this here? Blue jyze?)

[Jyzemelt]

11

    Just at dusk and right where jyze began, except for
certain differences, or one big one anyway. And there's
this: a new era's underway. It appears. And I hope.
    More than one big difference. The grass outside
the sliding glass door here, I cut it myself. This was
my first bit of bona-fide solo mechanized lawn-mowing in
almost twenty years (since the summer in Gatewood after
Dad's death). And for the rest of this year's grass-
growing season and I hope next year's too the job will
remain all mine. Right now the much larger backyard
awaits me, already almost comically overgrown. But it's
drizzling out there. Every day for four days straight
it's been drizzling all day long. (Dad, do you hear me,
still coughing up the same old excuses?)
    But the new era. The lady isn't home at the
moment; she's off deep in the woods at the camera
factory. This is her very first day at her new job.
And for the first week she'll be doing her training on
the swing shift, from three to eleven-thirty p.m. For
those hours I've got the house all to myself.
    And another difference: I'm working at the redwood
table. This is the one I assembled myself while D was
away visiting her parents shortly after we first moved
in here at U Acres, one of any number of domestic
surprises I put together for her that first summer of
country living. (I liked it so much, this table, I went
back the next day and bought a second one, since they
were on sale at a ridiculously low price and I was
relatively flush then -- and that second one now stands
out on the deck.) Working at the low coffee table was

80

starting to hurt my back again so I decided -- because
this is it, the make-or-break JIFTing-of-Mentoka year --
I'd better get serious and set up a real worktable in
here. So here it is. We passed it in from the utility
room, D and I did, lifting it over the ancient stereo
console (inherited from Andy and Tera) and the three-
shelf particleboard China bookcase. And we set it down
on the same sheet of plywood Papa U laid out for me, and
I fetched from the parlor one of the creaky old wooden
public library chairs (a brass plate affixed to the
underside of the seat attesting it's still my old
employer's property, back in my city No. 11, if I've got
the number right, the one where Lady U and I met; but
we did actually buy it, along with five others, for ten
bucks total as I recall) -- and on this chair I now sit.
    It's a good-size table, a work surface of thirty by
fifty inches. Eight redwood planks running lengthwise.
A calendar blotter. A desk lamp, fluorescent type
(maybe I should substitute the other one with the
standard bulb -- yes, I will, because this one bothers
my eyes a bit since its width requires me to look
directly into at least part of it no matter where it
stands on the table -- and so now I can say that much is
decided).
    And meanwhile dusk's gone black outside the glass.
    -- But I promised to feed the outdoor cats at eight
and I see it's now past eight-thirty. It'll take me a
while to adjust to all my new zen-househubby duties.
Still to do tonight: wash the dishes, make the bed,
clean the bathrooms, start a load of laundry, maybe a
couple of other chores I've lost track of (but we did
draw up a list together, the lady and I, and it's
propped up in a conspicuous spot on the kitchen counter).
Already I've done a fine job brewing a pot of coffee and
rustling up breakfast. (And right now I'm doing a fine
job as well ignoring a ringing telephone: until nine
o'clock it could be Employment Security and I definitely
want to avoid them for a few more days until I can
launch a new batch of employment-inquiry letters.)
-- But the cats. They're yowling at the door up there.

Makes me want to clap my hands over my newly sensitized
ears all the way down here.

*

Two minutes later and I'm back. It wasn't that
hard! Filled all five bowls even though only three cats
showed up. And clamped the three wooden clothespins
back on the nearly depleted twenty-five-pound sack of
Mouskies or whatever they're called. And back down here
started up the washer which is whirring busily in the
next room. Closed the curtains with an accidentally
overstrong tug on the cord, then feared for a moment
that the whole apparatus, rod and all, was about to come
crashing down. And disinterred a dark cherry candy from
its hiding place deep in my backpack and popped it into
my mouth and just now broke through to the deliciously
sweet hit of "juice" at the core. And all is well.

Or is it? Well obviously it isn't. But still it's
looking better than it has for some time. We've got Mom
in remission (of a kind anyway) and we've got Lady U
bringing in some bucks -- and we've got all fingers
crossed (except the J-stick-clasping ones).

We've even got (and I have to unscrunch my
disbelieving eyebrows over this one) a letter from
sister Barb. It's belated and it says very little of
substance (is it that she's just colossally concerned
about maintaining doctrinal purity or what?) -- but it's
handwritten words on paper. Not many words, but some.
On a card hand-fashioned, in fact, by her admirable
live-in boyfriend Keith from glossy movie-ad cutouts
featuring a gaggle of mega stars (among them Rambo,
Gump, and the Terminator) and some wildly inappropriate
words which I forget. Is it worth checking what they
are? Sure! -- But I won't. The card's upstairs. (And
Barb mentions that Keith had advised her, when she
stalled out while trying to get started on this letter,
"Don't fake it." I like that too -- even though I
think Barb might have a lot easier time in life if she
could lower herself a bit every now and then to doing
exactly that: faking it. As for myself, I have no doubt
at all that faking it, like it or not, is mainly what

82

it's all about a significant (highly) part of the time
in my life or just about anyone's. Certainly it's one
of the best ways I know to make something more real
that's not already real enough.)

My next task is to mail down the Russian poet's
book of essays. I bought a second copy but because I
don't want Barb to think I ignored her instructions
("Don't buy me any books -- I'm the one who has money
now") I'll send her the copy I've just finished reading
and keep the shiny new one for myself until she gives me
the old one back, if that ever happens, in which case
I'll pass the new one along to brother Rob.

But an interesting ten days leading up to May Day,
which this is. Out in the world we've got the aftermath
of the horrific heartland bombing in which bodies are
still being pulled from the smoking ruins of the federal
building and here and there people are finally starting
to ask some pointed questions about these rabid
"Christian Identity" militants. Let's hope this is the
event which finally reverses the flow of the rightward
tide -- but as of now such a hope looks rather more
plaintive than promising. (And things could get very
nasty, maybe something like the wars lasting decades
between left/liberal/cosmopolitan/moderates and right/
conservative/nationalist/reactionaries in certain Latin
American countries, say Colombia or Chile or Argentina.)

And for us, the job climax. All of a sudden Lady U
had four different options on the fire at once, or
almost at once. Say three at once. Ophthalmology
assistant was a no-go, as already noted. So then there
was stocker at the bridge market (just two and a half
miles south of us), receptionist/salesperson for a
women's weight-loss clinic in a mall maybe thirty
minutes away (one way) by car, and finally disassembly
worker for the funky camera factory (twenty minutes'
drive into the forest).

Yvonne at the bridge market called with an apology
for the delay in processing D's application, but she had
a truly solid excuse: her husband had killed himself.
And she still wanted D bad. But -- again not enough

hours, D decided. And the pay was very low. And no
health insurance. And her biggest concern of all: the
heavy lifting might restart her back problems.

The weight-loss clinic, it did offer a health plan
and a slightly higher salary, but this didn't outweigh
(sticking with the lingo) the cost of the long commute
and the strong likelihood of mandatory split shifts.

The camera factory is small and independently owned
and the company slogan is "It's a Snap!" What they do
out there is disassemble, reload, reassemble, and
package throwaway cameras on a contract basis for larger
companies. Disassembling is called "shucking" and the
real klutzes do that. When D went in for her interview
she said she wanted to do shucking but they told her
with her background in art and also her stereotypically
presumed-nimble fingers (but they are just that) she was
"too good for shucking." That's been the joke of the
week around here. When she brought me the tweezers and
lifted her sweatshirt I couldn't resist: "Hey you, Too-
Good-For-Shucking, how come you can't pluck your own
nipple whiskers? What happened to those nimble
fingers?" Too-Good-For-Shucking Lady U, like Too Tall
Jones. (But of course I plucked anyway; it's one of my
all-time favorite domestic chores.)

The factory, such as it is, is ten miles southwest
of here just outside a small town a lot like ours, which
is to say it's basically just a clearing in the alder/
cedar/fir forest containing a few score homes and shops
(probably it's a little bigger than our town but for
sure it's a lot more isolated). A cluster of ramshackle
barnlike metal buildings, a deeply rutted gravel parking
lot looking literally like an auto junkyard, with about
twenty beater cars belonging to the employees pulled up
in wild disarray therein. Just about the last stop on
the job line. Five bucks an hour, which is fifteen
cents over minimum wage in this state. Required
overtime during rush periods. Health insurance "after
six months on the job" but somehow no one ever seems to
get any. Long slow periods in winter during which
shutdowns and layoffs may occur at any time.

[Real Jyze]

    But this is the job the lady prefers. In fact she
declares it's her employment dream: pure mindless rote
work, like the old assembly lines. (Of course she had a
dream about rural life too and that one hasn't turned
out too well as she sees it and also as I see it. Some
bitter jokes. And she's not real happy about having to
go back to work. But she's doing it and trying to be
cheery about it and what more can I ask?)
                              *

    -- It's several hours later (one thing arose and
then another and another) and the new addition to
workforce USA is now home. The car came crunching up
the driveway through drenching rain at one a.m. "I'm
sure they won't all be like today, but if they were --
it's not that bad!" Most of today she did "poking":
removing cutout sections from the camera's cardboard
inner wrap. Nobody hassled her. Her only problem came
on the way home when she missed a turnoff in the dark on
the twisty forest road. And she showed me the four
"tools of the trade" she was issued, all cheapos and
very small (the largest a standard razor-blade knife).
    Looks fairly promising. Now if only her health
holds up -- or I should say if only the inevitable
health collapses aren't bad enough to get her fired or
force her to quit.
    Yes, I like it. Knowing she's out working to keep
us in vittles may even help me be more focused while
fictojyzing, I'm thinking. Nor do I mind doing the
chores around the house. They fit nicely into the
breaks I like to take anyway. Lend them a surprisingly
virtuous new meaning -- even folding the laundry does
this. Even scrubbing the toilet bowls.
    For right now I'll try not to think about the
many things that could go wrong.
    What else? -- Well, a few matters, yes, but
better to yield to a persistent distraction: the
excited new factory worker is dying to spin out (act
out too no doubt) another batch of stories about the
quirks and crazinesses of her first day on the job.
                              *

85

[Jyzemelt]

     All right. Consider today just about all jyzed
out. Already! -- But I must mention a former U.S.
Secretary of Defense's revolting new mea-culpa book on
Vietnam: the guy who ran the war and even had it named
after him (by journalists). Now more than a quarter
century ex post facto he sheds crocodile tears and says
it was all a terrible mistake. Fesses up. This rips
open lots of old wounds but not for people like me who
were calling for this man's scalp back then. We can
even crow a little. We can even dare to hope this too
heralds a turning of the rightward tide.
     And mention this: one night at the bookstore in the
city I met the painter whose work I was raving about in
these pages last week. He, Anton T., was taking down
his canvases from the brick walls in the basement cafe
as the exhibition came to an end. Just him and me in
the back area. I told him how much I liked his stuff
and we got to talking and went on with it for close to
an hour. He's a former stockbroker, of all things --
surprisingly diffident as an artist and winningly self-
effacing. Wife and kids to support and little income
from the art. Not a single call resulted from the
bookstore showing -- in fact my comments were the first
feedback of any kind he'd gotten.
     How far out of it am I? Aside from Lady U and her
mother, this was the first working artist I've talked
with like that in years. More than a decade maybe, I
don't know. I was almost as tongue-tied as he was. I
couldn't help but be struck by our similarities as
isolated lone-wolf "outsider artists." Even in this
hang-loose society the artist may encounter a very
different kind of fate. Who wants a "community of
artists" anyway? Still it can be bracing (and touching
too) to see up close, even exchange words with, someone
who in many ways walks in your own chucks (as indeed he
was doing and black-and-white ones too, just like mine,
but his featuring colorful laces as only befitted the
visual artist -- the jyzer's laces being more
prosaically vanilla just as one might also expect).

12

The depot. Yup, Jyze City train depot, five minutes before seven in the morning, and I'm not even going anywhere. Today, that is. Except back to the woods.

July 6th is when I'll be seeing Mother next, a change from June 7th -- because Aunt Shar will be visiting her on June 7th, it now becomes known, with Aunt Shel and brother Jeff arriving later that month. Much easier for me than for any of those others to change dates. And July's preferable for me anyway because I won't be facing a conflict with office work then, and probably not with Employment Security either.

(This morning the depot's packed, and mostly with teenage girls. It's still about a month too early for anyone to be going off to summer camp, so I wonder what's up. But now I see a few boys scattered among them, so maybe it's a school field trip. Possibly to a fantasyland theme park of some sort -- do kids this old still go for that kind of thing these days? Or I suppose they could be headed for the state capital, an in-the-flesh civics lesson which itself might prove somewhat fantastical if not downright phantasmagorical.)

-- But there's good news. Yes! That, and there's vindication -- and so a double yes! (The adolescent high spirits raging away on all sides seem to be contagious.)

It happened like this. I phoned dayscoper Doris at the office to check whether reporter Naomi had returned yet from out of state with the grand-jury finals for me to correct (in other words, would I have to go in to the office that night or would I get to wait another day or two). Doris was all glum and gloomy: business was terrible and what's more, get this, reporter Verna had lost her grand jury. The feds called one day without warning and said from now on it would be handled by another firm. No further explanation.

But we don't need further explanation. We know. Back during the RIF crisis last summer I warned partner Fran this might happen if they took the nightscoper -- me -- off GJ. Verna's a great steno writer but she's too sloppy in her English usage (grammar and such); it was only because a diligent scoper was spending extra-long hours cleaning up her stuff that her work was acceptable to the feds. She knew it too (and told him, the scoper, so) but then after a while she forgot.

"You're shooting yourself in the foot, Fran." -- Not that I'm crowing. Not that I'm gloating over someone else's misfortune. Not that I'm indulging in the old I-told-you-so. However I will admit I'd be justified in doing all those nasty things -- and more! But instead I'll extend my condolences and slather Verna and the whole firm with commiseration for the lost business. Oyez.

(Last night I even ran into partner Una in the hallway -- first direct contact with her since well before I got axed. Did she have a kind word to say? No. An apology? Not hardly. All she could talk about was the dwindling number of pages the firm is cranking out. And of course here too I earnestly commiserated. -- This conversation lasting all of a minute or so before she had to hurry off.)

So then I called Naomi at home and found she'd just gotten back in town. And learned this: she intends to take only three months off for the "birthing." And when I asked if she wants Jyzer Ink to keep doing her government scoping when she returns she said, "Please please please." And she said she expects to keep her grand jury. She didn't come right out and say, "Thanks to you, nightscoper G," but that's how I chose to hear it regardless.

Why is this good? Because, first, I'll be able, after the three-month interlude, to keep feeding my own stuff through the office machines -- though I'll still have to be very cautious about it -- and this in turn means I won't have to be using Papa U's cast-off machine except in emergencies. And second, I'll be able to augment the bucks D will be bringing in from the camera factory (augment by a factor of half to two-thirds maybe) while still keeping most of my time free for working on -- the Mentoka series!

Yes, the series. But it's not "Jyzer," at least not at the moment, that's the series book in play; it's "Mentoka Dreams." And it's happening. It's the real thing. It's terrific. All of which I can say because it's utterly and wholly unJIFTed. Nonetheless I'm working hard on the reJIFTing. (And this does make sense in the world of fictojyze, a/k/a JIFT, except that here I'm working not from jyze or protojyze but from the chronbooks (a/k/a urjyze) of decades back.)

-- And there they go, the teens, swarms of them, lining up for preboarding at Door 2. All juniors and seniors from a local suburban high school, it turns out (I've been listening -- no other choice really). Dressed to travel. Fancied-up grunge gear and backpacks galore. Here and there I spot an actual hard-copy-type book. All Cawks, these "upperclassmen," except for one guy who looks South Asian, "India Indian." (And do they realize the shame of this racial near-purity? Would I if I were in high school today, living where they live -- which probably isn't all that different from the lily-white burbs of my own adolescent era?)

Meanwhile it's almost time for me to pack up for the next stage in my own journey. The usual course. But things aren't at all usual most of the time these days as D and I grind through our transitional period to becoming a smoothly functioning two-worker set of zen spouses. One sign of this: my clothes are still damp (shoes even more so) from last night's two-mile hike through a pouring rain to the county bus stop -- most of it along a muddy, puddly, gravelly road shoulder.

[Jyzemelt]

    Every time I go in now I have to do this trudging,
although it's not always in the rain. Just usually, it
seems. But strangely enough I don't mind all that much.
I even like the exercise. Now I can say I walk at least
six or seven miles a day and be sure it's true. (Sore
muscles the first few days because you walk differently
on soft gravel, to say nothing of when you leap on, and/
or onto, soft gravel to elude splashes from passing
vehicles. -- No rifle shots from joyriding pickups to
dodge as yet, but those too may come at any time.)
    And much else is new. But later for that. -- With
the depot now empty, the doors still open, conductors
glancing at their watches, the same continental I was on
last month (even the same train number), and maybe will
be on again in July, trembling in place with all those
kids aboard and due to pull out any second now.
                    *   *
    This too is unusual. One of the super-jumbo
ferries is looming out there in Slip No. 2. That's the
suburban-island boat, too big, too fast, too fancy for
our run. But there it is in our slip. Presumably some
repair work's being done on the super-jumbo's normal
slip, No. 3.
    And here I sit on the Slip No. 3 side, because with
the crowds for both boats crammed mostly into the No. 2
waiting area no seats were available over there.
    The mirror image of the usual setup as I see it and
also as it sees me.
    Am I sharp today? Am I sharp? At the office-
supply store the clerk told me they no longer carry the
brand of pens I use for editing. So I nosed around a
bit and found a dusty display of those very pens
partially hidden behind another display on the highest
shelf atop a corner stand. She laughed, the so-called
Latina (maybe Nicaraguan, I'd guess, from her
resemblance to Unk Erik's Consuela in looks and accent)
-- very warm and friendly and always able to coax me
into buying a few more of their special comp books,
which to my mind are simply the finest there could ever
be for jyzing purposes. She and I can goof around a lot

90

because at eight a.m. I'm almost always the first
customer of the day and the only one in the shop.
-- And I say "so-called Latina" because why should
descendants of the Maya and other indigenous peoples in
that area be called "Latin," an antique name for the
European tribal confederation that massacred many of
them and colonized the rest? It's something like
calling descendants of the Mentoka, or for that matter
any other tribe on the northern seven-eighths of this
continent, "Britas."

A few flashes of sun as I walked over from the
depot. Straight north. Already dozens -- or no, more
like scores of homeless men were standing or sprawling
on the sidewalks outside the missions and in other
isolated spots all the way to the stationery shop, about
eight blocks to the north.

Oops, gotta go. Ferry's almost in. It snuck up on
me because I'm not used to looking out from this Slip 3
angle.

*

Peaceful nine o'clock run. A/B's, short for
ablebodieds, swabbing the deck section in front of me,
having previously blocked off access to the area with
high walls of stacked deck chairs like something out of
a major French street demo. Little talk -- most folks
reading newspapers and sipping coffee. Tap-tap-tap of a
laptop with its key-sound button on (for many people
brought up on typewriters, myself included, it's
comforting to hear the taps -- and useful too, when it's
your own keyboard; you can often tell by sound alone if
you've misstroked while your eyes were tending to
something else). And now someone's talking in an
obnoxiously loud voice on a cellphone. Neither cells
nor laptops were commonly seen on this boat until just a
few years ago. Technological progress and its
pernicious side effects, the old story. (And you
certainly don't want to try to come up with a new slant
on it during a fifty-minute ferry ride.)

Here's a big rustbucket freighter looming up close,
straining leeward on its anchor chain like an irascible

overgrown pit bull in an ill-fitting harness.

     -- And about those editing pens mentioned earlier,
I should say I bought all they had, ten of them at two
bucks apiece. All the blue-ink ones, that is. I go
through them like...like...what? Like so many straws in
the wind, I guess I could say. (But straws portending
what, O Jyzer G? Construction of straw men perhaps?)

     -- Three weeks went by before Mother called again,
or almost three anyway. This time the news was not so
good: the doc could find no shrinkage in the masses.
Accordingly Mother was feeling pessimistic. "I don't
know, Glennar, I don't think it'll be twelve to twenty
months -- a lot less than that, I'm afraid." She also
reports most of her hair's fallen out, although she
hasn't yet gone shopping for a wig (and so I suspect
she's exaggerating). And she's been out, on her own,
walking, shopping, even riding a bus -- the very thought
of which makes me shudder with fear for her (much as she
must've done for me on my earliest bus rides alone, back
when she was just about exactly half my age now and
slightly more than a third her own age now). She even
did her laundry at a neighborhood laundromat and then
dragged the bags home along the sidewalk (and described
this proudly, of course).

     How long before she breaks a hip? I beg her to be
cautious but I know she's not hearing me. Better to
take the risks, she thinks, than to give up all activity
-- and so she heedlessly throws herself into it. Argh.

     Aunt Shel's visit, she says, was a disaster. It
took her, Mother, days to get over it to the point where
she felt strong enough to talk with anyone. -- But no
details. She uses their relationship as a cautionary
tale for me and Barb. "Don't let it happen to you."

     Ho. Ho ho. But at least Barb and I are still
trying to avoid such a fate.

     (And maybe I'm learning a little more about Barb
from reading a magnificent Portuguese protojyzer of
sorts who happens to be a bit on the depressive side,
I'll say, in much the same way she often is. Now I've
hunted down the man's second book published in English,

and to my astonishment I find a blurb printed on the
cover describing it as "the most beautiful diary of the
Twentieth Century." In fact I've located two different
sets of selections from this diary and I've bought them
both. I love the cover photo on one of these showing
the huge old steamer trunk in which the man's
unpublished writings were discovered after his death,
including the makings of the diary. Even in Portuguese
it wasn't published until half a century after its final
entry. And I'm still wondering how I missed the first
English version when it came out ten years ago.)

And getting back to the transition period: I'll
just say I've been mowing the lawn and washing the
dishes and making the bed and scrubbing the tub and
doing all the other chores in such fine fashion I almost
feel I'm fourteen years old all over again. The lawn's
the toughest because I'm a rookie with the trimmer-
mower, which handles quite differently from the types of
mower I've used before, both reel and rotary. And the
yard is marshy, hilly, bumpy, and, above all, huge. And
of course I'm whining about it nonstop. But no, not
really. Guess I could even say I've grown up since back
then, just as Mother and Dad, no doubt much in the way
of mothers and dads everywhere, often said with a sigh
they hoped I would someday manage to do.

During the five days a week she works D needs all
her waking hours for the job and all her sleeping hours
for sleep. That's just how it is and so I'm trying not
to squawk too much. She drives off at two-thirty in the
afternoon and returns at about one a.m. or so after
working an hour or two of overtime and crashes
immediately. So far the work itself's been easy. I'm
just praying nothing upsets the apple cart.

Life goes along in periods of drift with only
slight changes, though over time these changes can
accumulate in surprising ways when you compare how
things are now to how they were a year or two or five
ago -- and then there are the sudden large changes.
These latter are what so-called catastrophe theory is
all about (one of the hot realms in popular math/science

over the past few years). Right now for D and me is catastrophic in this sense of sudden great change. What we want to do is confine the catastrophe as much as possible to this mere superficial mathematical sense.

The turn. There it is, unlovely downtown navy burg. And there, first in the row of big gray ships, ominous, awesome, is the most famous dreadnought of them all, this summer's primo local tourist attraction (because coming up this August is a major anniversary of the end of World War II, and the Evil Axis Empire East, which is to say the U family's ancestral homeland, officially capitulated on its deck -- and a model of that very ship floated atop my dresser, as part of a small but mighty and, to my mind then, stainlessly virtuous task force, for most of my childhood).

13

Well why not one more time aboard the ferry going in. Things just happen to fall this way if I abide strictly by my jyze schedule for this year, and that's what I'm trying to do whenever possible. And besides -- though I'm aware I've said this several times before and always been wrong (which actually is pleasing in a way, indicating I may not be in as much of a rut as I thought, or at least a different kind of rut) -- it could be I'll soon stop riding the ferries altogether, or almost so.

Had to rush up the exit ramp to make this one. "DO NOT ENTER" says the big sign at its base -- but lots of people do enter there, and frequently I have no choice but to do so myself because otherwise I'll miss the boat. The connections with the foot ferry are very

tight timewise; and owing to the way the docks and
parking lots are laid out, foot-ferry riders constitute
by far the largest group of transgressive boarders
charging up the exit ramp.

Useless arcana. Jyze on, fool! And didn't even
remember to bring your bottle of ink! (And you thought
you had it so together today.)

Large popcorn -- why not? And, by a stroke of good
fortune, an official state-ferries plastic thermal mug
bearing an image of a ferry accompanied by a pod of
leaping orcas with the city skyline and mountains
sketched in for background (greens and purples and blues
looking good on the gray mug but alas the artwork is
awful) -- this indestructible future archaeological
artifact, its lid firmly in place, jumped up into my
hand from the trash barrel. Maybe a tourist thought it
was just a run-of-the-grinder coffee mug and tossed it?
But at the canteen they cost $2.75 apiece. And if
you're carrying one of these mugs all coffee purchases
on this or any other ferry are charged as refills, and
refills are surprisingly cheap -- a concession (in both
senses) to complaints lodged by regular riders
concerning last year's astronomical across-the-board
boost in canteen prices.

Efficient -- because I have to be. By the time I
get up D is long gone to her job. I must shower and
shave, make breakfast (including coffee), throw
together a box lunch and snacks, and leave home in time
to complete the two-mile hike to the bus stop before
half past five when the last bus of the day pulls out.

I can still get my ducks in a row if I have to.
It's even fun in a way. Even when it's raining. (And
today -- it's not!)

Tonight's the first round of another cycle of
grand-jury scoping. Probably there'll be just one more
such cycle before reporter Naomi goes on maternity
leave. Therefore I'll soon have to put a stop to the
fun of being so organized.

The pattern for the new era is already emerging and
I'll just go ahead and say I'm delighted with it and

hope it will last forever. Two, three, four years --
any of those would be acceptable too. Given even the
shortest of them I'm pretty sure I could do what needs
to be done. Meaning: "Jyzer," "Dreams," and "Ghosts":
the Mentoka trilogy. What's more, if my body holds up
long enough I think I can still hope to complete the
rest of the lifework I started planning roughly half a
lifetime back. All is not lost! Maybe even nothing is
lost!

   And I get to do a lot of reading too. The thirty-
inch-high triple stack of books by the study couch which
I retire to for my late-night nap, this is my new secret
pride. At the top of the stacks are about a dozen books
which I'm trying to dip into a bit before nodding out,
each with a brightly colored tape place-marker. Among
the active dozen I jockey and scheme to keep a wide
variety of genres well represented: fiction, poetry,
lit crit, biography, autobiography, science, politics,
anthropology, philosophy, among others. As with the
lifework, if I can keep this up for two, three, four
years -- if not, again, forever -- I stand at least a
slim chance of becoming, finally, passably educated and
informed and up to date. (Miss T, college-prep scourge
of Gatefield High, do I hear you cheering?)

   (The main drawback with this approach to reading is
that one of the dozen books may grab you to the point
where you ignore all the others. Then by the time you
finish the grabber and get back to the others, you may
have forgotten what they're all about and have to start
over. -- But then is this really so bad? Obey your
passion! Even if it's a bookish one! -- And the parts
of the other books you've forgotten while going at the
grabber, they may leave a slightly more lasting
impression from being read twice, or more than twice.)

   -- We're looking across the bay at a ferry perched
atop stilts inside, but also well above, one of the
massive dry docks. Which means this stage of my
infamous ten-stage commute (five each way) is close to
its end.

   Next: the usual hike over to the ORB cafe (only

real bookstore).

Weighing down my jacket pocket is the Portuguese depressive's magnificent diary, replacing the sampler of his works which I finished yesterday. I'm simultaneously chipping away at the other translation of this same diary at home, so this is my high Portuguese-depressive period.

*   *

Root beer. Glass of ice. Blue table in the back corner. "Poppa's Got a Brand New Bag." Of books!

A mixed bag this time. Seated on the USAn-classics chair (an ordinary but puzzlingly uncreaky wooden library chair hidden deep in the literature section) I checked out all the titles. It's a kick I'm on. Only two authors was I unfamiliar with and I bought a book of "confessions" by one of them. The other was a guy also, like me, writing about a USAn harbor, his being on the far coast. (A second work of his is truly a classic of this century, an assured brick in the canon at least according to the intro. Shows the staying power of the literati in that same very large city. Shows as well that some harbors may be better than others to write about if you want to peddle the words.)

Also in that bag is the novel I'd been trying to recall the title of for Barb, the one set in Italy about the time she was there during her post-college "wanderjahr" (two years actually as it turned out). By sheer luck I came across it on the remainder table.

-- And (segue here) when I called Mother on Mother's Day Barb was hovering in the background, along with cousin Lars, and when I had Mother ask Barb if she'd received my second package containing the Russian poet's essays, Barb said yes and then threatened to deluge me with books. "You wait and see!" (I heard her say this in the background.) And I thought: hmm, is this not strange? Will she really send me some books? What would they be? Will I have to buckle down to the magnum opus of some nineteenth-century theologian? The complete works of a major twelfth-century enabler of the crusades? What have I set myself up for?

[Jyzemelt]

    With Lars Mother resorted to the old thrust-it-at-
you gambit and I could hear him mutter as he approached
the phone, "I'm really not very good at this." I guess
we managed all right, we two stodgy eldest sons, except
for the three or four occasions when we both started to
talk at the same time and then lapsed into mutual
embarrassed silence. But still -- I like the guy.
Right away noticed his apparently ineradicable Mentoka
twang. These days he's a law professor at a far-coast
state university. For years he worked in the field of
poverty law and probably still is doing so. And he flew
all that way to see his dying Aunt Georgie. And I've
known the guy since a few hours after his birth and
remember very clearly the excitement of that day.
-- And so, thinking of these things and appreciating his
good-spirited and almost deferential modesty on the
phone, I later asked Mother to send me his address.
Maybe we can find some matters of mutual interest to
write to each other about. (Or more likely: not.)
    -- As for the grand ol' lady herself, things are
going as well as can be expected or (I'd say) quite a
bit better than that. I find myself thinking: she may
well survive another two or three years. Probably this
was the last Mother's Day I'll be able to speak with
her, but maybe not. She wasn't coughing at all (though
she said the coughs were lurking "just beneath the
surface" at all times). The call itself was rushed
because it took me half an hour to get through to her
and by then it was almost my departure time for another
surreptitious appearance at the office. (Earlier I did
try to recall exactly what presents I'd given her on
Mother's Days as a kid and could come up with nothing
specific. I'd intended to ask her on the phone but then
in the rush forgot.)
    And the next morning on the way back home (moving
on now from Mother) I did my first major bit of grocery
shopping for D and me since our city days (when for ten
years I did virtually all of it and almost always hauled
the bags home five to ten blocks on foot). Monday
morning at eight a.m. is a good time for marketing, I

recalled from before, and this apparently remains true.
Empty aisles, full shelves, cheery, unrushed checkers.
I zipped through it all in less than an hour and didn't
miss a single item on the list. From now on this is my
job as long as D's still working and I'm not, or mostly
not.

How's she doing? Seems to be adapting well to the
new working life. To the majorly increased presence of
a zen hubby in the house, and a zen househubby at that,
maybe it's a bit more of a stretch for her. If so, it's
a matter I for one am willing to be as patient about as
she wants or requires or demands.

-- But it appears the ink's nearly out and what's
more it's late; I could be up there punching in edits.

*

-- And now it seems the alarm on ink was false.
Held up to the light the ink window on the J-stick is
dark, meaning plenty's still in there -- either that or
the light down here's weaker than it appears to be.

Ah well...if a rule can't be broken it's too
draconian for jyze.

*   *

Aboard in the a.m. Will the ink last? Only three
pages to go after this one before I meet the notes
coming back the other way. (But the drama on the ink is
false because I've got backup brand-X BB-nib J-stick No.
4 ready to tag in from my bag. What's more it's been
there or in my shirt pocket all along. Yet I wasn't
being intentionally misleading. To me it always feels
like drama when the ink's about to run out -- and doubly
so if at the same time the J-book is about to fill up.)

This morning I've somehow wound up configured in
the booth in such a way that I can eat only by reaching
across my right arm with my left. This beneath another
framed blown-up black-and-white photo, the "midget
grocery" in the state capital, again roughly sixty years
ago. (If it's a forerunner at all of the supermarket I
shopped in the other day it's a remote one -- not much
more than a thousandth the size, I'd guess.)

A long night's work -- half of a 225-page grand-jury session fully scoped and the rest scanned and set up for tonight. So far I've worked on a methamphetamine bust and two frauds, one small-business and one postal, six witnesses in all. This means even if today's session is as long as they get (about two hundred and fifty pages) I still won't be too pressed for time over the next two nights. In other words I should be able to squeeze in a nap each night. This is important during the transition period with Lady U because, owing to the hours lost to preparing meals and walking to and from the bus stop, I can sleep only about four hours at most at home.

A lightly overcast morning. Quiet boat. Not much traffic out here -- we're zipping across. No oceangoing freighters plowing by to complicate matters. Straight shot. Piece of cake (wish I had one).

And here rests the Portuguese depressive's book of true protojyze (promoted from "sort of"). It's written, supposedly, as it turns out, by one of the actual author's so-called heteronyms, defined by the translator as a group of "imaginary authors to whom he [the actual author] gave complete biographies and who wrote in styles and attitudes different from his own." This particular heteronym, Bernardo Soares, is described by the actual author as only "a semi-heteronym because, although his personality is not mine, it is not different from but rather a simple mutilation of my personality." I quote this latter passage because it's also a good description of the narrator of the Mentoka series, Jyzer G, whose full fictive name also will appear on the title pages and covers (thinking positive here) as the author of all three books. Like Soares, as it happens, Jyzer G is keeping a diary/journal (but in the more idiosyncratic and infinitely more exciting form of a jyzebook) and just as Soares's life in most respects is identical with the book's actual author's, so Jyzer G's, again as it happens, is much the same as my own when I was his age (except for a certain amount of fictifying designed mainly to disguise the real-life identities of other characters, and also -- maybe even more -- to justify the use of the term "jyze fiction" as opposed to "jyze" alone. -- And of course "jyze nonfiction" would be not only a tautology but also, at the same time, and paradoxically, and much more interestingly, a contradiction in terms, but in any case irrelevant for the Mentoka series.)

So -- another reason I'm enamored with the Portuguese protojyzer, depressive or not.

As for this volume right here called "Real Jyze," I'll say at this time (because most likely the topic won't come up again) it's about as far as you can get from jyze and still be counted as such. Events have taken over. Fortunately the tragic moment has not yet arrived, but its seeming and indeed highly probable imminence -- whether a matter of days, weeks, months, or even years -- has kept me from launching into true unrestrained jyzing, in which all things of the moment except those physically present are left behind. And this may be the case as well for the next volume or two or more. In fact it may be so for most J-book volumes or perhaps even all, since events will likely be taking over more and more and life will be producing a plethora of tragic moments for us -- not just for Lady U and me, I mean, but for everyone -- as the years go by and ecocatastrophe pushes in ever closer. True "real jyze" may only rarely make an appearance. That may be the nature of the beast. You keep the J-stick moving on a regular basis to give that authentic, unalloyed jyze a chance to appear. Its actual arrival is sheer serendipity and rare at best.

But even this low-grade jyzing I like to do. It's fun. It keeps me alert and alive. It adds some meaning and order to my days while also injecting some unpredictability and excitement. It's hard to beat, jyze is. Yes it is!

With splendid timing too as we turn dockward. Glory be. To jyze! Hip hip hooray! And again!

BOOK II

[Jyze for Mom]

14

Where else but the baddest new bar in town? Where
else but beneath a painting titled "Dancing with Oneself
VI" (not II) (but selling for $225)? Where else but a
joint whose music for the night is advertised as "acid
jazz" (not jyze) (and sounds more like protopunk
hiphopified or rapsodized -- or maybe sodomized).

Dark. Lots of black paint. Bizarre art, macabre,
grotesque (words popping up like paint bubbles) -- campy,
kitschy, neo-Gothic, neo-Beat, neo-Baroque. Dada and
decadence -- fractured. Intentional derangement of the
senses -- rederanged. Or maybe closer to -- dederanged.

I noticed this place several weeks ago but tonight's
my first chance to stop in. Two blocks west of the
office, a block and a half north. What was here before
I'm not too sure. A video game arcade? Heart, I know,
of the old dope-dealing "war zone," also known as "the
Blade," which has now shifted to other places -- or some
of it has anyway. Or so word has it.

(Someone else who's also confused is being told the
"acid jazz" is later, live. -- But acid jyze, of a sort,
is right now, yes, eating away at these pages.)

I can be over here doing this because I don't have
much work at the office, neither their stuff nor my own.
And besides, partner Fran's up there. I saw her talking
on the phone when I dropped off my packages. She waved
but then spun away from me on her desk chair. Then I
left. And because she remained facing away from me, she
couldn't see me wave goodbye, and that was fine by me.

Another excellent walking day. Splendid weather.
Most of spring's been like this. Trudging along the

road to the bus stop I saw -- a snake. Slithering in
the shoulder sand and gravel. What kind I don't know,
but big. Maybe about as long as I am when stretched
out horizontally and thick as my forearm, black with
brightly colored bands, I think green and red (but I
was moving too fast trying to put some distance between
me and it to be sure about the colors or the extent of
the contribution of my overheated imagination).

This will be the summer J-book. Already it seems
we've moved past spring and I've scarcely taken note of
its arrival in jyze. Or in the rest of life for that
matter. Spring was just a blink -- though it may be
back. But one day it was no longer necessary to burrow
under all those jackets as I napped. I didn't need
heavy long-sleeve henleys -- indeed, couldn't bear them.
Flowers popped up everywhere. Rhodies and hydrangea
and, truly everywhere (especially as seen from rural bus
windows), the yellow flower I want to call goldenrod
though it's almost certainly not that. But it's a lot
like it, so I hereby christen it goldenrot. And that
takes care of that.

A book of summer and a book of grace, because we've
still got Mom with us. Knock on wood! (Though I doubt
there's any wood in this joint. Or no, I'm sure there's
plenty but it's disguised and hidden. This is the
intentional antithesis of a fern bar. Lots of punk
spirit in here. Postmod is here too, or maybe even
post-postmod. Display cases of brutal jewelry for sale.
Walls hung with numerous paintings, all cold or fierce
if not savage in subject matter not to say impact.
WHAM! SLASH! OUCH! In decor this establishment's not
even faintly warm and fuzzy. But it sure does beat your
average bar. Just to see the colorful neon sign outside
announcing the presence of "Art" -- much like the bright
blue neon "Jazz & Blues" at the fictive Nick's Place in
Mentoka Falls -- it scores with me.)

She called last night, Mother did. This is an "up"
week, with Doc B. waxing positive about her bone marrow,
the way it's "bouncing back one hundred percent" after
the treatments. Not much breathlessness or coughing, or

so she reported. (But the babytalk persona appeared
from time to time, usually a sign she's drugged herself
up pretty good.) Only once did things get a little
dicey, and that was when she called me "the most
powerful man I've ever known." Though she swore she
meant it as a compliment or a simple statement of fact
(flip-flopping between the two), I know better, or
strongly suspect. -- But it's not a matter either of us
wants to pursue at this stage in our tangled lives, and
so best to let go of it in here too.

     -- Only six paying customers in this bar right now.
The space is narrow and deep and high-ceilinged, with a
couple of pool tables dominating the raised section in
back -- seems about half a city block from the front.
I've got a little round table here more or less in the
middle, and atop the table a chubby little devotional
candle flickers in a netted round red jar (even the most
brutal "Art" cannot banish such candles from its bar).

     -- This is an interesting time for my shadow life.
In less than three months narrator G and the rest of the
fictive gang (traveling not just from the M. zone but
from a nonfictive time zone exactly one Glennarian cycle
back) will be arriving right here, this city, to live
out "Mentoka Ghosts." Among other projects for the
months ahead will be furnishing said gang with a local
life: places to live, work, love, fight. This will
entail visits to parts of the city I haven't seen for a
while. The old haunts: can I find new uses for them?
Will at least some small part of my local research
conducted over the years prove not to have been in vain?

     The high age of grunge has pretty much passed
around here. It peaked a little more quickly than did
the equivalent high age of flower power back in my city
No. 2/7. But the parallels are close enough to be
useful for family histories in "Ghosts."

     (Across the aisle we've now got a picturesque group
of five souls examining a vacuum cleaner that's standing
atop their table sort of like an early modernist
readymade sculpture on a pedestal. At least two of the
five work here and the other three may be owners or band

members or both. Long dresses, big hair, big cleavage,
dreads, tattoos, storm-trooper boots, a nose ring, a
priestess look. Also gold lame' and a torn black-denim
jacket apparently held together with huge safety pins
and clanking with chains. Tips for the employees on how
to use the machine, which has a droopy maroon bag and a
big steel snout like a cowcatcher -- tips on how to
clean the floor with it, I do believe, but possibly also
on how to show the thing as a work of art, or "Art."
Indeed all five examiners look quite artist-like, at
least to me, and this too is a happy surprise.)

What's new? Certainly (I was thinking) as a matter
of jyze virtue I ought to take occasional note of
construction projects appearing along my path. Not too
often but once in a while, and especially if they might
someday be causing changes in the path itself. So: at
the city ferry terminal a new concourse is going up just
south of the slip I use now (big cranes moored out
there). And across the street from the terminal the
waterfront streetcar is out of commission as its tracks
are being dug up -- I know not why. And halfway between
home and the home port the south-county express bus has
begun making regular stops at a new park-and-ride I
never noticed while it was going in. And therefore
ridership on that route is up by maybe ten or twenty
percent, which is to say: one or two riders per trip.

And that's about it. Because of the crazed
overbuilding fostered by the market free-for-all of the
previous decade no big buildings have gone up in the
downtown here since then.

"Acid jazz," I'm discovering right now, is weird.
Bizarro. Not my kind of stuff. A few too many
intentionally annoying and ugly sounds -- it's all in
the aesthetic, dude. Summer of Love this emphatically
is not. (But it sure does beat top forty, country, just
about everything else of our current era.) (If I could
come here regularly I might start to groove on the music
too, including even this abomination playing right now.)
(Occasionally someone strolls by checking out the scene
-- "Wunnerful, wunnerful!" I heard a shaven-headed Nazi-

looking thirty-something in a yellow plaid sports coat over camo pants and shiny black combat boots exclaim just moments ago -- and you can tell they think I fit in all right, most of these passersby, although by my own standards I'd have to say I don't -- yet. To do so I'd need to sharpen and harden my nastiest nightscoper edges by a factor of about ten. -- But then I seem to recall announcing at some point way back that with jyze I could hone me a new edge -- and who knows, maybe it's already doing that on me by itself, jyze is, and others are seeing it even if I can't.)

And speaking of city living, the last of my shirts from that era -- beloved tough Pacifics, so called -- is about to give out. I'm wearing it now. Light brown cotton with blue pinstripes. Patched elbow and shoulder and pocket -- but at several worn spots elsewhere it's too threadbare to take more patches and it clearly needs them. At one point I had six of these shirts. They may still be sold somewhere but if so they're too expensive for me. My main shirt type of the current era is the hickory-striped workshirt from our local farm & forest outfitter. Ralf, the foot-ferry pilot, likes them too -- "They wear like iron and don't show dirt -- what more can you ask of a shirt?" (But he favors zipper pullovers while I go for standard buttons or snaps.)

And nobody's hassled me here. So I like the place even more. I think I could prosper in it. At no time ever will you find more than a few places where you might prosper, and that's doubly or triply true if you want to be jyzing for a lengthy spell while you're there.

And with that I suppose it's time to go. Will I ever make it back here? Will the bar itself make it back here after its shakedown cruise? Is that dubious-looking vacuum cleaner (now returned to its closet, presumably) -- is it really up to either of its appointed, or maybe I should just say potential, tasks? For answers to these and other crucial questions raised at the top of this fourth J-book in the series -- follow the jyze! (But even there the answers may be few.)

[Jyzemelt]

15

What I neglected to bring along is the insect
repellent. But maybe it won't be needed so early in
the season.

Should make clear at the start this is nothing like
a normal excursion. D and I came here once shortly
after taking up country living and never returned, or at
least not together, despite an occasional vow to do so.
Certainly we've never visited the place on foot. We did
pedal by once, the single time D rode her foldable mini
bike outside the safe confines of the dead-end (and
level!) street in front of our house.

All right, nix with the hinting around. This is
our town park. A picnic table, open-sidedly sheltered,
beneath a huge old tree that I take to be a cottonwood.
It's ten a.m. on Memorial Day.

More fine weather. Spectacular even. Bright sun,
forecast in the eighties. If last year (or was it the
year before?) was the spring from hell, this must be the
spring from -- yeah. Or nirvana in contempo-speak.

So after yanking myself up from my nap I hiked over.
Took the long route in order to drop off an important
piece of mail at the post office: my unemployment claim
for the past two weeks. Left Lady U (a/k/a "Stretch"
and "Skeeter" at the camera factory) still asleep in bed.
Greeted four different horses, one goat, one fisherboy,
and one shotgun-bearing rumored militia leader along the
way (the last-named being the aptly sobriquetted Captain
Brick, our neighbor three houses to the south, who
honked and gave a mock salute). Peered down into a
creek six times, and in four of those six a prominent

sign named it as the same creek, and yet in all six one
could easily step into it (so take that, ancient
philosopher of flow).

I'm the only one here today. And this is not
unusual: in all the scores of times I've driven or biked
or walked by I've never seen anyone using the facility.
This is the kind of park you dream of: a retreat for you
and you alone. (Will someone drive up right now or step
out from behind a tree just to confound me? -- No one
does. A bird scrabbles high in the presumed cottonwood.
Lots of cheeps and chirps and chirrs and chirrups around
here. It buzzes, it hums, it skirrs -- but no squirrels
thrashing about. No squirrels anywhere in our town!)

As I recall, the size of this chunk of timberland
bequeathed to the town as parkland is forty acres -- or
maybe twenty or sixteen or twelve, because memory is not
speaking in a single voice. Most of these acres,
however many, are still "in timber," and if it's not
original growth it's got to go back at least ninety or a
hundred years to the time of the original socialist
experiment, soon failed, though its traces live on here
and there in the town and probably in this park too, or
maybe even as this park. Had not some social idealist
of means (or land-rich anyway) been smitten by the
experiment and seen a bequest as a way to honor it, no
park. But that's just a guess.

A ravine cuts diagonally through the center of the
property. It's primordial down there -- while
clambering around a bit on the near slope when I first
got here today I was strongly reminded of those wondrous
redwood groves farther down the coast. A hint of them
here. Tall old trees, widely scattered slanting shafts
of sunlight looking solid enough you could walk right up
them (or down them, I suppose, for those starting in the
canopy or even higher), trickle of a brook, abundant
ferns, a refrigerator-size boulder or two and lots of
smaller ones. Flickering wings. Snaps of twigs. Look
out, that right there (and there and there and there)
could be poison oak! But no skeeters so far. -- And
more on that other Skeeter, the a/k/a, in a moment.

[Jyzemelt]

     And then the northeast corner of the park, in which
I sit, is largely open except for half a dozen shade
trees. Two ground levels here, and on the upper one, a
few feet higher, is a funky old softball field with a
triptych metal chain-link backstop behind home plate and
a small permanent wooden bleacher on the first-base side
capable of seating maybe thirty at most. The bleacher's
rickety, painted forest green (blends in well), and at
the moment a single soda can, visible from here, stands
on the top plank, of five. And the can is half-full of
rainwater, I know, because I checked, inspired largely
by the fact that I myself was carrying a can of the same
brand of soda, black cherry flavor (am sipping on it
right now). And so we can deduce that this baseball
diamond, field of dreams though it clearly is, is not a
beehive of activity, since it hasn't rained around here
in more than two weeks. -- And for corroboration I'll
note that a pyramidal truckload of sand rises on the
diamond itself, in fair territory about ten feet behind
third base, and from the visible erosion patterns you
can tell it's seen a good deal of rain.

     In chasing a long ball to left you're in danger of
plunging into the ravine -- perhaps one reason the
diamond is little used.

     Down here in the lower section of the open area we
have four picnic tables, two of which squat beneath the
shelter, which looks rustic with its rough-hewn timbers
and slanted cedar-shingle roof. Not a barbecue in
sight. A few yards to the west stand a rusty set of
swings with chains but no seats and, beyond that, a
single splintery-looking wooden slide about four feet
high. And to the east, facing the fence, is the piece
de resistance, installed during our time in the area and
dedicated in a ceremony written up in the south-county
weekly paper: a thirty-inch-diameter, ten-foot-long log
bearing our town's name followed by the word "Park," all
of this chain-saw-carved into it with impressive skill.

     Also there's a gravel parking area with enough
space for maybe a dozen cars, its boundaries marked by
upright bald tires sunk halfway into the ground, their

top halves almost completely hidden in the weeds. As a
newly certified expert on lawn mowing I can venture a
guess that this place was last mowed about ten days ago,
and whoever did the mowing didn't bother with the
intricate picnic/playground area where I'm sitting now.
     And we've got us an outhouse. It's a small wooden
one partly hidden back in the trees right on the edge of
the ravine (for obvious reasons), with a door on each
side, presumably one for men and one for women, although
the structure itself is so small you'd think it could
contain only a single room, a single seat, a single
hole. And that's where I'm headed now.

*

     Just one room and seat and hole inside, I was
right. But also just one door, so I was wrong too. I
must've become disoriented when I was first exploring
the ravine and mistaken the front side for the back.
-- In any event I pulled open that one door and was hit
by a cloud of stench, which by outhouse standards I
suppose wasn't all that bad (though still plenty bad by
any other standard); but also I saw a labyrinth of
spider webs which looked sturdy enough to snag a bear.
So I took a pass on the outhouse and instead stepped
behind a big old stump hulking a few yards down the side
of the ravine -- stump about six feet high and maybe
five feet in diameter -- and watered it.
     -- Aha, human activity! No, I mean someone else,
an intruder: the caretaker. Or at least the person in
charge of unlocking the gate to the parking lot, which
until now I hadn't even realized was locked or lockable
(I came in via a smaller gate for foot traffic). An
elderly Eurusan lady who apparently lives in the first
house to the north, barely visible through the trees,
was heading this way with tiny steps after swinging open
the gate and then stopped in her tracks when she spotted
me sitting here. Was stunned, it appeared. Wearing a
pale pink bathrobe and matching slippers. I waved but
too late; she was already shuffling along again, now with
her back to me and going in the opposite direction, and
moving a lot faster than before. Smokin' pink slippers!

113

[Jyzemelt]

Memorial Day: when we honor those who've given their lives for their country. Or no, for this, underlined, country. Vietnam vets are still squawking because they see themselves as insufficiently honored (I heard some grumping about this on public radio just last night). Of course I'm one of those hoary dissenters who think the fools, knaves, dolts, and belligerent self-proclaimed USA superpatriots (them especially) who killed and maimed millions of innocents in Vietnam should be even more "insufficiently honored," right along with those who planned and ran the war. I don't buy for one second the right-wing argument that any of these guys, regardless of their position in the war-mongering pecking order, are heroes of the empire. It's beneath contempt, it's so absurd. Ignorant and/or bamboozled victims of the empire's propaganda is the best I could say for them.

(And now -- surprise! -- comes a shiny black convertible sportscar. It's parking crunchily on the gravel beneath a big shady overhanging limb thirty feet away. A pair of spiffily dressed Cawk suburbanites, it would appear, a man and a woman of roughly my own vintage, unfold themselves and head off into the densely wooded grove beyond the baseball right field. They're jointly carrying a large wicker picnic basket sideways, one on each end. Could be they didn't see me over here. Perhaps even as a matter of principle they didn't.)

-- But what's been happening in the world? Weeks or maybe months have rolled by since jyze has taken a look in that direction. And here during the long holiday weekend as we make the turn into summer is certainly an appropriate time for such a look. To firm up the deteriorating context a bit if nothing else. To rough out the big picture if only at its sketchiest.

Well, we've got the murder trial of the football hero, it's been going on for months, the nation hanging on every word. We've got the continuing right-wing political assault on the capital, now turning into a disgusting hypocritical campaign to balance the federal budget (on the backs of the poor, of course, by cutting

social programs) after completing all the hoopla of
their utterly meaningless "contract" with their swarms
of crazed supporters. We've got a "national dialogue"
about right-wing hate radio -- did it help cause the
heartland bombing of six weeks ago? (Gosh, I wonder.)
We've got millions dying of AIDS in Africa and also an
outbreak of Ebola virus there, hundreds dead. Ongoing
war in Bosnia, aftershocks of war in Rwanda, the supreme
leader hovering near death in China, arrests made in
terrorist gas attacks on a Japanese subway. We've got
squabbles over regulation of e-mail and the internet.
We've got the former-out-party-controlled congress
rolling back regulations protecting the environment,
water quality, air, endangered species. We've got ---
     But no, I'm bailing right there. Let the
context creep in indirectly if any more is needed.
     What about Lady U? Better to move on to the last
remaining mystery of this entry. (And by the way, the
skeeters never have shown up here at the park. Nor have
the butterflies or the bicyclists or the beavers. But
all these are around, and more.) -- "Skeeter," to
repeat, is what they call her at the camera factory.
Because she's so small and does a lot of buzzing around.
That's when they're not calling her "Stretch," for which
also her size is, to be sure, a prime inspiration.
     She's astounded by her fellow workers: a motley
melange, virtually all Cawk, of rednecks, punks,
derelicts, jailbirds, farm wives, city street people,
suburban high-school dropouts and rebels. Finds many of
them likable and tells lots of funny stories about them.
(The best so far sounds apocryphal but she swears by it:
a new employee, a grungy city kid, sees deer grazing out
in the company parking lot, hollers, "Look, look, deer!
Anybody got a camera?" -- They're all up to their necks
in cameras, of course, and a big howl arises.)
     Nor am I unaware a lot of things could go wrong
with her gig out there. She may even run off with one
of the numerous guys she tells me are panting after her
-- and I believe her. All I can do, really, is trust
her. Or anyway, that's all I intend to do. If it's

over, it's over: that's how I try to look at it. We've
had -- by and large now to be sure -- a helluva good run.
No kids to suffer if we split up. I always want to be
ready: this may even be the secret of our longevity.
     -- Hey, how'd I get onto that?
     Be nasty. Buckle down. Cast a skeptical eye.
Chew rattlesnake hide, or the hide of whatever kind of
serpent that was I saw slithering along last week.
     (A white butterfly just fluttered by. And this
whole time, unnoted by jyze, barking dogs. An
occasional whinnying horse, even some bellowing cows.)
     Last Friday night one of the jazz station's late-
night DJs who's also a talented blues vocalist performed
at the very bar where jyze held forth earlier last week,
so it turns out the joint's open to different types of
music and that's very good news. Also its name got
bandied about a lot on the air. Maybe it'll make it,
who knows. It's just two blocks from the downtown art
museum and right across the street from the probable
site of the new downtown library (as if that's relevant
-- by the time it's up and running art itself may be
dead, except for the domesticated variety acceptable to
the reactionary new congress -- but no, no, no, art
ain't gonna die, it will know what to do).
     And I keep chomping away at the amazing Portuguese
diary. In disposition the diarist appears to be about
as far from me as anyone could be and yet I love the
guy. His despair is wonderful, his pessimism amusing,
his disquiet a laff riot. I'm not playing here. And at
the same time it's all achingly beautiful. Such
succulent sadness! Such mellifluous melancholy! Such
tantalizing tedium! (The pages on tedium are among his
best, and he doesn't even have to resort to, say, hokey
alliterations, as I'm doing here.) As for the way he
believes one ought to think to see life truly -- the
absurdity, the meaninglessness stamped on all things by
that spoilsport death -- all I can say is I just can't
do it. Sure, he's right, I'll concede that much (not
that it would make him feel better if he knew, since by
definition it couldn't, given his disposition and

beliefs) -- I'm just temperamentally incapable of it.
     You could almost say this is what life itself is:
an emotional or constitutional inability to accept the
true meaning(lessness) of death. And of course of life
as well. We dance on the high-tension wires strung by
that paradox. Cavort. Shudder. Refuse to look down.
Laugh. And in the end fry. Or just fall and go splat.
     -- But lookit all the leaves -- some wiggling.
Lookit all the pinecones -- some rolling on the ground.
Lookit all the intricate powdery-blue cutouts of sky
visible through the trees -- all tirelessly shifting
like kaleidoscope shards. Shape-shifters! And that one
very expensive convertible, top down, still shinily and
trustingly parked. It's almost as if they'd seen me as
a street kid and flipped me a couple of coins to guard
their wheels. (Is a picnic table hidden somewhere in
the grove up there? Perhaps an elite bed and breakfast?
Next visit I should explore that quadrant.)
     -- My bedtime coming up. Old Skeeter might be
wondering where I've disappeared to. I'm going home.

16

     Git on that carpet and ride!
     Am so doing. Because this is (once again) maybe
the last time ever. Without doubt it's the last
legal time for at least three months unless something
extremely unexpected pops up.
     So I'm sprawled atop my old green sleeping bag.
It's spread out on the gray carpet in the main
conference room, between the long oval oaken conference
table and the wall with the two large windows which hang
above countertop level and look out on the bay (along

with a good portion of the waterfront and the urban
hillside leading down to it). The sprawl space is about
three feet wide. What's good about it is if the guard
arrives to check out the office interior, he can't see
anyone lying down here unless he comes all the way over
-- actually enters the conference room. And no guard's
ever done that yet while I've been in this spot.

My trusty old windup alarm clock says it's 2:39
a.m. Usually the guard makes his next round on this
floor about 3:30 (one every ninety minutes). -- And in
reality the alarm clock ain't so trusty. The tick is
feeble and uneven. If I wind the clock too tight it's
liable to stop entirely. It loses anywhere from fifteen
to thirty minutes a day. But so far it's always done
the job. So maybe one could say in the reality that
really counts it's trusty after all.

I fold the sleeping bag over on itself widthwise to
make a better cushion against the hard floor (the rug is
not so plush), and therefore the surface I snooze on is
about fifteen inches wide. For a pillow I tip over one
of the conference-table chairs and lay a freshly
unrolled paper towel atop its upholstered backrest.

Actually the firm owns this sleeping bag. I bought
it one winter when severe snowstorms marooned me
downtown for several days in a row. The firm kindly
insisted on reimbursing me for it (and thus anyone who's
here during the day in theory has access to it too --
but none of them, I'm sure, would ever dream of touching
the scuzzy thing).

What's it like down here on the carpet? It's
always reminded me of just what you'd expect: hiding out
under the dining-room table of early childhood days.
Also brings back movie scenes of people playing footsie
at fancy restaurants, shot from just this perspective:
calf level, say. Sometimes the full moon shines in and
brightens the whole room, even down here, and I have to
shield my off-pillow eye with the back of my fingers
(same way I do at home during daytime sleeping hours
unless the black washcloth is serving the purpose).

If I look up from my recumbent position I can see,

at an interesting angle, the top few floors of the
fifty-story tower looming half a block diagonally to the
southwest. I can hear traffic on the streets down below
right at the core of downtown. I can feel the building
shudder whenever a heavily loaded truck passes by. I
can hear yells and screams floating up from the post-
office bus stop. I can hear the elevator ding at the
far end of the hall when someone gets on or off. I can
hear the guard's footsteps and the clanking of his gear
as he marches down the hall in my direction. At four
a.m. a launch revs up down by the ferry terminal and
buzzes out into the bay, bound for I don't know where; I
can hear it leave. (I never hear it come back, but then
by the time it does I've probably chugged off from that
same area myself on a ferry.)

Dreams. Lots of vivid dreams right here and I tend
to remember more of them than I do in other places
because, no matter how tired you may be, it's impossible
to sleep soundly or for long in a setting like this.

If a little wind starts up you can hear the
building creaking. I like when rain's falling because
the drops patter against (sometimes pelt) the windows,
making a noise something like popcorn popping, and that
drowns out many of the other night sounds.

-- Right now I should be sleeping. I'm beat.
Yawning like the bottom-feeder I am, as if waiting for a
school of krill to swim into my mouth. But I've always
wanted to jyze away a bit in this spot and I may never
have another chance. So I'm doing it. And it's coming
out feeble to the max. But that's okay. Jyze doesn't
fear showing itself at its worst. Jyze welcomes critics
and delights in giving them plenty of krill-like tidbits
to chew on or swallow whole as the case may be.

Empty metal shelves to my right. And built into
the counter above them is the hated temperature-control
unit, part of a buildingwide system. If it's running,
this area is too hot or too cold and the air's too dry;
if it's off, as now, the air's too stagnant. The system
groans and wheezes and hisses, especially when it's just
been turned on (usually about five a.m. unless the

weather's exceptionally hot or cold).

Who knows what kind of bugs might be lurking in this carpet down here. I do know the shampoo the janitors use to clean it is lethal stuff: it's probably taken years off my life and may be taking off another small, or even big, chunk right now (as if, in theory anyway, any remain to be taken).

Have I ever brought a lover here? -- Ya kiddin' me? A lover? I told ya, I'm a fidelitarian! -- Well, but come to think of it, Lady U herself has napped here a few times over the years and she ought to count. She heads the lifetime pack! -- But even with her there was no serious hanky-pank. Too risky for that. (I'm not saying fantasy was out of bounds, then or now.)

-- Better quit. Is this all it's going to amount to, then, the magic-carpet jyze jam? Guess so.

*   *

Shameful, this. Got to, got to, just got to jack it up. Yet the fact is I'm not feeling so hot. Might be coming down with something. "Got a headache tonight, mate" -- not normally a good excuse for failing to jyze.

It's too hot forward of the midship fire bulkheads this morning; everyone's coming back to the aft side.

And speaking of shameful acts, I just laid out seven bucks and change for a ferry sandwich, a banana, and a miniscule bag of chips. First time I've ever fallen so low as to buy a food item, to say nothing of three food items, aboard one of these floating extortion chambers. (Popcorn doesn't count as a food item. At popcorn the ferry system is very good and for some unfathomable reason doesn't grossly overcharge.)

The sandwich is roast beef and Swiss cheese on whole wheat. Not too bad except for the price. But since a customer base could scarcely be more captive, or at least not outside the prison system, what's to expect? In an unabashedly "market fundamentalist" country even government agencies (and the ferry system is one such) must practice price gouging.

I'd prefer to be preparing my own meals these days and packing them to save money. But the time factor

makes doing so too hard. This particular trip it didn't
but in general it does and so I said to hell with it for
this trip too, since it's my last official work commute
for a while if not ever.

For me to restart these torturous ten-stage round
trips a number of conditions must obtain:

(1) Naomi must survive the birthing more or less
intact and abide by her vow to return to work;

(2) The office (the firm itself) must survive;

(3) The feds must extend the remaining part of the
firm's contract to do grand jury and related work; and

(4) The firm must continue to be willing, despite
its dwindling workload which is forcing its full-time
salaried scopers to sit idle, to send its government
scoping to an outside "independent contractor," i.e.,
vendor 173, i.e., Jyzer Ink, i.e., me.

How do I read the odds? About sixty/forty against.
But I won't worry too much about beating them so long as
D can hold onto her job, and thus far she's managing to
do that. (And even seems to enjoy it. She still can't
believe a crazy rogue operation like this camera factory
with its bizarro cast of urban/burban/backcountry pokers
and shuckers could exist anywhere outside network TV.)

The big drawback is that for at least the next
three to five months (and of course maybe longer,
depending on when the U's next come calling) I'll be
lacking an up-to-date word processor. Therefore I've
decided to do at least the raw draft of "Mentoka Ghosts"
(which is to say the first fictive draft) by hand just
as in the olden days. Pen and ink. Just like jyze.

And why shouldn't I? (By the way, in browsing
through a book about jazz history at the bookstore last
night I noticed that the etymology for the word itself
is just what I had speculated it must be: from jizz.
That is, the white seedy stuff, spermic and semenic.
-- When you get right down to it it's all just a matter
of semenics, Jack, jyze is. Semenics and oogonics.)
(And then this delicious note: in the birder world the
term jizz refers to a bird's "wild essence." Yes!)

-- Meanwhile about two-thirds of a thus far

unexceptional voyage has chugged on by. Looks like a
decent day lies ahead after roughly sixty hours straight
of rain -- but those were preceded by an unusually fine
three weeks so no one's complaining.

On the health-tragedy front the focus shifts
briefly, I'd guess, to D's side of the family as her
Auntie Alice suffers a heart attack. She went in for a
triple bypass yesterday and we don't know yet how it
came out. (This is Papa U's younger sister who moved
back home after her marriage, the first ever in the U
family to a gaijin/haole/Eurusan/Cawk, broke up.)

As for mere annoying health problems I took the
laurels myself for most of the week with a sore toe. It
turned my three days of hiking to and from the south-
county bus stop into sheer hell and forced cancellation
of the fourth. Wearing some ratty old shoes for lawn
mowing seems to have caused it.

Two startling events:

(1) Bicycle cops "take down" a matched pair of
alleged bicycle drug runners in the historic quarter,
right outside the only real bookstore, and one of the
runners lands on the sidewalk about five feet in front
of me as I'm hobbling along, with a cop then diving on
him something like a cowboy dragging down a roped calf
-- but instead of lashing up limbs, snapping on plastic
cuffs. (If I was startled, what did the group of maybe
twenty Japanese tourists right behind me, a tour guide
with megaphone included, think?)

(2) The deer family is back! Same papa deer, same
two mama deer, one lanky adolescent, and two brand-new
baby deer (true white-spotted fawns so recently whelped
as to seem still glistening). They strolled by right
outside the shed window. Had it been open I could've
reached out and touched them -- except with the window
open they probably would've smelled danger as they came
up the path from the creek and hightailed it back into
the woods.

I hadn't thought of it before, but what fine
contrasting stereotypical and also utterly misleading
pictures we have in (1) and (2) above: urban grit vs.

boonie pastoral. (Furthermore, making the bust even
more disturbing, both drug runners were, in Mentoka
lingo, Afrusan brown and all the cops Eurusan pink.)
     -- And here's my stop. What's more, the only one.
                   *   *
     Home-port saloon across the inlet. Dark. Empty.
I was rattling the iron bars of the gate on the cafe
side when Vi approached from inside to open up. Now
she's turning on the TVs as in stagger the first half-
dozen morning regulars (I as a sporadic don't qualify).
I keep as far away from this belligerent "jingo lounge"
retired career-military bunch as I can (and still be
inside the place once in a while).
     Several small launches packed with inspectors and
flunkies were buzzing around the shipyard containment
booms as we waited to disembark the auto ferry. Another
radiation spill, a ferry guard said, this one apparently
not too serious except for timing (all these tourists
pouring in to see the dreadnought) (speaking of which,
paintings of it now adorn the sides of local buses --
even my south-county clunker -- seemingly based on the
same plastic glue-together model I revered as a kid).
     The Portuguee (as D refers to him, pidgin-style): I
took another deep drag of his protojyze on the foot
ferry as we crossed. About fifteen minutes at a time is
the best way to read him. How sorry I'll be when I've
run out of fresh pages of his stuff to which I can grant
quarter-hour bursts of absolute adoration.
     Jyze riffs. I'm trying to think of each paragraph
as a jyze riff. (This week I again found myself
puzzling over jyze theory. Jyze seeks the edge yet it
also seeks vagueness -- but wait, isn't that a
contradiction? And now the notion of "wild essence,"
doesn't that complicate matters still further? Well
sure, on both counts, but this is jyze and jyze loves
contradictions and complications just as jazz loves
counterpoint -- or loves the backbeat -- or no, loves
dissonance, let's say, or anyway should, though not,
paradoxically, to excess or maybe to too much excess.)
     Or is it all just another unacknowledged category

error? When it starts seeming to be that, best I stop
talking about it for a while.
     (And tip the glass to the ceiling, mouth a couple
of small ice cubes and put on a scathing face for the
jingos as I run the gauntlet on my way out to the bus.)
                    *   *
     Unlock both locks, slowly open the door about four
inches and slip an arm through the gap, bending it
around in time to catch the falling "burglar-alarm"
broomstick before it hits the floor with a loud WHAP.
And I'm home. Home after the last walk home.
     Now it's the brown armchair in the "parlor," as
Mama U still calls our living/dining area, and therefore
we call it that too. The J-book is spread out on the
chair's broad right arm and bathed, as is most of the
room, in bright sunshine angling in over the carport.
It's 9:35. The refrigerator is humming -- or better to
say rattling. Or better yet to say it's doing a vibrato
hum with light arrhythmic percussive accompaniment.
     And a fine walk home it was. Even the bus ride was
good, although it was delayed a few minutes at the start
while teachers shepherded maybe two hundred frolicking
grade-school kids across the street to the foot-ferry
dock. June: the month of field trips. Can I say that?
Or anyway: June, the month of long days. Of course the
really long days don't hit until what I call the deeps
of June, which is that part of the month -- usually from
the 12th, 13th, or 14th until the end -- in which the
days are all longer than the days of any other month.
The next two or three jyzedays will fall in the deeps of
June. This we're in right now is still the shallows.
     During the bus ride I took off my right shoe and
sock (as far as I could tell offending no one) and
discovered I was probably wrong in what I wrote before
about the cause of my sore toe. It's not a mower's toe
after all; it's a buyer-of-cheapo-socks's toe.
Sometimes the cheapos I favor have knots in the seams
that run across the front of the toes. This sock had
one over the next-to-last toe (ring toe?). That other
sock that caused the injury had one over the little toe,

I'm all but certain. I also noticed for the first time
that the cheapo socks shed a lot of lint which builds up
in the interior of the shoe near the toes, leaving the
toes less maneuvering room and no doubt increasing the
friction they absorb.

Quite a discovery, surely one of the more notable
ever made on the county bus, at least by me. What's
more, it led to immediate remedial action: I whipped out
my handy pocketknife and sliced off the protruding knot.
True, the sock will probably unravel sooner or later,
but meanwhile my last walk home was made pain-free in
the area of the toes of the right foot -- except, that
is, for leftover pain from the misdiagnosed mower's toe.

(As for the extraordinary Portuguese protojyzer,
even when he goes off on his reactionary rants I still
can't help loving the guy -- such a motherless child he
is, so wonderfully senseless and achingly solipsistic
all his ideas -- the oversensitive kid creating a gang
of imaginary playmates and dreaming up a rationale for
doing this that's so transparently pathetic and hopeless
and yet so gorgeously expressed I'm just, as the title
of that first collection of his prose promises, ALWAYS
ASTONISHED.)

And then the walk itself. Well no, first Tina lets
me off (none of the other drivers will do it) at my
special place by the pull-off for the truck weigh
station, near the hole in the fence through which I
clamber down to one of our local roads, saving about
half a mile of mostly uphill trudge from the official
bus stop. And then I hike along parallel to the lagoon,
whose high-water marks come to within a few yards of the
road (and the lagoon is quite stinky when the tide is
out and the wind is right) -- on and off the road, seven
steps on but here comes a car, twelve steps off and now
no cars are coming so back on, with a four-step diagonal
between road and far edge of treacherous gravelly
shoulder, and once in a while scrambling to avoid
slipping down into the lagoon or a muddy ditch.

The daycare center, built in a stretch where the
shoreline veers out thirty or forty paces from the road,

features not only ducks, geese, chickens, peacocks, and human children -- every last one of the last-named Eurusan -- but also a small herd of Vietnamese potbelly pigs which zooms around at high speed among all of the above. To be exact, a herd of three. "The three little potbellies." They're all solid black and they make quite an amusing sight as they trot briskly about in tight formation. They'll even dash over to the fence and seem to be, and probably will be, sensitively parsing what you're saying as you murmur sweet nothings to them (as I did today and do whenever I can, and especially if they're being given a rest in their little human-playpen-like pigpen from being chased around by the swarms of kids in the main yard).

And that's just one of the numerous points of interest along the route. (Last week three large deer bounded across the road about fifty feet in front of me. That was at the deer crossing, which is officially marked as such, and it was the first time I've ever seen deer there or at any other official deer crossing that I can recall. -- It's right before you get to snake territory, which isn't marked as such but maybe should be, and which I now hurry through with my eyes glued to the ground.)

And onward. The way I think of the town's layout, it's a classic T highway junction with two loops appended. The larger loop, the church loop, bulges up across the top of the T's crossbar, with several blocklong dead-end roads branching off it like tangents, one of which is ours. The smaller loop, the post-office loop ("town center"), swings down from the far right-hand side of the crossbar and connects at its end with the stem of the T, skirting the tip of the lagoon along the way and featuring, in addition to the all-important post office itself, the weathered old cedar community hall built back in socialist days. (The stem of the T is actually two parallel westbound roads a block apart; the park where jyze was going down last week stretches out between them a couple of blocks west of the main north-south road, which is the T's crossbar.)

[Jyze for Mom]

    All in all the town is about twelve square, or in
most cases only partly square, blocks. The houses are
distributed in this area almost stochastically, so it
would seem, like a few dozen arrows shot with minimal
skill at a bull's-eye; and most of the land is either
wooded or, if cleared, used for pasture. Many of the
houses are completely hidden from the road and from
their neighbors. The main local creek, which bears the
town's name, winds down diagonally from northeast to
southwest right through the heart of town and then
empties into the lagoon.

    Why is there a town here? Because at one point
people coming from the south who wanted to head west on
the peninsula had to skirt the bay and the lagoon before
they could turn west. But then a bridge was built
across the lagoon at the point where it meets the bay
two miles south of the town (near the county bus stop),
shortening journeys to the peninsula by a few miles, and
the town quickly sank back into obscurity -- in fact did
this well before it had emerged from obscurity. (Except
for the socialist experiment, which made it notorious in
some quarters. But that's a story for another time.)

    -- Holy moly, this walk home is taking forever.
I'll sprint the rest of the way: to the post office
(check Box 289) and then back to the main road (the T
crossbar) and north to the far end of the church loop,
east one block to our street, north four houses to our
driveway and up that and around to the back door, keys
out. (First, though, backpack off. Mop brow. And
usually on the way up the driveway converse a bit with
Topper the horse and Goat the, yes, goat, maybe feed
them a few weeds pulled from our side of the driveway,
which is the only side weeds grow on, because Beryl and
especially Ben have annoyingly low tolerance for weeds
on their side. -- And by the way, for the past ten days
B&B have been gone on a trip somewhere and the task of
feeding their critters, including also three dogs and a
cat, has again fallen to us, and this time almost
entirely to me, and until the dry spell ended I was as
well the one delegated to water their garden and

extensive flowerbeds daily.) -- And then in.
     Actually it's good to get this basic geographical
description out of the way. Now this J-book feels much
better grounded. At least to me it does. It's homed
in. And as of today it's on vacation, which means it
can expound at greater leisure about its own true nature
and maybe even experiment a little in hopes that this
nature won't stay too static -- for the truth is that no
authentic true nature is even slightly static, which is
to say it's all shifty and paradoxical, including even
the parts that are homeostatic. Yes! (Vacations also
being great for straining at profundity only to fall a
prat or two or three short of it. I mean, why not?)

17

     Here comes a jyze trance. 'Long about midnight.
In the early, the cool, the drizzly deeps of June.
Right here where it began -- and tonight begins again.
     The new life. Definitely feels like it. I did
have one more genuinely work-linked trip to the city
left in me, and I got it out of me last night. Just a
matter of backing up my last batch of grand-jury
transcripts onto a storage diskette for the feds. Now
no more to do, although there'll be another trip anyway,
in fact tomorrow, to pick up all the stuff I've
accumulated down there "over the centuries," as my note
for the day crew mentioned. And it's true there are
slippers, sandals, cornstarch powder, a sweatshirt, the
infamous alarm clock, an electric blanket, padded wrist
guards fashioned from basketball kneeguards (to protect
against carpal tunnel -- my own adaptation, and they
seem to have succeeded so far) -- and much more. But

the only thing that really matters is my lockbox full of
hard-copy files and storage diskettes, along with the
computer paper and toner cartridge I use when printing
my own work. The box itself, with my initials painted
on the outside in red, I may leave there just as a
reminder that I might be returning in a few months. The
contents of the box I'll bring home where they'll be
safe -- or anyway safer than they'd be there.

(Meanwhile Stretch has slipped in. Except when
working overtime she always rolls up the driveway at
about eleven-fifty. A few minutes before then I'll have
finished making the bed and doing the dishes; the
kitchen counters will still be slick from their sponge-
down. And tonight is no exception. what's more I've
got the washer and dryer going simultaneously. I tell
you, and ain't joshin' either: this right here is the
good life.)

And about three weeks from now I'll be making
another visit to the office, or at least I hope I will,
to stay there overnight before catching the train in the
morning for my next visit with Mom. Otherwise no more
office appearances by me until Naomi starts up again,
and maybe not then either. In any case: no more
sneaking in. No more scope-firm contributions to my
jyzerly operations. I'm truly on my own now. (Though
yes, no question, I'm hoping to be able to return to the
Jyzer Ink "independent contractor" setup, maybe as early
as October or November. But more likely it'll happen,
if at all, sometime after the first of the year.)

-- Trancelike owing to exhaustion. And that
stemming from a late return home this morning after last
night's trip in. But soon no more such arduous
commutes.)

By coincidence on my very last day of being at
least partially employed I came across a magazine piece
about a guy roughly my own age thrown out of an
executive job -- just read it tonight. Chortled a lot.
In this era of rapid technological change it's happening
to many a highly paid corporado with plenty of working
years left. It could've been my fate too if I'd had

that kind of upper-echelon job: the panic, the
interviews, the headhunters. How pleased I am my life
didn't go that way! I just shake my head. I wallow in
sweet inarticulacy about all this. That world! (All
these misbegotten folks who let themselves be inveigled
into it, the success and status games, power trips,
money, toys, the works -- and now suddenly it's too late
for them. Or so they feel. Because it really isn't:
you can always rip the scales off your eyes.)
     Now I ponder my options in my own much less
traumatic transition. For a span of at least three to
five months (I know I keep mentioning this but I'm
obsessing right now) I won't have access to a word
processor capable of handling my storage diskettes:
that's the main hitch. Maybe I'll have no word
processor at all, depending on whether I'm able to crank
up my old "insurance policy" machine. If I'm not able
to do that, I'll have to fall back on Lady U's partially
digitized typewriter for certain tasks. In either case
I'll be starting afresh -- and that's fine. I'd even
say that's just how it oughta be. And even more to the
point, that's how I want it to be.
     I already have a project for this gap period fully
laid out. It's to do a complete rough draft of all
three volumes of the Mentoka trilogy, in reverse order:
first "Ghosts," then "Dreams," then "Jyzer" (which is
already about an eighth done -- but I'll probably just
start over). Meanwhile I'll be making a few trips into
the city to revisit those parts of town which will serve
as the setting for "Ghosts," and I'll be doing this
while the story itself is supposed to be taking place
there (under the Glennarian-cycle-delay plan, which is
much too elaborate to try to explain here).
     "The one bright book of life." At the moment
anyway my confidence is all abubble that I can come up
with something pretty damn good for this three-volume
version. -- And in truth I see the urjyze and the
protojyze and now maybe the jyze series itself as three
more such bright books -- huge ones for me (and
literally, meaning physically, huge as well, or in other

words lots and lots of words).

   -- And here's some hunger. The gut kind. Should I
finish the ham or go ahead and open the roast turkey
right now? -- In the months ahead we may be skimping on
turkey, ham, anything else that bumps the cost per meal
over about a buck and a half. Savor those tasty cuts,
my man, while you can. While the unemployment checks
are still rolling in. (Yes, they're still doing that.
It's a miracle. It appears about a thousand dollars
remains in my ES account, which amounts to another
month's worth of checks if I play my cards right. As of
this point I'm still paying all the bills and Stretch --
just can't resist calling her that! (maybe because I see
her doing lots of dance-type stretching and she always
looks so good doing it) -- Stretch is saving her own
checks for the rainy days of next winter when the camera
factory will likely be laying her off for a month or two
during their slow period. Her lamentably puny checks:
only slightly more than half of what I'm making on
unemployment. So when we have to depend on those checks
alone the living will not be easy. But I'm still
figuring we can do it -- and this is so even if I don't
go back to part-time scoping for Naomi in October or
November or after the first of the year or ever.)

   Might as well stick with the ham. It's not even
necessary: just tasty: so do it. Obey your hunger!

*   *

   And roll the curtain back some eight hours later to
reveal a damp gray June morning. Actually just a little
gray is visible and a whole lot of green. Bright
dripping green. At which I've been whacking for twenty
or thirty minutes almost every day, though not yet on
this particular day.

   Yes, to hell with the lawn mower, because he's
baaack: Mr. Whacker! The craziest sumbitch in the whole
damn forest! Whips that thing back and forth, back and
forth, switching hands every so often (sometimes every
five cycles, sometimes every twenty-five, depending on
circumstances, the most crucial being the lay of the
land and, even more, just where the clumps are, the

131

outliers, the patches of unusually high grass or whatever else happens to be growing high out there).

The whacker itself is the same one with which I kept the relatively tiny lawn of our previous city house in check. Essentially it's a long-handled, lightweight sickle with a straight, double-edged footlong blade serrated on both sides so you can slice off the bastards just above ground level both going and coming, and without bending down. It's shaped like a hockey stick and to deploy it is almost like "dribbling" a puck down the ice and slapping off passes or shots, sometimes forehanded and sometimes backhanded (not that I've ever even touched a hockey stick that I can recall).

I never would've dreamed I could be so happy with keeping the grass manageable, but so it is. I'm like a kid again knocking stones into the woods with a stick. And sometimes I do take baseball swings: when stalking along the borders beating back the blackberry brambles up to shoulder level and even higher. The growth tips of those proliferatious vines come whizzing in high and low, in and out of the strike zone, and I gleefully knock them back, spray "frozen ropes" in all directions as runners circle the bases and the fans go wild.

(A big old blue jay just landed on the sidewalk outside the glass. Handsome crested "Steller feller" with his two-tone color scheme, coal black on top and bright blue below, and frenziedly vigilant -- jizzy, could say -- as he hops about pecking at -- what? Bare concrete, it would seem. Some stray grass blades or grains, maybe, sent flying by my whacking, but those wouldn't be all that appealing even to a ravenous jay, would they? But then think chickens. What's good for chickens could be good for jays. Even for jyzers and the mates of jyzers, maybe, under certain extreme conditions, possibly now looming, or soon. Might even qualify as "whole grain" or "grass-fed" humanfeed.)

And a few surprise gusts of wind and all the green above eye level is on the move. It was rustling earlier too, but now it's no longer subtle about it. Wild thrashings. Old hat to trees no doubt but still quite

impressive when you mull it and especially, as now,
observe it from maybe twenty-five or thirty paces away.
A little puff and the whole forest breaks into a frantic
bougaloo forty or fifty feet high (and in some places
up to twice that or maybe even more).
     -- This being Father's Day weekend, I pause to
consider what my father would think of me now. Mr.
Whacker -- very appropriate name, yes. Had my father
lived another twenty years would he have become wise
enough, flexible enough, humble enough to recognize the
merits of my current way of life? Perhaps not. Most
likely he'd consider my life (up to this point anyway) a
sadly wasted one. I see it thus myself when I look at
the world as he did, and I can't deny I still do that
wholly on my own at times. Not very often. But the
voice is always there if I want to listen to it. One
of a chorus with a very wide variety of opinions -- not
a Greek chorus or a Norwegian or Austro-German or Scots-
Irish one either, really. A motley European and Eurusan
chorus. Conscience is so much more complicated than
it's generally made out to be! I for one am glad to
have this chorus around -- it's like a lively,
perverse, skeptical, cranky, unpredictable companion.
Very entertaining. Good for lots of laughs and also
the occasional intriguing sorrow, not to mention a
useful critique here and there, along with, alas, a
sprinkling of the overly harsh kind.
     Dad the lawyer. Dad the hardworking family man.
Dad the guy usually not at home and if at home usually
closed up in his study. Dad the Old Bull. Dad the
baiter and dinner-table arguer. Dad the old roue, the
ballroom dancer, the flirt. Dad Mr. Debonair and yet
"just a country boy." Dad the youthful tennis bum.
Dad the deceiver and the outrageously unfaithful
husband (but I didn't know about that, and neither did
Mom for the most part, until he was gone). Dad the
sarcastic. Dad the guffawing fan of old radio comedies.
Dad the stern army reserve officer and World War II vet.
Dad of the wicked backyard curveball. Dad at the head
of the table, carver of meat, pourer of wine, proposer

of toasts.

And: Dad who's Santa at Christmas. Dad who's the eternal devil's advocate. Dad the cautious driver and lover of adventurous shortcuts. Dad with his gag gifts and goofy cards. Dad with his overly formal and more than slightly tortured prose. Dad the PTA president and township attorney. Dad the knower of the meaning of words and the immediate consulter of the dictionary when stumped, especially at mealtimes. Dad the man without much hair up front, even way back when. Dad the bumbling but game weekend sailor. Dad with his somewhat idiosyncratic splayfooted stride. Dad the melancholy in his later years gazing glaze-eyed at police shows on the study TV. Dad the mischievous. Dad of the deadly two-handed set shot in the driveway still wearing his leather-soled street shoes after the commute home, slipping oddly sideways on the asphalt with each launch.

-- This list could continue a long, long time. And on some other occasion maybe it should. But to add even one more item right now would somehow make this entire entry -- unbalanced. (Life goes on.) (And Mother's life is still doing just that, going on, as far as I know. She's failed to call for a couple of weeks. But this is understandable with both of her sisters and middle son Jeff in town this month and my own visit coming up soon, and she's probably thinking I could use the break, and she's right. No doubt she's sparing me from at least some bad news -- perhaps much. For this kindness I'm nervously, apprehensively grateful.)

And where's Ripper? Disappeared. Been gone more than a week now. For Ripper, like Hoppy, life probably ain't goin' on. Only the delicate and supercautious Taro remains of Blur's sawblade brood. Taro the survivor, just as we all predicted.

(The zen of whacking, that's the part I forgot to mention. It's reassuring to get out there and do it a little every day. It's both restful and inspiring. It builds strong bodies twelve ways, especially hands, arms, and shoulders -- though it may also bring on bursitis or some other form of repetitive-motion injury.

And I should note I have no John Henry delusions. With
a yard this big you've got to mow at times. What Mr.
Whacker can do is reduce the frequency of mowing by
about two-thirds. You just hustle around chopping off
the outliers, the fast-growers, those overachievers
among grasses and dandelions and other kinds of weeds
that outperform themselves right into the category of
"the nail that sticks out gets hammered down." -- And
how's that for mixing not so much your metaphors as your
implements? Tools of the jyzaphorical trade! -- But I
can do the front yard entirely by hand-whacking, and
this is very good because only in the front yard do
appearances matter. No other part of the yard is
visible from the road or from neighboring yards unless
any would-be observers fight their way in through
thickets of brambly forest strips. -- And you can whack
in most kinds of weather, including light rain.)

But -- can I really strop a sharp edge on this
thing with all this whacky talk? Restore that perverse
spirit? (As a flock of robins, if four or five -- five
-- counts as a flock, hunts-and-pecks its way through
the dense, vividly green whacked-off grass right
outside. They're visible only from midbelly up except
when pecking, at which time the head vanishes down into
the grass but the tailfeathers flip up, that is,
"present," as in "present arms!" or (as with us
simians) "present ass!" -- Reminding me that I
encounter some truly magnificent feathers of the tail
variety as I ramble along the road to the bus stop, real
ones, on those peacocks at the daycare center, though
more often than not they, the feathers, are dragging
through the mud -- the potbelly pig mud. The sensitive
quivering noses on those pigs are also delightful.
-- Flock of "presenting" robins having long since
departed but now up in the big apple tree three jays are
flitting about with brilliant flashes of blue. Call it,
yet again, jays-burst. Lookie there! -- And they look
even better doing that when the apples have fully
ripened to a vividly contrasting candy-apple red.)
Meanwhile my first reading of the great Portuguese

protojyzer has regretfully come to an end. But what a
wondrous spring it's been for reading! You expect to
discover a writer this good maybe once a decade -- but
two of them heaving into view in a six-month period,
this must be my lucky year (readingwise, that is). And
mixed in there two other inspiring finds from my own
era: the first guiding me through haiku country, the
second offering a female Japanese perspective on the
Mentoka zone intriguingly resembling Lady S's Korean
view. (Whoa -- and here come sheets of rain! Slanting
in and undulating maniacally: it's hard not to stare.
Gaze in awe. Nature sure can do it! And so
effortlessly! Birds diving for cover and a roar in the
trees and squawks too, or more like caws: probably those
rowdy crows down by the street.)

   (And now loud knocking at the kitchen door. Most
likely the damn evangelicals again. I heard a car door
slam. But only three sets of knocks and then the car
came crunching back down the driveway. But they'll
return. They're relentless, and they're based only
about a quarter mile from us as the crows fly (or not).
-- And they're doubly relentless now, the evangelicals,
because old Stretch encouraged them by not daring to say
no to a proffer of literature.) (And it was a typical
squall for this area, having already raced through, into
history, leaving the eaves frantically a-drip and the
windows beneath their five-foot-wide veranda overhang
wet nearly to the top from the intense wind action.)

   I was saying -- what? Talking about reading.
Every night I go at the books for an hour or two,
shifting them around among those same three stacks on
the floor by the couch, deciding on the night's order
pretty much by impulse, seldom getting to all the active
volumes as indicated by sticky page markers -- fifteen
or sixteen in that category right now, though many are
close to dormant -- both numbers keep growing -- and yet
nothing's really grabbed me lately to render them all
dormant except that one, the grabber -- and then the
exhaustion wave hits and I flick off the radio and the
light, usually just as dawn's stealing in or during

those faintly crepuscular moments just before dawn as
the first birds are awakening. Not to mention the
raccoons thumping atop the veranda just outside.

The impermanence of all things, but occasionally
some serendipity while this or that or the other thing
is still hanging around even as some new things start
popping up. Think of the horror of the Russian poet's
life (the woman whose essays I was reading). Or, say,
the lives of Russian poets in general of that era. Or
billions of other lives of all kinds now ongoing. This
right here is paradise and I'm blessed. Dressed in
rags, though. Eating, in fact, mostly peanut butter
even now, despite the occasional slice of turkey or ham.
And health? Well, I feel fine but I'm probably in dire
straits or at the very least I'm sure as hell running
big risks. And so, like I say, wallow in it while you
can. Thank your lucky stars. And most important of
all, no matter what your field or lawn (as a new squall
blows in -- right now!): KEEP WHACKING.

18

Am I just gonna sit on my laurels? Hell no! I'm
gonna rush out and embrace new challenges!

And so here I sit (where? -- wait!) all sweaty and
I've exchanged night for day and squeezed it in what
I'll call the versa vise, which is a kind of
antimetaphysical juicer. This on the morning after the
longest day of the June deeps, the solstice itself not
even ten hours past -- or not even thirteen hours
anyway, now that I recalculate (but I ought to be
forgiven the bungle, I think, because I've got a lot on
my mind).

Topsy-turvy, hoo boy, am I. Unless I'm mistaken
again this is the first time in fourteen or fifteen
years I've been up and operating at this hour when not
on Nightscoper Upside-down Time -- the one exception
being the Mentoka research trip, which probably
shouldn't count because then I was completely outside
the realm of the quotidian -- whereas here (and now)
(and maybe even regularly for a while) I'm back into it.

Not just a little either. Way back. A decade and
more back -- six years more, almost exactly.

Where I sit now (the mystery unveiled) is -- a
picnic table. In a corner minipark which didn't even
exist at the start back then. Looking across at the old
homesite. In fact two of them. Both now occupied by a
single bulky four-level gray apartment building
festooned with "for rent" signs because the semester at
the nearby U is just coming to a close. Furnished rooms
starting at $275 a month -- which is more than we were
paying for the entire so-called carriage house,
including a large yard and patio and garage, back then.
(Even in those days I prattled on about what a great
deal it was, so this isn't just the usual old-timer kind
of nostalgia -- though it's partly that too, to be sure,
or why be here at all? Other than masochism. Or how
about simple curiosity? Or how about still more Mentoka
research, this time for the third volume in the series
whose first two volumes, much like, back then, that
apartment building over there, don't even exist yet
except for a few scraps hither and yon.)

-- And the students keep meandering by just as
before. Not much change at all really. They still
carry books or wear bulky backpacks (like mine) and
dress casually or outrageously according to the going
demand, which itself is unlikely to be too different
from era to era and certainly not as different as they
think (and we did too). Except for this one new
apartment house -- well, and one other much like it but
pink, just to my left on this side of the street -- the
whole neighborhood looks almost exactly the same.
Except, again, for the office building standing where

the big restaurant/nightclub used to be, and the massive
expansion of the motel (which put my former favorite
morning coffee shop out of business) -- but in the
larger picture even these latter two alterations are
minor since both are a full block or more away and I
have to turn ninety degrees to see even a small part of
them (and that's top floors only, of four or five).
    Yeah. "So here I sit." At the edge of the
basketball court, which is pretty much as it was when it
first went in, still tiny, although now boasting an
authentic twine net on the hoop, though probably not for
long. Old Stu, used to go one-on-one against him here,
hour after hour, day after day, semester after semester,
though I scarcely knew him otherwise. Took photos of
the house from here during one of Unk Erik's visits and
also during the U's' first stay (a blowup of one of
those photos still hangs in their den at home).
    And right here I sat writing the last entry of a
crisis-driven protojyze volume. If Lady U wasn't up
there in the house, I knew it would be over with her
forever. And in a sense that turned out to be true.
She wasn't up there, and what we've had since then,
though it's been plenty good enough at least in my view,
hasn't been what we had before. (And so I'm glad they
tore the whole thing down -- the house, yes, but the
love too. Why not? Throw up something new and
different. I won't say better. It might be, though.
-- And as always, only a little more than that, it might
end at any time. So best not to dwell thereon.)
    And then over to the right of the carriage house,
also gone now, the big old redwood farmhouse, remodeled,
which had stood there more than a century, with the
first-floor apartment in which we lived for the first
two and a half of our years on the site around on the
far side and D's friend Jo's on this end overlooking the
power-relay station inside the vacant lot which became
the park where I now sit. And Philly Frank's down
below, until he moved. And whozit's upstairs, the Far
Eastern scholar who always played Western classical
music, often with the volume extremely high. And the

old house to the left of the carriage house, that too was
torn down to make way for this big gray uber-entity.
     Almost six years of my life right there. Or was it
five? Without doing a series of complex calculations I
can never remember what year it was we moved to the next
place (exactly eighty blocks due north of here, and I do
mean due, the number of its street address identical to
that of the carriage house). -- But my feet remember
this area all right. On my tour today they carried me
around blind-milkhorse-like (neigh you say!). (A stop at
a used-book store -- I bought a beat-up copy of a book
about writerly dreams. Seems like I'm always looking for
new ways to goose up my dream life and get some of the
good parts down on paper.)
     Among the vehicles parked within view along the
street here is an ancient microbus spray-painted in
colorful counterculture fashion -- red lettering, lots of
it, mostly unreadable from this distance except for the
words "out of campus!" A sight that warms my heart --
like a Confederate veteran, say, returning decades later
to an old Civil War battle site and coming across a
rickety munitions wagon bearing the weathered words
"Yankee go home!" -- except I ain't no Confederate.
Other than, that is, by half my ancestry. And that I
would disown forever if such were possible. -- And
surely it is and I mean in some very real sense.
     -- Up this morning quite early: five o'clock. Hit
the road at quarter to six -- on foot. Of course on the
shortest night of the year it had long since been
daylight out there. All the traffic was going the
opposite direction from what I'm used to and thus most of
the time I could stay on the hard surface of the road
and cut maybe five minutes off the hike. (And along the
way our local worker-driver bus for the naval shipyard
roared by. Its livery is county but the bus itself is an
old diesel model originally deployed in my city No. 2/7,
and displayed on the destination panel above the front
windshield is "Municipal Zoo" -- as has been the case for
the six years or so we've been seeing the bus.)
     -- Since I sat down here the sun's broken through.

[Jyze for Mom]

A squirrelly rustling of leaves draws my eyes to the
small trees to the left -- back on squirrel turf again!
A seaplane buzzes overhead, very low, bound for the
nearby urban lake. A few birds hop about. If I strain
my ears a little I can hear those same damn loudspeaker
announcements blasting from the pole-mounted outdoor
P.A. at the auto dealer's lot a block northeast. (If
the wind were blowing this way they'd be a lot louder.)
       Should I be moving on here? With lots of errands
to run and a yen to beat the rush-hour crowd by catching
a two-thirty ferry? I should. But first -- in case I
don't make it back into these pages at one of the local
cafes as I hope to do -- first I should at least mention
(A) Mother finally called and all's about the same as it
was the previous call; (B) I printed up what will be my
last set of job-inquiry letters and mailed them off and
kept copies, as always; and (C) the main goal of this
mission to the city has already been accomplished in
that I'm carrying with me a copy of a Sunday paper from
my lifetime city No. 4, the one just outside of which I
grew up, mostly, meaning for twelve years of the first
seventeen (which newspaper I need because in "Dreams"
Ciara D. -- who's Lady C in real life -- is visiting
that very city right now, and not just in fictive but
also in real time: Centropolis I'm talking about, yes).
       And so -- onward. To the main bookstore and
several other old hangouts in the quarter. One of which
will not be, sorry to say, the franchise record shop
where brother Rob works. Turns out today's his day off.
Therefore next time for Rob.
                         *   *
       Jyze brings it on home. Or tries.
       I did just barely make that two-thirty ferry, but
only because I skipped half the items on my "to do"
list. Finally staggered in the kitchen door here a few
minutes past six, with new walking blisters on both feet
to match the whacking blisters on both hands.
       Wotta day! Mainly I was struck by the sheer number
of people out there inhabiting the daytime, the Sunny
Side Up world. And also by the odd choosh that I'm no

longer the same person wending his way among them. It's
Rip Van Winkle in reverse: I've aged by about fifteen
years and they're exactly the same as they were. -- But
no, no, no, no. Just the opposite! I'm pretty much the
same person I always was but I no longer fit in as
before -- or I should say I fail to fit in just as I
always failed to fit in, but now at least some of the
ways in which I fail to fit in are new. (I've become at
once less noticeable and more categorizable -- weird
street person of circa-counterculture vintage. In my
jeans and chucks and hickory-stripe shirt and hauling a
black shoulderbag as well as a backpack, and somewhat
longhaired with a few gray hairs cropping up (all but
invisibly!) and hiding behind shades too and with no
fewer than five -- count 'em! -- pens and markers poking
out from my shirt pocket, although I do inexplicably
lack the requisite nerdish plastic pocket guard.)
     Wotta apparition! And I figure once every couple
of weeks or so it'll be reappearing on the streets over
there, the apparition will, as I go about collecting
details for successive chapters in "Ghosts."
     My descent on the bookstores yielded several
promising items, including one weighty tome on the
delusions of so-called analytic philosophers. And a new
issue of my favorite tabloid book review with its cover
screaming "Fin de Siecle." And a dozen new editing
pens. And when I get home I find in the day's mail the
summer fiction issue of a certain glossy far-northeast-
coast weekly mag and it contains all sorts of good
stuff, including a scene (never before published)
involving Huck and Jim cut more than a century ago from
the canonical novel -- and also a batch of journal
entries composed by a number of first-rate contemporary
protojyzers (though these may be bogus -- I haven't
actually read any of the entries yet).
     At half past two in the a.m. Things more as they
should be, except I'm wasted from the big day and lack
of sleep tonight (just three hours and I woke up all
sweaty and seemingly feverish because upon arriving home
I plunged right into bed without undressing or noticing

the thickness of the covers D'd been using).

But I popped back in for this kwikjyze postscript mainly so I could note the really big event of the week. This was the successful firing-up of my "insurance" computer, the very first one I ever owned, and also a printer which had never even been tested in the ten years I've had it (the box was still sealed). Miraculously it took me only a single frenzied afternoon of ransacking the premises to locate two missing cables and a bundle of missing manuals. Eureka! Three separate eurekas, and I mean widely separate.

So now the two machines are set up on the dining-area table. My next task is to relearn the old word-processing program -- basically a waste of time, true, and not just because the computer's so slow; but I have no other options. -- My new fear being that either one or both of the machines will conk out (all these years of inactivity can't be a plus) and repairs will be either hideously expensive or impossible because of lack of parts for such ancient equipment.

Yet there's no doubt about it: I'm much better off than I expected to be. The old computer "insurance policy" has finally paid off!

*   *

(As the year starts to wind down lightwise. And some other ways as well, most likely -- so achingly sad to say. So close this down right now.)

19

Haul one of the old wooden barstools downstairs and set up in the utility room. Because it's hot out there, I mean as hot as it ever gets in these parts (or at

least at this hour). And in here it's cool. It's cool
in more than one sense of the word. Jyzin' atop the old
clothes dryer, what could be cooler than that?

     I've long been meaning to add this room to the
roster of jyze sites. The hope is it will bring a kind
of utilitarian slant, as it were, to the ever-developing
perspectival jyzosophy.

     (And now take a few steps to turn on the radio in
the next room (where it all began). Another radio's
already playing but I can't hear it very well because
it's up in the kitchen. -- Until moments ago I was
ensconced in the armchair in the parlor, sipping my
wake-up brew (a Kenya blend nowadays) and finally
getting into the "Fin de Siecle" issue. In just my gray
shorts and mottled sleeveless green henley. Sticking to
the plasticky simulated leather of the chair in various
places because of the heat. -- And then the thought: my
god, if any jyzing's to be done tonight, now's the time!
And leapt up, miraculously without losing any skin.
Because at eleven or a little after I'll have to switch
over to chore mode so the house will be just as it
oughta be when the new bacon-bringer brings it on home.)
                        *
     Very good. Big-band swing music surging in. Not
that I particularly like the "evening jazz" this station
plays. An hour ago after four or five atrocious tracks
in a row I let out a loud howl. What's especially bad
about certain popular jazz singers of our day isn't
their vanilla singing per se but their evident belief
that they're engaged in an act both elegant and highbrow
(not to say chichi and recherche). The pretension!
It's enough to make me want to beat a mad path to the
punk/grunge station at the other end of the dial. They
too take obvious pride in singing that's not necessarily
all that commendable but at least they don't pretend
they're creating high culture in groaning it out.
(Well, maybe a few do. How can anyone know for sure
what they're pretending? Can't punks/grungies dream
too?) -- And besides, there a listener must also put up
with long spells of nonstop hard-sell ads. And I refuse

to do that. At least for now. (And it's too hard to
retune Andy's old radio. Once I've got it locked in on
something the bias against any kind of change is high.)

     This coming at the far end of the June deeps. At a
few minutes after ten p.m. dusk is still visible through
the windows. And wafting in almost visibly through the
screens is the scent of freshly mown grass from next
door, where Ben is home on vacation this week -- meaning
I have to pick and choose my hours to play Mr. Whacker
in the front yard or otherwise I'll be drawn into orgies
of gratuitous neighborliness. (And yes, earlier this
afternoon that was our miscreant neighbor Captain Brick
calling out, and from the window of his forty-year-old
pickup no less, as I trudged along the broiling macadam
on the last leg of my journey home from the big city --
six hours plus of commuting so I could once again, just
like last week, buy the necessary out-of-town newspapers
and jot down a few pages of notes for "Ghosts" and
glance through new arrivals at the bookstore -- Brick
called out these words, and in a way I don't believe
I've heard since I was raised up back in the heartland:
"Hot enough fer ya?" -- followed by a bizarre cackle
that sounded something like botched overdubbing.)

     And speaking of bacon: the three little potbellies
were again thundering around at the daycare center. But
in addition, more significantly, this is it, this week,
or it is if I'm reading the numbers right: it's my very
last week on unemployment. As the new sole source of
support herself observed when I pointed this out: "Get
ready for the real poverty to hit the fan."

     She's hanging in there. She's even being
moderately good-natured about it. The one problem is
most or even (sometimes) all signs of love and affection
have vanished. I have a hunch I'm being blamed for this
new work regime, even though she acknowledges it's
certainly her turn. It's just that underneath -- and
she's not shy about fessing up to this -- she doesn't
think bacon-bringing is a matter on which she should
have to take a turn. And this despite her generally
progressive politics. (Will the love and affection ever

fully revive? I hope so. But I'm not counting on it.
As always I'm figuring things could spin out of control
at any moment, and I have more reason for thinking so
right now than I've had in quite some time.)

Next week she faces a major decadal birthday.
Little Stretch turns twice the age she was at the start
of the year before we met. This is helping her
underlying frame of mind not one bit. Suddenly she's
exercising like crazy -- pounding so hard on those
stair-steps in her room overhead that sometimes I fear
the jyze-central ceiling will come crashing down. And
like I say: in one way or another it just might.

But who, me worry? Now? When I've got this jyze
thing rolling? And all systems are go? My life's as
close to ideal as it's ever likely to get? And I know
it can't last? I should worry now during this moment of
splendor? On a day when I'm perking with new ideas for
the next go-round on "Jyzer"? And the revised outline
for "Mentoka Dreams" is nearing completion?

Not likely. Tonight I possess in abundance the
power to suppress. I may or may not be using it. Don't
want to give the matter another thought if I can help
it.

(I'm sitting with my right side pressed against the
front of the dryer and jyzing away on its glossy white
top surface. The elbow of my jyzing arm is resting on
the lid of the big old freezer which we use as a
horizontal storage cabinet, unplugged, because keeping
it running is too expensive. And this area in which
I'm seated is part of my nerf court, an open patch of
cement floor about six by twelve feet in which at more
or less regular intervals I jump around and fire shots
at the hoop mounted six feet eight inches up on a
centerbeam-supporting post just behind me now -- and so
most shots taken from more than about two feet have to
be line drives, "frozen ropes" again, and the longer the
shots the more true this is, because the clearance
between hoop and ceiling is a mere sixteen inches.)

(What else is in this room? At the far end squats
my one remaining fire safe, two-drawered and black, in

which I'm storing backup disks and completed J-books, among other things. And here's a spillover stack of books about Mentoka. And a seven-foot-long wooden five-shelved fiction bookcase. A sink. A washer. A workbench with a big four-by-eight-foot wall-mounted tool pegboard. Papa U's big gray power band saw. A water heater. Brown packing boxes stacked here and there, along with bright plastic boxes of various hues. Pails, clothes-drying racks, hand saws hanging from hooks on ceiling beams, a mop, poison for pests, bulk detergent, out-of-use portable electric and kerosene space heaters, an upright ironing board -- all the typical utility-room stuff and then some.)

If I were really into it -- doing right by the highest jyze standards -- I'd launch into a description of the intricate patterns made by cracks, stains, discolorations, paint splatters and other forms of wear and tear and use and abuse on the concrete floor, say as I was first trying to do just about a quarter century ago in city No. 2/7 regarding the basement floor at what was then my favorite bookstore of them all (and is now my mother's!) -- but can't. It's time for my chores. And though I'm hoping to return later tonight in these pages, I won't be doing it here. This stool goes back upstairs to its accustomed spot by the parlor counter.

-- Lots of pesky little bugs down here, by the way, something like fruit flies only quicker and nastier. Just the past few nights they've arrived on the scene. They're new to the area as far as I know, so I'm wondering, is this it, the apocalyptic fin de millennaire? As announced by the forerunner bugs of a horrific new plague? -- That "Fin de Siecle" special edition, I want to mention, it turns out the writers featured are just the usual bunch riding their usual hobbyhorses. In all their tens of thousands of words only one paragraph touches on the truly boggling issues you'd expect millennial thinkers to tackle. Just for starters, consider the appalling trade-offs we'll all, or nearly all, have to be making because of impending ecological catastrophes. -- So sez I anyway. Though

[Jyzemelt]

I, just like most of those writers, may not be around
to witness the real horrors or acquiesce in the real
trade-offs. Or rather the real horrors and real trade-
offs to come, I should say -- as if the ones we're
already acquiescing in aren't real enough and horrible
enough to corrode the soul way past the core.
     -- And now, make that bed! Scrub them toilets!
Get up in that kitchen and rattle them pots and pans!
                    *   *
     -- How could it have turned so cold so fast? All
of a sudden an Arctic Express rolls through. I was
shivering -- had to pull on sweatpants and sweatshirt.
Thought hmm, must be because I got sunburned today,
these strange chills glissandoing up and down my spine
and electrifying my forearm fur. And no doubt sunburn
did have something to do with it. It was in the mid-
nineties out there this afternoon! And I was trudging
along in the sun for hours! -- But then a moment ago I
stuck my head out the back door and I could see my
breath! So it would appear this amazing bit of weather
news is for real, yes. (The chores took only forty
minutes and I came right back. It's not even midnight.
Stretch isn't home yet. I do expect her momentarily.
And we'll rave about how many cameras she loaded today,
how many smiley faces she was awarded, what wild and
crazy things happened -- how many gift film cans the
besotted older-dude shuckerman laid on her today.)
     I'm curled up on the couch in jyze central. A new
lamp has shown up here -- it wasn't doing me much good
up in the shed with the power out. And we've
transferred the lamp that was here up to D's room so she
won't go blind trying to read the alternative grunge/
punk/rock weekly on the couch in that same room (at her
request I fetched her a copy of the new issue while I
was in the city today). Since starting the job she's
taken a new interest in youth culture -- she wants to be
able to talk with the young guys she works with, many of
whom of course continue to be going gaga over her and
assume she's only a little older than they are. (The
older-dude shuckerman, by the way, is almost my age --

148

the only one within a dozen years of her age on either
side, she says.) She's even talking of returning to
school in order to take up the teaching of youth. Or
grooming of youth maybe? (I hear the crunching of
gravel -- that's her. In the wagon. Or should be.)

(Yes, is. "Got cold fast, didn't it?" So we're at
least back on speaking terms, it would appear.)

-- And Mom. Under the new regime she and I talk
every other week. If she doesn't call Monday or Tuesday
night at nine-thirty I call Wednesday night at that same
hour. In theory at least, this means we can both be
well prepared to talk. But when I called last night she
was in tears -- took ten minutes to pull herself
together. It was because Jeff had left earlier in the
day at the end of his five-day visit and my call had
caught her as she was immersing herself in his babybook.

And: now she wanted my help. Jeff had said she
should talk with me about the bitterness she still feels
at times toward Dad. She wrestles things into a more
bearable perspective but then she loses her grip on it.
"The Fritsch wall" -- she and Jeff had been pondering
all the things Dad had been "holding in." The financial
scandal Gramps S. was involved in: Jeff wondered if Dad
had ever gone back and checked out the newspaper
archives on it as I did during my Mentoka-zone visit a
couple of years ago. How much did Dad really know? He
always referred to the scandal as involving a "gray
area" of the law (and he never called it "the scandal";
I think I'm the one who started that, long after he
died), but in Jeff's view there's nothing gray about it.
What, Mother asked, did I think about all this?

Do I need to spell out how I answered? Very
carefully, that's how. The complexities of the
situation. The tortured politics of that era. The
extreme difficulty of our knowing more than half a
century after the fact what really went on. The tangled
roots of Dad's conservative turn. (The more he turned
that way the more he, like Gramps himself, could believe
the whole case was just a liberal plot fomented by the
Depression-era feds and their Mentokan "stooges.")

        -- But that's enough. I can agree Gramps doesn't
come off looking so good in retrospect even if he did
escape prosecution (just exactly how he did this remains
a mystery to everyone, but he was known to have a friend
or two in high places and Mother thinks one of them
saved his ass -- though I doubt she'd ever put it so
crudely). And I can feel for Dad facing all that and
thus I can forgive him for things that once looked to me
-- well, I was going to say unforgivable but it was
never quite that bad, not even during the worst period
(which was after finding out about his marital
infidelities -- and by that time he was gone -- and now
I see I'm repeating myself, again, so for a while at
least I'll just let all this fade out...).

        Anyway: the call was relatively short because next
week I'll be traveling down there and she and I can talk
at length about these things face to face and no doubt
will. Unfortunately she has to go in for a chemo
treatment on the very day I arrive, and she's now
conceding there's some truth to the standard observation
that it takes about a week to get back to normal after
each treatment. She apologized in advance. I feel I'm
ready. As much as I can I'll be trying to look on the
bright side. And I'll be proofreading the genealogy
while I'm there and also doing some reconnoitering....

        Fades. The old "Dot Dot Dot (a Lament)" (that
being the title of a poem I wrote many eons ago to a
girl called Dottie whom I felt had done me wrong). The
fade is also a current popular hairstyle, or anyway
recently was. And I'll just say I've built up some
nasty calluses from my daily whacking bouts, including
an itchy black one, a fascinating blood callus it's all
I can do to keep myself from picking at as it fails to
fade on its own. -- And now that I don't have to worry
so much about keeping my hands in tiptop keyboarding
shape, maybe I'll just let myself have at it after all.

                              *

        But -- but -- before signing off for this week I do
want to mention a calendrical oddity. Here we are at
the far end of the June deeps -- and yet still in them

-- and even so the incoming grooveyard jazz jock just
said to the outgoing jock, "Happy holiday." It's still
June but because it's Friday night and the Fourth of
July falls on Tuesday and many people will have Monday
off, the unusually long weekend is already upon us. And
that would help explain why I heard several strings of
firecrackers and some whistling skyrockets go off while
I was up there doing the chores. -- And since Lady U's
birthday is the 5th, our holiday will be even longer
than most, and before the 5th is over (by NUT time
anyway) I'll be on my way to visit Mom (barring some
emergency like last time), and if I am on my way I'll be
right back to jyzing -- so what we have here is just a
sort of preface (and now, I really mean it, concluded).

20

-------.

   The conductor tells us (over the P.A.) about "a
brooding snowcapped presence" off to the left at ninety
degrees and indeed such a presence is out there -- I
twist my neck about a hundred fifty degrees to take it
in. This is a lot closer to the monster than I usually
get.
   As we roll into the exotic city of -- next city
south. South of Jyze City, that is. At half past eight
in the morning. Sun slanting into the observation car.
My seat is canted forward about thirty degrees and this
means I'm looking more or less in the direction of our
abode, which stands about fifteen miles northwest of
here. "U Acres" I'm talking about, yes. What I see,
though, is just weedy green summer fields and a jumble
of typical evergreen-serrated ridgelines and a small
patch of water which I happen to know is salt water.

[Jyzemelt]

     So I guess a correction's in order: these are among
the outermost outskirts of the next city south.
     Of course it would've been much simpler to catch
this train at the station down here -- just a half-hour
drive from U Acres instead of a two-and-a-half-hour
commute (my usual one, though at an hour very unusual
for me). But D would've had to drive me in at a time
inconvenient for her, and what's more during the morning
rush, and she'd've had only minutes to get ready for
work when she returned. So I rode the bus and ferries
instead. Got up at three a.m. to be able to do it.
     (And now here's the city itself. First came the
infamous sulfuric aroma, then the sight of the downtown
buildings perched on their hillside to the southwest --
ahead and to the right -- across acres and acres of rail
yard. Rows of classic weathered boxcars -- an excellent
near-Mentokan specimen right outside -- and farther back
in the yard a train's on the move, its high round-topped
livestock cars sliding slowly above the roofs of the
stationary boxcars. Several tiers of animals in those
cars: sheep maybe. -- But reminding me that as the
county bus pulled away from our stop at five-thirty this
morning in the predawn dark three stray horses came
galloping riderless up the middle of the empty highway.
Two white, one brown -- belonging, I suddenly realized,
to our neighbors living over by the bible church.
Somehow the critters had gotten loose and they looked
wild-eyed, frantic. A stunning sight. The driver
phoned it in.) (For me it recalled, as I thought about
it on the bus, the celebrated poem about sighting a
moose from, yes, a bus. A sudden shocking access of jizz
in the birder sense -- "wild essence" -- but in the case
of these horses even more foreboding than that provided
by the moose in the poem because this was jizz breaking
out of seeming domestication.)
     -- Grand old station here. Waterway. The downtown
skyline featuring half a dozen highrises that aren't all
that high -- the tallest maybe twenty stories. Chemical
plants belching steam and smoke. And now water, the bay,
a huge old freighter being loaded a hundred yards away,

152

a crane swinging its load, another freighter moored a
bit farther out awaiting its turn.

So...here we go again. Deathwatch trip number two.
(Not by coincidence, one of the books in my bag -- down
by my left foot -- is a French near-protojyzer's
fictified tale of his journey through the USAn night.)

This trip doesn't feel anywhere near as urgent as
the last one, I should say, nor do I think it ought to.
Not only have I had another four months to absorb the
shock but also the death itself has been put off into a
future distant enough and indefinite enough to make it
seem almost like anyone else's future death, including
my own -- or sometimes anyway.

(As we glide through a lengthy tunnel and emerge
running alongside the narrows at just a few feet above
water level, chalky cliffs on the far side and the big
green suspension bridge up ahead -- and perhaps
accounting for the deja-vu feeling I'm getting, we just
drove over that bridge a couple of weeks ago, D and I
did, and marveled at the sight of a silver passenger
train snaking along down here more or less where this
train is now and headed in the same direction.)

It seems probable that all three of this year's J-
books will feature a journey like this one. Structural
sameness. A high point each time. And I'm delighted it
can be so: six months ago things looked nowhere near
this hopeful. (Best I say this now because by tomorrow
night I may be seeing things a lot differently. Maybe
not, hopefully not, but regardless I'd better be ready.)

Salt water continues out there, with many small
evergreen-studded islands. Beyond them, my home turf
(current) from a slightly different perspective. I even
know the names of some of the islands. (This account
threatening to fall into total incoherence because the
lady next to me is trying to talk "journaling" with me
-- is angling to find out if I'm someone she might've
heard about -- just because I'm jyzing!) (The P.A. is
now telling us about the mountain range hidden in the
haze to the west. Even without being able to see it I
can visualize it to a high degree of resolution. -- Or

anyway like to think I can. It'd be interesting to
check my "imaged" mountains against the real ones. They
are, after all, the same ones I see every day, but now
from a significantly more southern perspective. The
parallax effects might prove to be seriously confusing.)

     The past week (as now we abruptly leave the
shoreline and plunge into a hundred or so miles of
forest) has been -- strangely peaceful. (Those last two
words took a long time to arrive.) Preparations for the
trip. Warm, sunny weather. Lots of grass-whacking and
a tank's worth of mowing until some "bad mowjo" hit and
the mower broke. (Luckily we have a replacement part --
the so-called "mow ball" -- but no bolt to attach it
with, so the repair job will have to await my return.)

     Despite the long holiday weekend -- just coming to
an end right now, really -- D and I saw little of each
other. Her landmark birthday ("D-Day") came as close to
passing unnoticed as any such signal event can do with
us. (I gave her a book of haiku and a pro-hoops puzzle,
both of which I'd bought long, long ago, before I lost
my job and of course well before we'd agreed to forget
about gifts and to skip birthday celebrations in this
year of minimal income. Under no circumstances were the
"balloon people" of the past few family birthdays to be
puffed back into existence, and they weren't.)

     (Here's the state capital and its new depot. We're
trembling in place. I've heard about this building but
never seen it before. I must've been snoozing when we
stopped here on the way up last time. It's small,
wooden, and quite spiffy-looking. A rarity these days
for USAn railways.)

     -- To try to continue with this right now would be
futile. (But I do have a new cap bearing the name of
this train. Six bucks. Not at all bad for the price.)

*   *

How'll this work? A few hours later -- a bit of
dozing and some of that fictified French near-protojyze.
And some mags. A couple of my own homemade peanut-
butter sandwiches. Passing through all the utterly
predictable places. (What else is train travel all

about if not, first and foremost, predictability?
"Getting the trains running on time" -- timeliness,
however, being their least predictable quality these
days, on this run anyway, or I guess I should say in
this country and in this era.)

And now as we approach our last stop before
climbing into the mountains, I face laterally with
respect to the direction of travel. This is new for me
in a club car. Always before I've been able to grab one
of the canted seats. Now it's sideways gazing at the
mountains to the west. At my back, out the windows on
the other side of the car, a trio of famous peaks, far
off: they look like small horns growing out of the
ground-hugging clouds concealing their lower slopes.

Two cars ahead (coach No. 1113) I had two seats to
myself for the first several hours, then had to give one
up briefly to a sullen cap-worn-backwards teenager whose
girlfriend was sitting a few seats in front of us. Then
our attendant came up with adjoining seats for them.
Probably my luck won't hold much longer -- not even two
minutes longer (as we pull into a familiar station --
and right now I'm looking at the very parking lot where
the "hippie bus" stopped and I hopped out and shopped
for snacks at a nearby organic market back just about
exactly thirteen years ago, if I'm not misremembering)
(and if I can arrange it I'll be returning home ten days
from now on that same bus line -- if it still exists).

Nine hundred twelve is the passenger count on this
thing today ---

*   *

It didn't work. On a train this crowded
distractions are almost inevitable. But I'm trying
again, now in a canted seat across the aisle. Same one
I sat in on the way up three months ago on the other
half of this round-trip ticket.

Nor did my luck hold. Some weird Cawk dude in
ultra-low-hanging "sag" pants exposing a band of hairy
lower belly dropped into the other half of my coach seat
-- friendly enough but I soon knew I didn't want to be
talking too much with him if I could help it. And he'll

be there most of the rest of the way.

Meanwhile it's dusk and the spectacular gilded "volcano named after the soft drink" dominates the territory up ahead, its snows still sunlit as the plain goes dark beneath it -- the volcano as a whole looking less like a soft drink, I'd say, and more like the upper reaches of a giant butterscotch sundae -- even though it must still be thirty or forty miles away. We're rolling through flat terrain with dark isolated round mountains huddled on both sides and an occasional cone-shaped one popping up for variety. Mostly at my back what must've been a gorgeous sunset (given all those odd-shaped clouds hanging about on the western horizon) is now fading quietly away.

How fine it is to become absorbed in a good book on a long rail journey. The vibration, the rhythms, the sense of the journey itself transfer somehow to what's going on inside the book (with the peripheral flow of scenery as a constant reminder of this) -- all these as well as the isolation from the concerns of daily life, the temporary severing of attachments (or rather the illusion of such severing) and for that matter the aura of romance of the long-distance ride (all those novels and movies with scorching train scenes -- Myshkin meeting Natasha, I think it is -- Anna Karenina squirming lustily in her seat as she recalls Count Vronsky twirling her at the ball -- not to mention a lesser-known blockbuster in which Jyzer G scopes out the "woman in purple" at the far end of the lounge car -- and that one, for me at least, no mere fiction).

-- And if one book's fine, what's three? In addition to the Frenchman's hyper-jazzed protofictojyze I've got an impressively lyrical contemporary indigenous USAn poet ghost-dancing in prose and a perverse contemporary Russian historian strolling in imagination 175 years ago with his country's reputedly finest poet. (And a couple of quarterlies!) I love reading too much -- way too much. Especially considering I can't stand being a bookworm (meaning one who primarily reads instead of acts) and also can't stand to lose too much

jyzing time, whether JIFT or JIRT. But for the past
month I've been on a tear to make up for having been
short of reading time over the past decade. Can't help
myself. Probably it'll soon be leveling off -- finding
its own level, that is, what I need for basic writerly
sustenance. (Just as I feel the journalizing has done
-- via the crucial limits imposed by the jyze rules.)

     -- And we roll on into the night. The looming and
brooding "soft-drink" volcano, lightly cloud-wreathed,
grays fading into blacks, up close now yet barely
visible. The interior of the club car brightening and
coming alive because it's summer and lots of courting-
age folks are aboard. Beer, earphones, laughter, dice,
laptops -- and a number of books too. And ladies on the
make, a couple of the older ones maybe hoping for a
quick score in this very car. But count me out, ladies,
just in case I'm reading you right and I've made your
short list of potentials. -- But absolutely I wish you
a torrid sleeping-compartmentful of good luck otherwise.

     Earlier the trip across the high country was all I
expected and more. Today's tunnels numbered not twenty-
two but hundreds or even thousands, gray tunnels and
white tunnels and semiopaque ethereal tunnels because we
were boring through the clouds themselves into isolated
patches of sunshine. And the wild roses numbered in the
zillions. Snowcapped peaks popping into view, awesome
vistas, stacks of new railroad ties and then suddenly
scatters of old ties (of just the type I'd love to
buttress the shed with back home). Best of all: the
flickery alternations of white cloud interior and eye-
blasting panorama as we glided by the concrete columns
inside the snowsheds.

     A beautiful ghostly scene right now with the snowy
and still ever-so-faintly glowing volcano passing by
extremely close up. You have to lean forward until your
nose is pressing against glass and look almost straight
up to glimpse the summit or something close to it.

     Or those roses -- the biggest surprise. They're
still wowing me. Mountain roses by, okay, if not the
zillions, at least the tens or hundreds of billions.

[Jyzemelt]

Pinkish-red -- rose colored! Mile after spectacular
mile of rose-colored wild roses! A wild rose is a wild
rose is -- wild! Wild floral essence! Yeah!
                    *   *
     Just dawn -- rosy (of course), misty dawn and we
come barreling westbound out of the brown hills and hit
the flatland -- bright lights, water, a tanker being
loaded, another looming just offshore -- and out onto
the bridge with a thumping roar (oh, such a fine clatter
-- must be the same bridge that made that very same
sound, I'd swear, last time on the way up) and now on
the other side we've stopped at a station I can't see
and folks are filing down the aisle next to me to
deboard, a crossbuck and gate with flashing red lights
is energetically ding-ding-dinging right outside my
window (our coach is oddly stranded at a diagonal in the
middle of the street and I'm looking down across the
gate into the sleepily expressionless eyes of a truck
driver wearing a camo cap and now lifting a bright
yellow thermos to his lips) and a few feet to the left
of the truck stands an ancient black steam engine and
coal tender, No. 1258 it looks like (in the shadows),
permanently on display on its own little model-train-
like section of track -- but now we're moving again,
southbound, starting to parallel the shore to the west
and a brightening orange sky to the east and lots and
lots of tank cars on both sides lined up for the
refinery -- glistening water (the mirror effect) and my
eyes are still creaky stiff and my green raincoat is
pulled over my lap and my belt's unbuckled, my jeans
unbuttoned and unzipped beneath the coat to give my
similarly creaky-stiff and dream-swollen and heat-droopy
genitals some room to stretch out, and my shoes are off,
I'm feeling greasy and grimy and in a moment I'll be
gathering my stuff, getting myself together because my
stop is just a few miles down the line (and last night I
missed an attempted child molestation involving the
obnoxious little girl half a car up, some guy was
arrested and hauled off the train by local police but at
the time it happened I was back in the observation car

lost in fictive realms) -- and that's it, there's the
bridge whose name I forget -- not that I could mention
it anyway -- but it goes across to the notorious prison
-- and I'm thinking I'd better pack it in now -- this
clearly being the end of the night through which, and in
another sense into which, I've been journeying.

*   *

    -- But not the end of the day. So I'll tack on an
extra paragraph or two. -- And here's a way to do it in
style. For this is the very same spot where I whipped
out my J-stick when returning home several other times
way back in the protojyze era. Heart of the city. The
antique fixed-track conveyances I rode daily to work for
a few seasons a quarter century ago, they're still
clattering by. The monument to an imperial USAn
commodore (not the one I was named after -- middle name
-- but the one whose last name is shared by the
philosopher on whom I wrote many a college paper despite
being unable, then or ever, to read more than a page or
two of his ruminations at a sitting) -- this monument
towers almost directly overhead. The inscription on the
east side of its base is laid out a few feet in front of
me, with three tiers of pigeons treating it suitably
from above. And I perch on the concrete edge of the
next planter over because my old favorite bench is --
missing! And not just that one -- all of them! This
may be because a so-called "Career Fair" is about to
commence for the lunch crowd, but I doubt it. I suspect
it's part of the crackdown on transients I've been
hearing about from afar for the past couple of years.
And what a shame if it's so. What a commentary on this
country's ways in the era of the conservative backlash,
phase II. (Thinking of the celluloid-cowboy era of two
administrations back as phase I. -- Not failing to
realize, of course, there were earlier such phases and
will be later ones as well, probably even worse.)
    The usual banal first impression: mixture of
continuity and change. As always, except for the rare
catastrophic occasion, continuity far exceeds change but
change stands out more (well, hey, bookmark that!). My

159

favorite art-supply store of them all, source of my very
first protojyzing brand-X fountain pen and also recently,
by mail order, of fictive Jyzer G's "DREAM" cap and much
else, has left the downtown -- that's the other big one
for me (along with the missing benches). And regardless
of the balance of the change/continuity formula there's
nostalgia. History. Ghosts. Memory. Lots and lots of
all those here for me -- civic kind as well as personal.
But forget the civic. And forget the personal!
-- Because I gotta be moving on.
       -- I trudged all the way from the ferry terminal to
Mother's apartment carrying my bags (on a sunny, crisp-
yet-warm, most excellent morning just as the sidewalks
were beginning to come alive with downtown workers, and
I felt as though I vaguely recognized a surprising
number of them and certainly would see a mix like this
nowhere else and what's more I fit right in, though at
the fringe, just as I always did, or felt I did).
Stealthily I let myself in using the keys Mother mailed
up and I deposited my luggage on the landing and snuck
back out, knowing she'd be needing all the rest she
could get on this day when she goes in for chemo (and
normally she stays in bed until noon or close to it).
And then I hiked around nearby districts all morning,
getting as far as the heart of downtown before starting
to work my way back. Then this quick stop, now ending.

21

       Suck it up. Narrow them eyes and grit them teeth.
Got to if I want to pull this off.
       Talk about wallowing in it. The corner window
table at my onetime prime hangout in this city No. 2/7.

[Jyze for Mom]

And it's still called Mac's, although the succeeding
words are a little fancier than they used to be. Same
location, though, same interior configuration as existed
after the big remodeling carried out while I was
overseas, and really not much else is different either,
including the menu. Is there still a Mac M.? Seems
unlikely -- but I won't ask. No need. For me there's
always a Mac M.
     Ordered a burger and fries, I did. For old time's
sake. Dig into some real indie (nonfranchise) grease.
     Tail end of the noon rush hour and for the past
ninety minutes or so I've been wandering around some old
hoods, starting with the one where I shared the top
floor of a house with Unk Erik and then moving outward,
that is, westward. I hiked up to 1616, checked out the
scene. Marveled all over again at the view up there.
(How could it possibly be that the three-story apartment
building newly constructed on the site has so few view
windows on its north side? The gulch, the park, the
military sanctuary, the downtown skyline, the bridge,
patches of the bay, hills of the county to the north --
none worth an unobstructed picture-window look from
maybe two hundred feet up?) Found trees grown to full
size in the vacant lot by the school -- they hadn't even
been planted yet when Lady S and I moved in up there.
     But here it is, the Mac's Special. Beautiful.
                         *
     -- Most of it I managed to force down. Bad meat
and cardboardlike fries. -- One of those "small
changes" you immediately notice, no question.
     Sitting three tables back is a rather bulky salt-
and-pepper-haired Scandi-looking lady I took at first
glance, then even at second, harder glance, to be
partner Una of my former firm in city No. 12. She
stared right back at me rather imperiously as if she
thought she was still my boss. But of course this is
not partner Una. Just another ghost. But definitely
not one of the ones I expected to encounter down here.
     Meanwhile throngs of homegrown city No. 2/7
phantoms battle each other to win the right to haunt me.

In this part of town especially. Most are incarnations
of Lady S or Lady V -- or not incarnations but more like
misty intimations. Or sometimes vivid mirages. And the
rest of the cast of thousands of that era turn up too,
or a small portion of them though it seems like most,
including some I'm pretty sure I haven't thought of a
single time in all the years since then, except maybe
during my five or six previous return visits.

On an expedition like this one you sure do get to
pondering the quirks and idiosyncrasies (not to mention
idiosync-holes) of memory.

Off to the southeast a mile or so is the crown of
the forested hill I could see looming almost directly
overhead by leaning out the bedroom window of my last
apartment in this town, the one just down the hall from
Erik's. From here the orange upper reaches of the TV
tower rising from that hill's verdant summit appear to
be nimbly dodging an endless series of big raggedy fog
puffs as they tumble by headed due east. Owing to those
same puffs, the light on the street here just outside is
constantly changing, the scene flickering and shimmering
like an ancient silent film (but in color) running half
out of the sprockets.

We've got a fine sampling of human diversity
traversing the sidewalks just as before, a tolerably
modest base of normals of all races (but more Cawk than
not) and then numerous overlays and underlays of
eccentrics, New Agers, punks, geeks, grungies, hip-
hoppers, students, drifters, motorcycle gangsters,
transsexuals and unambiguously "out" gays and lesbians,
and some truly superb specimens of hippies preserved in
amber. I still find it a very likable neighborhood, yes
I do. I'd move back here in a flash if I could.

But -- cain't. Not now. Probably not ever.
Except, if I'm lucky, maybe in the fictojyze realm -- in
jyzoscope.

So this is what? Tuesday. I came in Friday. Is
the world still hanging together despite everything?
Just barely. On Saturday night sister Barb came over
(leaving boyfriend Keith behind at her place, where

they're now living together, because Mother and Keith
are barely on speaking terms after Keith's "crack-up"
during Aunt Shar's visit a few weeks ago) (while nobly
chauffeuring Mother and Shar around town he suddenly
started loudly imitating their no doubt hard-to-take
sisterly backseat chatter and for several minutes could
not be made to stop) and what started out as a lovely,
lively, even splendid three-person dinner party,
nostalgic as they come, featuring two dishes Barb and I
loved as kids (hamburg spaghetti, cherry pie -- though
made with cherries from cans, not from the backyard
cherry tree which, incidentally, has now fully fruited
into legendary stature) -- this blew into smithereens.

    Mostly it was Barb and Mother, as I saw it, with me
attempting to mediate, but then Barb went off on me as
well, and then when Mother tried to defend me from some
outrageous charges, Barb accused us of ganging up on her
-- "Everything he says is great and everything I say is
horrible!" -- which is to say she simply repeated the
same line, more or less, she's been taking on me since
about second grade. And it's as unfair, exaggerated,
ridiculous, preposterous, horrifying now as it was then
-- only much more so, of course, owing to the
circumstances of Mother's terminal illness. But then
this, obviously, is just my view of things. Once again
the big brother pontificates.

    Until almost two a.m. this battle went on. I had
to crawl through all kinds of mud to get Barb to stay on
and enable the three of us finally to reach an extremely
shaky accommodation. No apologies from Barb, of course.
We just all have to see things her way -- or pretend to.
So that's what we're trying to do.

    Rather than compromise, rather than admit the
possibility that the other person in an argument may
have a legitimate reason for disagreeing with her on
some moral issue, my sister becomes personally enraged
and indignant, demands capitulation, flings wild
accusations, and finally Jly threatens to break off all
relations -- stomp out. Bolting up with flared nostrils
and heading for the door: "I don't have to take this

anymore!" Same thing's happened numerous other times --
most notably when she made a quick fiery exit from
Gatewood right after Dad died.
     Why is this?
     Well. To hell with it. I've done all I can to try
to get along with her and it's just made matters worse.
Instead of jockeying to effect a reconciliation with
Barb, from now on my major aim will be to keep the
tensions between her and Mother from flying out of
control, because Mother depends on Barb's help. I know
Mother understands my situation with Barb well enough to
accept this. (And I won't make a point of it. Just try
to get along.)
     Is any of this clear? Probably not. Nor do I want
to put any more effort into trying to make it so. How
it is is how it is is how it is is is. Amen.
     -- The world as seen through the greasy and
imperfect lens of the front picture window at Mac's
upscaled burger emporium. It never was very clear seen
this way -- somehow I just know it's the same glass --
but I loved the view anyway. And I'll take it now too.

*

     Last night's dinner guest at Mother's was Jim Q.
Leftover hamburg spaghetti and cherry pie but we had a
delightful time. Sister Barb was not present. -- Or
no, this was two nights ago, what am I thinking?
-- Jim Q. arriving late because he'd been whipping up a
batch of whole-wheat pancake mix which provided the
basis for our brunch yesterday.
     Jim Q.'s new apartment (he's moved again) is about
five miles southwest of Mother's place. He goes home
after his visits; he does not as a rule sleep over. For
my part, I go downstairs to Rikki's apartment where I'm
staying while she and her kid are housesitting somewhere
out in the burbs. I listen through the ceiling to
Mother coughing upstairs -- but it's not at all bad at
this point. She's faring remarkably well. (The
mosquitoes are a bigger nuisance these days -- owing to
those drenching spring rains followed now by a spell of
warm sunny days.) We even walked over to the post

office yesterday, Mom and I. She scurries right along.
The danger is that she'll overdo it -- as overdoing it
has always been her danger -- and now she loves to show
off what a tough old babe she can be.

Rikki's place reminds me a lot of Lady V's.
Attractive foreign-oriented young single mother with one
child, a boy. In this case all the foreignness (the
packed bookcases offer scarcely a volume in English) is
German instead of, as in V's case, French and Chinese/
Vietnamese. But I could swear the abundant kid's
artwork on the walls and fridge is a knockoff of V's boy
Danny's. And Rikki herself is within a few years of V
in age and just about her size and build, though she's
not particularly athletic or artistic as V was (both)
and her hair's brown instead of black.

Friday was tough (just as forecast) because Mother
was drugged up by the chemo, too excited, too geared up
-- almost unbearably so. (This is why it's forgivable
that Barb would crack, Keith would crack, anyone would
crack -- if only Barb herself could see things this way
regarding the rest of us cracking.) But in the end
Friday too may have contributed to our well-being --
because I think Mother came out of it more clearly
understanding why she'll do better to stay as low-key as
possible in her relations with Barb and Keith -- meaning
when the shit starts to fly.

(Didn't I say to heck with all that?)

-- And the editing of "Chandler-Hutcheson Family
Memorials" is underway. It too is tough going -- four
to six pages an hour with a total of about 225 tightly
packed pages to slog through. A genealogy press on the
far coast, southern sector, set the type and will do the
printing. To ease the eye and neck strain I'm using the
tiltable bedtray I sent Mother as a Christmas gift a
year ago, setting it up on the kitchen table. An
excellent gift if I do say so -- and I'm glad I'll be
inheriting it someday. Up until now it hasn't gotten
much use from her -- all right, no use -- but it still
could come in handy when she hits the bedridden stage.

-- Riding the bus downtown this morning, then

transferring to the streetcar underground and zipping
right out to the old turf. The house where Erik and I
lived in our divided-up "garret four stories high" (at
that time did I ever even notice I was living out my own
thesis book title's forecast of almost a decade earlier?
-- Can't recall), it still stands and not only it but
the entire hood looks virtually unchanged (including the
missing stair on the wooden fire escape in back going up
to my "window of tears," as Lady V christened it).

     -- Discomfort factor growing here though no one's
pressing too hard so far. But still: Mac's upscaled
burger emporium, it's time to bid you adieu. The pages
I've just jyzed into being increase the total I've
churned out over the years in this honorable
establishment by a mere fraction of a percentage point,
I'm sure -- probably a very small fraction. Or do I
exaggerate? Does it just seem like I spent thousands of
hours in here scribbling, that is, journalizing, that
is, protojyzing? How many was it really? Five hundred
maybe? A thousand? Fifteen hundred?
                    *   *

     -- Now for the first time ever jyzing on a
photographic view shot from space of the very spot I'm
jyzing in. It's a large blown-up color satellite photo,
and it's laminated atop one of the ancient oak tables in
the first of the branch libraries I ever visited in this
city. Yet another familiar old setting for me, musty,
high-ceilinged, a single big room, arched windows up
high. (And it probably never did get back those books
Lady C and I took out shortly before our breakup.
-- Well, no, it was Lady C who took them out and later
admitted she'd intentionally tossed them in the trash.
But they were on my library card and the overdue notices
followed me for years. Nor was it simply a matter of
principle that I refused to pay for them, because I
would've done so if I could've. But I was chronically
broke and therefore principle prevailed.)

     When I paid my bill at Mac's I noticed an eight-
by-ten color photo on the wall behind the register, a
tall man in a ridiculous turban and rajah's outfit.

Said the caption under it, barely readable from that
distance: "In Memory of George 'Mac' M.," with his date
of death four years ago (and his year of birth one year
after Mother's). Saddened me but also warmed my
cockles, it did. When I asked the college-age woman at
the register if she knew him, she said, "I'm sorry, all
that was before my time." So of course the period of my
patronage of the place was also before her time --
possibly even before her birth -- and I didn't ask
anything more. But it was good indeed to know that
someone who'd packed away as much of Mac's cooking as
Mac himself doubtless had done could've reached the age
of seventy. All by itself this news makes my own
longevity prospects look significantly better.

So then I walked ten blocks west on the gently
declining slope toward the beach. Everything appeared
the same en route except in small ways mostly not worth
noting under current jyze constraints. The old
laundromat. The magnificent Catholic church with its
Spanish-style double belfry. The masquerade shop. The
ice-cream store. The supermarket -- now bearing a
different name and differently configured, the entrance
facing a new direction. The big apartment complex where
Al and Sherry E. briefly lived. Several new coffee
shops, all tiny. (The proliferation of these coffee
shops, many if not most of them franchises, constitutes
probably the single biggest visible change over the past
two decades, here as in so many other USAn cities.)

Pass this library and cross the main road and enter
my old hood A, I'll call it, here in city No. 2/7.
Homeboy. (Mac's joint and 1616 are in hood C, speaking
chronologically. B, a couple of miles due east, is too
out-of-the-way to visit this trip. Where Mother now
lives is D; Erik's place is E. And I think of the last
of Lady V's hoods as F though I never actually lived
there -- just stayed there with her and Danny for a
month while preparing to pull up my own final stakes and
head overseas. I'd like to visit that one, F, again,
but at this point it appears beyond reach owing to those
same jyze constraints.)

Hood A, I'm happy to report, looks just fine.
Better than ever, I'd say, because now it boasts a much
greater racial and cultural mix and is much livelier,
more like V's hood F twenty years ago. Lots of folks on
the sidewalks, lots more small shops than before and
maybe half or more Asiusan-owned and -operated. Mothers
and kids (a number of the mothers in short-shorts or
microminis to knock your eyes out on this warm afternoon
-- I was far from the only older guy in dark glasses out
for a stroll, pretending to be philosophical or lost in
harmless-older-guy thoughts while actually gazing hard)
(but of course I'm well aware it's only a trick of the
hormones that's telling me I could easily fall for just
about any of these stunningly attractive young mamas --
a trick I hope the hormones will never lose the knack of
successfully playing on me) (but I suppose they can't
keep doing it forever, so I'd better enjoy it while I
can, and I'm trying to do just that, but discreetly).

The two-story building at 1222 is almost exactly as
it was in Lady C days except now it's painted gray with
blue trim instead of mono maroon. Several of the
apartment houses nearby are up to three or four stories
instead of the former uniform two. I looked at the place
from all angles but the gate to the side passageway was
locked and so I couldn't reach the outdoor stairs in back
to peek in our old living-room window to get an idea of
what kind of mischief's playing out up there nowadays.

Step across the boulevard a few doors north of 1222
and stroll over to the old escape spots in the park. The
glen. "Glen's secret glen." No bench there now -- some
sort of ecology experiment is underway (according to a
sign). But still, what a splendid location for an
apartment, right by the park. No wonder Lady C and I
were so thrilled to be moving in there. How could a new
marriage possibly fail in a setting like that? (Answer:
very easily. And quickly. In our case it took well
under a year.)

Up and down the main shopping street, both sides,
eight blocks each way, poking my nose in dozens of the
old hangouts. Only a few are pretty much as they were,

but almost all still retain some aspects I recall. Thai
restaurants, Vietnamese video stores. Korean, Japanese,
Vietnamese, Cantonese, Mandarin, Thai all spoken here
now along with some others I couldn't identify
(Cantonese dominating along with English in most areas).
-- And when Lady C and I moved in, there were no
Asiusans at all except for the ones operating the
laundry and a restaurant or two, as if strictly for
stereotyping purposes. The color line for residents in
this area still hadn't been broken (though as newcomers
to the city we weren't even aware such a line existed).

The old soda fountain lives on. The stationery
shop too. I dropped in there for a moment, told the
fiftyish Italian-looking gent at the counter I used to
live nearby roughly a quarter century ago. He joshed,
"So I guess you were one of the kids who used to buy
candy from 'Our Mr. Brooks,' eh?" And then went on:
"Well, if you think you can squeeze a free candy bar out
of me, forget it. I'm not such a soft touch." And then
from behind the counter farther back a college-age
Korean-looking young woman piped up mischievously: "Oh
yes, he is too soft. Now he's the new 'Our Mr.
Brooks.'" (But neither of them produced any free candy
for the visitor from a far province, who had indeed
accepted a free jawbreaker or two back in the day while
buying supplies from "Our Mr. Brooks" (who actually was
not Mr. Brooks; he had bought the shop from someone of
that name and left the sign up -- it's still up now --
and enjoyed playing the role; in looks he was closer to
Mr. Conklin of the old TV show) -- but the nostalgia hit
of all this, I'll say, was plenty all by itself.)

Even before leaving Mother's place this morning I
had hoped to do some jyzing at the old corner saloon two
doors down from 1222. A saloon is still there, now
called something different although looking much the
same (it's a restaurant as well), but it has a
handwritten sign on the door announcing a one-day
closing for electrical work: today.

I had no fallback plan. Wandered around in a
quandary. Jyze-friendly spots are still few and far

between out in this area. Asian restaurants won't do,
nor will tiny coffee shops (both kinds of establishment
needing the few seats they have). Ice-cream shops won't
do either (people who stay longer than the melting time
of ice cream being pegged as loiterers). Laundromats
won't do, at least not at this hour -- too busy.

     Then I remembered the library. I didn't even know
whether it was still standing. But here we are -- I
could stay on until nine, the closing hour. About half
the seats are occupied. Bright sun's streaming in at
ten to six. An impressive "Family of Man" diversity is
on display among us the recalcitrantly print-oriented.

     -- And this photo from space. The park shows up on
it as a dark green rectangle the size of a J-stick nib
(mine). Easy to see where the main roads intersect,
even the block our 1222 building stands on. 1222 itself
I can't make out. But the old turf, here and in hood C
a few blocks to the east, psychic center of a decade in
my life and in some ways of the whole damn show -- at
least as I know it so far -- it's all on display, and in
suitably reduced form: I can cover it with the outer
phalange of my thumb. (And that's pretty much what I
had to do with it in real life for a while, after things
went south for the last time with both Lady V and Lady
S, one right after the other.) -- And over here on the
far side of the map just above the top edge of this J-
book something's snaking along which I'd wager is the
rail line I came in on a few days ago. And not far from
it is the highway I hope to be traveling on aboard the
"hippie bus" when I leave again in a few more days.

     Next, though, walk an uphill block south to the
streetcar stop; and the first thing I'll do there,
before heading back in, is find a good spot to observe
an outbound car disgorging its load of downtown workers
into that dazzling late-afternoon ocean-amplified
sunlight. For some reason it still tickles me to watch
those comical unloadings -- as it did even in the days
when I myself was one of the staggerers.

     But it's a kick being back in this city. Tai chi
classes in the park near Mother's place (where seven

stories of scaffolding cling to the eastern steeple of
the church named after two top-tier saints -- and which
steeple represents which saint is a question I've never
even stopped to ponder before this moment). The
ubiquitous flowers. The mom-and-pop groceries with the
colorful sidewalk produce bins. The fresh breezes and
wondrous shifting natural light. The near-total absence
of visible lawns. The arts consciousness. The tourists
agog. The little old ladies in tennis shoes limping
along so feistily -- one of whom is now my very own
mother, a ringleader even, the baton twirler out in
front of the marching senior pom-pom crew.

     And the lovers. The gay couples not even slightly
self-conscious about being openly gay and openly loving.
The dozen streets recently renamed for literary figures,
the huge mural painting of the most splenetic of all
urban poets -- the French one -- glaring from a wall
facing one of those renamed streets right outside my
former favorite bookstore of them all (still Mother's
also, and Barb's too for all her years here) and
overwhelmingly visible from the balcony tables at the
bar next door where I hope to be holding forth when next
jyze resuscitates itself and roars back into action.

22

     So I do get to vamp on the grass in the park.
Along about six p.m. on a gorgeous Friday evening, very
warm, refreshingly breezy -- folks sitting and lying
nearby in singles, pairs, small groups, paddleballers
and frisbeeists at play (a pair of each) and several
dogs frisking leashlessly, the tail end of rush-hour
traffic rolling and strolling by on adjacent streets and

sidewalks, sun hanging just above the trees in the
children's corner and blazing down like an exceptionally
powerful stage spotlight on the jyzer of these very
lines as he scratches away right here at the center of
all the action.

I'm stepping out for a few hours. Said I wanted to
see how the district looks on a Friday evening these
days -- my excuse. "Of course, darling, feel free to
come and go as you like!" That's Mom. But I feel bad
if I leave too often or stay out too long. And then
again realize I'll be better company for her if I can
air myself out at least once in a while. So here I am.

White trolley-buses gliding along in unfamiliar
livery, an orange horizontal stripe itself inner-striped
with a narrow yellow band. Honks. Applauselike flaps
of dozens of pigeon wings as a marauding mutt startles
the grazing flock. Voices, laughter -- somersaults.
Above it all to my right the steeple on which the seven
layers of scaffolding seem to have been spiked -- or the
scaffolding itself could be seen, perhaps, as a quirkily
skeletal pagoda. Which might well symbolize the Itausan
unhappiness with Chiusan expansion into this area and
the subsequent exodus of the Itausans (but not their
restaurants or churches). (Or did the Itausan exodus
precede the Chiusan arrival? My hunch is a good part of
it did. Of course the Itausans who stayed on are
squawking the usual ethnic or maybe even racist squawk.
This is the USA! Viva Italia! Viva Old Cathay!)

-- I'm leaning back against bark just as I always
liked to do here. An acquired taste, this. The trees
are new, a tight grove of five replacing the three in
the same spot that died a few years ago, and the statue
standing among them, though old itself, is newly
refurbed (and rededicated three years after the last
time I lived in this area); but the feel here is much
the same. One of the best. (No building taller than
three or four stories anywhere in view from this low
perspective, the church steeples excepted. Italian flag
rippling above the old hotel to the south. Delicious
whiffs of both Chinese and Italian cooking coming first

from this direction, then from that. Fluted off-white
concrete tower much like a lighthouse poking up on the
high hilltop four or five blocks directly behind me if
I twist to look around the tree trunk. In the hillside
greenery near that tower is where we'll one day scatter
my mother's ashes -- as she and I were discussing again
this afternoon. It's definitely what she wants.)
        Ghost of Lady V lurking in the shadows, ready to
charge out Valkyrie-like as she actually did do in the
flesh and more than once. Ghosts of Dan and Leslie B.
strolling across the grass. Fiona, Marn, Miko.
-- Lengthening shadows of the trees over there creeping
across the grass and reaching almost within tickling
distance of my happily squirming bare toes. (Now a few
paces away five guys and one gal struggling to keep a
beanbag aloft with just their bare feet -- in the middle
of this sentence the bag lands six inches from my knee
-- I apologize to the gamers for my slow reflexes in
allowing it to hit the ground, then serve it back
volleyball style, lefty -- instinctively preferring to
drop the J-book, I notice, rather than the J-stick.)
        -- And because the "Memorials" editing has been
going extremely slowly I've decided to stay on in this
burg a few extra days. (Oops, there's the bearded Cawk
dude who sold me two pounds of coffee earlier today --
cutting across the park diagonally. And here's a punky
guitar player, another Cawk dude, plucking out classical
(surprise!) riffs. And I should mention: a large part
of the excitement of this park comes from the way the
big-city density intersects with the small-scale setting.
The taxicabs jockeying for an edge, the racial mix, the
derelicts -- and right here's a wino of the old school,
also Cawk and also bearded; he stops, observes the group
still playing keep-it-aloft with the beanbag and
announces, "Hey, I used to do that in the joint."
-- And here's the shadow, it just swallowed me up whole
with a sudden breeze-impelled pounce -- then let me go,
like a cat playing with a mouse -- now pounces again.)
(And the chattering in Cantonese of groups of elders
slowly circumambulating the park on the curvy asphalt

path. Only occasionally do you see the old Itausans who
used to circle the same way or perch like veteran friars
in black on the benches flanking the path.) (A pedicab,
a young gay couple holding hands in back, less interested
in the sights of the city, it would appear, than in the
ripply-muscled exertions of their shirtless pedal-man --
and all three clean-shaven Cawks.)

The hippie bus service still exists. They run two
buses a week between my old hometown here and my current
hometown some eight hundred miles thataway if I look
over my left shoulder -- Monday and Friday. I've signed
up for Friday. Mostly I want to travel by bus -- and
especially this bus -- for the sake of jyze variety.

Lady U, by the way, appears not to mind at all that
I'll be coming home later than expected. She's partying
with coworkers -- plans to join them at a big alt-music
festival next month. Clearly I'm not invited. This all
reminds me so much of our pre-blowup months of thirteen
years ago I shudder to think about it. (Do I have to
think about it anyway? Of course! But not in these
pages. Or at least not yet.)

-- Now only the highest part of the park in the
corner farthest from the sun remains ablaze (northeast
corner). But the crowd's just as big and as evenly
scattered as before. The shadow that's been playing
with me is scaling the trunk of the tree whose bark is
scoring my back -- I tilt my head rearward until it too
bangs against bark and I roll my eyes upward and think,
hey, green leaves fluttering in the breeze, vast numbers
of them, all brilliantly lit up in those same dazzling
last rays and kicking like a chorus line of thousands!
Like the card section at a football game! Like
thousands of miniature stuff-strutting tree sprites!

No more deplorable incidents with Barb. She and
Keith dropped by late one evening to deliver the ancient
typewriter I'll be using to type up Popeye's unfinished
article ("Fact and Fiction in Genealogy") for the
publisher. All went well -- warily but well.
Regrettably, Mother's already losing the perspective she
gained from the argument the other night when Barb

attacked us so nastily. But I suppose such losses must
be expected. In any event I'm resigned to them -- and
everything else.

     Tomorrow night Barb and Keith are coming over for
dinner. This time everyone will be on best behavior, I
expect. And hope. Already Mother and I have talked it
over for hours, how to handle things.

     -- As for the editing, I'm enjoying it more now.
It's slow but I'm learning. We're all "direct
descendants" (is there any other kind?) of the "Poet
King" of Scotland back in the 1300s -- well waddayaknow.
Makes us fairly declasse' now, does it not? The madcap
parade of the generations. -- And what about the
snobbery angle? -- Well, who wants to get into it. I
do a lot of private wincing but try to keep in mind how
much all this means to Mom. The tales of slaves and
aristocracy and all that, "royal blood"...oh well.

     (Even Mother herself says it: "If I'm a snob, well
fine, then I'm a snob" -- with reference to her sister
Shel's comment about "Memorials" being largely an
exercise in snobbery. -- A streak of which undeniably
lingers on in all these Hutchesons and Chandlers, and
the Garretts and Taits on Nana's side as well -- these
southerners who lost so much in the USAn civil war and
then came north to what was almost a foreign land and
therefore they needed more than ever to hang on to the
old ways and the old airs. -- But couldn't, and didn't,
or at least didn't for the most part. Some exceptions,
yes. And those can be lived with. And it better be so,
because I'm no doubt riddled with them myself.)

     (About a third of the tree above is now shadowed.
And though I've already run half a dozen errands for
Mother this afternoon, I've still got a couple to go.
-- Picked up medicine at the drugstore, bread sticks at
a French bakery, four different types of ground meat at
the butcher shop, two bottles of her favorite chardonnay
at the liquor store right over there kitty corner from
the park, coffee at a local shop, vegetables at the
supermarket -- and now back to the drugstore for the
kind of cookies she likes and several more boxes of

kleenex to help restore everyone to temporary dry-
eyedness in this abundantly lachrymose time -- and
abundantly merry as well, you better believe it!)
                          *   *
     Here's a surprise. A couple more errands and a
quick circuit of the district at sunset on this happenin'
Friday evening and now I find myself holding down a back
corner table at -- yes! -- the same funky little caffe
with the two F's where so much went down in my own
private soap opera back in the day I'm embarrassed to
think of it. In fact I'm embarrassed to be doing this
in here -- jyzing away among the tourists as if I thought
being seen going at it in this way could get my wax
statue added to those of the immortals posing at
virtually every table in here -- as seen by mythologizing
eyes now, this is -- but I can overcome it. And will.
For the principle of the thing. For the warm fuzzy
dimly-lit feeling. In front of the old black stove with
its intriguingly elbowed stovepipe. Across the room from
the wooden phone booth, inside which during those earlier
times I did a truly unwholesome amount of anguishing and
pleading and heavy sweating.
     The heat. The heat is on weatherwise and that's
why I get to sit in here. It's on without even being on
-- that stove has become, contrary to appearances, a
cooling influence right now -- and therefore at least
half the customers, both tourists and locals, are
sitting at tables set up outside on the sidewalk -- as
at numerous other places along the old circuit. But not
at the saloon where I'd intended to set up, which is
accordingly packed on both levels inside (I pushed
through all the way to the back of the balcony as if I
were looking for someone -- which I always did like to
do in that hormonally supercharged earlier era) and
therefore I had to scratch my plan to jyze there (for
now) and thus happened to stroll by here and notice that
half the inside tables were empty.
     Aroma of some very good coffee (roasted next door).
Photos (framed) crowding the walls all the way to the
ceiling maybe twelve feet up. Newspaper rack containing

the latest issue of my old weekly rag standing just
outside the door (and I don't even want to be thinking
about this aspect of my former life during this stay --
or otherwise I'd be breaking every jyze constraint in
the book). Espresso machine putt-putting away a few
feet to my left. No familiar faces behind the counter
and few elsewhere -- but regardless this is still a kind
of homecoming for me.

Crucial scenes right here with all three romantic
heavies of that era. Several other contenders of
serious but lesser eventual impact I actually met here.

So what about it -- how does my life look now
compared to what I thought it would someday be back
during the time when I was protojyzing here (and
frequently haunting the joint on lonesome nights)?

Despite some big superficial changes, not so
different. That's what I'd say. -- And yes, I still
look upon myself as a kind of successor to the wax
statues here. I'm carrying on the tradition. Doing it
my own way and to highly uncertain effect, no question,
but still doing it. The immortals would dig jyze,
surely they would. -- Though also think it a bit
square, I suppose, if for no other reason than its
extremely high likelihood, at least for this jyzer right
here, of being conducted in an ambulatory dope-free
zone. (Sorry, immortals, just can't hack the hard stuff
and that's that. Never could.)

The tables and chairs appear to be the very same
ones, possibly resurfaced. The squeak of the accordion
door of the telephone booth as it opens and closes is
the same -- and the light inside still isn't working, I
see, now that someone's actually in there making a call.
I'd wager a bundle the burned-out bulb is the very same
one that came into view back then when my eyes rolled
heavenward during particularly exasperating moments in
the nearly endless phone dialogues of that excruciating
yet also exhilarating era.

Good crowds everywhere except on the strip itself.
Several of the old clubs are gone and one is literally
boarded up. Several small storefronts belonging to the

[Jyzemelt]

Beat ministrip along the side street we're on here are
similarly closed down and empty. Topless/bottomless
appears to be on its last legs, as it were, or its last
overstuffed mammaries perhaps. Yet the crowds keep
coming to the district -- apparently. (Mother asked me
to see if I thought the main entertainment drag was
"coming back up again." And I'd say it appears to be
doing just that, though not necessarily with a bullet.)
    The mysteries of the aging male human organism. At
times, no doubt as one ought really to expect, I catch
myself hoping a Lady V or Briana T. or Marn T. or Miko
S. will pop around the next corner -- and preferably in
a form or shape still recognizable to me. (Why isn't
Lady S on that list? For some reason she doesn't
possess that kind of ghostly power in this district. In
most other parts of town she does but not here.)
    Chewing on an ice cube. Asking myself should I be
moving on? Getting back to Mom's place? Finishing this
up later when I go down to Rikki's? I think so. Don't
let ol' Mom sit home alone on a Friday night. Only in
the last few moments is the evening turning full night.
                    *   *
    Just let it fly. All right -- a nightcap. And at
the top I'll say it's been a damn tough night with the
old lady. Was it the effect of the chemo? The coffee
which she knows she shouldn't be drinking but drinks
anyway, and lots of it? A long-running "nervous"
illness that's gotten out of hand (that is, some sort of
craziness)? I don't know what it was.
    -- So just sit back and take it then. The way you
said you could.
    All right.
    (Hard to do, though, when it seems she's
intentionally twisting everything you say into the
opposite of what you mean -- keeping up the attack no
matter which of a hundred different ways you try to
disarm the situation.) (Just ain't no magical solutions
here. Got to accept this. You said you could!)
    -- This in Rikki's bedroom directly below Mother's
living room. At noon today Rikki and her seven-year-old

boy Mischa popped in unexpectedly as I was stepping out
of the bathtub with the bathroom door wide open. "Well
hello!" After I'd toweled off and donned some clothes
she and I talked for an hour or so. (Barb had told
Mother she thought Rikki and I would be good for each
other, "almost as if she were wanting to fix you up" --
or not "fix you up," Mother wouldn't say that, but some
similar phrase.) (It is almost three in the morning.)
I like Rikki but the sparks are not flying, certainly
not on my side and I don't think on hers either, and
this despite her glimpse of me in my rosy/hairy/full-
frontal-nekkid/hot-bath-loosey-goosey glory (although
she pretended to have seen only "a long arm reaching for
the door"). -- But I do sense we could be friends and
perhaps allies of sorts. At least she doesn't seem to
tilt Barb's way, though she's Barb's friend as much as
Mother's and has clearly been exposed to Barb's views on
my life and is well aware of the tensions between us.)
    No doubt it's the good bourbon allowing me to spew
all this nonsense. -- Let's see if I can zoom in on
something else.
    Down here, Rikki's place, what will I remember?
The new trick I've devised for trapping skeeters (the
real things now; this has nothing to do with that
shucking and poking Skeeter far to the north) -- the new
trick for trapping them by covering all exposed flesh on
my body except my hand, which I press flat against the
side of my head with palm facing out and thumb and
forefinger loosely encircling the ear. Thus I can hear
the skeeter as it approaches and lands on the only flesh
available and can simply close my hand around it. Like
catching a fly, only easier. "Not with honey or vinegar
but with real human flesh." And it works. I've nailed
at least five or six so far. (But I don't want to think
about how many hours I've wasted doing it.) (Of course
the skeeters would've kept me awake anyway -- if not by
their buzzing and biting, by the subsequent itching.)
    Washing my hair in the bathtub -- reminds me of the
long soaks in the bathroom I shared with Erik. Giving
Mischa the railroad hat I bought on the train. Rikki's

touchingly earnest and sincere words about how terrific
Mother is (and she's right!).

Scariest of all for me, I was supposed to meet
Mother upstairs at noon today but didn't get up there
until quarter past one. The apartment was eerily silent
and the door to her bedroom was still closed. To my
knowledge she had never stayed in bed anything like this
late. Twice I called to her quite loudly right outside
her door -- no reply.

Was she dead? Had she suffered a stroke? I've
often thought it's a miracle she hasn't so far. -- What
to do? Break in when she might be badly needing the
sleep? (All morning a jackhammer had been tearing apart
the street up toward the intersection.)

Right or wrong, I decided to wait an hour or so.
And while waiting I realized I had no idea what to do if
she was dead -- or, say, unconscious. "Call 911."
Nothing else came to mind. And the same's true now.

Forty-five minutes later she sailed out. She'd had
a bad night, she confided, and had needed a little extra
sleep. And it isn't at all uncommon for her, she
further informed me, to stay in bed this late when no
one's visiting her. She was surprised to hear I'd been
worrying. And for sure she didn't want me to be
alarming Barb that, as I confessed I feared, a stroke
might leave her, Mother, unconscious or unable to speak
or move or make any sound at all, and that the chemo
might be increasing the likelihood of a stroke. (Well,
she needn't worry that I'd be alarming Barb -- certainly
I wouldn't be doing anything to upset Barb if I could
possibly help it.)

"Certainly." Who am I kidding? There's nothing
anything like certainty anywhere in sight around here.
Period. (And so I'd better not say this negative
statement on certainty is itself a certainty either.)
(But here's another big fat mosquito zipping around.
It's craving my blood. By this uncapped skeeter, at
least, I can say it's very close to certain: I'm wanted.
My flesh is hotly desired.)

-- But anyway. I've still got a week to go in this

town and so I'll have at least one more chance to jyze
this damn jyze. At another of the old hangouts maybe?
I hope so. In any case I'm yawning -- I'm bone tired.
I need some real sleep. Got to suck it up tomorrow.
Got lots of things to read (from Mother's files). Got
editing to do. Got to face a long evening with Keith
and Barb. Whew. Whew! -- And none of this will ever
be getting any easier. -- So then find some positives
and accentuate them as you've never accentuated before.

23

     Made it. Right here. Where you got to want to be.
     Midafternoon and no one else around. Had to clear
three wineglasses from the table with my own delicate
keyboarding hands. And a fine table it is: round and
featuring an original painting, or several probably,
enameled right on, or affixed somehow so you can wipe
down the surface without damaging the painting(s).
Framed artwork of various kinds hanging at my back and
over my head and on the walls all around beneath the low
dark ceiling. A laminated leaflet probing the eternal
UFO controversy. A tiffany lamp with a flickery bulb.
A pipe-cleaner stick figure. A quasi-fauvist reclining
seminude. Everything colorful, worn, warm, funky,
lived-in, quirky, just the way you want it if you happen
to want the way I do.
     This is the balcony table in the triangular area at
the very front overlooking the street. Four large
windows open right next to me or nearby, starting below
knee level and reaching above head level as I sit here.
Saloons familiar from the old days stand directly across
the street (six lanes including the meter parking on

both sides, the street angling down toward the main
business district to the right) -- and just outside the
window, a few inches below the level of the table, a
shiny new street sign pokes up honoring one of those
aforementioned immortals, one whose active days in this
district were already a decade in the rearview when I
first arrived in town. And, in smaller letters above
the immortal name, "End." I could lean out and touch it
with a yardstick. And if I did that I could also see,
while doing it, uphill just one door to the left across
the newly renamed street (which is only a very short
block long -- a stunted alley really), the entrance to
the former best bookstore of them all (which is still
pretty damn good -- even if my own sister and mother
happen to think so too).

     And to the right, next to the open window here, a
sign sticks out from the building so it can be read by
sidewalk and street traffic stopped for the light maybe
a hundred feet up the hill.

          A gathering place...since the days
          of 1948. Always serving drinks at
          reasonable prices.

(Those extraneous words "the days of" -- are they there
for sheer echoic effect, I guess? Something like "since
the days of wine and roses"? Poetry in stasis, say? Or
was the sign-painter being paid by the word?)

     The window through which I view that sign swings
inwardly on side hinges like a door and like all the
others up here is open now and in the inward-angled
glass I can scarcely miss seeing darkly reflected an
image of -- the jyzer himself. Up close. At work.
Blowing. Vamping. (As the music on the box switches
from classical to bluesy rock. And a couple of
conventional Eurusan bent, that is, Cawk male and Cawk
female, probably around half my age, appears and takes a
table along the side facing the bookstore -- the two-
story-high face of that same most splenetic urban poet
of them all depicted in the wall mural outside glaring
in at them with, as it seems to me, a little extra
dollop of his very most scornful stuff.)

[Jyze for Mom]

    It's Monday. It's foggy. It's my three-hour
break. At six I'm due back and tonight I'm determined
to finish off the "Memorials" proofreading. Then I'll
start revising (lightly!) the essay and then I'll type
it up and then I'll be more or less done with all my
appointed tasks.
    (When I left, Mother was hunched over her twin
filing cabinets in the little pantry behind the kitchen,
seated on a footstool, searching for photos of ancestors
to consider for inclusion in "Memorials." A big stack
was mounting on the floor in front of the fridge.
Eleanor of Aquitane. Pepin the Short. John of Ghent.
Not to mention the real ancients, including the most
snobworthy of all: Charlemagne. -- Earlier she showed
me an article from today's paper about an exhibition of
Mongolian art going back to the era of Genghis Khan and
I pointed out to her that in Elgie she has a grandson
whose ancestry might well trace back to both Charlemagne
and Genghis Khan -- opening myself to thirty minutes of
interrogation about exactly what Lady S had told me
regarding the Genghis Khan part.) (And the jyze rules
permit me to use all these surnames because these
worthies are all -- supposedly -- family.)
    -- Where this very straight Cawk couple previously
referred to is sitting is exactly where I sat when I did
the "utamakura entry," as I think of it, eleven years
ago this fall. Back when I was wrestling mano-a-womano
with the fearsome warrior of a mama of the mixed-race
alleged descendant of matched tyrannical megalomaniacs
from a millennium back -- Lady S herself being the mama
I'm talking about, yes. And here we are eleven years
later, the kid is a full-grown stranger to me, Lady S
has become a kind of reclusive Taoist elder-in-waiting
now living somewhere unknown to me back in her
ancestral land; and my own mother, blessedly informal
though she is under most circumstances, suddenly lets me
know she objects to my use of "kid" in place of "child"
and "mom" in place of "mother" and various other
shocking colloquialisms as flagged by her in the ms. of
"Jyzeburst." Egad! (As she would say herself.)

(Roar of buses. -- And growling by out there now,
a blue motorized cable car of a type I've never seen
before. -- Also one frequently comes across open-top
double-decker tour buses on the streets here these days,
red, knockoffs of English omnibuses.)

   -- Last night I read Mother's diary until four a.m.
Finally I've gotten all the way to the end. It's the
story of her "best years," as she says, again, herself:
her last three years of college and first two years of
marriage -- my very own birth being the highest point of
all in this period or maybe it's one of two -- judging
in part by the length and tone of her entries, but
mainly by what she's told me this past week -- the other
high point being the wedding about fifteen months
earlier. It makes for fascinating reading -- poignant
and often quite amusing -- and as I pointed out to her,
it's full of the colloquialisms of the day, as is only
proper, not to say winning -- but yes, winning!

   One detail in particular in her diary stopped me in
my tracks -- and I mean my very earliest tracks. Many,
many times I've heard the story of how my name was
Jeffrey Chandler Sandefjord for the first few hours of
my life (until Mother, awake for the first time after
the birth, opened the letter Dad had sent weeks earlier
from Australia expressly to be read on this occasion
and found he'd reversed himself: now if the kid was a
boy he wanted him named after his father -- and if a
girl, after her mother, with even the nickname specified
to be the same, the primary one, Georgie -- so if born
female, the jyzemaster would still have been, and would
still now be, G). And in reading Mother's account I was
astounded to learn that my given and middle names for
those first few hours before she opened the letter were
not Jeffrey Chandler (her father's given and middle
names) but Jeffrey Vincent. Vincent! Dad's maternal
grandfather's first name!

   -- Yet Mother swears this is wrong, it was never
Jeffrey Vincent, she can't imagine why she wrote such
nonsense. (Personally I believe the diary. I suspect
Mom's memory has revised itself over the years in

response to later developments and judgments. Perfectly
understandable. At around the time of my birth her
relations with Dad's side of the family were still
pretty good. A few years later they were very bad --
maybe even as little as a year later. At that point the
idea that she'd named one of her kids after a Fritsch,
if only for a very short time, started becoming
increasingly intolerable unconsciously -- sez I. She
would doubtless deny it. Maybe even with a howl of
outrage. -- As, come to think of it, I might too, as it
dawns on me now that she and Dad named Barb after Gram
S., maiden surname Fritsch, when Barb came along three
years later. Oops! So: best not to bring this matter
up again. Scratch this graph! Go with the unknown!)

But we've been doing fine. The archetypal scene of
the past ten days: I'm laboring away on proofreading
"Memorials" at the kitchen table and she's working at
some other task on the other side of the table, or maybe
at her filing cabinets in the little pantry right behind
me, or at the kitchen counter, or at her desk in the
living room, and the jazz station is turned up loud. If
it's after six or seven I'm nipping at bourbon and she's
sipping at wine. To allow me to get lots of work done
she's trying not to bug me too much (as she says) but
she just can't help herself, there's so much she wants
to talk about. And me too! So for long periods we turn
the radio down and talk and that's another reason why
the proofing goes so slowly.

Of course the painful moments are plentiful also.
She has a big hole gouged in the back of her thigh where
tissue samples were taken for biopsy and her chemo
treatments prevent it from healing and it bothers her
constantly. I've bandaged it numerous times but it's in
an area where bandages just won't stay put. Also she
often becomes breathless, especially when trying to talk
while excited or moving about -- sounds almost like
someone being interviewed right after winning a marathon
(the thrilled, frantic, geared-up quality being part of
this). She breaks into coughing spells, often caused by
"reflux" (something like regurgitation combined with

heartburn). She gets cranky, irritable, cantankerous,
disputatious -- starts taking everything you say as a
personal insult or near insult in one way or another (in
its extreme form this has happened only a few times and
not for long, with one roughly six-hour exception). And
she really is losing her hair now, her skin is getting
blotchy, she stumbles, she suffers arthritic pain in
ankles and knees, back pain, shoulder pain, tailbone
pain -- on and on.

And yet, almost miraculously, and certainly
testifying to her courage and positive spirit, she's
usually a pleasure to be with, full of life, highly
responsive, curious about everything -- doesn't even
seem much different from her usual healthy self of the
past fifteen years since getting over (somewhat) Dad's
death. It's almost too easy to forget what the real
situation is.

-- I glance up and see the writer's name on the
street sign and "End" in smaller print right above it
and naturally I think the man himself would approve of
this focus on Memere (but would surely urge far more
extreme sentimentality). The king of spleen over there
I suspect would urge just the opposite. (And never mind
what either of these supreme masters might say about the
quality of the prose.)

The dinner Saturday night with Keith and Barb: as
predicted, no problems. Best behavior on all sides.
Barb had been down for a couple of days with a touch of
the flu (or was it, as it should've been, shame and
self-disgust over her previous bad behavior?). Even so
the condescension implicit in a few of her remarks took
my breath away. What was I intending her to get, she
sniffily wanted to know, from this book on neoprag
aesthetics I'd laid on her? She was used to reading
superior stylists and thinkers such as X, Y, and Z (her
same old august standbys, all three being male literary
so-called modernists of politically reactionary and
antisemitic bent); she just couldn't be bothered with
this lightweight stuff. Could I maybe sort of summarize
it for her? And several more remarks of that ilk. The

urge to strangle. But safely suppressed.

    -- The more important point being that Mother was delighted with the way the evening came off. Not a single open expression of hostility from anyone! She's now thinking she might be able to move past the latest rough patches with both Barb and Keith without too much longer-term damage done (though she worries that she and Barb will need to have it out yet again to clear the air after I've gone home).

    And then last night we talked by phone with brother Rob. At times this was a little awkward for me (and no doubt for him too) because of our impasse over his failure to return a certain book of mine on Mentoka history (how preposterous -- but I need it badly!). Yet we gabbed on for a good long while and on the whole I think we're still doing fine. He's in the process of rewriting his entire journal, some sixty-five volumes, trying to compress it to about one-fifth its original length and thus make it readable for his kids. And he's doing this by hand -- pen and ink! Two-thousand-plus pages in the compressed version!

    (He also asked my advice on whether he should throw out his original handwritten journals, the sixty-five volumes. I advised him not to. After all, his purpose isn't the same as mine: he's not trying to come up with what I call a literary diary/journal. Myself, the only originals I intend to keep around are these J-books. Of course this is also in part because no matter how badly I write now, I'm sure it's seldom as bad as it used to be virtually all the time in the protojyze and -- yeek! -- urjyze. This stuff here, stodgy and plodding though it often is, I can actually bear the idea of other people reading. The originals of the earlier forms, no way.)

    -- Been nursing a single soft drink this whole time. And life's been going on out there on the street. Couples putt-putting by on motorscooters just as Lady S and I used to do -- and Lady V and I too, and in fact on the same rinky-dink scooter for both (though never all three of us aboard at once: perish the thought!). Lots

and lots of cars, vans, pickups, SUVs, buses rolling by
as well. What, a hundred vehicles a minute? For a
hundred minutes? The proverbial ten thousand then, and
each one motivating along on its own daily path that
just happens to pass this point. The magical myriadic
mass of yore -- "the ten thousand pilgrims" -- but
motorized now and therefore, at least for me from this
vantage here, pretty much faceless, just as I am, of
course, for them.

(And I called home at one a.m. last night. No more
sign of "that loving feeling" from Lady U than any of
the other times -- meaning the other calls as well as
the times we ran into each other at the house during
previous weeks. Teasingly I asked, as I did last time,
about the element I was missing, that is, where was the
old love and affection? Again instead of reassuring me
that I was misreading the situation she was openly
irritated that I would ask. This time she even had the
gall to tell me she's been "too busy to feel anything."
What a crock! All she's been doing, at least according
to what she's told me, is going to work at the camera
factory and hanging around the house.)

(I'm quite sure I'm not misinterpreting her. I'm
just wondering how long I should keep putting up with
such blatant displays of indifference. I'm not
confronting her at all -- yet. Will I want to later?
If so, how much later? These are questions I'd rather
not be dealing with right now. I'm hoping she won't be
ratcheting up the discord to the point where I have to
call her on it -- but that may well be her very purpose
or intent in doing the current long-distance telephonic
ratcheting, whether conscious or otherwise.)

-- But a big group's filing up to the balcony here,
I see, and soon will be crowding me into this corner,
making escape awkward. I'm thinking I could volunteer
to leave right now. And I'm not happy with where this
account is going, so why not. A bold move. And sudden!

24

--------·

-- Just pulling out. On the "hippie bus," No. 503.
Packed and rollicking. And on a rocky road at the
moment, as the shaky J-sticking makes obvious, at least
to me. And I have just an hour to go at it here in the
mid-bus canteen section (with its two fold-down wooden
tables) before it's time for what they call "the
miracle" -- when the entire interior converts into, in
effect, a single gigantic mattress. For overnight
sleeping purposes, this will be.
    Golden oldies playing. My three Cawk boothmates
rapping, each with a different but very strong variety
of English accent: David from Ireland (circuitously
returning home after two years Down Under); Andre from
England itself; Adrian from Australia -- all three
around the age of Jyzer G in "Jyzer" days. Friendly
dudes, especially David here at my right elbow. (Soon
to be moving on, after Ireland, to Nepal.)
    A fine way to travel, this bus. You gotta smile.
"Alternative travel," written in script on the side
panel, along with "The only trip of its kind" and --
some other slogan. Check. Because I jotted down a
note. Oh yeah: "Arrive inspired, not dog tired." Old
green diesel bus -- city type, but refurbed in the
traditional hippie-bus way, with a big luggage rack on
top. One of the few surviving "sixties institutions,"
as everyone calls anything involving more than one
person that's still hanging on from that era.
    Introductions to the farthest corners of the bus.
Lots of thick accents, some all but impervious to me.
A few leftovers from the early days -- two laid-back

bearded Cawk counterculture vets playing cards in the
booth across the aisle, one carrying a beat-up copy of a
totemic sixties text (by a Russian anthroposophist, I
believe it is, or maybe I should just say spiritualist),
the other traveling with his Boston terrier Ziggie and
wowing a much younger German woman with tales of his
adventures in Bali and Java.

(Here's the big bumpy bridge at -- what is it again?
I couldn't recall it either time we crossed it by train
and still can't now. Near or maybe in a city that used
to be at the outer margins of my own hippie-era antiwar-
journalism beat. -- Booth talk now turning to shiny USAn
tanker trucks -- hey, you dudes oughta see the ones in
Japan! -- But no, I'm not playing that well-traveled
grizzled-vet role. I'm a modest and wide-eyed and
helpfully friendly quasi-local. "Full of freaks and
weirdos, this boois, innit?" ("Boois" rhyming with puss,
sort of: the Aussie Adrian's words.))

The city was gorgeous at dusk with the lights just
coming on, a flaming orange sunset silhouetting the hills
across the bay as we rolled over the bridge and forked
northward. The tower on the hill above Mother's place
floodlit white -- the hilltop where Dad, while hugging
the rail aboard a troop ship bound for the South Pacific,
spotted crowds gathered to observe the departure -- while
Mother (with Aunt Ida) watched from a point farther west,
and I was about five months along "in the oven" -- as
described in the letters and diaries I read so avidly
late at night during this stay (just as during the other
stay) -- that very tower, yeah. The one which all too
soon will be serving as a kind of glorified headstone for
ol' Mom's ashes. So know what you're seeing up there,
blithe companions in travel!

A rushed departure, Mom and I occupied with dummying
in pictures for "Memorials" up until the last possible
moment. Stress. Quick decisions. Reminded me a whole
lot of newspaper deadline days.

Vintage late doo-wop on the P.A. "Everybody's got
a brand-new dance now." We're locomoting! Several
riders getting into it while settled cross-legged on

cushions -- in effect, again, one big cushion, or half of the gigantic one to come. Behind us, cones of light, swirls of talk (here's another one, let's twist again like we did back in the late Pleistocene!) -- with amazement lingering over the wild band of transsexuals that descended on our crowd as we waited for the bus to arrive in the alley behind the terminal. "I don't mind 'em so long as they stay away from me -- a good distance away" -- proclaimeth the most uptight of the bunch at the table here, the Aussie, again, who's currently studying ag economy at (I've learned in the last few miles) a university in my own primary state of upbringing (and I'm recalling Popeye did postgrad work in that same field, ag economy, before switching to sociology and then deciding he could make a name for himself in this new discipline only if he moved north; and so it was that eventually Mother and Dad could meet in the heart of old Mentoka and the jyzer himself could soon be popping out of that same aforementioned oven).

Heroic bus jyzing. Jyze is beating steep odds to make its appearance right here and right now. (Just one more bus rolling north on the freeway, though, on a muggy summer evening, six lanes of traffic flowing heavily in each direction. But wotta bus! A merry prankster of a bus, or almost. Close enough. Close as I'd ever want a bus to get to that, in fact, and myself still be aboard.)

Both drivers are Eurusan women. They switch off at the wheel from stop to stop. The off-duty one sleeps in an eerily coffinlike wooden box suspended across the back of the bus. (Here's a popular folk tune from the time I was living at 1616 -- hood C, if I recall right, city No. 2/7. Tune about a restaurant where you can get anything you want. My boothmates recognize it, or rather two do. Not the Aussie. He nodded at first but then sheepishly admitted ignorance. David on the other hand has seen the movie inspired by the tune and is now expounding with enviable erudition on the distinguished family lineage of the folk singer in the lead role -- even knows the name of the actress who played his

Chiusan ol' lady (so Briana-like to me).)

Best to stop now before dizziness sets in (more of it). Plenty of chances later to add to this. Now we're approaching the core of the old antiwar-journalism zone near the evil Air Force base, which of course is still there and still flourishing. (Boothmates laughing at the way folks in passing cars are agog at the sight of this maverick bus -- waving up, flashing peace signs or flipping the bird.)

       *   *

I guess if Andre can do it I can too. (Hey, it works much better this way!) -- Now that we're into the "miracle," I'm stretched out on the front portion of the giant mattress, sideways, perpendicular to the direction of travel, which remains more or less northward -- I along with eleven others. Six are already sacked out (a couple of these sacked more or less literally in sleeping bags, the others swaddled in bus-provided quilts and blankets. -- Though it's not at all cold).

And then there's me and Andre. I'll call this session "My Jyzing with Andre." He's to my left, we're both leaning back against the windows, and it's almost like one of those old-time Japanese linked-poetry-writing parties. "At least one page every day," declares Andre, "that's my slogan." He's nineteen or maybe twenty, a medical student just starting out on the long academic grind -- but first traveling for a couple of months to prepare himself for it psychically.

-- Now (pursuing the hall-of-mirrors effect) I show him the "My Jyzing with Andre" sentence and he informs me I'm appearing in his account as well (we've already talked about jyze) and reveals that his name takes the Russian form and therefore sports an "i" at the end. As with a certain great Russian novelist of almost a century ago, who's unknown to him. But he, our Andrei right here, is reading a pretty damn good contemporary novel so he must be okay. And especially for a medical student. (But he's soft-spoken and his accent is not always easy for me to decipher.) "We jyzeslingers have to stick together," I josh him, "whether ur, proto, or

the real thing." He agrees. Yup. (Actually I'm trying
to do my bit to pass along the art. This is probably an
effect of my two-week genealogy immersion. The
cavalcade of the generations!) (And he was pleased to
hear I'm well aware the English have produced more than
a few great protojyzers. I mean I brought this up and
as I threw out some names he very nearly blushed with
pride. Yes! Protojyze superstars each and every one!)

Now off clicks the reading light directly across
from us. It's the vet still in search of the miraculous
-- the miraculous seduction, that is (with the Russian
spiritualist as his hoary stalking horse). He and I are
playing footsie, in fact, or could be, or even kneesie,
like it or not. Looks as though his ear's being talked
off by the same young German woman whose eyes were
previously dancing in response to the other vet's tales
of Indonesian shadow puppets. And on the whole bus only
three reading lights remain on: one far to the rear and
the pair we dueling jyzers share.

All shoes off -- it's the rule. It's kind to
cushions but nasty to schnozzes.

Rolling along. Windows rattling. Through the
dark. Little red embers of aisle lights burning steady.
(How come the bus is shaking and they're not? -- Might
have something to do with string theory, maybe, or
possibly Vedanta.) (Lots of heavy talk going down in
this forward zone right now, my own written efforts in
here struggling to keep up.) -- And our bus headlights
piercing ahead and rank after rank of velvety black
curtains parting and sweeping by as we plunge ever
deeper into, and in a different sense as, the night
stage -- "stage" in the theater meaning but also
referring to the Wild West stagecoach in an updated
version. Grain elevators romping by too, admirably
floodlit to best advantage. The driver still listening
to oldie tapes but all other speakers shut off.

(And Andrei has rolled into his cocoon, his daily
page done -- and then some. So why jyze on alone?
Switch modes. A ramble with an up-and-coming neoprag.)

*   *

[Jyzemelt]

Now the new camp. Up in the mountains near the
halfway point of our epic journey. I'm sitting on a
stump some twenty or thirty underbrushy yards downhill
from the main eating area. It's all very rustic (except
for the shiny bus -- not ours -- which serves as a
kitchen) and sure does make you nostalgic for earlier
eras -- just as was noted by the bushier-bearded of the
vets who bushwhacked me with gab or I would've been down
here stumping away at the jyze a long time ago.

A fun night trying to sleep on the bus. Hot and
then as we got into the mountains suddenly cold. For a
while a dirty yet shapely bare foot stood tall about six
inches from my nose (Delilah's foot). A rockhound Cawk
jokester fresh from the deserts of Mexico -- more like a
redneck mountain man, except laid-back and at the same
time politically a self-declared libertarian -- pressed
against me on one side, Andrei the med student and
promising young protojyzer on the other. A window was
cracked open just above my head and I often dangled my
hand outside in the stream of night air to cool off.
(I'm slapping away mosquitoes as I write this. Just as
Mother and I were doing for much of my stay with her.)

Tumbling white-water mountain stream down below. A
sauna too -- with clothing optional, just as in the bus
company's former camp (which was washed away in "the big
floods," someone said, which to me would mean this past
spring, but then someone else said they've been using
this one for years). Our bus did a lot of grunting and
wheezing as we pulled in to this site on a heavily
rutted gravel road, winding, hilly, steeply canted first
this way then that. I should be able to see it, the
bus, parked down there to the right at a level maybe a
hundred feet below us but -- can't. So I must be
disoriented. Or could be it's hidden behind the large
knoll. Lots of forest around here but not thick enough
to hide a bus at such a short distance, I'm pretty sure.

A memorable half hour at a huge truckstop. Two
a.m. Brightly lit like a dozen night baseball games
going at once on adjoining blacktop fields. Another
monster rig pulling in every thirty or forty seconds.

Hundreds of them parked for the night in parallel lines,
all idling, all facing the same direction -- reminded me
of photos of the U.S. invasion force ready to roll into
Kuwait first thing in the morning. And then off to one
side our antic little hippie bus with its bicycle-
bearing wooden luggage rack on top and its ragtag troupe
of misfits and aliens spilled out on the tarmac, trying
to take it all in. Huddled together, as it were, for
protection against the big bad truckers, who were doing
plenty of gaping and inspecting of their own. Loud
antique rock'n'roll blasting from P.A. speakers
throughout the lot. Showers, sleeping rooms, phones, a
big store, restaurants, porn on TVs in the men's room --
the whole authentic triple-X-rated U.S. truckstop scene.
     -- I glance up, I see remnants of that same motley
band from the truckstop now huddled about the main
campsite with its picnic tables and pergolas and huge
geodesic dome fashioned from bent saplings and
transparent plastic sheeting -- "the hippie bubble,"
call it (and how long before it bursts for good?) -- all
waiting for breakfast. Blueberry pancakes. Can sniff
'em now. -- And in fact the triangle's ding-a-linging
and I'd better get up there pronto to lay claim to my
three bucks' worth.

*   *

     Try now a low stone fence at our next stop. Perch
thereon. (And hear the blond driver saying to the tall
Cawk dude in khaki, "If you do wind up writing anything,
leave my name out of it." So that's his secret! He's
of the dreaded journalist breed! To which breed a note
is addressed in the company flyer: "We have no interest
at all in more articles about 'tee-hee, look at all the
hippies.' Our riders can't be categorized.")
     U bookshop a block up the street -- I thought about
hunting down a German-language book there for the kindly
single mother Rikki in whose bed I slept (always alone!)
for fifteen nights in a row. But we're allotted only
half an hour here. -- Jyze or shop? Jyze of course.
     College town! Once D and I viewed this particular
variant of the type as a highly desirable place to live.

Now I see it as having mutated to something more like an
oddly misplaced semi-suburb, sadly upscale and
conventional and both politically and digitally super-
correct. As the bus crept into town behind a long line
of high-end traffic a shudder of anticipatory dread
bumped up my spine at the very thought of moving here.

     -- Rolling down out of the mountains I flashed back
to my last trip on one of these buses. Then too I was
trying to read a demanding book and having difficulty
concentrating, and for the identical reason: an odd
mixture of creeping dizziness and sleepiness, both
enhanced by diesel fumes.

     And I should note: I've let myself be hooked into
becoming the de facto editor of "Memorials," the family
genealogy book. This means I'll be called upon to
perform various tedious tasks over the coming few months.
In a way it's a labor of love -- and certainly an act of
devotion -- but I still hate the prospect of wasting
time and draining energy on such a project when I could
be and should be working on the Mentoka series. It's
exactly this kind of gruntwork (and some other kinds
too) I was attempting to get away from in quitting
journalism myself lo these many years ago. And I
succeeded! -- But here's a brief relapse of sorts.

     (And it's been useful already in teaching me
something. I see now my writing's become much different
-- but here's the call to the bus.)
                    *   *

     -- Last stop en route. It'll be a short one
because we're running half an hour late and need to make
up the time by curtailing the scheduled layover.

     All the way here from the previous stop: rapping
with David, the young Irish doctor. Wotta yakker he is.

     -- And I was starting to say back there (picking up
the thread now at an outdoor picnic table) I write much
differently these days and this makes grinding out the
old kind of journalistic mumbo jumbo harder for me. I
want to do only jyze style, whether the fictive offshoot
or the "pure" jyzebook stuff, JIFT or JIRT -- to revive
some neglected terms. It's like "How can you keep 'em

down on the news desk after they've scoped out jyze?"

And looking back further I recall a trip to the laundromat and a walk to the drugstore, both with Mom. She's now one of the "frail elderly" even though she does everything in her power to avoid doing anything that might cause anyone to draw that conclusion. And: Thursday night Barb came over for dinner (without Keith) and not a single bad moment ensued. I felt for Barb, the difficulties she's up against. (At least for a couple of weeks my presence spared her some of the daily pressures, although undeniably adding a few new ones.)

This city. Here too it's unlikely I'll ever live. Ain't got no magic for me. ---

*   *

A quick farewell to my partners in travel, a city-bus ride crosstown, a mad rush down the hill with suitcase bouncing in one hand, travel bag in the other, backpack right where you'd think, and all of a sudden here I am aboard -- my usual commuting boat! In my accustomed booth! We haven't even pulled out yet! My heart's still pounding and I'm filmed with sweat! And my backpack and suitcase are still warm inside in a totally unexpected way from the heat buildup in bus No. 503's luggage compartment!

(But here we go. Rumble, rumble. Another kind of big old green tortoise -- maybe even about the same age -- but of course much, much bigger than the bus. It's hard to get used to all this roominess all of a sudden. Not to mention the abundance of fresh air.)

This is an earlier boat than I thought I'd be catching -- the nine o'clock rather than the ten-thirty. Last traces of sunset dead ahead. Now if my zen-wiff-whose-devotion-has-come-into-serious-question has been able to avoid, as she thought she would, having to work tonight, and if she chooses to answer the phone when I call from the transit port, chances are good I'll be home before midnight. Maybe forty, even fifty minutes before midnight.

Meanwhile I'm pleased to have this chance to sum up the trip. Fasten what might pass for an ending on the thing -- a jyzey kind of ending if at all possible.

These long "hippie bus" journeys, I suspect they usually wind down in a similar way. By the last quarter or fifth of the route -- the home stretch -- at least two-thirds of the passengers have already deboarded. The remaining group bonds simply from being survivors, perhaps something like cross-continent pioneers in wagon-train days. And a shakeout process has occurred. You've had plenty of time to meet and talk with anyone who interests you (and probably some who don't, including perhaps a few who at first seem they do). In any event, for this last portion of the trip you tend to hang with those of the survivors you like best.

And so it was today. As we crossed the river and roared ever closer to our final stop I moved to the front of the bus with my pals David, Andrei, and Adrian and stayed there the rest of the way. Also with us was Sonia, a young German factory worker I'd met early on (not the easily wowed one), and Gunter, another German who was shadowing Sonia the whole trip (and they'd just met for the first time while waiting to get on the bus). And finally, sitting in one of the midsection booths and right next to me for a while was the comely and very bright Lisa, a former Ph.D. candidate in psych who turned out to be, at least by my reckoning, more than a little -- strange. Only by a hair's breadth, and reluctantly, did I manage to arrive at this diagnosis in time. Even so it was a bad scene of sorts as I half-turned my back on her and talked with David and Sonia and the others and gradually put a little space between myself and Lisa. Eventually she returned to the back of the bus and continued reading there while carefully avoiding all eye contact with me. Whew.

(Even so I liked her a lot. Too bad she was so... odd. Maybe I'd've had a candidate for a replacement paramour should it turn out Lady U has decided now's the time to hand me my walking papers.)

Sweet Lisa. Brunette and Eurusan and resembling the one in the movie that had her name in the title. By which analogy I become a David and crazy as a coot

myself, I guess, even before noting that Lady K also was
a Lisa, although a fictive one. And that fact may
account for part of my fascination with this authentic
one, who knows. (It's "Middlemarch" she's reading, also
a favorite of the other Lisa.) In any case, this Lisa
of the bus finally gave up her reading and was lying
facedown on the cushions while the rest of us scoped out
the landmarks of the final approach. I felt bad -- but
not bad enough to risk trying to include her in.
(Another part of the equation: she, Lisa of the bus, is
in the process of moving up here. Alone. With no place
to stay and only a single backpack and a briefcase
stuffed with coffee-stained library printouts of
esoteric psychology monographs which she'd started to
explain to me in numbing, monomaniacal, ever more
fervent detail. -- Until finally I had to turn away.)

     Of those remaining on the bus at this point I was
the only one (except for the drivers) who'd ever, before
today, ventured within five hundred miles of my current
home city. By the time the city itself came into view
I'd been pressed into service as a kind of reluctant
tour guide, trying to answer salvos of questions coming
from all sides. (Not that I didn't enjoy playing the
role in spite of myself.)

     By the time we reached the bus depot I'd never felt
older in my life. The main reason for this, I'm sure,
is that in normal daily existence I'm seldom around and
still more seldom have a chance to talk at length with
anyone younger than my own (reluctant?) housemate --
much less a near-full busload of such sprouts. Suddenly
it's clear I'm not just another dude of uncertain age,
I'm a goddamn fossil. (And I say again: yes, I was
aware of this before. Of course I was! But I didn't
really feel it, or at least not with the same painful
intensity. This trip was pounding it home.)

     Also it was a return to the world of my own
foreign-travel days. Several times I flashed back to
the Korea-Japan ferry with its similar consignments
of international travelers. And even at my age then
I'd still be an older dude by the standards of most

of today's "hippie bus" bunch.
     -- Hey, somehow we're here! I don't believe it. I
thought we were just creeping along! I gotta call it
quits! A foot ferry's just coming in! Jyze full stop!

25

     First I had to beat back the blackberry stickers.
Then I figured I needed a loaf of bread and a jug of
wine, or something close thereto. Next it occurred to
me I'd better slather myself all over with insect
repellent. Finally I made a detour to pick up the mail
and beheaded some offending dandelions along the way.
     But now. And now. Here I sit: in the shade of the
old (yes) apple tree. The oldest one around -- trunk
close to three feet thick -- and what's more it's a
special variety of apple. I forget the name, but it's
French-sounding. It was Andy's father's pride and joy
-- he who built most of our house.
     And ten feet to my left, barely visible in the
unrecently mowed or whacked grass, is this year's first
fallen apple. Or first to my knowledge. This apple
itself representing knowledge, of course, as well as sin
and wholesomeness and healthiness -- "an apple a day" --
as well as being the fruit, literally speaking, of the
old-timey USAn way, from the legendary strewer of
appleseeds right up to the legendary strewer of chomped-
on-apple-logoed computers. Most likely this particular
apple right here, as opposed, of course, to any of the
merely symbolic and/or commercial ones, is rotten to the
core or at least significantly eaten away by worms. And
by birds and deer and slugs too, maybe.
     I lean back against the trunk. So does the

whacker, the actual implement, a quarter trunk turn to
my left. A fly lands on the thumb which is clamping
down the top of this very page (the J-book is resting
against the jyzer's upraised right thigh and knee) and
then zips away with an almost audible screech of horror.
I guess the repellent must cover him too. Or her.

Sunny day -- shadow-dappled page. The best kind of
day, the best kind of page. The dapple of the apple.
Shadows slowly shifting and interlacing. A gentle
restlessness underlying these lazy jyze licks.

What else is in the picture? Across roughly twenty
paces of shaggy grass, the house. It's a two-story
(viewed from here), two-toned (both tones a shade of tan
or light brown) box with a moderately peaked roof, and
I'm seeing it head-on from one of the gable ends --
opposite to the uphill, single-story one I was seeing at
the time of the barn-jyze entry a few months back. And
down in the lower right-hand quarter of the box is the
sliding glass "pocket door" directly behind which --
jyze first burst into being! And directly above that
the double window (twice as wide as high) of -- the
jyzer's study! And to the left of that the picture
windows of the bedroom from which -- the jyzer has now
effectively been banished! It seems! (But what the
hell, he's no whiner -- and jyze is patient.) And below
those, the gray door and opaque four-paned windows of
the utility room, a/k/a -- the all-seasons nerf court!

To the left of the house, the "corral." Then the
wetland woods. Toward the near end of that side of the
front yard, a much smaller apple tree, one still
protected by a few strands of sparkly silver "bird tape"
(supposedly it scares off the birds because they think
the tree's on fire). To my left and right and behind me
as well as behind and beneath the large apple tree,
great tangles of blackberry vines up to eight or nine
feet high hung heavily with berry clusters, among which
some glistening black early ripeners stand out. Also to
my right, parked on the grass just across the driveway,
its flatbed backed up against a real corral fence,
neighbor Ben's red pickup (from which he probably

[Jyzemelt]

offloaded a couple of bales of hay last night). Topper
and Goat at this moment are out of sight, but not out of
whiff, behind the blackberry patch. Part of B&B's
ranchhouse is visible beyond the pickup. Otherwise it's
more trees and bushes between their house and ours.
Overhead power lines looping by parallel to our driveway.
A chunk of ridgeline with evergreens standing sentinel
all across the horizon (as a row of picturesque Apaches
might do in an old Western before the U.S. cavalry rides
in for the slaughter), or rather the part of the horizon
that's straight ahead a few hundred yards to the east.
Right here, on and above the front lawn, birds hopping,
flitting, warbling, perching, screeching, twittering,
clicking, soaring -- robins, crows, blue jays, sparrows,
finches, hummingbirds, and some others I can't identify.
A few fluttering butterflies. Sound of a babbling brook
(the one burbling westward on the far side of the
driveway) and a distant chain saw, an occasional barking
dog (mostly it's Buster next door).
     -- So I'm back. Made it. Paradise regained. High
summer now. High noon. High jyzer too -- because why
not celebrate the whole damn array while I still can.
     So I open the jug and gulp some down -- not wine
but actually, yes, close to it: grape juice. One gallon.
"100 percent pure," it says here. Regardless of the
truth content of that claim, it's splendid stuff. And
so's the bread. About eighteen slices short of a loaf,
alas, but it's enough for now. Tasty stone-ground whole
wheat. I gobble tons of it. For the next year I expect
to be pretty much living on it -- and damn well pleased
to do so. (Of course that's the best-case scenario.
The lesser cases, never mind for now.)
     (Also resting here is today's mail, which consists
of two Mentoka daily newspapers and a note on a piece of
pink rabbit-shaped paper from the mail lady, Peggy,
thanking Lady U for the can of soda she, D, left for her
in the mailbox. When not delivering mail, which she
does only part time, Peggy is a coworker of D's at the
camera factory. From attentiveness above and beyond the
call of duty Peggy knows more than anyone rightfully

202

should about the folks who live around here. Me, for
instance. She asked D: "Is your husband a Communist or
something?" -- because of all that subversive literature
I get, some of it from as far away as, horror of horrors,
England. Book reviews even! D's reply: "Oh, that --
that's his brother. There's Glennar and there's Glennor,
one with an A and one with an O. My husband's family is
so weird." -- Which wasn't a reply to tickle me to
conjugal bliss. But who am I to complain as long as the
"It's a Snap!" bucks keep rolling in.)

    Loafabread, juggawine -- what about the missing
element of the trinity? Just before I retired to the
shade here "thou" drove off to an eye-doctor appointment.
Another missed day of work. The bucks don't roll in
today -- but I should just be thankful she hasn't been
laid off yet, as a number of her coworkers have. It
could be the Mexicans have finally discovered the secret
to recycling disposable cameras, she tells me, as her
boss tells her, and the factory will soon be shut down
for good -- and then what? (But we don't worry. We
take it one day at a time. And we thank our lucky stars
D's health insurance doesn't run out until next week.
This visit to the eye doctor, at least, will be fully
covered, except for the damnable copay.)

    So last Saturday night when I arrived back in the
city she was home. It took a while but she did answer
the phone. She wasn't at all happy to have to interrupt
her exercise routine but she did come pick me up. She
did greet me with a peck on the cheek even though that's
the hottest it's gotten for us so far, speaking, again,
conjugally. She is at least attempting to keep up a
facade of good relations -- not warm, not loving, but at
most times mildly cheery though warily so -- and I'm
resigned to the fact, or rather to the high likelihood,
that this too is as good as it's going to get for a
while. And that's at best. At worst -- but never mind
about worst. Accentuate the negative in the shade of
the old apple tree? Ha! Ain't gonna happen!

    (This morning I awakened to "the hottest new
[vocal] group in jazz" circa my college days belting out

a longtime favorite tune of mine on the radio. All day
I've been compulsively humming it, singing it, whistling
it. "The more I'm with you, pretty baby / the more I
feel our love increase...." Going by the sheer number
of this group's cuts capable of taking me over in this
way, they're still number one on my all-time hit parade.
I can think of at least a dozen. Maybe more like two
dozen. "We'll build a house and garden somewhere / along
a country road a piece....")

      Home and right off the bat a different kind of hit:
of good news! Employment Security will be sending
another check! Another five-hundred-dollar windfall!
Astounding! (But this has just got to be the last one.)
(My big worry now stems from a widely publicized IRS
plan to step up audits of tax returns nationwide this
fall, especially those of so-called sole proprietors
such as myself. "The audit from hell." The newspaper
stories I've read suggest the odds are turning against
me -- and the first question the auditor will ask is,
"Where's your marriage certificate? Let's see it."
-- But the jyzer doesn't worry too much. Not now. And
maybe shouldn't at all, being so low on assets. Of
course they could attach our salaries, D's and/or mine,
if, that is, she and/or I continue to have a salary.
And if the old zen marriage falls apart we'll both soon
be needing a salary for sure, and especially me.)

      -- And now I'll say discomfort's starting to set in
under the old apple tree. Bugs. Cramps. Hot sun
incubating little proto-cancers all over my dapple-
patterned exposed parts. -- Meaning it's time to stand
up and stretch. (Last night for the first time in years
I tried to do the exercise I've always called the side-
stretch -- probably that's not the right name -- and was
shocked to hear some potent wheezes. What's going on in
my lungs? Whatever it may be, will it soon be getting
the rest of me too? Just like Mom? And while I'm in the
home stretch -- with Stretch? The last and final race?)
                           *
      While I was up I figured I might as well take a few
whacks. This is the lowest part of the entire yard and

therefore the wettest and therefore the grass grows like
gangbusters down here -- gangbusters on growth hormone.
And after a long dry spell the rains rolled back into
town for a couple of days right after I did. And that's
why I stayed away from this J-book for close to thirty
minutes just now -- because a lot of rain-enhanced
whacking fun was to be had out there. All within thirty
or forty feet.

(Best of all was slicing the apples. "The scrapple
of the apple." I came across at least a dozen more
specimens hidden in the grass, and all but two or three
I chopped cleanly in half, more or less, on the first
stroke. I tell you, the man's got his whack back!
-- And just to prove he ain't no Buddhist either, he'll
admit he often fillets slugs too. They hide in the
grass by the hundreds. The only way, incidentally, to
avoid slaughtering lots and lots of slugs is by (A)
smothering the grass with tarps instead of mowing or
whacking, or (B) letting the grass "have its way" (which
I might note is a famous fictochronicler of suburban
life's catchphrase for saying he's done the raunchy deed
with his wife: "and I had my way with her") (a phrase I
wouldn't ordinarily think of using in that fashion
because I like to believe she's having her way too --
though I'd concede that on any particular occasion this
belief may well be fostered by sheer feel-good delusion
on my part and/or, possibly, kindly deception on hers).)

And then when I came back to the foot of the old
apple tree after hacking apart all these fallen Edenic
symbols what did I see slithering across the very spot
where I'd been sitting? That's right: a serpent. A
cute little garter serpent this time. Fifteen inches
long, maybe, and quite skinny. It skedaddled straight
into the brier patch. Brer Snake. It could be peering
out at me even now as I jyze away. "The Garden of Jyze"
-- whence cometh the good book, which is, of course --
but of course it's of course! (but I wanna say anyhow)
-- the J-book! Born again! As on every eighth day!

Meanwhile: catchup time. Jyze duty. What since
last jyze? (And to be reported with a dash of the old

jyzematyze.) All right. Therefore: whacked the whole
goldang lawn. Talked three times with Mother by phone
and once with Barb's Keith, mostly (all these calls) on
"Memorials" biz. It's a pain and it's highly unorthodox,
our production method, but we're moving right along.
Keith will help and he knows about book editing, so
that's good (but he won't be able to help all that much
-- too many tensions with Mother and Barb) (and for some
odd reason he calls Mother "your mo," which made me
blink the first couple of times; and not least because
it put me in mind of the battleship that's docked eleven
miles north of us here with its sixteen-inch guns
pointed this way -- we're easily within range -- and
goes by the same sobriquet, with an adjective denoting
great power preceding it to be sure).
        -- And as well this week I helped Lady U work out a
complicated shift schedule for the camera factory. Mr.
Consultant. From thin air (while saying it came from a
factory I once worked in) I conjured up a new type of
arrangement which I dubbed the "six-day short." Now
they're all seriously calling it that. They've decided
to adopt the thing immediately without change. I've
been chuckling over this for days.
        End of obligatory catchup.
        (Topper makes noisy lip-flapping breath-blowout
phlizzzzzes, like a wet whoopee cushion. Does that
sound have a name? Other than, ugh, horse mouth fart?)
        A last swig of the grape. ("Unhand that bottle!")
        -- It's warm now. And the tongue of the jyzer is
purple, as he can see for himself when he sticks it out
to the max. As a cartoon kid just observed a couple of
days ago (but I should note I'm currently reading the
comics page, like the rest of the paper, a week or more
past publication date and in the Mentoka version mailed
from Wachute -- "currently" being strictly so-to-speak)
-- the kid observed, to paraphrase, "It's not summer
until your tongue is purple." Around here in
ollalaland -- which is to say, in local indigenous
tribalspeak, very-berry-land -- that's doubly true.
        Meanwhile the shade of the old apple tree (which

indeed "seems to whisper sweet nothings to me") has
shifted eastward and deepened as the sun passed directly
overhead (its rays having to fight their way down
through the most densely pulped and leafed and fruited
part of the tree to accomplish a single measly dapple)
and is now lightening up again as we move toward
midafternoon -- and past my usual crashtime. (These
days my crashings happen mostly in the study. The lady
seems happier this way, since hers continue to go down
in our bedroom. It's not the first time with us for an
arrangement like this and it means little by itself. If
it turns out this is also the last such time -- the
arrangement, that is, becomes permanent and I never make
it back into the bedroom at all -- well, "so be it" --
as -- wow, what timing! -- up the driveway rolls the
dusty gray wagon with herself behind the wheel. Crunch
crunch. "Yoo-hoo!" I hoot, but she's not expecting
anyone to be holding forth over here under the tree --
glances in a couple of wrong directions at the sound of
my voice, slowing down but not stopping, then continues
onward -- past the high bushes, momentarily out of
sight, then hangs a left -- emerges from the bushes,
peers down this way and spots me, cries, "Hey!" As in
"what kinda mischief you up to down there?")

26

     Am I wrong? Maybe? I'd like to think so.
Nonetheless I'm not thinking so. Looks to me like it's
over. Don't see any way back.
     Seventeen years -- somehow work in the phrase
"seventeen-year locus."
     Eighteen is just a couple of months away. The

immediate goal is to make it that far. Not as mates,
though. Just hanging on as strangers in the same house.
That's how it looks.
     -- "107.7, The End." It's playing on the kitchen
radio and all too fittingly -- so fittingly that I'm
suspending the jyze rules and citing the name. The End
Fest, the big alternative rock festival at the county
fairgrounds, that's where she is right now. Rode off
with her camera-factory buddy Jason and I don't know who
else, if anyone, at eleven this morning while I was
intentionally making myself scarce up at the shed. Now
it's dusk and she may or may not be back before long.
     I'm fresh out of the shower. Wearing just a yukata
robe and my new blue shorts salvaged from a remainder
bin in the city for $2.99 a week ago. The brown chair.
The overly bright lamp (when reading here at night I
have to shade my left eye with my right hand --
sometimes the right eye with the left hand -- by
dangling the appropriate hand over the top of my head
and resting the forearm between crown and brow). The
box overbrimming with consumed periodicals. I'm finally
just about caught up on what came in while I was away.
     Now a live radio report from the fairgrounds. To
my surprise it's still going on out there. I thought it
would end, the End Fest, at sundown. Wishful thinking,
this? I'm not even sure.
     Will I be able to stop myself from obsessing about
this sorry situation with D? Not at all times, clearly,
but at least for periods long enough to get some chunks
of the real work done? I'm hoping so. I continue to
believe things are different now. For sure there will
be no repeat of my actions during the Marco crisis of
thirteen years ago but still gallingly fresh in memory.
     The Marco crisis. I'd been wanting to keep that
sorry episode out of these pages. Looks like it's
jumping back in anyway.
     (Hair wet still. Towel draped around neck. The
towel with black and white stripes and brown borders. A
towel that's been drying off our naked bodies for almost
our entire seventeen-year locus -- dare I say? Just

this once? Like those earlier citations?)
     The complexities of breakups. I'd like it to be
no-fault, perhaps because back in a previous era when I
was the one engineering the split with someone else I
wanted it to be that. Such admirable consistency!
Nonetheless I think the record should be clear: Lady U's
the one pushing for this one (just as during the Marco
eruption). I'd rather we stay together and try to patch
things up. But this time the impetus for reconciliation
won't be coming from me.
     Not that either of us has said a word about any of
this. That's not the way we do things. Not anymore.
Gradually over the years I've yielded to her preferred
style in the amatory realm. No direct confrontations,
no straightforward conflictual soul-baring.
     Right now no rage either. No fury. In me I'm
saying. Just sorrow and regret. Some disgust that
something like this could be happening again, and so
closely following the earlier pattern. But let's face
it: little is left anyway. We've "grown apart." We've
discovered we don't have so much in common after all.
     At this point it would seem the only truly live
question is: does she feel she owes it to me to support
me for long enough that I can finish the "Dreams" draft?
"Ghosts"? "Jyzer"? Any of these? All of them? That
is, will she hold to her word? "Well, don't get me
wrong. I'm not saying it's not my turn. It is my turn.
It's way past my turn." (Her shaky assurance of last
fall, more or less verbatim.) -- But does she still
care enough? Can she hang on for another few months? A
year? Two years? Should she? Should I let her try to
do so? (The answer to this last: yes, unless the
atmosphere were to worsen considerably: become unlivably
bitter, say.)
     It's no picnic right now having a whole new set of
dreads to deal with -- no matter how old and familiar
they may be. The dreads always lying there dormant even
at the best of times: of returning to the job market and
the courtship bazaar, of facing loneliness and poverty,
so on and so forth. However, I want to believe I'm

tough enough, savvy enough, deep-spirited enough to face
all this down. Yes, I truly mean it. And able to keep
moving ahead on the things that really matter to me,
excepting the one for which this is apparently no longer
to be the time: meaning love for a particular woman.
And in particular for this particular (very!) D woman.
     Hair just about dry. Time to step into the
bathroom and take it the rest of the way with the blower
(because the night's turning a little chilly).

*

     whew. The mark of dispirit. I hereby vow I won't
let it keep marring these pages. Any hint of weakening,
simply recall that jyze won't permit it.
     Now back where it all began. The blues show is on
down here. Sounds even better than usual to me;
scorches all the way down. -- And I'm dressed. In
sweats. My uniform for the duration here at home. So
long as it's still home, that is, and I'm still here.
     Tomorrow I won't be. Tomorrow's the scheduled
start-up day for "Mentoka Ghosts" and for a long time
I've been planning to hit the chosen sites in the city
on this day and I see no reason to change that now. In
fact I see additional reasons for going over there. And
will do so. Even if old Stretch doesn't make it home at
all tonight.
     It can't be mere coincidence that this was the week
in which Employment Security sent out the Dear Jyzer
letter. "All benefits have been exhausted." It's a
release and it's a wake-up call. Destitution begins.
The current reverses. Lady U takes over paying the
bills. (And we cancel cable TV, which with rare
exceptions only she uses. And we reduce her health-
insurance coverage to the minimum, which will still cost
much more than we can afford. -- And I continue to have
none. This is just how things are and I'm not even
grumbling about it.) -- And I start living on bread and
water. And that's only a slight exaggeration.
     (Crunch of gravel, a car rolling up, dogs barking.
But it's one of the B&B vehicles. We share the same
driveway up to the point parallel with this jyzeroom

210

where theirs forks off to the southeast while ours
continues straight east for another fifty feet before
turning ninety degrees to the north toward the carport.)

   -- And Mother called several times. "This is your
podner...." More "Memorials" stuff. Meanwhile I find
myself wondering: have I seen her for the last time? I
left in such a rush at the end of my most recent visit I
scarcely had a chance to think about it as we said our
hurried farewells on her front landing.

   And flurries of interest in a news-magazine cover
story on "the overclass" and a long review by "the most
interesting philosopher in the world today" according to
one of the more influential literary critics in the
world today (and I'd agree with him, except I think of
the philosopher himself as an antiphilosopher). And a
few other lesser periodical pieces. A three-day stay on
the yard-maintenance injured list owing to a strained
ligament in my right elbow (from sparring too
enthusiastically with legions of spear-wielding
blackberry invaders). On the book front laying the bio
of the Russian poet/essayist to rest (along with a
contemporary Japanese novel which I just can't finish
right now) and starting up in its place a Pakistani-
English contemporary novel, among others. A quick
letter, to an author of historical works about the
Mentoka zone, inquiring about the tragic story of Great-
Uncle Roar and his cross-race (Afrusan) inamorata Sadie.

   -- And now here she is. Wants me to let her in.
Unusual.

*   *

   Rain. At the shed. All plans for the day canceled.
Not that I want to be too melodramatic about it. I just
couldn't bear the prospect of hassling the trip into the
city and all the crowds in this kind of weather. It's
the peak of the big summer festival over there and the
ferries would've been jam-packed. And I'd intended to
do a lot of walking in the northern districts. This
rain would've taken most of the fun out of it.

   And then there's the crisis at home. Wouldn't want
to miss a moment of that either.

[Jyzemelt]

(This is going down in the old green shed armchair
with the window immediately behind me raised only half
an inch and still an occasional splinter of rain reaches
the back of my neck some eighteen inches above the sill.
-- And does so by a kind of grenade action, I just
figured out: big drops from the eaves shatter on the
wood surface of the flowerbox a millimeter or two
outside the window pane and some of the shrapnel has the
angle to spray all the way up to my neck. If I'd put up
the damn gingerbread trim it would've prevented this.)
     Actually nothing much has happened. When the lady
arrived home last night I opened the door for her (while
eyeing Jason's car as it pulled down the driveway) and
when she dawdled with the outdoor cats I went back
downstairs. I had no greeting to offer her and she had
none for me. Then she went up to the bathroom --
presumably to take out her contacts, which she'd been
wearing (again presumably) for a longer-than-ordinary
period -- and then I heard her clomping around for a
while up there, and then no more sounds. A few minutes
later I went up to the bathroom and found she'd already
gone to bed and closed the bedroom door.
     That was it for last night. Then this morning I
heard her using the toilet and talking to Fred the cat
and I went in to tell her I wouldn't be going to the
city today after all. She'd already returned to bed and
she offered no response to my statement; instead she
said something about how Fred was being bad.
     "Did you hear?" I asked.
     "I heard," she said.
     I could've stomped out right then but actually she
didn't sound too hostile so instead I stuck around for a
moment to see if she might have anything else to say.
She did, but only to Fred, whose neck I was scratching.
He was perched on the blanket atop her chest (his
customary spot at this hour) and pushing hard against my
hand. "See, I told you he was bad," she said, as he
slid halfway off her chest in his effort to elicit a
better scratch. (Or "chichis" we'd both say for "chest"
in more intimate times.)

"Are you recovered from yesterday yet?" I asked.
"No," she groaned.
"Well, keep working on it," I said, or something
to that effect -- no bad vibes in it, I swear -- and
then left and came straight up here, to the shed.

So that's all I've got to go on. And after a few
more pages of this entry, jyze will be shutting down for
another eight days. A lot can happen in eight days.
It's not impossible one of us will be living elsewhere
by then. Most likely it would be me, except -- how
could it be? I have no funds and no hope of coming up
with any. So it would more likely be her, even though
this is her parents' property. She would perhaps be
staying with a friend or a lover temporarily while
waiting for me to decamp. Except -- what about Fred?
She wouldn't want to leave him behind and she'd probably
think him too old and too set in his ways to be uprooted
so abruptly.

Fred. The cat I gave her as a six-week-old kitten
shortly after the Marco brouhaha had passed (or anyway
had peaked). It's no exaggeration to say it's at least
in part because of her attachment to Fred that we're
still together. And now he might be the main reason we
survive the next eight days, if we do.

The inadequacy of jyze to all this. At least so
far. Because jyze wasn't around for the Marco events or
the immediately subsequent several years, this is its
first real domestic crisis. It needs time to adjust.

Unfortunately all this is happening just as I'm
finally about to get started on the actual writing of
"Ghosts." Tuesday or Wednesday of this coming week was
to have been the (rescheduled) big day. Will it still
be? I'm hoping so. I'm gonna give it my best shot.
And speaking of shots: maybe this crisis will give the
fictojyzing a shot in the arm. One can dream anyway.

Drip-drip-drip on the flowerbox. So steady! And
pattering on the roof. Dozens of tiny taps per second.
-- Is it dozens? Maybe not quite that many. But this
is real rain. Light but real. Not just drizzle. (And
speaking of light: dim gray light and it's mostly coming

in the window right behind me and I'm contorted in the
chair so I can catch as much of it as possible on these
pages to see by -- because there's still no power up
here and thus no working lamp -- and my hand and the J-
stick are casting annoying fuzzy shadows.)
     The crisis feeling. It got a good grip on me after
D's arrival home from the fest last night and I didn't
like it one bit. I had new doubts about whether I could
be stronger than it. The baddest of the bad Marco
moments came bubbling back up. You forget how easily
all this badness can bring you to your knees.
     -- This session is about to sputter to an end. Ten
pages of jyze pain. Or eleven I guess. And so: one
more. Make it a non-baker's dozen. Why the hell not?
     I ask myself: do I have any strategy? And the
answer is: not really. Just a few tips to myself.
Things I want to keep in mind. Like, for example, don't
confront her on anything. Don't be sycophantic but
don't be nasty either. See if she can pull herself out
of this. -- And don't get caught up in trying to
second-guess either her or yourself. And for god's sake
don't go crazy trying to find out if she's actually
cheating on you (if cheating's the right word -- and I
say it isn't, and I say I don't even want to think in
terms like that). But don't stoop to spying and
snooping and stalking and all that self-demeaning hooey.
Try to stick to the high road. And if it turns out to
be true the gig's up (not the jig, I'm thinking, but
the gig, the seventeen-year-locus gig) accept that fact
as proudly and gracefully as possible. No pleas. No
attempts to dissuade or argue or strike back.
     Is this ridiculous? I suppose. Jyze is frowning
and shaking its head over it. For this pathetic
rejected lover's pep talk jyze entered the world? (I
hear an unfamiliar male voice coming from down by the
house and leap up. But it's someone at B&B's place.
Or I think it is anyway. -- But see, this is what I'm
up against. Am I about to be challenged? Will some
desperate lovesick type be showing up? Lurking about?
-- But actually this is just a small part of it. The

obsessing is what I fear most. I have no idea how to
handle it, how to beat it. Tell me, jyze gods, what's
wise? What do I do now? -- But the jyze gods, for the
moment anyway, and no doubt wisely, go silent.)

27

     This is not the old mill stream. This is not the
height of summer. This is not the way things ought to
be -- except the blues are playing on the radio and the
jyze is cranking up again.
     The rainstorm which was just getting underway when
I last came to this J-book begging for relief turned out
to be the real thing and not just symbolic. Roaring
trees and power knocked out for eight or nine hours,
Christmas candles and kerosene lanterns brought forth
to fill the air with some confusing unseasonal whiffs.
For a couple of days the blow continued and then for the
rest of the week we were mired in misty/drizzly (so say
mizzly) darkness and coldness worthy of a nasty November.
A real storm -- but still its symbolic aspect was what
most interested me. (And certainly is most useful now
no matter how pathetic the fallacy.)
     For gleefully masochistic reasons I'm at this
moment jyzing away where I've never jyzed before: our
bedroom. The one we no longer occupy together at the
same time but rather in shifts. With my better half (or
somewhere between a quarter and a third, actually, by
body weight, of our combined total) -- with the lady off
at work, I say, under her new "six-day short" schedule
(which I myself drew up!) this becomes one of my bedroom
shifts. One of the few where for me something is going
on in here, on our very zen-marriage bed, other than

lonesome storm-tossed sleeping or semi-sleeping or non-sleeping.

Shining with misleading warmth, symbolically speaking, are both wall lamps and also the bedside one hanging above the radio with its two-person alarm setting and single radio setting, this latter now always tuned to her station rather than mine -- except I just changed it. The six-hour weekend blues show, Sunday-night version. Keep pouring out all that sorrow! (Or rather: those courageous and inspirational and even joyous wrestlings with sorrow -- though I haven't heard anything truly moving so far -- but I'm smiling anyway. Sure! All of a sudden life pummels me into eyes-rolling, stars-flashing vertigitude!)

An odd perch here. I'm sitting on the spot where the inimitable Lady U lays her special orthopedic pillow; I'm twisted around so I can rest the J-book atop one of the cheapo cedar chests which, in two double-stacked pairs with a piece of plywood bridging the twelve-inch gap between them, make up the bed's headboard. Standing to J-book's right are an orange flashlight, a large jet-spray bottle of wasp killer (presumably intended for use against human male intruders, possibly including, these days, myself, a WASP to be sure even if an off-label all-caps kind), and two jars of snacks for Fred the cat: so-called triangles and so-called pellets. Then the radio, the overhanging extendable-arm reading lamp, and my ancient red windup double-bell alarm clock whose extremely loud ticking I use to mask daytime sounds with "red noise" during sleep hours. In the current era the big tin potato-chip can which serves to amplify that ticking sound still further is more trouble to set up than it's worth. First off, because I'm no longer doing boring work which always threatens to put me to sleep if I'm the slightest bit sleepy (that is, I'm unemployed), it's not so important that I get undisturbed sleep these days. Second, I no longer sleep in here that much anyway. Third, to repeat, when I do sleep in here, I sleep very little no matter what steps I take to avoid sleep disturbances.

[Jyze for Mom]

Sorrow, sure, but no self-pity. This is just how
it is. I've got plenty else to be grateful for -- damn!
Don't even have to work too hard at convincing myself.
It rolls right back in. The dark cloud, the sun re-
emerging. Where am I anyway? It's a new day! A new
field! A new twelfth-dimensional plane!

(Here's the blues jock plugging a festival the lady
and I once attended together. Blues fest, yes. -- Now,
alas, she's found a different kind of music she likes
much better. Doesn't have time for this old-timey stuff
anymore. -- And as far as jazz goes, forget it. Shuck
it. To her it does not speak at all. And probably
reminds her of my mother as well.) (My mother who is
well, still, this week, relatively speaking -- this
relativity being in its deep structure about as closely
aligned as any can be, between mother and firstborn.)

Pine-paneled bedroom. New industrial ceiling which
wasn't my idea at all but I had no right to protest,
really, and didn't. Two sets of drawable floor-to-
ceiling curtains -- Mama U's handiwork -- currently
closed, as they almost always are, but which when open
offer fine second-story picture-window views of front
yard and side yard and mainly of a great many leaves and
limbs and trunks -- you can almost feel you're bedding
down in a treehouse. In the middle of the room a set of
unmatched wooden his-and-her dressers, total combined
value fifty bucks tops, hers small and his large in
close mimicry of our actual physical proportions. And
to the left of those the long but shallow closet with
its double set of folding doors, again one set for him
and one for her. And behind me the bizarre extra
"bathroom," hidden by a doorless L-shaped pine-paneled
partition about six feet high. A sink and a toilet in
there. Andy's handiwork. Nobody's ever been able to
figure out why he put it in. (The regular bathroom is
just steps away on the other side of the wall.)

-- Well, but isn't there some news you ought to be
getting to, O jyzemaster?

Yes there is. And this is it: the thing is begun.
"Ghosts" is underway. Chapter one is in the can.

There's no turning back now. No use wasting energy on inconsequential stuff, not a single erg.

For the record, it finally began on the 12th of August of the year jyze two. A Saturday night. The prodigal Lady U was off at work or wherever it is she actually goes when she says she's off to work on a Saturday night. A couple of false starts had preceded this, or rather failures to start. But when it was finally set to go, it went. Hopefully, and with burning resolution I say this -- not that I think burning resolution can work miracles -- but who needs miracles? -- hopefully, I say, it will keep on going. And that's all I'll say about that. For now. Until next time.

And then there was the showdown with my mate of seventeen-plus years whose devotion has been waning. I didn't mean for a showdown to happen but it snuck up on us. I was just trying to understand why this sudden obsession with so-called "New Music" for which she had evinced nothing but scorn as recently as a couple of months ago. Why the metamorphosis? Was it an early midlife crisis or what? Was she really resenting me down to the bone or did it just appear that way?

Lots of insulting questions, as she herself didn't fail to point out. This was three nights ago -- as I sat halfway up the basement steps and she on the couch below in front of the TV which was playing a borrowed video featuring performances by several of her newly favored groups. She reluctantly put the video on hold and listened to what I had to say. Didn't argue much, didn't really protest. What could she object to? I was just pointing out the obvious. No signs of loving or caring from her, lots of signs of resentment, and now this new passion for a kind of music she'd had no interest in previously. What was going on? And didn't she realize the effect all these things taken together were having on me and on us? Didn't she realize we were growing apart and our relationship was under extreme duress? And all kinds of pathetic things like that. Didn't she realize that to me this might look like the Marco crisis (I didn't use his name: couldn't bear to

say it aloud after all these years in which it's gone
unmentioned) -- the Marco crisis all over again?

    She acted as if none of this had occurred to her
before. But at the same time she showed no sign of
being upset or concerned or of wanting to repair the
damage or to set me straight on anything. She tossed
out a few "theories" to explain this or that but then
quickly backed away from them when I tried to pin her
down on consequences. Indifference, blankness, lack of
curiosity was the overall impression. Understanding
causation in emotional realms doesn't interest her that
much -- never has. Explore the roots? Why bother?

    She did say she thought maybe she'd been depressed
-- perhaps that was why this kind of music with its
"teen angst" and "depressive rage" suddenly appealed to
her so much just as she's moving beyond her own self-
defined (as of a few months ago) youthful pursuits.
She's just pleased she's found something that interests
her. She agreed "alienation" might be a relevant term.
She cited her longstanding "cynical streak." And
finally she said, "Well, it sounds like you're saying I
should be doing something I'm not doing, so what is it?"

    Hostility. I said no, no, she should do what she
wants to do. If our run's come to an end, so be it.
"So be it!" And then she said, first, she had no new
love interest or anything like that, and she said she
thought in time things might work themselves out for us.
She said she didn't want to split up. With no sign of
love or caring or real concern she asked me to be
patient with her.

    As she was spouting all this stuff I was thinking,
yup, it really is over. There won't be any recovering
from this. -- But I also was thinking, well, what the
hell, give it a chance. Suspend judgment a while
longer. Try to focus on other things and see what
happens. Why not?

    -- As I sit now on the spot where she lays her head
to rest. My spine twisted in a way she can no longer
twist hers without pain. My whacker's elbow throbbing
(but not too badly). On the radio a blues singer,

female, growling out her hunger for "a little meat on
the side." Do I believe Stretch's disavowal of any
outside love interest? Not quite. She seemed to be
phrasing it a little too carefully. But she is being
somewhat friendlier now (though still neither warm nor
affectionate, and as for loving lust -- forget it, not a
chance). Yesterday she attended the camera factory's
company picnic for a couple of hours before going to
work, and though she didn't invite me -- not that I
would've gone; no way -- she did bring home a chunk of
cold barbecued chicken breast and some tooth-rotting
carrot cake "just for you." Unbeknownst to her, I wound
up flinging both into the woods out beyond the corral.
Catapulted the damn things as far as I possibly could
with my bad right arm and probably aggravated whatever
it is that's causing all the badness there.
     -- So who knows what's next. Jyze doesn't know.
Nobody knows. The lady herself doesn't know. (Her
little green slippers down there on the floor. Worn. I
mean tiny. In past eras I might've worked up great
clouds of sentiment over them as they look right now --
not to mention what might've been stirred up by a piece
or two of her more intimate apparel -- twisted myself
into knots of a true belated teen angst of my own. And
I may yet so twist myself -- if not over the items in
view here, over something. The whole beloved ensemble,
say -- if it still is beloved. Time no doubt is
gleefully cogitating on what it will tell about this.)
     Meanwhile, what else? Poverty tightens its grip.
So far, though, no real pain on this score. An old
switch-hitting baseball slugger dies and so does a
somewhat less old guitar-picking rocker of celebrated
psychedelic propensity, but neither has ever been a hero
of mine (unlike many in my generation and the ones right
before and right after for whom these are two of the
gods). I shop for groceries in three different towns,
proudly managing to stay within our newly tightened
weekly budget. I eat lots of bread and potatoes. I
curse the rain because it makes the grass grow. -- Oh,
and right at the start a big emergency arises with Fred

the cat. It delays the showdown with D for a few days
and also heightens it a bit. Fred the furry and fuzzy
Marco surrogate, one might say, the one I foisted on the
lady myself some thirteen years ago -- then gradually
became rather fond of despite everything -- Fred was
frothing at the mouth. An overnight stay at the vet's,
a frantic Lady U, an unexpected forty-six-dollar bill
to pay (which will pinch later if I'm unable to resume
work at the office). -- And the so-called golden
anniversary of the monstrous USAn nuking of two Japanese
cities slips by and the one for V-J Day is coming up
tomorrow or maybe it's the next day, with a big
celebration scheduled aboard the mighty dreadnought
which is still docked over at the transit port. And our
cable has been shut off now so I guess we've washed back
out of that particular current of the mainstream, or
rather D has. Only one TV station comes in out here via
the airwaves, it turns out, and that usually with a lot
of flickering and static.
     -- Stream did I say? As in old mill? I had wanted
to find a perch by our town's main creek, a rock I could
sit on. And jyze this good lazy jyze -- ha! Up a lazy
jyzestream! But maybe it will still happen. And maybe
someday I'll be welcomed back into this bed right here
on which at least I can now stop tormenting myself in
this sadly warped fashion. "She wouldn't listen to my
jyze...." (But that's so twisted!)

- - - - - -

28

- - - - - - - .

     Silent house. "Utterly." Had enough of that radio
station the lady likes so much even though I now figure
I'm almost required to listen to it and not just as a

matter of self-protection but -- for art! What else
would our "Mentoka Ghosts" newlyweds be listening to if
not "alt rock"? (Except the station and the kind of
people who listen to it like to say -- and no doubt I'm
being repetitive about this, just as, lord only knows,
they are -- the music is New Music, and so-called
traditional rock, like God, the novel, the switch-
hitting baseball slugger and the keep-on-truckin' guitar
picker, among lots of other people and art forms and
deities, is dead -- and maybe even, since they're
probably not required to listen to the New Music all
day, gratefully dead. And also dismantled. Ho ho.)

Dusk decaying into night. I'm seated sideways on
the couch in my study. For once the curtains to the hall
are open. Two lights on in here, one on the facing wall
and the other directly above my head, so close it heats
up my inner skull, or seems to; otherwise the world is
dark. Darkening windows bearing weak secondary
reflections of the row of blown-up black-and-white photos
of the lady herself in lissome pre-back-injury black-
leotarded dance mode, all just over a decade old now.

Eight more days gone by. Or probably it's nine.
But in any case the slogan of the day is the familiar "On
the eighth day he jyzed." It's a crossover hit now,
having made it into "Ghosts" during its first week on
the JIFT chart (again, that's jyze in fictive time, as
I'd almost forgotten myself).

-- All but the last two of these eight days (or
actually nine, yes) having been rainy. What a bad spell
it was. And in August! And chilly too. Right at
climax growth stage. Or no, I should say right after it,
because most things had ceased or slowed down in growth
as they always do in true high summer -- the time of hot
and dry. This nasty aberrational wet spell had a bizarre
split effect: nudging some of the surround back into
growth, some of it into premature yet still terminal
autumnal decline.

Meanwhile I kept hacking away. Hacking and
whacking. A stroke a second, back and forth, moving

right along. In an hour that's a lot of hockey games
and tennis sets, a lot of vicious cuts in the batting
cage. Pain in my left wrist (aggravating the old proto
carpal tunnel syndrome) now arising to rival that in my
right elbow. Thousands of slugs neatly filleted. Deer
bounding blithely about -- it's gotten to the point that
they stick around for long periods while warily ignoring
me (don't come too close, pal, or I'll tell my fleas to
shoot you full of Lyme disease). Actual gunshots, every
time I hear a burst of them I think that's the end of
our little herd, but so far it's kept reappearing. The
twin fawns boing-boing about in tandem like cervidified
Chinese love ducks on springs but without wings.

And the mate crisis. It percolates right along in
the same suspended form. As the deer do with me, I
warily ignore it, the crisis, insofar as possible while
secretly wishing all kinds of plague upon it. I pretend
a lot. "The great pretender." Wail it, doo-woppers!
The lady's continuing to be at least somewhat friendly.
No doubt this too is a matter of pretense, but it's far
better than open nastiness. Real warmth she's not even
pretending to show (that could be dangerous). So we
mostly do our own things.

It may go on in such fashion for quite a while.
And I hope it does. At least that would be preferable
to facing all the hassles of a breakup during this
extremely inconvenient period. So what if my heart is
broken -- it's always been broken, or at least for most
of my adult life. The point is it still pumps. Or the
pieces do, who knows. They run a few hopes up the pole
too, the equally broken pole, these pieces do, once in a
while, still, just out of habit. As long as the lady
and I continue living in the same house I guess I might
as well go on hoping. Squeeze those hopes out like
ditties from a wheezy old accordion (then run them up
the broken pole powered by the broken pieces).

So I turn grumpy in private. This is not
necessarily bad and neither is it continuous.

And I push ahead with the experiment in JIFT, that
is, the fictojyze. Three chapters of "Ghosts" now.

Complete. In their raw ficto-form, that is, of course.
Yet in rereading I've thought a couple of times, you
know, this thing just might fly. So I suppose I ought
to be jumping with joy. But I'm too grumpy these days
to be doing that (despite what I said one paragraph up)
and I also recall too many previous jumps of that sort
which later proved embarrassing -- or premature might be
a better term, as with the brownness of the otherwise
vividly green surround -- too many of those, I say, to
be hopeful about the prospects of going airborne again.

And be sour. Yeah! You can do it and fie on all
future readers (there it is, though, hope sneaking up
the broken pole again, in the guise of hoping for
readers).

Forty chapters still to go. I'm focusing on it.
On them. Every three or four days, one less to go.
Please, I just want to get to the rewrite stage, because
that I believe I'll enjoy much more and maybe even do
well with.

What's made the difference? No question about it:
having the outline. That's what I work on for the two
or three days leading up to each session. Study my old
chronbooks from the appropriate period and take brief
notes, then review previously distributed notes for the
chapter and revise the outline as necessary, spicing it
up with a few sure-thing boffo details. Having this
expanded outline to turn to when a rough patch crops up
enables me to keep blazing away at a good clip, and that
seems to be the secret, for me, of getting all the way
to the end of something -- and especially of something
fictive. Don't let myself bog down in absurd quests for
perfection. Not even in reasonable quests for progress.
Be happy for now not so much with what you've got as
with the mere fact that you've got something. Keep
trying to get more.

*

Stopped right there. Stretched (but without a
capital S). Hit the head. With JIRT you can do this,
no problem: jyze in real time. Start, stop, go do
something else for a while, jump back in.

224

[Jyze for Mom]

     The old brown sleeping bag is spread atop the
couch. Soles of my bare feet pressing against each
other. Hairy legs making a diamond shape and genitals
impudently (not to mention impudendally -- sic) drooping
out from leghole of new blue shorts, left side, for
airing. Had to pull them out, actually, because the
shorts are fairly tight around my thighs. It's warm
again -- finally back up into the eighties today. Also
humid. "Now let's make them all sweat a bit."
     Let's see, 10:06. (Red digits glow on the clock
radio to my right.) Or make that 10:07. But either way
I've still got about an hour. Not many dishes to do
tonight. Then, after completing the other chores, a
couple of hours at the redwood table in the library
downstairs prepping for chapter four. Then back here to
the couch for a two-hour reading orgy before I crash.
Right here. A light blanket pulled over me and an
overloaded bookcase hanging directly above, rising all
the way to the ceiling. If a serious earthquake ever
hit while I was lying here I'd be buried alive in books.
Which in my case is one of the better ways, or rather
say one of the apter ways, or even the aptest, to go.
     I left out dinner. Something quick and simple
about two-thirty a.m. Meanwhile Lady U would probably
be shut up in her room doing exercises. I don't mean
exercising in any necessary or even healthful way; I
mean vanity stuff. Muscle stuff. Body beautiful stuff.
And then before going off to work tomorrow another hour
or more applying makeup. To me this is just craziness.
What happened to the art lover? What happened to the
lover, period? Or the artist, period? Or the reader,
period? But never mind.
     Besides, she's off tomorrow -- I just remembered.
This ridiculous camera factory. Just pray she can hang
on to her job. "For the nonce." Don't worry about
anything else (if you can help it). Try to be as
heartfully and also mindlessly trusting as possible. Go
out there and do, woman, what you gotta do!
     And I go shopping. Southward this time. She wrote
out a check for two hundred bucks to cover two weeks'

groceries for both of us and miscellaneous expenses,
among them coffee and gas and lens solution. Her
paycheck this time -- she gets paid every two weeks --
was $276. So we're cutting it a little close, there's
no denying. (And today the yearly registration bill for
the wagon came in -- $213 all by itself.)

Eat lots of potatoes. Try to stretch the two
weeks' grocery money out to three weeks.

-- Stacks of papers. Stacks of books. Stacks and
stacks and rows and rows, and none of this arrangement
is anywhere near as neat and tidy as those words might
suggest. It's clutter is what it is, most of it, the
state of my mind reified. And I curl up in the midst of
the whole ensemble -- or dyssemble? -- quite comfortably.
-- Starting in on the big fat book of haiku commentary
tonight, and that fact all by itself makes a lot of
things seem bearable. Or would do so if I even thought
about things needing to be bearable. Actually, except
for attacks of grumpiness over the mere demise of a
long-running love connection, I'll call it, I'm floating
along quite obliviously in jyzeworld.

As for Mom. No communication in a week or so. I
did talk to Suzanne, our contact at the publishing
house, and we're now waiting for them to set some
corrections so they can work up an estimate on the cost
of a second proof. Mother and I talked several times
earlier and everything was going as well with her (Mom)
as could be expected. After a week of recovering from
chemo she experienced a surge of energy. She's hopeful
about the effects of a drug called chlorella -- it's a
kind of alga (or, in groups, algae) and it's supposedly
the most popular health booster in Japan these days.
-- Oh well. I hate to write about this sort of stuff.
If taking chlorella gives her a boost of some sort, even
if only psychological, great.

Out in the world, what? As a newly ordained full-
time recluse I now can report only what I read in the
papers, usually with a parallax effect (the week to ten
days' delay), although every seven or eight days I do
pick up a current local daily paper (city paper)

because I may need it someday for "Ghosts," which is
supposedly unfolding in our city right now even as I
jyze this real-time jyze over here -- the fictive
marriage of Jyzer G and Ciara D. rapidly disintegrating
much like the current one of Jyzer G and Lady U, except
Jyzer G and Ciara D. 's hitch-up is an authentic,
socially sanctioned one, not the mere zen kind.

Trying to ride out the right-wing craziness
currently raging in the national capital and across the
land. Hopefully it will self-destruct and never reach
the stage where I'll feel I must drop everything to take
up the struggle against it. I'm monitoring it but as of
now it doesn't seem to merit a whole lot of focused
thought much less drastic action. It's clear as can be
what's happening. The nation's tawdry triumphalism.
Post Cold War throes. Casting about for new enemies
upon whom its ongoing failures can be blamed and its
war economy restoked. (Or, of course, even those old
enemies of the internal kind might do in a pinch, such
as for instance us lefties, sixties rebels, bohemians,
not to mention gays, feminists, racial minorities,
environmentalists, disabled folks, immigrants, welfare
recipients: the list is long and all too obvious.)

Scratch scratch. My deadline approacheth. I
acknowledge I've so far failed to show any evidence of
how strenuously I've been meditating on things -- many
things. I dip into a fourteenth-century volume of
zuihitsu (a kind of protojyze itself) and a twentieth-
century thinker's notions about time and I realize I'm
really not doing anything greatly different from what
these gents are doing, thoughtwise, speaking generally
and not going too deeply into actual content, except I'm
failing to write down most of my own gems of wisdom.
-- The reason being, or at least the rationale, that it
seems they must all be already written down. I get more
pleasure from coming up with new ways to avoid writing
down those same things while writing down something else
that maybe hints at them via extreme indirection which I
might not even be able, or in some cases all but
certainly will not be able, to parse myself. It's the

only pursuit that doesn't seem utterly pointless.
(Which doesn't mean I don't enjoy uncovering the various
ways in which others have articulated the wisdom.
-- Which is odd, I guess. So maybe I need to be
thinking a little more seriously, if I have to be
thinking at all, about these things. And it seems from
the evidence of this tortured paragraph right here that
I'm not yet ready to do this.)

    Last minute. Last few lines. Look away from the
page, tip my head back so the ceiling floats into view
like the underside of a flatbottom boat. Close eyes,
inhale (it's air!) -- and welcome the three little
invisible stars. Like the three little raccoons, the
three little potbellies, the three little love ducks,
even the three little U's (because they're all quite
short, the U's). (Huh? Say again? Where you gonna go
with this?) (Away, that's where.)

29

    Bong bong bong -- the maximum number of bongs, all
the way out to evening's end -- and we're on, it's a new
day by Gregorian reckoning and therefore it's the Jyzer
G Birthday Jyze & Blues Party.

    Down here in jyze central. Why the hell not? (It
pains me to be unable to beat back this Neumanic "Why
not?" gambit more often than, say, nine times out of
ten.) No big grandfather clock bonging out the hour --
no bongs of the hallucinatory kind either, or at least
not literally -- but I'll still try to do some smokin'
anyway, of the jyze kind. And hope I still know how.

    Bong bong bong -- I hear them, deep and vibrant.
Like train whistles in the night, I want to say,

probably just because I've got this album of women's
railroad blues playing. Great staticky sorrowful stuff
from the twenties and thirties. And stacked up behind
that, or actually above it on the turntable, two other
albums featuring great blues masters from the same era,
one album per master, and then finally a compilation of
more recent work of the Centropolis electrified kind.

So could any party be finer? I say no.

Yeah, I've cranked up the old stereo. It's an
antique now -- miracle it still works. (Here's a master
I'd all but forgotten about -- ooh she sassy!) A loose
wire somewhere -- you have to jiggle the chassis (it
sassy too) until you find a spot that gets results and
then be careful to stop jiggling real quick. Stack of
four on the spindle, one down already and three still to
flop. Will they flop right? Don't know. It's been at
least five years since I've used this thing. The good
old obsolete Japanese brand Mother and brother Rob laid
on me for my birthday the year Dad died but after the
actual death (or otherwise it would've had to be one of
his own company's models).

First album I spun tonight, two of my favorite cuts
of all time, venerable South Side C-town piano man in a
collection from my Mezzu days. Sweetest, soulfulest,
pain-filled-est growl ever. ---

*

-- Nope, it sure didn't work. Disaster. Album
number three slowly slid down as the tone arm started
working on album number two. Pinned the tone arm
against the record with a godawful screechy yowl. I
lunged for the damn thing. Lifted number three back up.
-- But now it's spinning out all right again, number two
is. -- Disaster only seeming, it appears.

And can I say anything similar about my own sorry
situation? Disaster only seeming? Not likely.
Scarcely a chance at all. But that's how it goes. No
room for self-bad-mouthing in these pages. Not tonight.
Not anytime if I get to have any say about it, conscious
or otherwise.

Blues masters, show us how it's done!

[Jyzemelt]

        And this one does. Hard-feeling blues, yeah. Or
any of them, hers or the others', they all show you how.
                See he drives so easy
                I can't turn him down.
        Two cardboard boxes of old vinyl. I lay on the rug
in the tight quarters back behind the China bookcase and
fished out a dozen favorites from the olden days. Then
stood in front of the blasting speakers resonating with
the pain and the irrefutable transcendence thereof.
Even danced the joyous misery-stomp dance.
                You know the things we used to do,
                Little girl, we don't do no more.
        So what am I complaining about? The little girl,
she's out there in the deep woods packing cameras
overtime just to pay our bills. To pay for the juice
powering the stereo and also this lamp right here.
Powering this whole goddamn raucous party which I'm
savoring to be sure. Bite into this and grind away
until everything's how you want it to be, that's what.
        So another year's gone -- or added onto the pile.
And lots else added on with it. And I'm all grizzled
and sore-lipped (stupidly tried to tear off a flap of
chap, I guess I can call it). -- Oh but you're right,
Mr. Bluesman groaning it out right now, it's a hard hard
feeling just as the jyzer was saying moments ago in
those very words, hard hard hard -- and now let's roll
on into this next one about the bus station, the high-
energy walking bass -- how can you help but cackle?
With delight! This is one helluva fine party and I'm
gonna stomp anyone who says no. (So speak, talent!)
        It's just the right time. She's driving home now
over those dark, twisted, forest-clamped roads.
                Bye-bye, baby.
                Bye-bye, baby.
                Baby baby, bye-bye.
        -- A successful flop this time! No pause at all
and up pops the one about the steady-rollin' man:
                Ooo, you hear me howlin', baby,
                Down on my bended knee.
The howler howlin' too. Howlin' Jyzeman Jeep.

[Jyze for Mom]

Jyzin' Howler G.   Scratch it out you gravelly-J-sticked
son of a C-town "mouthpiece" you.
     -- Here and there a dark night of the howler soul.
Let's fess up.   The shrieks.   The stabs.   And yet the
lawn's still passably a lawn and the dishes always get
scrubbed, the chapters always get scribbled.   (Over to
my right, perched on a wooden bar stool, a
posterboardful of jyze slogans meant to light the way
through the labyrinth.   Nothing looks too helpful right
now, though, I must say.   A lot seems a touch -- off.
Superfluous.   "Push it"?   Really now.   "Make it
strange"?   Or how about "Be fractious"?)
     Eight more days gone.   Where'd they go?   No use to
mull this one.   Any high point in there?   -- Don't get
around the forest much anymore, that's for sure.   One
major grocery run to the nearest supermarket to the
south (I'm trying to balance out all the years of going
mostly north).   A few minor runs to the bridge market.
A few others even more minor to our tiny town store and
of course always, daily, sometimes twice daily if the
first trip proves premature, to the post office.
     Aw, but..."I could not help but cry."   But...but...
the train that leaves the station.   The two lights on
behind.   Sears.   Scalds.   Rips you apart.
     Tossing around on that couch up there.   Its hard
wooden frame.   How stuffy the air gets in that room.
The nasty nightmares jolting me awake in a heavy sweat.
     Is the lady jerking me around?   No doubt.   But to
what extent?   And to this I say: don't wanna know.
Because if I find out something really bad I'll have to
do something I don't wanna do.   Something even hard-
hard-harder to do than what I've been doing.
     (She just slipped in.   "I got a wonderful feeling,
people / my baby just came back home."   South Side
C-town piano man observed thusly right at the instant I
heard her.   Serendipity!   "You know I love my woman /
Don't want to see her go."   But why slipping in?   "I got
a wonderful feeling, people / my baby gonna treat me
right."   Sounds good, sounds very good -- but I don't
think so.   Hey Mel Bear, gonna come join the party?

-- Not too likely, no. And certainly not yet. A faint
faint, I mean really faint chance she's setting up the
cake, the candles, readying the funny hats and
noisemakers -- puffing up the balloon people -- haw!)
        -- But I can keep on partying anyway. Rip this
chip off my shoulder and hurl it like a discus into the
woods. Crawl out through the hole torn in my own skin.
Hose down my pink and wriggly new self. Give the hollow
old self a tap, see it collapse in a powdery puff.
Squeeze out a swaggery new-man sneer. Rattle these new-
man bones. Jyzify this new-man soul.
                Well I feel so good -- gonna boogie!
                Gonna boogie till the break of day!
        -- Or then again, all parties must come to an end.
For one thing, you get hongry (at a party like this one
with no spread at all). You get tired. You lose that
maniacal spirit. You see the last cut on the last album
in the last stack is about to spiral to an end. You say
to yourself it's time to burst this little bubble and
head yourself on out there. (But -- out there where?)
                *   *
        -- Thought I'd stroll up the hill and try a hit of
morning jyze. See if I could chase away this ugly Jyze
& Blues Birthday Party hangover. Do it at the shed just
as I did last year on birthday morning. (Because fine
memories do linger of sprawling on the shed threshold
that morning -- of a plunge into serious thought which
turned out to be -- a bizarre pleasure! -- And this
was, and is, a morning every bit as naturally gorgeous
as that one was. And will forever be, if I can make it
so, in the annals of the Jyze Age if nowhere else, or
anyway until the acid-free paper crumbles to dust and
the storage diskettes degrade beyond retrieval.)
        But before returning to the threshold I thought I'd
better get the blood moving a bit. (It's not just a
birthday party hangover -- it's a study couch toss-and-
turn hangover as well. That's where it got really
ugly.) So, go out there and whack. And where whacking
was most needed was the footpath up to the barn. This
passes through a field of very high (six to eight feet

in places) and tough weeds which grow that way (but not
necessarily greener) because they're above or nearly
above the septic tank. The path hadn't been whacked in
at least a month. In essence it needed to be reblazed.
And so I attacked it. Howling like a true zen howler.

     And when I got all the way up to the barn door,
which is on the north side of the structure (rather than
facing the house, which is to the west), I noticed "the
other shed." This is an attached open-sider with a
corrugated plexiglass roof (covered with fallen leaves
and branches) which runs the entire length of the back
-- east -- side of the barn. And sitting under the near
end of this other shed, still wearing its battered blue-
and-white-checked vinyl tablecloth (attached with
staples on the sides), was my old picnic table. The one
Mel Bear gave me as a birthday present six years ago.
-- Or no, make that seven years ago, because it was in
place when Mother and Barb came up for their visit that
fall. For which occasion we bought the tablecloth.

     It beckoned me. Those more loving, more innocent
times. So, yes, this would be the spot where I would
try to chase away the hangover. And never mind how
dirty it, the tabletop, was. I mean it was filthy; I
had to bulldoze it clean with a scrap of two-by-six
before even attempting to wipe it down with an old rag.
And then I noticed that both of the benches that came
with the table were missing. So for a substitute I
turned over one of the ancient half-stumps lying in a
row like barrels just under the edge of the overhang --
and exposed a massive infestation of termites. Had to
bulldoze the flat surface of the stump too. Off came a
layer about two inches thick of rotten wood and silently
shrieking termites (inside their science-fiction-like
white pods). Stood the refurbed stump up next to the
table. Yes, this would do just fine.

     So here I perch on the refurbed stump. Looking
pretty odd, no doubt, were anyone watching, like a
derelict banished to a tall dunce stool, because this
stump is almost as high as the surface of the table.
I'm hunched way over with elbows resting on the

tabletop and knees almost pressing against my chest and
feet dangling several inches above the ground -- but
this is, again, just fine. As good as it gets. "Take
him out to the woodshed and larn him some jyze sense!"
     Birthday morning. Sun making for leafy shadow
patterns on the plexiglass above, two layers, one
shifting about and one not, because the tree limbs are
in motion with the breeze but the leaves and twigs atop
the roof itself just sit there, well sheltered from any
wind action. Scrabbly blue jays flash incandescently in
classic "jays-burst" fashion. Beyond the edge of the
shed on all three sides is a clearing twenty to thirty
feet deep which used to be part of the lawn but under
Lady U's mowing regime became high weeds, and under mine
is staying that way. Beyond the high weeds, forest.
Tall trees. Big Bushes. Blackberries. Shafts of sun.
All gently in motion, though to be sure going nowhere.
And in the middle of the former clearing a big old tree
stump stands with stolid dignity, half a dozen upright
sections of unsplit firewood logs gathered around its
base for seats. -- And a jay just materialized on the
nearest of these. Poof and there it quivers. Vivid
shimmering blue body, punky black spiked crown. Steller
feller, you're back! On the scene! You da jizz! -- At
any second this splendid feathery apparition might break
into "Happy Happy Birthday Baby," whistled version.
What you say, J-bird? (Nope. Because poof, it's gone.)
     Stretch, she saw a bear up here once, a real one.
Swears she did. And now another species of nasty old
grizzly is hanging out in the area, perched on a stump.
Red-eyed, no doubt. Ready to tear her apart limb from
limb, the D-woman, and chew the pieces to grossly
unspeakable hominid mush. (Well, she did remember to
say happy birthday. That was nice. But that was two
hours after she got home. And that was it. And that
will be it, one suspects. -- But no, I still won't tear
her to pieces. "Turn your head and spit me out" -- line
from a popular tune on her favorite station. One of her
current fave alt raves. -- But I'm saying to hell with
all that. Wrench things back to the long view. It was

a great run while it lasted, much of it: yes it was. So
be grateful for what you got. Me I mean, I should be
grateful, but of course same's true for her. She'll
realize it someday. Or if not, that'll mean she found
something better, so in that case what will she have to
complain about? Not a goddamn thing, that's right.)
     Blue and white checks. They bring it all back.
The city shed. The little house. The wild roses. The
tall pines. The squirrels. The bed up on the loft --
the beautiful hand-crafted loft! Which is now part of
my backwoods shed of dreams. Right down the hill.
Where in recent times I've been holing up for hours
every day.
     Wonders galore. "Sometimes I wonder." (Moans Mr.
South Side C-town piano man.) But -- sometimes wonders
do happen. Do materialize. For me, you, everybody.
You gotta remember this. -- Especially when the
remaining termites lurking in their invulnerable bunkers
down below the seemingly solid stump surface are sending
out patrols fixing to chew your ass out, literally. Or
could be. Telling you it's time to get up and moving,
you've worked off your ugly birthday-party hangover as
much as you ever will. Or anyway seems as likely as
anything else if not a whole lot more so.
                    *   *
     -- Tack on, Jyzeman, a last birthday riff.
Kwikjyze encore. At thirty minutes before midnight, the
end of the big day. A very fine and very productive day
if I do say so. And that just happens to be exactly
what I'm saying and mean to keep on saying.
     So it's another blues riff, a last spasm of party.
Because the lady did lay a gift on me after all, "a
little tiny one" (which is only as it should be
considering our straitened financial circumstances, as
we've in fact previously agreed). And what it is is a
tape featuring an excellent contemporary blues dude,
also a Centropolite though originally from nowhere else
but the bluesily autochthonous delta (and both sides of
the great river -- same great river that runs more or
less straight north all the way up to Mentoka and

235

vicinity). And on this tape the dude shouts like so:
          You're damn right I've got the blues
          From my head down to my shoes!
And why does he have those blues? No mystery there:
          Lord, have you ever been mistreated?
          Then you've got to know just what I'm
               talking about.
And exactly how mistreated?
          Lord, I worked five long years for
               one woman
          And she had the nerve to kick me out.
And I say: Only five? And this dude thinks he knows
the blues? (Oh but he does, he does.)
     -- Old Stretch, from here on out she'll be seeing
nothing but high spirits from me. No more mope, no more
grump, no more surly or scowly. Highest (heist) of the
high and that's it.
     -- Thinking what the heck, it might not be such a
disaster for me to go back on the courtship market. All
this whacking is turning me into quite the physical
specimen. Shoulders and arms like Tarzan of the Apes.
And not only that. Every time I'm sitting here in jyze
central and my brain seems to stop functioning I head
over to the utility room and start jumping around on the
nerf court. The hope being I can jolt a few ideas loose.
And my brain ceases functioning often enough these days
that I do a helluva lot of jumping. And so it is I'm
developing a ripped bottom half to match the Tarzan top.
     So keep that in mind, little Ms. Playaround. Ms.
Post-Post-Teen Angst. (Were any balloon people present
they'd start madly clapping now because I just flashed
the "applause" sign.) (Gobbled down close to half an
apple pie, Dutch-crumb style, my birthday "cake," ala
mode but lacking candles, picked out by me and paid for
by me during a solo journey to the bridge market.) -- As
bong bong bong, a most pathetic birthday passes into
history. Jyze history. And around here, for better or
worse, there is no other kind, at least that I know of.
Or want to know of.

[Jyze for Mom]

30

    Gonna lay this J-book to rest right here. Town
cemetery. I'm parked just outside the gate, beneath the
sign with its oddly showy and old-timey lettering
(almost as if it were a vaudeville marquee), and I'm
holding forth inside the car because it's wet out there.
Raining. As indeed I knew it would be, or strongly
suspected, since it was also raining at the house less
than a mile from here -- but I couldn't resist the easy
symbolism. If something's got to go, this is a damn
good place and time to dispatch it.
    Even brought along my old Bat Masterson rain hat so
I could take a maudlin graveyard walk in the drizzle.
(Is it rain or is it drizzle? Already this story is
going wobbly on me. But I'd say right now it's drizzle
with occasional showers -- and when the showers hit,
it's as if I'm sitting inside a tin drum. I guess this
is because slight gusts of wind accompany the rainfall
and these gusts dislodge much larger drops, along with
numerous needles and the occasional cone, from the big
old pine beneath which I'm parked.) -- And I wore my
high rubber barn boots as well. First I had to shake
the pellets and triangles of cat food out of them. And
the hat, it creaked when I pulled it on. It's been a
long time since I've gone for a walk in the rain (or any
other kind of weather) wearing this thing (now resting
all soggy-looking on the floor in front of the driver's
seat). (Bat Masterson up there a few lines, I know he
was legendary but was he fictive? If not, I need to
fess up that I've broken the jyze rules again.)
    Our funky little country graveyard. It's the

237

hillside variety, high enough up that it should command a good view of the town center down in the valley directly to the east and of the lagoon to the south of that, but you can't tell for sure if it does because lots of tall trees have grown up downslope and blocked most, and in some areas all, of the view. The graveyard itself is rectangular, about forty paces deep (I stepped it off) and about twice that long. It's surrounded by a white three-rail picket fence. Through scattered gaps between downhill treetops you can see the usual misty serrated green ridgelines off in the distance. You can also make out through the lower parts of those same trees a couple of nearby houses dug into the lower hillside. Farmhouses I guess you could call them since both have pastures nearby where animals are grazing -- horses, cows. But who knows whose pastures they are. The real farmhouses attached to them could be somewhere out of sight. The houses in view may just be commuter residences or country retreats -- like ours, say, which has served both of those functions over the years and come to think of it is still doing so right now, or would be if I were still commuting or if Lady U's twenty-mile round trip into the forest were considered a commute (and why shouldn't it be?).

    The cemetery appears to be old but it's not. As far as I can make out it's entirely a product of the twentieth century, with 1910 the earliest death date I could find. The elements, however, age things fast around here. A certain virulent local variety of moss especially likes to chew away at any arrogant human presumptions regarding permanence. Of the fifty or so grave markers in there I was able to read fewer than half. Only two graves show any signs of being maintained -- and the signs they show are plastic flowers which may have been in place for a decade or more. Ironically enough, in their plasticity that same arrogant human presumption noted above may prove itself justified. The elements may have met their match. (But not to worry: in the slightly longer run they'll wreak their revenge and then some. Which is to say: worry!)

Aside from the entrance sign, it's as unpretentious a graveyard as you'll ever see. Not a single fancy headstone. One small eroded stone spire about three feet tall from 1920, 1926, or 1928 (hard to read that last number). Everything else hugs the ground, and maybe a quarter of the markers are what I suppose must be "pauper" type -- a slim metal or plastic stake about a foot tall with a hand-printed label attached, encased in still more plastic. (Can paupers specify they'd rather just be incinerated? I mean of course they can, but will anyone pay attention if they do? In any event, I hereby so declare for myself, just in case.)

So what's dying here today? Or rather: what's being lowered into the earth? It's obvious. I won't even say it.

Body blows all week -- to the heart. Then last night the demise. Empty house at three a.m. Weird lightning flashes and booming thunder. Lots of sorrow. But I found a way out that worked for me. From here on jyze is all. Jyze from here to the grave.

Simple! Why didn't I think of this a long time ago? (As another mosquito slips in through the narrow cracked-open gap at the top of the passenger-door window, clambering over the rounded edge of the glass sort of burglar-like with long needle snoot and skinny legs and wings akimbo; I happened to be looking up when it did so. -- I'm sitting on the passenger side because the steering wheel would get in the way of the J-book. With the book itself I'm pressing down the annoying automatic shoulderbelt which does not want to stay put -- damn thing's still trying to strangle me.)

Quiet up here. As it should be! Like a graveyard! A few birds. Crows? Probably. If not ravens. Or buzzards. And every ten or fifteen minutes a car goes by on -- what's the name of this road? Doesn't matter and can't be noted anyway. But it was one of my favorites for bike riding because it's hilly yet not excessively so, little traveled, well maintained, twisty, scenic as it snakes along maybe as much as two hundred feet above the lagoon (farther south it boasts a

number of spiffy water-view homes). And by pedaling
east across the bridge spanning the entrance to the
lagoon and then heading north you can complete the loop
back to our town. Total distance is almost exactly five
miles.

And speaking of mortality: I never did hear from
old Mom for my birthday. Not a call, not a present, not
even a card. This is so unusual -- unprecedented -- I'm
sure something must be horribly wrong. Her memory
couldn't have deteriorated this much this fast. She did
mention the possibility of taking a jaunt with Jim Q. to
help him ready the winter house for sale. (Is that a
crazy idea or what? A sixteen-hundred-mile round trip
with Jim Q. at the wheel in that cramped "heart attack"
sports car of his!) Surely Barb would've called me if
something truly horrific had happened. -- Or would she?
Maybe not. One failed attempt at reaching me by phone
and she would probably feel she'd done her sisterly duty.

Well I don't know. And I've been too caught up in
these other death agonies; no spirit to look into what's
going on with Mom.

But I'll be all right now -- I want to say. And is
this true? Will I be able to handle the emotional
storms sure to be rolling in over the weeks and months
ahead? But how the hell would I know? I just know this
one death is now official and I'll grapple as best I can
with what's yet to come. And with the post-death
adjustments and revisions as those become necessary.

This, by the way, is the morning of Labor Day. A
very slight amount of autumnal yellow has infiltrated
the ambient green. Here and there a brown leaf is
caught in the weeds. Up this high the August cold spell
has had a much less obvious effect than it's had in our
yard. A steeper hillside, better drainage, different
soil, possibly a whole different contingent of plants in
a whole different ecological niche -- who knows why.

(A car passing, I glance up and see an elderly lady
in the passenger seat peering at me with slightly
swiveling head and brief warm sympathy, I suppose
believing I must be a devoted son come to pay his

respects at his parents' graves. -- And I am that, a
devoted son! In the Mentoka zone two years ago I even
hiked down the Buena Vista hillside to the grove where
we scattered Dad's ashes and I meditated there for an
hour or more -- some forty or fifty feet beneath great-
grandpa Bendyk's monument dedicated to the Hermit of
Twist Ridge. And I'll note this: that book-besotted
recluse of a century and a quarter back is the person I
may come closest to emulating in the years ahead.
Though not to the point, I hope, of living in a cave as
he did. Not to mention dying at an age somewhat younger
-- I think -- than I am now.)

So gory. So ghoulish. And me with a whole lotta
living still to do. But in jyze, nowhere else. Or at
least not for a good long time. And never again with
the particular companion of the era now passing. Here
lies the body. Died at age seventeen, seven weeks
short of eighteen. -- But by and large had a good run,
most definitely: I'll second myself on that. -- But
I've come to bury this love, not to praise it. Right.
Later for the praise too. Or at least so I hope.

-- In the meantime. Well, let it be admitted
"Ghosts" has suffered a setback. I'm calling it a
midcourse correction but in point of fact I'll be
starting over yet again, one more time just once yes.
A-one and a-two and...but seriously, folks, I know what
I'm doing here. I like what's been going down with the
all-new fictojyze, the turbocharged JIFT/JIRT. I like
it enough that I'm aiming to expand it, that's all. Now
I see how I can fit in most of the stuff I was unclear
about before and so decided to leave out. In a week
I'll be ready for another sustained assault. It'll take
that long (but not one minute longer!) to distribute my
massive collection of apropos "running notes."

A single spot of color visible out there -- it's
one of those plastic bouquets. Fire-engine red. All
else, except for the chalky white of the picket fence,
is blurry greens of various shades along with scattered
browns and tannish-yellows. "Earth tones." Mr. Haiku
Master (whose pen name means Mr. Banana Plant), what

would you make of this scene? Sabi and wabi enough for
you?

(Reminding myself this vehicle in which I sit is
not mine. I've paid off about half of it. Maybe
they'll reimburse me for that, the U's, although I doubt
it. In any event the vehicle will revert to them. I
have nothing. Books and papers, and I'll probably have
to give away most of the books. Maybe a few I can sell,
though I'm sure not for much. And: no place to go. No
one to take me in even temporarily, except maybe Mom --
and in the immortal words of yet another modern-day
blues hero, "she may be jivin' too." No job either.
All I've really got is this right here. Jyze! And I'm
jyzin' now. This is the real thing. It's happening for
sure. -- As my feet overheat in the barn boots and my
toes start to go squishy. My elbow aches, and it's my
jyzin' elbow too. And my stomach growls.)

Figuratively, Mr. Banana Plant, I'm already sucking
on ice. -- But that itself is a recondite reference in
a truly haiku-like spirit -- and without bitterness!
-- For in his famous "sucking on ice" poem to which I'm
alluding Mr. B.P. was accused of unseemly bitterness by
several other haiku greats of the era.

I'd be happy to move into the shed. It would serve
as a fine "thatch-roofed hut" for makeshift internal
exile. I'd sleep on a mat on the floor and use the
woods and the creek for amenities. For the next week or
so I might even be able to survive by sucking on
blackberries. This is the season for it -- and I've
been having at them too, more so than ever before.

Everything, not just me, sucks these days. I
should note this. In the past week I've had a couple of
run-ins with Lady U over her sudden extensive
teenagerlike overuse of the S-word. Not to be coy about
it, but regardless I refuse to elaborate further on the
matter. Or on anything else related to it, or to her.
Here vagueness is once again it. And in truth I don't
know a whole lot myself and would like, as mentioned a
few times before, to know even less.

-- It's odd I'm the only one to have shown up today

to honor the dead. But then it's not Memorial Day,
even though for some reason I keep thinking it is.
Memorial Day, that's when I was blithely holding
forth over at the town park, at that point having not
the slightest inkling things might be turning out
this way by summer's end -- the next seasonal turning
point. I was hoping, though, I remember, to be able
to round out this volume at the end of summer with a
matching entry from the city bar with all the art.
"In the end is the beginning." No big loss, I guess,
that this aspiration should go unrealized.

And I never was able to squeeze in a jyze session
"down by the old mill stream." (Or trout stream, or
salmon creek.) Maybe I can do it next volume if I'm
lucky and if the spirit moves me -- which itself would
be a form of luck, of course.

Pain. Oh I just know I'll be blasted with lots of
pain. Pain and sorrow. It's gonna hurt so bad. "It's
nine below zero," cries still yet another exemplary
blues hero, "and mama, you kicked me out!" Could happen
to me too. In a way I'm flying through the air already,
right now, booted out the door by the U landlords'
resident agent and self-appointed enforcer.

How about pride? Got any left? Well sure I do,
and it's the best kind. Jyze pride. Yes, that's
exactly right.

Forget Lady U. Didn't I say? Instead -- stretch.
(Not that Stretch!) -- Roll a shoulder. It cracks.
Press feet against the mat. They squish. Roll eyes in
their sockets. They creak. Swallow. There's a catch
in my throat. (Is this another way, a new way, I'm
dying, maybe related to that sore spot I felt back there
not so long ago?) -- And if that skeeter's still in the
car (not that other Skeeter!), and if it comes after me,
I'll just have to give it a good swack. Simple. No
more of those complicated ear traps of earlier times.
Hard-guy solutions. BIFF! BAM!

Or more likely I'm swacking myself. -- Whatever
gets you through the night. And the day too. I may no
longer be a nightscoper, but for me the day is still

the night. And yet the night is also still the night.
     When I leave this boneyard I'll have to start up
the windshield wipers even if the rain's stopped -- to
sweep aside the thick layer of newly fallen pine needles.
"Local unemployed man's body found in car buried beneath
mound of pine needles outside cemetery gate." -- And in
this way too the forces of impermanence can prevail over
the immutable red plastic and all other forms of human
hubris (however temporarily convenient its workings and
products may be in some eyes -- or why not go for
accuracy here: in almost all eyes and at just about all
times at least in recent centuries but not for a whole
lot longer as we dig dig dig dig dig our own graves).
     Three, six, nine...some twenty-two pine trees
standing in a neat row in front of the funky white
picket fence. Hard to tell how many for sure because as
the perspective lengthens, some trunks may be hidden
behind others. Planting pines in our village, though,
is like hauling coal to you-know-where (and a town by
that name lies within easy coal-toting distance a few
dozen miles to the east and, like the original, is
itself the site of coal mines, convenient for any locals
worried about keeping warm during the coming super-
carbonized end-time). -- But you wonder who could've
cared this much. Why this cemetery? What's the story
here? -- As motion flashes and a big brown dog lopes
smearily across my upper peripheral vision just inside
the fence. How many heads on that dog, may I ask?
Three by any chance? And how'd he/she get in there
anyway? And how can we keep him/her from getting out?
     So there's the best answer I can come up with for
the moment -- and probably for all moments. That's it.
     The burial and then a jyze wake, now ending. All
the participants involved will sniff away their tears,
crocodilian or not, and get on with the disposal of the
remains, the shoveling of the dirt. (Does the
jyzemaster mean these words in the scandalous "dish"
sense? Certainly not.)

BOOK III

[Jyze to the End of the Night]

-------- -

31

-------- ·

It's a struggle this time. Got to drag myself
squirming and grumping onto the page. Never wanted jyze
to be like this -- never thought it would be -- but then
of course the notion that it could always be otherwise
was and is absurd. Especially given the disciplinary
aspect of every so many days the jyzer jyzes (still
every eight and meaning to remain so), sometimes you're
bound to catch yourself in an unpropitious mood.
Did I say -- what? Surly? Sour? Morbid?
Hopeless? Disgusted? Downhearted?
Oh well. "Here I sit." And even though the day's
not bad for it, and another like it may not come around
anytime soon, this is not the bridge spit. Nor is it
the bank of the old mill stream. It was all I could do
to push myself half a dozen steps outside the door of J.
central. To the old Grover's Corners "Town Manager"
bench. The one with the two black plastic dishes nailed
to it at the far ends to minimize conflict at feeding
time for the outdoor cats, back when we had only two.
Peering at the front lawn. Straight ahead is the
big apple tree and it's in full heavily laden red-
spotted sunlit early-autumn glory. Magnificently
measled, I'll say. Its thick trunk tilts rightward
maybe fifteen degrees and splits into a near-perfect Y
about eight feet up -- could make a fearsome slingshot
if a Goliath happened along. No flashes of blue
lighting up the foliage thus far but I expect them (the
jizzy jyzey jays) at any moment.
Off burned the fog. Much earlier than yesterday.
Along about midmorning it finished evanescing. That

puts us now at roughly thirty minutes past midmorning.
Birds tweet, trill, chirp, squawk, whistle, warble,
mostly off in the main body of wetland woods to the
right of the big apple tree (and halfway between the big
apple tree and the woods stands the much smaller apple
tree, even more heavily laden, with half a dozen ribbons
of bird-chaser tinsel dangling from its limbs and
twisting in the breeze -- the same sparkly stuff I
mentioned a few entries back -- and for some strange
reason I just can't stop being surprised it's still
hanging around).

"Autumn in the air." The breeze picks up a bit and
scarves of yellow leaves detached from on high go
sailing across the road down below to the west and a
couple of apples go kerplunk onto hard dry grassy ground.
Or I presume apples. What else is lurking up in that
tree to take such a tumble? (Almost a dawn-of-science
kind of question -- or Edenic even.)

Caw. Very loud and close. Now three more caws.
From up on the power line paralleling the driveway.
Right at the center of the sag. And here comes Goat
wagging his ridiculous little tail -- he's patrolling
just inside the fence right under that same sagging
center. He contorts himself into some godawful postures
to poke his snout through holes at the bottom of the
fence so he can nibble at the luscious green grass which
tantalizes him out there (it being "always already," as
certain theoreticians might say, greener on that side).

Rustle of leaves. Actually most of the leaves
around here are still green themselves. But sometimes
when a dead one works loose you can hear it tumble all
the way down through the canopy interior, limb by limb,
branch by branch, almost like a body falling down a
stairwell, sometimes pausing at the landings -- or if
not tumble all the way down, tumble as far down as it
can get. Leaf corpses sprawl on landings all over the
place up there waiting for the wind to give them another
kick.

When two or three of these internal leaf-falls
occur simultaneously the forest almost seems to be

rattling. More than that and it's applauding. Still
more and it's on its feet roaring.

-- But what is this, the second coming (as farce)
of Mentoka Pete? The jyze dude as (fictive) ecofreak?
-- Well, but they say this is what happens when you turn
fossil: you withdraw to your hermit's hut and you
observe nature and you jyze about it. And I'll say
right now it's not a bad way to go, hut or no hut. "In
the autumn of his years." (But hang on. Just scratch
all this. I'm not ready to wax autumnal.)

So then what's new and wonderful? Hoo hoo. Gross
me out! (At least I'm starting to wake up a little.)
-- Not a good goddamn thing, that's what. (But in
addition to the bridge spit and the mill stream I did
consider the root-beer joint ten miles to the south as a
spot to make this week's jyze stand. This during
yesterday's special mission to pick up D's disposable
contact lenses and lens solution on deep sale at the
discount mart down that way -- all in an effort to be
doing my fair share around here -- and I even took this
new green J-book along with me. With such high hopes!
The blank slate! Alas, just like today, I didn't have
it in me. But then yesterday the procrastinatory excuse
was still available: knowing this morning would count as
part of the eighth day according to the NUT calendar,
which I do still resort to in emergencies. This
morning, by the same calendar, no such excuses remain.)

I can report the horrifying news that I seem to
have hit another snag in the writing of "Ghosts," and
this time a truly major one. In that realm the supply
of procrastinatory excuses has suddenly become boundless.

-- I remind myself it's now almost September 15th,
the date reporter Naomi thought she would return to work.
I've heard nothing from her.

My feelings on restarting the scoping are strongly
mixed. I also have considerable doubt that the firm
will permit me to do so. And if they don't, who would?
But the main point here is if I do take it up again I'll
be forced to make some big changes in my approach to
working on "Ghosts." But then again I don't think those

changes would be fatal. I'd lose JIFTing time at home
but I'd gain revision time through access to the office
computers. And I'd gain income. And I'd gain freedom
of movement. Should I need to depart permanently from U
Acres, for example, as I expect I soon will, I could do
so. Though to be able to finance that, Jyzer Ink would
need to find more clients than just Naomi.

As for the collapse of the big love, no changes to
report. Not a damn thing. This may or may not mean the
odds that we'll be able to continue dragging on as we've
been doing are improving. But I'm still determined to
keep trying to do just that -- i.e., keep dragging on --
as long as possible. Not that I'm making any attempt to
persuade the lady to change her mind (or force her,
entice her, trick her into doing so -- anything along
those lines). I'm fully resigned to our probable sorry
fate. Which is to say, I refuse to suffer once again
the indignity of having my reconciliation efforts
scorned and rejected. I'm not going through that post-
Marco ordeal again. Any impetus for reconciliation will
have to come from her. Period. And at this late stage
the impetus required would be massive.

(Not that I think she'll come up with any impetus
at all. I don't. As far as I can see she's finished
with me. Just like that -- and never mind the causes
of all the years of internal rot presumably leading up
to the collapse. As I say, much better to believe we've
"grown apart." I don't have enough energy left to me
in this life to squander one joule of it on anguish over
trying to figure out the real causes. Let them be.
Maybe I'll look at them again if a time ever comes when
I want to try to redeem this mess by turning it into,
say, a story about itself. Beyond this one, that is.)

So here I sit, yeah. Old jeans, heavy blue long-
sleeve placket-neck riverman's henley (or whatever kind
of shirt it is -- the kind I wear almost always), and
dark blue rubber-soled slip-ons, the cheapo type that's
surprisingly durable for indoor use (and this is true
even if you jump around in them an hour every day, as I
usually do for exercise -- up from thirty minutes daily

in the pre-high-reclusion era). Feet crossed and
resting on the concrete walkway that borders the entire
west side of the house. Right in front of my toes
squats a portable half-stump just large enough to make
an alternative resting spot for my feet when they tire
of the concrete. To its left sits an oak whiskey half-
barrel of admirable vintage bearing a bumper crop of --
not marigolds. What the hell are they? Amazing I can't
recall the name. -- Except it isn't; as noted before,
I've never done well with flower names. Anyway, they're
thrusting out an encouraging profusion of pinkish to
rosy-hued late blooms. -- But encouraging with regard
to just what, they give no hint and I have no big ideas.

     As up putts the mail jeep. White. Clink of Ben
and Beryl's box closing eighty or ninety feet down at
the end of the driveway (out of sight), followed by the
clink of ours closing. -- And there goes the jeep
already zipping along in the opposite direction after
making its other deliveries (two) and turning around at
the end of the street. (We live on a dead end. A sign
even says so. This is a fact which I've fought off the
urge to make hokily portentous use of -- until now.)

     And since Beryl will soon be ambling out to pick up
her mail and since I don't want to be getting into any
neighborly scuttlebutting at this particular time, and
especially not about the little tiff she may've heard D
and I are engaged in, I'll close this down temporarily.

*   *

     Came whacking my way up to the shed, lopping heads
off stray yellow-flag-waving dandelions. "Me! Do me!
Take me out!" -- Doing them left-handed still, because
my right elbow remains "out of whack." The thought even
occurred: what if the damn thing needs an operation?
Isn't that sometimes the case for so-called tennis
elbow? And me with no health insurance and insufficient
funds to buy even a box of bandaids. And what if it
gets so bad I can't push a J-stick?

     No sign of that yet. I can push this stick just
fine. What it leaves as its trail, that's something
else again. But then it always is, bad elbow or good or

251

anywhere in between. Especially on a day like today.

No matter. Push on regardless. Knowing even on a bad day you're apt to surprise yourself with something good once in a while.

This is going down at my inner-sanctum writing desk. Despite the presence of seven handmade windows, the trees overhanging the shed's back side make it a little dark in here. Papa U has said on the phone we should call in an electrician to do whatever's necessary to restore the power, but I don't want to run up more bills for Papa U when we can't even keep up our payments (to him!) on the car loan. And he's also paying the taxes on the place. Yet he fears the outage could lead to an injury or fire, and though the odds of its doing so are slim, it still might happen. What to do? But if it turns out we don't summon an electrician, I figure this could be my last chance to have at it here jyzewise until next spring -- or ever.

So just do it. Sit right down and jyze myself a J-book. (And make believe it came from -- who? Or what?)

Because soon it'll be too cold with no power up here. And even if I break out the kerosene heater again (as in the pre-electrical era) this inner zone will be a whole lot darker most hours of the day and most days of the week, depending on weather and what time I get here.

So fetch the key from its hiding place up in the eaves and unlock the door. Raise a couple of the plexiglass windowpanes and slide blocks of wood under a corner of each to hold them up. With forearm clear adequate space on desktop. And go to it, you jyzeslinging devil you.

(Yes I do love this shed. That doesn't change at all, other than deepen with time. And become more energized from the panic of knowing I'll soon be losing it. Therefore I must cultivate a Buddhist detachment toward it -- and maybe that's part of the reason why these past few weeks I've been finding the writings of Mr. Banana Plant more moving than ever. -- But a modern Buddhist travel book, raved about by the critics a few years back, no matter how hard I tried to detach myself

I couldn't get jiggy with that. Finally tossed it
rudely aside. Make space for the new! In this case the
new being quite old: a Eurusan explorer's travel
journal. A whole different kind of guy, no doubt about
it. The first Eurusan to check out the Mentoka Valley
and the namer of Parapet Bluff, and that was long before
he came upon his famous soon-eponymous peak a thousand
miles to the west. And if he bombs too I've got another
Eurusan Mentoka explorer of the same era in the wings.)

A fine-filament net in which green starfish flop --
the bigleaf maple branch thrashing outside my window.
(Dedicated to the memory of Mr. Banana Plant, those last
two phrases, despite their eight extra syllables.)

-- So I drove off to the post office to pick up the
mail. Admired the long row of head-high, almost
incandescently bright flowers lining Captain Brick's
driveway. What are they, I wondered. And still do.
(Lady U doesn't know either. But she told me the
flowers brimming out of that vintage whiskey half-barrel
by our front sidewalk are some sort of wild geranium.
This strikes me as being wrong. I had even thought of
the name geranium on my own and summarily dismissed it.
If there's one flower I know, it's the geranium. Just
on principle I insist I could recognize it even in its
most obscure and wildest and jizziest form.)

Three men perched on the roof of "the hippie house"
near the post office, hammering, lining up shingles,
scrambling about. "Men patching steep roof sprinkled
with slippery brown leaves -- my life doesn't seem so
hard." (The haiku approach to things is sometimes tough
to resist.) Postal window closed because it's noon
hour. Bend to unlock Box 289. -- No doubt because the
box is just one tier above floor level we find a lot of
misdirected mail in there, stuff that should be going to
the boxes immediately above or below or to either side
of ours -- for what postal worker would want to bend way
down to check those three long rows for distributional
accuracy day after day, for weeks, months, years?

A good haul today. A mag, a review, a weekly La
Chevalle County newspaper. Lots of junk too, but this

time for a change each piece with a tiny cachet of its
own (the very first of Lady U's many colleges extending
its annual homecoming invitation -- and I'll just say
it's a lot less likely than usual that we'll be going
(and we never have attended a reunion of any kind --
hers or mine -- or even seriously considered doing so)).

Then on the way home stop at the house mailbox for
the second haul, almost always a larger one because this
is where all the Mentoka-zone dailies arrive. -- But
within a week such will cease to be the case because I'm
letting my subscription to the last of the dailies, from
Wachute, expire as of September 13th, which is, by
Gregorian reckoning, today. For almost exactly five
years I've been reading this paper faithfully (and for
four of those years a second daily from Menard, seventy-
five miles farther north, and for one of those years a
third daily from a city 150 miles to the southeast --
Lahontan, burg of my birth) (as the first, Wachute, was
the burg of my father's birth and the second, Menard,
the burg of his father's birth, or close to it).

Open the rubber-banded home mailbox haul and a
front-page banner hits the spot. "JACKSON COUNTY COMES
ALIVE," it proclaims. It doesn't know this but it's
talking about what Carver County's doing in the first
chapter of "Jyzer." Or anyway I take the coincidence as
a good omen. I might even clip the page and tape it on
the wall above my JIFT setup down in J. central.

Then there's this. Mother's failure to write or
call on my birthday was simply a matter of slipping
memory and mind-dulling anti-pain medication. She was
shocked by the lapse. I was too, although in retrospect
I realize I shouldn't've been. "Me of all people!" she
cried -- almost in both senses -- on the phone. Chemo,
stress, all the other meds she's taking, and these on
top of advancing age -- it's little short of wondrous
she does as well as she does (and continues to do). A
warm, sad, even sometimes happy talk, and we both were
all too aware, and quite open about it, that it may turn
out to be, and probably will, our last such birthday
conversation, even if a bit delayed. A cascade of

birthday memories. I ought to be writing these things
down -- and am, a few, in quick notes, but I just don't
have time to do more. Most of this stuff -- even the
very best -- you've got to let go. What else is dying
about? Why else does it hurt so much? (As rhetorical
questions those are both real doozers, eh wot?)
        -- And so it goes, another chunk of jyze jyzed and
another new J-book opened, that is, inaugurated, in the
expectation of much more and many more to come. But
sameness with a difference! As meanwhile down in the
house my sweet honey-dripper continues to buzz away from
me at warp speed. For I have sinned! For I have ceased
to provide! For I have moved on to wrestle with my
destiny! -- And as a venerable jazz singer growls on
her new CD (she one of my "hottest new group" beloved
for so many years, she so fine and so twisted): "To hell
with love." -- But does she believe that? Or mean it?
I say no. And I say I don't either. How obvious could
even something so obvious be? It's obvious! But
regardless I can't be fooling around anymore. "Got work
to do." "That's what I'm here for, that's what I'm here
for, that's what my livin' all means." But then again:
"What is this pause in between?"
        Which is the last word or bunch of words. Until
next time. Until the jyze once more, like those good
Mentoka cows, comes galumphing ho-ho-ho -- sez you you
jyze ho you -- galumphing ho-ho-ho-home, that's right.

32

        For the first time ever (yes, another first) it's
standing indoor jyze. And kitchen jyze. With not just
the kitchen sink thrown in but also the dish drainer

next to it and the microwave next to the dish drainer --
the massive brown first-generation microwave atop which,
laid out flat, rests this J-book. Along with a bottle
of ink and a stack of whole-wheat crackers. Down the
hatch with all this!

Jyze in a high lather. The true stuff about to
flow I do believe and hereby predict. After all, like
firecrackers they've been going off, the epiphanies, not
just all night but all week. So toss some in here!
Change targets for an hour or two -- keep in jyze trim.
Because soon I'll be back churning out the JIFT and now
more than ever I'm convinced I have one heckuva fine
tale to tell. Or fine fiction to fictojyze. The otter
muse has got me by the cojones now and won't let go.
Not until the last drop of "Ghosts" has been drained
out. Milked out. Inked out. (Words fail me! Yee-ha!)

Leaning in against the front of the microwave. The
overhead light above and behind my right shoulder makes
for an awkward trembling hand shadow that lurches along
the page -- resembles a gerbil on the move, nervously
chewing. Or a squirrel minus the big bushy tail. Each
word a nut, an endless supply, nut after nut after nut.

Of course other than in the JIFT arena my life is
an across-the-board bummer, more miserable than ever.
Some of the time I feel it and most of the time I don't
-- because most of the time I'm in the JIFT arena.

Tonight, for example. Chances are good the
aforementioned chief caretaker and landlords' agent/
enforcer for U Acres is out messing around on me again.
I mean right this minute. She came up with some highly
dubious cock-and-bull story about starting work three
hours late and finishing up the same -- i.e., two-thirty
a.m. -- because of a rush job that must go out tomorrow.
More likely she's gone to the county fair to see a star-
studded lineup of so-called New Music bands with Dean,
the camera factory co-owner who I'm now assuming is her
current heartthrob. However, I could be wrong. It
could be someone else. It could be almost anyone,
except, to be sure, me. Still, I'm putting up no fight
and I'm trying to show not the slightest concern (and

mostly succeeding, I think). If this is how she wants
our final chapter to read, fine. Or if she doesn't want
it but just can't help herself, that's fine too.

It does improve my spirits to be reading a
biography about the "miracle years" of one of the great
nineteenth-century Russian fictionists. And were those
years ever just that for him and so for everyone!
Especially when you consider the horrors of his personal
life at the time. If he could produce two of the
towering classics of world lit and several other lesser
but still undeniably great works while enduring such
extreme turmoil, his pale, pale shadow of an epigone can
surely squeeze out "Mentoka Ghosts" while experiencing a
few puny torments. -- And I'm fiercely focused now and
feel things in that realm could not be going better. So
to hell with everything else.

Once more with feeling: TO HELL WITH EVERYTHING
ELSE.

Now, as for the other parts of EVERYTHING ELSE,
I'll just say I'm cooking, I'm sweeping, I'm laundering,
I'm bed-making, I'm dish-washing, I'm plant-watering,
I'm grass-whacking -- I'm doing whatever's required and
insofar as possible I'm doing it cheerfully and without
complaint. Meanwhile the lady is, at least as it seems
to me, griping, moping, snapping, festering, blaming,
begrudging, self-pitying. Even so, the only time, by
and large, I get my back up is when she starts issuing
orders implying I've been demoted to flunky status. A
couple of brief spats over this. Otherwise little but
purely perfunctory passing contact.

-- And with stakes and two-by-fours I buttress the
rotting grape arbor, up behind the shed. The grapes in
their bulging hive-shaped bunches are too heavy for the
arbor (they're an untasty wine-making variety) and the
deer worsen matters by rising on their hind legs and
propping their forelegs against the spindly midlevel
crossbars to get at the higher bunches. (I've seen this
happen from about ten feet away through the shed's east
window. Could make out thistles caught in the deer's
scraggly underbelly fur.) (Each morning I go up to the

shed for an hour or so, weather permitting -- as it's
been doing all week, with the continuing spell of foggy
mornings giving way to sunny middays and afternoons --
and I work some on getting my cache of personal papers
(future "nachlass") ready for the day when evacuation,
possibly of a very speedy kind, becomes necessary.

Jazz playing. Stove light on. Sink light on.
Floor lamp on at the parlor end of this long triple-
purpose room. Let's throw another party! sez I. -- And
as I swing the J-book to the right side of the microwave
top suddenly the J-stick-and-hand shadows become highly
complex. Well lookie there! Javanese almost!
(Thinking it was famously Mr. Androgynous Macho Literary
Papa himself who liked to write standing up but was
there anyone else? No doubt there was. The forever-
homesick giant out of the USAn southland maybe?)

Everything sparkling in here. Looks better than
it's ever looked before. I take a gory pleasure in
showing up poor Lady U, who's surely one of the worst
ever at housekeeping. This deficiency never bothered
me, though, until suddenly now she's demanding that I be
much better at it than she ever was. Oh, okay. You
want immaculate? So take this! And thanks, Lady U, for
understanding how badly I need all the free time I can
muster now to chip away at my masterpiece. But never
mind. It's famously good zen fodder, housework. And as
noted a few times before (I'm pretty sure), I like to
take brief fast-moving breaks. Sitting for long
stretches does not sit well, so to say, with me. I like
to leave the floor smoking with that broom. (Like the
premier USAn ecoscribbler of our era in his published
protojyze likes to get out there with the ax and lay
into the firewood logs until they're reduced beyond mere
kindling into prematurely smoking matchsticks.)

(Mother not feeling so good after this round of
chemo. The point at which her tolerance for it runs out
may be nearing. At least the "winter house" is sold.)

-- Twist back to the other side of the microwave
and now drawing my eye to the left is the shaded window
looking out on the carport. D's old yellow car, the one

she was driving the night we met, occupies the far spot,
its tires almost flat; it's unlicensed and hasn't even
been started in months. The near stall, the much newer
gray wagon's stall, is empty. It's now one-twenty a.m.
But I refuse to start counting the minutes. The
countdown on this relationship is already complete.
(And she doesn't even care! That's what really burns me
up. Right now the only thing I don't quite understand
is why she's not telling me to vamoose immediately. I
can't believe it's guilt. Yet perhaps it is. Still I
don't doubt the eviction notice could come at any moment.
And if it did I'd be in very bad shape, just as was the
case last week and the week before and so on and so on.
No place to go, no money, no nothin'. But rather than
refuse to leave I suppose I could swallow my pride and
ask my poor dying mother to lend me a few bucks. What
other option would I have?)
     -- Reporter Naomi still hasn't tried to reach me,
or at least not so far as I know. Starting now the odds
that Jyzer Ink will have her as a client for part-time
scoping work shrink a little with each passing day of
silence. But I won't be the one to break the silence.
If she doesn't want me back badly enough to come after
me I'd rather look toward other options should I be
forced into taking a job. (I say "options" mostly from
habit. My only real option is pounding the pavement.)
     Today is the 20th. That's notable because as of
tomorrow my remaining ferry coupons become worthless.
And I still haven't returned to the city to check out
the new settings for "Ghosts." In part this reluctance
to go over there right now stems from absorption in
"Jyzer" and "Dreams" planning, in part from lack of
money, in part from a growing sense I won't be losing
much, if anything, if I simply make up the settings --
invent my own fictive hood, that is, and not worry too
much about how representative and up-to-date it is. In
"Ghosts" I think I could get away with this because most
of the focus is directed either inward to Jyzer G or
tightly outward to Ciara, the Lady C character.
Probably the newspapers I'm laying in as source material

for the projected jyzedays of the novel will be
sufficient to provide a few authenticating touches.

Ach, or agh, I say this is enough for now. Maybe
more in the morning. I want to get back to "Dreams."
I'm halfway through the distribution of the running
notes -- some thirteen hundred of them still to grapple
with. Again and again I'm flabbergasted by the stuff I
was scribbling in that binder as long ago as three,
four, even five years. It almost makes a semifictional
work all by itself. And a lengthy one too. How many
words there, I wonder. Couple hundred thousand at
least. And they're concise. Packed with life. Simply
great stuff if I do say so. Howlingly funny at times.

I've flipped out -- no doubt. It's the way to be
right now.

*   *

Parked between a wheelbarrow and a lawn mower.
Seated in the "Mowjo Queen" director's chair. Beneath
the deck overhang in what we call the corral. Just back
from the late-morning dandelion patrol. And with
blackberry-stained fingers evoking the peak leaky days
of J-stick No. 3.

At the top (almost) I'll note the shifty-eyed
little cheatin' former mush-object finally did make it
home last night. At quarter to three. (Early
rock'n'rollers, take note.) And I was cool. No
questions. Did cast a skeptical eye at the unusually
heavy makeup she was wearing -- and I mean unusually
heavy even for this period in which it's heavy every
day. And this after she wore none for years, not to
mention her proud political reasons -- which I happen to
share -- for such abstention.

A thought struck me. The romantic interest,
whoever it may be, is what keeps her excited about going
to work. Without it she might've quit or been laid off
by now. So one could say it's what's fueling one's own
free time for JIFT. (Might as well be mercenary about
it. Mercenary is the order of the day.)

-- Today it's fine again. Not even any fog to burn
off -- not a single stray wisp. And I like sitting here

amid the junk and weeds and garden implements. The
rusty blue wheelbarrow, the classic wide-spoked, metal-
wheeled type found in Old McDonald's garden shed and
also in a certain midcentury poem celebrated for showing
that "so much depends on" just such items (though of
course that barrow's red -- and we lack the white
chickens to make our blue specimen seem to jump out at
you -- though Captain Brick three houses down has some).
     Rakes, hoes, a bona-fide pitchfork. Scrap lumber
sagging in the overhead rack along with our ancient
bamboo screens which we've been carrying around all
these years since the very beginning. Have we ever used
the goddamn things for anything but storage-space
filler? Not that I can recall. Weatherbeaten wooden
hanging flowerboxes in antic lopsided telescoping stacks
(we didn't hang them this year -- no time for that back
in spring). A box of old sports gear, mostly the
cantaloupe-size nerfballs I loved to hoop it up with on
the outdoor backboard at our second city rental house.
And here on the other side Andy's funky old wooden-
handled push mower (which I've never used). A burned-
out portable electric heater. A stack of rusty green
lawn chairs, cushions missing, which also goes back to
Andy and Tera's time here.
     Speaking of which: last Sunday we had unexpected
visitors. Up rolled a gray van as I was whacking near
the barn and out popped a white-haired Japanese-looking
man. Friendly. He strolled up as I strolled down.
Handshake. This was peculiar, this whole scene. Just
about the only unsolicited visitors we ever see here are
religious proselytizers.
     "This where Calvin U.'s girl lives?"
     "Sure is."
     Well, to heck with dialogue. In a nutshell, this
was Jerry O. who (like Andy) used to work for Papa U at
the power company back on the home island. For the past
twenty years one of his own daughters has lived in our
area here -- fifteen miles to the southeast -- and from
time to time he's visited this place, starting way back
shortly after Andy and Tera moved in (after inheriting

it from Andy's deceased father). "It was just a beat-up
country shack back then. You folks have built it up a
lot -- got it looking real good. Didn't even have a
yard in those days -- nothing but blackberry vines."

     The scene turned awkward as we ambled down toward
the van and I realized more people were cooped up
inside. The wife and a couple of hapa grandkids, it
turned out. And our house an utter mess except for
certain rooms where we couldn't take them and the
kitchen which has no place to sit. And Lady U still in
bed asleep at eleven a.m. -- catching up on zees lost to
a date last night with a man other than her haole zen
husband -- or maybe she was up but in hiding (as indeed
turned out to be the case). I mumbled something about
her working the night shift, still in bed, sorry I
couldn't invite them in, couldn't extend a little
hospitality of the kind they were no doubt used to
having lavished upon them during prior visits, heh-heh.
Fortunately they didn't seem too miffed and they did
take the hint. Parting amenities and off they rolled.

     Will there be repercussions when word gets back to
the U's? Rude inhospitable howler giving U. pal the
bum's rush from U. country estate? No one will say
anything to me directly but I'd bet a bundle I'll be the
fall person on this. (As on so many things. I've been
real good about taking the falls with D's parents and
she's been shameless about using me that way. The all-
purpose howler villain, that's me. The socially tone-
deaf nightscoper grunt oblivious to the nuances of old-
country ways and for that matter new-country ways as
well. The U's don't even know D agreed almost a year
ago to support me for a period while I try to get a
Mentoka book finished. As far as they're concerned I'm
just goofing off while their poor daughter slaves away
for me. And essentially this is the story she's been
feeding them for the entire time we've been together.
Even if she portrayed me as working, it was at some low-
level makeshift job and I could've done much better if I
weren't such a sluggard. Instead they had to send money
to help support their invalid daughter. -- Not that I

ever asked them for a cent. They and the daughter
worked everything out. I was never even consulted.
-- But fine, no problem; if that was how D wanted to do
things, she knew best. Go to it, kid. I was washing my
hands of all that stuff. "You take care of relations on
your side and I'll take care of relations on mine. Just
tell me where to stand and what I'm supposed to do and
what to say and not to say." -- And it worked all
right. I guess. Any other scenario and we probably
would've been blown out of the water ages ago. As we
almost were anyway, and more than once.)
     -- Taro wanders by, emitting a string of plaintive
little mews. Taro has stepped up with Ripper gone. The
survivor. Gentle and lovable but not too bright. At
night I usually work with the "library" sliding glass
inner door open a foot or so and Taro always comes by
once or twice and calls for attention, her nose gaining
a waffle-iron imprint from pressing so hard against the
screened outer door, and I take five and give her a
scratch-down on the Grover's Corners bench outside.
She's too restless and flea-ridden to be allowed inside.
     And back to the corral. Its grassy portion, out
from under the eaves, is about twelve feet wide and
thirty feet long. The wire fence enclosing it on three
sides (with the house on the fourth) is four feet high
with squared-off wooden posts and top bars, all well
weathered. Stacked firewood lines the inside of the
long dimension of fence (except for a few feet at the
far end where we've started to use it up) and most of
the stack is covered with tarpaper to keep it dry, with
a few large chunks of oddly shaped, extremely weathered
driftwood or stump portions holding down the tarpaper
(the cats like to sun on the heat-absorbing tarpaper in
the space between chunks). At the far right, attached
to the corner post and rising several feet above it, is
a driftwood birdfeeder with a steep A-shaped wooden roof
attached to it, and usually the action there is loud and
fluttery. The feeder is so situated that the cats can't
get at it without giving the birds plenty of warning,
but this doesn't stop the cats from trying every now and

then, and they do a lot of hungry staring from their
tarpaper resting spots and from posts on the deck -- as
does Fred from the bedroom window above the corral roof.
     And on the other side of the fence, a wall of
green. It's layered almost like geological strata
revealed in a cliffside: many varieties of plants,
ferns, shrubs, trees at various heights up to sixty or
seventy feet and more farther back in. Just behind the
fencepost at the far left corner this wall sports a
large hole in the middle strata where our best tree used
to stand -- an ancient super-gnarly cherry about thirty
feet tall. It went down in the big 110-mile-an-hour
windstorm four years ago, I think it was, and took part
of the corral fence with it (since repaired) and
narrowly missed the house. -- And way up in the canopy
you can see a couple of dead snag treetops maybe twenty
or thirty paces back in the woods where once in a while
a hawk or eagle will perch. But the colorful and
hyperactive jays are still the show-stoppers, here as
elsewhere. All day long bright blue wingflashes like
electrical charges jumping synapses. Or like the
flitting multihued parrots of Rima's green mansions,
which is to say: natural viridescence. Jizzburst!
     -- Right now all this greenery is basking in the
nearly shadowless sun of high noon. Stirring only
slightly. Only spottily yellowed with autumn. A few
dead leaves skittering down. Truly a fine and restful
scene. And I'm damn grateful I've got it to soothe my
nerves a bit at times like this. But still, all things
considered I'd rather be -- elsewhere, yeah. Anywhere
but here. And it's highly probable, what's more, I soon
will be right there: elsewhere. So savor this setting,
you lunkhead, while you can. And the jyzer sez all
right, yes, will. will try anyway.
     Deep breath. watch a spider inching its way down a
spectacular floor-to-ceiling web a few feet to my left.
This entire time the spider and the jyzer have been
laboring in tandem spinning out our best workaday stuff.
     All right then: enough. I can lay this J-book down
for another eight days. By the time for my return I'll

probably have plenty to complain about. But that's
then. Jyze breaks off while it's ahead or at least can
feel it is. Yes! So do it! Fast! Act now!

33

    The couch. Facing the two armchairs with the
reading lamp glowing atop the table standing between
them and the big black picture window looming behind,
the window glass there reflecting -- all of the above,
as well as the corny clipper-ship wallpaper behind the
couch (Andy loves sailing) and then next to the couch
the polelamp with its two bell-shaped white plastic
shades like stage spotlights, which in turn illuminate
-- the unkempt coiffure of the jyze guy!

    As the insipid golden-oldies station plays on the
kitchen radio. "It's the dance sensation / that's
sweeping the nation." How I loved it back in the hop
era, when hop was first -- hip! Yes! And Lady U, Dani,
namesake of the frontman of that hip hopping group, was
doing -- the diaper crawl! (And still do love that hop.
This particular tune at least a partial exception to the
insipidity rule -- not that you can't love the insipid.
Not that insipidity often fails to make the list of, for
instance, romantic love's primary qualities. -- But I
digress. And probably don't mean much of this anyway
were I to think a bit more on it. But won't.)

    Because -- news. Big news, relatively speaking.
No sooner did I holster my J-stick after the last J-
round than the phone rang and it was reporter Verna from
the office. She'd been trying to get me "for a month."
Was J. Ink still in business? Did it want work? Had I
heard the news about dayscoper Doris? And to cut to the

crux, that very night I was back in harness, scoping
away at the office. In fact for three nights straight I
was doing that, and the whole time dazed. The irony!
The repercussions! The sweet revenge! The absurdity of
it all! The boggling timing!

So what's happened? I don't really know. For some
reason Doris is no longer on the day staff; she and her
husband, Ralph, have moved back to their far-coast home
state as of mid August. She'll still be doing some
scoping by modem (for the sadly fumble-fingered reporter
Toni) but basically she's history (unlike the other time
a few years back when she seemingly quit in order to
return forever to that same home state but after two
years suddenly reappeared, whereupon her pal partner
Fran declared in retrospect that she, Doris, had only
been taking a leave of absence for those two years,
meaning she didn't lose her seniority, even though by
that point the nightscoper, meaning me, Jyzer G, had
been working there longer than Doris had in terms of
actual time in harness and should've been promoted to
senior scoper with a pay boost, but was not).

Thus the only scoper of any kind, day or night,
remaining on the office staff is Amy. And none of the
good reporters can bear to let Amy touch their work. Of
course this doesn't matter a whole lot since most of the
good reporters now do their own scoping, but Verna's an
exception when she's up against tough deponents or fast-
talking attorneys and also when she's taking grand jury,
which right now she's again doing every two weeks (how
she pulled off this coup I don't know). So I'll have
some work from Verna. But it won't be a lot, because in
a month "her" grand jury expires and the contract
specifies that a competing firm gets the new jury.

However, there's also this. From Verna I learned
that reporter Naomi will be returning from her birthing
leave as of mid October, and owing to Doris's
unavailability to scope her non-fed jobs she's asked
partner Una for permission to have J. Ink do all her
work (not just the fed stuff), and Una has granted it.
-- And the next day Naomi phoned me and confirmed this.

At first she'll be on call no more than two days a week,
but in January she'll go to three.

The work deriving from this contract (informal)
with Naomi should be enough to keep me busy three to
four nights a week on average, the equivalent of perhaps
a half-time or even two-thirds-time job, with the pay
averaging maybe eighteen or twenty bucks an hour,
possibly even more. And, equally important, I'll again
have access to the office computers and printers for my
own work -- for free. Just as before. (Not that I've
asked about this. I'm just assuming so until I hear
otherwise. And I figure I won't be hearing otherwise,
because both partners have likely long since forgotten
that they've given me carte blanche to use the machines
this way. In fact I'm counting on the firm's poor
institutional memory.)

Mixed emotions about all this. Of course! I don't
want to go back to work at all. I'll lose fictojyzing
time. But I should still have enough free hours to
allot to the Mentoka series. (Reading will suffer.)
And just as important, I'll now have something to fall
back on when (and dare I say if) breakup time comes with
our resident Alt Nation freak here at home.

The change was so sudden I'm still trying to absorb
the meaning of it. Did I say this already? I've been
shattered into near-total incoherence. My brain isn't
working right. For one thing I've had to turn my sleep
schedule upside down again to make myself available for
answering scoping calls -- and I have to be ready to
saddle up for the long commute on very short notice. I
need to be highly organized so the logistical
difficulties won't prevent me from getting my own work
done. Everything must become portable again so I can
work on the ferries, at the office, in bars and cafes in
the city and/or the in-transit port towns.

-- So it's now been about eleven months since I
lost my full-time nightscoping job and about four since
I stopped part-time contract work under the J. Ink
guise, and about two since unemployment comp ran out.
All in all it's been something like a one-year teacher's

[Jyzemelt]

sabbatical, I'll say, but a peculiar kind of sabbatical
during which the teacher must keep showing up at school
on a low-paid part-time basis during nine months of the
sabbatical year. And during this one-year period I've
had to deal with two of the worst catastrophes
imaginable in my personal life. So I guess I ought to
be pleased to have gotten as much done as I have.

        The irony. The very first night I return to work
at the office who happens to drop by? Partner Fran!
She doesn't attempt to hide her astonishment at finding
me there. She hasn't previously heard about Una's deal
with Naomi. (Will she try to scuttle it? Just might,
yeah. But I doubt she'll succeed.) -- Fran ran me out
of there so her friend Doris could stay and now look
what happens. He's baaaaack! If there's any justice in
the world, partner Fran did not sleep well that night.

        A good thing I recopied all my work on diskettes
after the upgrade last spring -- the old office read-on
device no longer exists. But the system itself is
unchanged (except it has two fewer workstations) and
after a brief shakedown period I've had no problems
using it. (A year ago Fran's main justification for
RIFing me was the putative need to save money for a move
to a whole new system. They still haven't even begun
gearing up for that move, and my hunch is they never
will.) -- Otherwise everything was just as it had been,
at least in my own tiny portion of the realm. My
building-entry swipe card and office key still worked.
The safe combination was the same and I nailed it the
first try sheerly by memory (surprising myself). My
lockbox and sleeping bag were right where I'd left them.

        Alas, dayscoper Amy is still there as well; may I
mention this once more? And so is Monique, the
relatively new office manager whom, because I've always
come in only at night if I've come in at all, I've never
even met. But a change in Monique's status may
eventually ramify on me: she's now a stockholder in the
firm, a partial owner. Therefore she's morphed into
partner Monique and has her own separate office, and the
ripple effect of this move has shifted around most of

the other room and desk assignments. And from notices
on the bulletin board I see the staff now meets weekly
and an "image consultant" is the main item on next
week's agenda. Sounds delightful. It's a shame I'll
have to miss the meeting -- that one and all those to
follow. (Which is to say: being a nightscoper on indie
contract does have its advantages.)

And the repercussions here at home? Sad to report,
it's not likely things will be getting any better. Lady
U is already at wit's end trying to handle an eight-hour
job even while I'm taking care of virtually all of the
housework; no doubt she'll become even more frantic and
harder to get along with once we have to start dividing
the chores again, like last spring. We scarcely see
each other when I'm here twenty-four hours a day;
what'll it be like when I'm gone close to two-thirds of
the time three or four days a week?

Not that I really think it matters. We're done for
anyway. The "if" I was daring to use earlier -- "if"
breakup time comes -- is just a kind of nominal hedge.
The lady is being totally indifferent at best and
extremely ugly at worst. In a moment of barely
suppressed fury over one of the uglier incidents a few
days ago I warned her she'd better change her tune fast
or the relationship won't make it. As far as I can see
she's made no attempt to change anything. I figure
she's trying to force me to be the one to end it.

(Why has this happened now? I can't say. I don't
even begin to know. And it's still true I don't want to
think about it any more than necessary. Why devastate
myself even further? I can think of a lot of things I
might've done better but they're all small things. In
general I'd say I've given it my best shot. And I'll
also say I'm not willing to do that anymore. My best
shot must go to the Mentoka books and any others that
may come along later. For D to pull the plug at a time
like this, after I taught adult literacy and then did
nightscoping for so long so she'd have her chance at
dance and theater and grad school and visual art,
roughly in that order, while she was also grappling with

[Jyzemelt]

various injuries and maladies -- well, it's hard not to
feel a whole lot of resentment. I mean, it's there. I
do feel it. But I've got to move on.)
    Duh.... Where was I?
    I'm looking across at the corner armchair where I
usually sit when drinking coffee or chomping away at a
meal. The three stacks of stuff to read: magazines and
reviews, quarterly journals, newspapers. The newspaper
stack is rapidly dwindling with no Mentoka dailies to
replenish it. (I suppose I could reup at least one of
my subscriptions now that I again have what appears to
be an assured source of income, but I don't really want
to. At this point I figure I know all I need to know
about the M. zone -- all and then some, by a factor of
hundreds.) -- The brown cushions, simulated leather
bearing body impressions. The sturdy bare wood frames
of the armchairs (and of this couch and the loveseat
downstairs), all two-by-six knotty pine, I guess it is
(and all originally bought from Ben and Beryl for a song
when they upgraded their own furniture). Farther to the
right, the old library-surplus table from our early days
together, D's and mine. The notepads, pens, self-inking
rubber stampers (red arrows), razor clippers. Stacked
vanilla-pudding empties. The large wooden box of read
newspapers to be discarded, the doubled-up brown grocery
bags for read magazines and mixed papers (all of which
we have to haul to the south-county dump for recycling).
The butcherblock floor (with a conspicuous grease stain,
ineradicable, hailing from the time I stupidly stored my
commuting bicycle in here for a few days during a nasty
storm, back before we had the carport). The bric-a-brac
shelf to the right with the blue hippo and the love
ducks and the Mentoka cow and much else. The glass door
to the left leading to the deck.
    Six and a half years we've been here. By a year
from now we'll be out, I'm almost certain, and (even
closer to certain) going our separate ways.
    What I've decided to do is this: try to tough it
out until roughly February. Two reasons. First, I
won't really know before then whether the Jyzer Ink

contract with Naomi will suffice to pay the rent on a
room of my own in the city. Second, I figure the four
to five months between now and then will be enough to
bash out a draft of "Ghosts." (A third reason would be
that perhaps D will come to her senses by then -- but
that one I'm not putting on the list. Even if she did
so awaken I probably wouldn't stick around. She'd have
one helluva lot of explaining to do first. And if she
succeeded at that she'd have to start in on the begging
and pleading and keep it up until her bended knee was
bloody and her face blue. No, it won't happen.)
     -- And all the above of course assumes that the
lady will let me hang around that long. She's said
she will, but she hasn't signed anything. She could
change her mind at any moment.
     And so at best I'll be living this way (and writing
like this about it) for the next four or five months.
Maybe even for the next year if I'm truly blessed.
     -- It's fall now, the real thing. Have I mentioned
this? A few days after reporter Verna's call the
weather broke and it's been rainy and blustery ever
since. Chilly. Break out the sweatshirts and raincoats.
(Oddly enough my first ferry ride back into the city
came one day after my old book of ferry coupons expired.)
Gird up the loins. Lock down the outdoor closets.
Settle in for some truly fierce fictojyzing.
     -- Saw all my old ferry buddies except for Tom T.
The daily back-and-forth. "Where you been, boy?"
Rather than go into the sordid details I usually spin
out something vague about modems and the trend toward
working at home. (But of course the federal work can't
be done at home owing to security requirements, and most
of Naomi's work is for the feds. The small volume of
so-called private-sector work she does wouldn't justify
the purchase of a modem even if I had a home computer
that would accept it, which of course I don't. And now
it's less likely Papa U will be sending us his used
machine or, if he does, that Lady U will allow me to get
anywhere near it. And I'd have to buy an expensive new
printer anyway to produce professional-quality

transcripts here. So no, it's back to the old ten-stage
nightscoper commute for me, with all that entails.)
     -- And there's this: I found out what happened to
the benches missing from my birthday picnic table up at
the barn. One day I followed the "garden path" a few
yards farther into the woods than I have in quite some
time and discovered a little retreat with those benches
and two of Andy and Tera's old lawn chairs set up in a
ferny glen by the side of the north creek where it
tumbles through a couple of small (maybe eighteen-inch)
waterfalls. D's parents must've done that during their
visit this past spring -- which is fine. Touching even.
But shouldn't someone at least have told me about it?
     Yet this shows how things are. It's their place;
they don't have to tell me a thing, much less ask for my
approval, if they don't want to. I'm powerless around
here, more like a guest or actually a kind of room-and-
boarder at this point, a hired hand down on his luck and
willing to take anything just to be off the streets. My
interests are of a whole different order than theirs and
over the years D has never tried very hard to make them
understand this. Now suddenly it's easier to see why
she's failed to do so: because her own interests are
turning out to be a lot less like mine than we both used
to think. I guess she just couldn't bear to keep up the
charade -- and most likely she kept it up for as long as
she did because she couldn't bear to let me know this.
-- And at what point did it become a charade? Maybe
when her efforts to sell her watercolors on the farmers'
market circuit fizzled out three or four years ago. Or
it could trace all the way back to the dance injury a
year or so after the Marco crisis. Or any time between:
plenty of options to choose from. Or even before Marco
came along, the period during which she tried to read
the works of my protojyze heroes -- which come to think
of it was mostly just before the play rehearsals started
and Marco appeared. After that I think she may've given
up in some crucial sense on the written word and
anything and anyone having to do with its production.
     Or better to see it as a gradual thing. Step by

step -- and with each step she was more reluctant to
talk about it. And I with my sureness about what I
wanted to do with my life (however badly I was doing it)
-- I was more and more a kind of live-in rebuke. Not
that she ever said so or acted as if she thought so. On
the contrary! She was as supportive as they come. Or
so it appeared. And of course I wanted to believe in
those appearances. And mostly did, except for rare
moments of doubt or suspicion, quickly overcome, and
usually at her strong insistence if I let any of the
doubt or suspicion show. -- Or no, not usually. Always.
Until now.

     -- A better post-chemo week for Mother this time.
Another talk with Suzanne of the genealogy publisher --
the "Memorials" proof will be arriving in a few weeks.
And that has to be it -- back to the real work.

34

     Aboard.
     "Get a life."
     "Got a life."
     Also got a large bag of popcorn. After a long wait
in line. Something wrong with the machine, they said.
But I stuff another handful down my gullet and say no.
Say that machine be cookin'! (And poppety-pop go a
swarm of motorsiccles...latecomers on the auto deck.)
     Mostly a quiet inbound ride early on a Saturday
evening. The previous boat was the raucous one, and
probably several before that, because right at this
moment our local baseballers are taking on their chief
rivals in the third game of the league playoffs and
they're doing it a few blocks from the far end of this

ferry run. The whole region's in a tizzy over the
first playoff appearance ever for our boys of summer --
now at last boys of October.

And earlier today the local footballers (college
level) lined up against another big bad rival a few
miles farther to the north and a jam-packed boatload of
folks returning from that game in the usual school-
colored gear, pennant-waving, souvenir-carrying, took a
very long time to disembark at the transit port before
any foot passengers could board.

How caught up am I in all this sports hullabaloo?
The football crowd appeared a little subdued and so I
assume "we" lost, but I didn't ask. And I'm wondering
how the baseballers are doing, but my curiosity's not
strong enough to spark a search for someone with a radio
listening to the game. As I mounted the ramp, though, a
white-uniformed officer up in the aft pilothouse leaned
out a side window and called to the ramp guard that
someone had just hit one out, cutting the bad guys' lead
to two. "There may still be hope!" cried the guard, a
new one I've never seen before, just as I was passing
by. "Ain't over till -- " the jyzer was in the act of
pointing out when the guard jumped in: "We can do it!"

Middle of the voyage. "Too damn much water around
here!" -- That's what one of the last of the
disembarkers groused back before I got on, a scruffy
old-school drunk, staggering out with a couple of
equally woozy pals, all three careening down the ramp --
no surprise at all if one or more had toppled over the
low fence and joined the gulls and propeller-filleted
fish parts floating down below.

And yet all week my curiosity's been strong enough
that I've listened to the games on the kitchen radio at
breakfast time. (Every day now I get up at ten to four
-- just like last winter and spring -- to be ready to
take a scoping call between four and five.) And some of
those late-afternoon breakfasts have dawdled on longer
than they should've or otherwise would've, just so I
could hear how the game came out.

While parking the car near the foot-ferry dock it

occurred to me I might as well start checking out what
rooms in that area are renting for these days. Even
though it's a right-wing military-dominated tourist town
("jingo heaven" in Tom T.'s phrase) and I'd prefer a
place in the city, it still has several things going for
it. For one, the combination of isolation with easy
non-auto access to the city. For another, the town's
smallness and self-containedness. For a third, the
setting itself, with its hills and stunning mountain
views and proximity to the water. And fourth, the look
and feel of the downtown with its frontier-style main
street (all-wood buildings of two or three stories with
sheltered plank sidewalks) and its lively marina with
small ferries chugging in and out all day and late into
the night.

-- As we rumble in toward the dock. But yes, if
rents in jingo heaven are significantly lower (as I
suspect), it might beat the city. "There may still be
hope!" -- Mainly it would depend on my getting enough
work from the office to provide a subsistence-level
income while Mother's still alive. Later the
inheritance from her should enable me to make up any
shortfall in that same income on a more or less
permanent basis, or say up until the time Social
Security kicks in. ---

*   *

Now that was some brutal truth I laid out in that
last paragraph. Jyze snatched it away from me before I
had a chance to put it in perspective. And I don't want
to go back and reread it. Let it stand. In the months
ahead I'm expecting such brutality to be the rule rather
than the exception. By necessity. Might as well get
used to churning it out right now.

At the broiler! (As far as I'm concerned there's
only one broiler.) -- With its disappointing new hours,
closing at eleven p.m. every day. And at ten p.m.,
which is to say right now, it's aswarm with exultant
baseball fans. Huge comeback victory! Even at the only
real bookstore most everyone was listening to the play-
by-play on the P.A. Have I ever before heard a cheer go

up in a bookstore, and not merely once but several times
within a few minutes? I think not. Then I walked north
just as the crowd came pouring out of the stadium.
Whoops and hollers. "Refuse to lose" delirium.
     (Enerjyze this thing! Got to do it!)
     A snooty, distinctly unfriendly note from the only
remaining dayscoper at the office -- try not to let it
bum me out. Hate to find myself back in a situation in
which I'm forced to deal with this kind of stuff. But
when I put everything in the balance, yes, this is still
the way to go. Grin and bear it. At least one of my
two dayscoper nemeses is now out of the picture. I'm no
longer outnumbered.
     (So far here in the broiler no one's even noticed
my presence -- half-hidden in a corner booth. Rubbed
down the table myself using a paper towel from my pack.
But I'm pleased to see many of the characters on both
sides of the counter are still the same. And so's the
view through the blinds. Night, neon, parked cars,
glint of traffic, scattered highrise hotel windows lit
up. Some nasty-looking sidewalk bypassers. -- A few
minutes ago someone in here no doubt thought I was one
of that same breed myself as I shambled by out there on
my way to the entrance. And that person was right!)
     (But that's because, or mainly because, I'm still
in a stir-fried state. Or I could say I'm broiling
myself alive over a double fire of what after all
remains only anticipatory, even if well-merited, grief.
And regardless everything keeps moving and shifting out
there, out that window, changing color, changing pitch.
Bearing down with furrowed brow I try by fierce
projection of resolve to make it all hold steady if only
for a few seconds. But it just won't do that.)
     (Maybe ten lines back I placed an order and
suddenly here it is already. You got to put it up (as
hoopsters say) if you wanna score! If you wanna some
justice! If you wanna some mercy! Mercy, mercy, mercy!
Refuse to accept anything less!)
                    *   *
     -- Not to mention hysteria. But that was then and

this is -- another old hang. It's the office conference
room. The big one with the westward view of the bay and
the mountains. Here tranquility reigns. I've already
laid out my old sleeping bag and electric blanket in
their accustomed spot on the carpet. My pathetic old
alarm clock is ticking away right here on the table. In
fact I'm eating into my nap time to eke out another page
or two of jyz-z-z-z-z....
     Wake up and smell the carpet shampoo!
     In a few days I'll be starting my regular Jyzer Ink
work for Naomi -- or at least so the plan has it. This
past week may prove to be the last I'll have fully free
for a good long while. My hope is to limit the scoping
to two or three days a week, or possibly four shorter
days. From my earlier attempts at churning out the
"Jyzer" and "Ghosts" rough drafts I know I'll need a
couple of days for organizing time (which is also
recharging time) between each actual JIFT session. I
don't see why I can't do most of that organizing while
commuting. It will require some ferocious concentration
but -- I think I'm ready for ferocious.
     Some of it I'll do right here. Some at the
bookstore cafe. Some on the ferries. Some maybe at the
library, either the local one by the dock in the home
port or the main downtown library on this side (and that
one stays open until nine most nights).
     Not just ferocious. I'm prepared to be ruthless
also. With myself and with anyone who gets in my way --
and it's mostly just one person I'm thinking about here.
(Only for old Mom will I do any bending. Probably I'll
be making another trip to see her at some point. And
I'll be editing "Memorials" -- or proofreading it
actually. That'll zap a few days, but it must be done.)
     Will my health hold up? That's another big worry.
Nothing I can do about it, though, except to assume it
will and plunge ahead.
     -- But the pathetic clock here keeps ticking and I
keep yawning, each yawn seemingly several ticks longer
and a centimeter or two wider than the previous one. If
I don't want to be rendered useless for tomorrow night

I'd better shut this J-book down for a while.

*   *

     Once again aboard. And rumbling in place. To say
screws turning in place might sound more nautical but I
guess right now the screws are not turning. Not for
about three more minutes. Or if they are turning,
they're doing it quietly, perhaps to keep the boat
pressed flush against the dock as the vehicles, each
with a distinct thump, roll aboard. (If a seismometer
were set up on the booth bench here it would doubtless
register each vehicle's arrival. -- And I am that
seismometer!)

     Just past dawn. When I left the office at seven it
was still night and the downtown streets were wet and
glary and empty. Now I look out the long row of windows
across the aisle to my left and straight ahead and all I
see is gray. Except for those orange container cranes,
that is, and even those look orangey gray. Low swirling
gray overcast. So dense is that soup up there you'd be
only slightly surprised to see a pod of orcas cavorting
in it.

     The rain began shortly after I hit the magic carpet.
As noted before, the first raindrops beating against the
conference-room windows sound like the early scattered
pops of a batch of cooking popcorn. Tonight it occurred
to me that this might have something to do with the
window being dry. Water on the glass may act as a
cushion and soften the pops into plops or something even
squishier and softer than a plop, so perhaps a splop.
(This may be elementary and self-evident. But somehow
in all these years of carpet-level analysis I've never
thought of it before.)

     When the guy sitting in the booth behind me took
off for the head a moment ago I stole a look at the
front page of his paper. A big photo of last night's
home-run hero, bat still in hand, gazing off toward the
spot where his dramatic late-inning game-winning grand
slam is presumably sailing into the stands. "THE MAGIC
NEVER ENDS!" asserts the huge headline. (And my guess
was right, the Otters lost -- I mean our local college

team here lost! -- the jyzer's got those Mezzu Silver
Otters on the brain! -- lost by a touchdown.)
      Has jyze ever before indulged in this ridiculous
sports scorekeeping practice? To this degree? I
think not. It's atavism or revanchism or just plain
old shameless recrudescence of jockish teenage
obsessions and compulsions not to mention delusions.
      The throb of the turning screws. Or maybe just one
screw, I forget; but however many, definitely turning
now that we're out in the middle of the sound. Suburban
island taking shape to the west and north in the row of
windows across the bow. As a fluorescent overhead light
dies in a brilliant neon nova, a lightning-like flash.
      As for relations with my cohabitor, the high point
of the week came when I acknowledged to myself I must be
able to accept losing her. I care about her, I want her
to be as happy as possible, I realize she's not at all
happy with me any longer and this isn't likely to change.
She's still of romanceable age, still looks very good.
Give her a chance to meet someone else. I know I'll
never win her back with pleas, not to mention sarcastic
quips. So let her go. I've had my time with her; be
glad for that. She gave me some -- probably most --
maybe all -- of the best years of my life. (Depends on
what's yet to come, obviously enough, if anything is.
In that realm, I'm saying.)
      What I mean is at times during the week I was able
to occupy the high ground of thinking this way. Never
for long, though. Sporadically at best. And of course
I say nothing to her about such matters. She has no
interest in talking about them. On the contrary (the
extreme contrary): she wants to avoid them at all costs.
      I'm still looking at February, preferably toward
the end of the month, as the best time to split for
good. Already I'm working on my farewell speech.
Unfortunately it keeps turning into a plea of some kind
-- mostly the falsely noble and badly disguised kind --
and she in reply keeps begging me not to go, at least as
I hear the dialogue playing out in fantasy. In dismal
fact I expect her to raise no barriers to my leaving --

rather she'll be doing all she inconspicuously can to grease the chute. (No, no, it can't be! She'll be devastated! She'll suddenly realize, as in a thunderclap, what she's losing!)

    Dream on. It's not even really a dream. I too can see we've reached the end. We've "grown apart," or rather through the accumulation of daily pressures we've had to raise barriers against each other -- and also to discard certain saving masks and roles. It just happens. For the most part silently, incrementally, insidiously. It's not at all unusual, especially in a relationship that's childless. You just wish this would've turned out to be the rare one in which it didn't happen.

    Ecch. Sentimentalism. I can't stop love from meaning a lot to me. (Sheesh, suddenly I'm even cringing to catch myself using the word. The L-word. The L-word for the D-woman. Love and loneliness, beauty and sadness, age and decay. Or no -- age and wisdom. Wisdom, that's it. The Chinese scholar-poets of antiquity holed up in the mountains. Jyzer G, recluse of the home port. Maybe. Or more likely, of some district close to downtown in the city -- an easy stroll to the office for a jyze isolato clad in nightscoper rags which after all do make for, as I always like to remind myself, pretty damn good street camo.)

35

    Jyze central. Another Saturday-night blues party. Eleven coming up, of the clock, and the lady of the house is off working overtime. Or so, before I went to bed this afternoon, she said she'd be doing. Maybe she's really doing it, maybe she's not. Maybe I care, maybe I don't. But tonight I'll say I don't. (As if it matters!)

   Big two-inch and three-inch binders spread out all over the place and every last one is chock full of notes. When you take notes for a book over a twenty-year period, or actually more like thirty in this case, and for more than five of those years you do so assiduously -- meaning that's just about all you do aside from what you must do to make a living -- you're sure to wind up with a helluva lot of notes. You get to a point where it's no longer a question of being able to squeeze all the good ones into a book or even a series of books; rather it's a question of being able to squeeze in a review of all the notes in order to be able to decide which are the good ones.

   Reviewing is what I'm still doing.

   A lucky break: I've had all this week off. Again! Naomi sent a postcard (addressed to "CEO, Jyzer Ink") postponing her restart until this coming week. The workload should be equivalent to about a half-time job, or hopefully a bit less than that, until January. Hardest will be the logistics. Lady U will still be working the swing shift and she'll be taking the wagon, meaning I'll either have to go in very early and do a lot of my sleeping on the conference-room floor or I'll have to do a lot of walking on country roads in nasty weather. But I figure I can put up with it for a few months, whichever way it winds up going.

   Meanwhile things may have taken a turn for the worse with Mother. The doc proclaimed her last x-ray to be a "mixed bag" and detected what he thought might be "new cancerous activity." This week she's undergoing a series of tests whose results she'll learn Tuesday or Wednesday. She's already hinting she may forgo further chemo if a regimen involving more powerful chemicals is prescribed or offered or suggested. She's afraid the side effects would be more than she could bear.

   And the sadness of all this is almost more than I can bear. But nothing about such a development is unexpected. The doc originally gave her a window of

six to eight months before the chemo would become
ineffective and it's now been about seven months since
her first treatment (the one I was present for).

You try not to think about it any more than you
have to. And then the time comes when you have to think
about it almost constantly. Is this the start of that
time?

*   *

Back from chores. And then the bacon-bringer
turned up, and now we're in the process of negotiating
the details on tomorrow's shopping trip. I'm being a
nice guy this weekend: shopping for both of us tomorrow,
then taking the wagon in Monday morning for its fifteen-
thousand-mile checkup. As soon as I begin working
regularly at the scope office I'll cease being so
accommodating. Maybe even start aiming for some mild
(ha) quid pro quo.

Things between us have improved not one iota.
Eighteen years (as of a week from today) down the drain.
Disgusting. I'm still in shock and I suppose at some
level in denial.

Well. Push on. Squeeze it out. Snarl. Growl.
Ooze bitterness. Do whatever's necessary just so long
as you don't give her the satisfaction of seeing how
badly you're hurting. No matter what no crawling to
her. Give no quarter. Exit with your head held high.

-- So this week. Out in the world. A fascinating
time really. We've got the verdict on the Afrusan
football star, the country going into paroxysms of
blatant racism as he "walks." We've got our hometown
baseballers in the league playoff finals after
dispatching the hated rivals in pinstripes, and around
here this is big, big, big. We've got lots of wet,
blustery, chilly autumn weather. We've got Ben next
door building an annex for his horse shed (in the corral
in his front yard bordering our joint driveway). We've
got a new cat, cream-colored, begging for scraps here at
the jyzeroom door. We've got endless V-flights of ducks
and loud-honking geese, many settling in for the night
in the field across from the town store (where a notice

is posted seeking volunteers to clean up the cemetery).

On the football hero I'm squarely with the defense
(and so is Lady U). He may have committed the crime --
we both think he probably did -- but the jury was right
to acquit based on the evidence it received. The
racism of the police department -- as revealed on tape
and in a hundred other ways -- is a matter far more
serious than even a brutal double-murder-by-celebrity.

Clamp down here. No use to work myself into a
lather over this. (Do I want to go into other
outrageous aspects of this trial? The class angle? How
money buys verdicts, whether just or unjust? And who's
been the primary beneficiary of this fact in this
country over the centuries, people of color or whites?
-- Decidedly don't want to be going into any of it.
Talk about stating the obvious.)

But neither be a cynic. "Hope lives!" Always the
sources for it abound as do the reasons to tap into
them. And then there's one's own personal hormonal
disposition. Who needs "reasons"? Whoever said life
would be one long easy coast? Conflict! Tension! The
wonder and the terror beyond! The indifference beyond
that! -- Not to mention the routine outrages.

Here's this J-book. Here's the J-dude hunched over
the J-book. Sighing. Scowling. Eyes rolling. An
errant cat whisker sticking straight out from his left
sleeve at the biceps and quivering loosely and
fascinatingly in time with -- what? Probably his
ricocheting breath bouncing off binders, blotter, lamp,
ferry commuter mug packed with pens and colored markers
-- bouncing in all sorts of complicated ways. Or maybe
it's his hitherto undiagnosed arrhythmic heartbeat, who
knows. Cat-whisker cardiogram. At almost one a.m. As
a mellow jazz tune gently caroms in (livelier blues
show's long over).

I did chop off some hair in front (the better to
see how it is out there). I did try to understand a
crusty analytic philosopher's decrees on consciousness
(but didn't feel too bad about failing since the man
makes no more sense than he ever has, which is to say,

for me: close to zero). I did chortle uneasily over the
in-your-face craziness of the reigning female faux-
feminist literatus (in truth, antifeminist). -- I did
just say "Busy -- two minutes!" perhaps a bit gruffly
when our resident alt-music fiend started to enter the
room right here (because I don't like the way she keeps
me closed out of her room all day and has done so for
months and sounds so hostile when I'm forced to try to
talk with her through the closed door -- and I mean talk
loudly, to be heard over the alt music blasting inside)
-- but I'd better go see what she wants.

*   *

And now, some ten hours later, it's the root-beer
stand. The morning's been thickly foggy until a few
minutes ago but suddenly we've got sun breaking through.
We've got scraggly dark evergreens turning, in the
brightening light, ever greener. We've got the eaten-
out red plastic shell of a strawberry shortcake -- first
one of these I've dug into in years. Guess maybe I'm
starting to learn how to live right all over again.

At the moment I'm kicking back between malls. Cat
food and gas and "alt weekly" scratched off the list,
bank and coffee and groceries still to go. Not to
mention a side trip for a dozen bagels for the lady.

No other customers in here. Once in a while a
vehicle rolls by in the drive-up lane just outside the
window to my left. The two high-school girls working
the counter are both listening to music on a "bud" in
one ear and talking a lot louder, including with each
other, than they'd otherwise need to. At the pet shop
an impressive green parrot was yakking even louder than
these girls and also had a lot more interesting things
to say, at least to my jizzy faux birder's mind.

This is the southward shopping zone. When we come
down here we call it "going the other way" -- south
instead of the usual north toward the home port. Either
direction the round trip for shopping is about twenty
miles. Lady U goes in a third direction to work, west
-- the mythical or maybe mystical "Third Way" -- and
about the same distance too, but out in that area no

malls exist. Not even mini-malls. Not even shopping
strips. By current standards it's untouched wilderness.
     A pretty little tourist town -- that is, it's small
and it's pretty -- but up here at the freeway end it's
neither of those. So maybe I should've gone down by the
harbor to perform my morning jyzercise. But that part
of town is a couple miles out of the way and I wasn't
sure what I'd find open on a Sunday at this hour. In
any event no root-beer stands down there with loose
dress codes and lots of well-lit empty booths. Instead
mostly dark waterfront bars and restaurants, and even
if open the restaurants wouldn't be right for jyzing.
It all came down to the bars. Did I want to gamble?
With not much slack in my schedule? I didn't.
     Maybe next time. It's always good to be holding a
few prime jyze venues in reserve.
     Fans spinning slowly overhead. Rows of plastic
booths gleaming with extra spit and polish under a
sudden surprise inspection by sunlight. A couple of
wooden picnic tables standing unevenly outside in the
grass just beyond the drive-up lane, looking so natural
and inviting it's hard to believe they're part of the
same root-beer operation. A bigleaf maple tree halfway
turned from green to yellow stands watch over both
tables and drops an occasional leaf -- very large, yes
-- on one or the other to make for something like half
a dozen quirky arts-and-crafts placemats. And there
goes a white balloon sailing by, the kind you buy for a
kid's birthday, though no kid is anywhere in sight.
     So: another venue to put on the list, "picnic
tables at 'other way' root-beer stand." (Done.)
                  *   *
     Jyze dives into the twilight zone hidden behind
those two little stars and resurfaces a full day later
at an auto dealer twenty-five miles to the northwest.
The waiting room, and though when the morning began
half a dozen other waiters were languishing in here,
now I'm the only one left. Voices of clerks around the
corner -- lots of voices, because this is one of the
larger dealers in the region, if not the largest -- one

voice having just wagered five bucks that the
baseballers will lose tomorrow's playoff game (and thus
bring their "miracle season" to a sad end).

Snatched a couple of hours' sleep. Crunched down
the driveway in the dark at six-thirty a.m. under the
mistaken impression northbound traffic would be heavy.
Then despite being stuck behind a school bus for several
miles, and despite a light rain that was slowing traffic
still more, and despite making two wrong turns (one a
block before and one a block after the street I wanted),
I still arrived here thirty-five minutes early. And so
backtracked downhill to a gas station boasting a twenty-
four-hour minimart and therefore good outdoor lighting
(as a night worker I sure am glad there's hardly any
other kind of gas station around these days) and sat
behind the wheel for half an hour relishing a fine chunk
of neoprag antiphilosophy. All by itself that half hour
made the whole ridiculous trip worthwhile.

Some sort of muzak is playing, sappy middle-of-the-
road rock of yesteryear. Gray clouds hang low above the
highly typical evergreen ridgeline dominating the
picture-window view along with several dozen rain-
glistening used cars of the expected make parked in
preternaturally neat lines out in the lot. Eleven
chairs in here, not one neatly parked. Lots of the
latest promotional literature and posters. Two small
potted rubber trees. Even a quasi-modernist painting in
four separate unframed canvas units, interrelated, of
what I take to be a multihued sports car chopped into
four parts yet still humming right along -- as if just
having undergone a highly unorthodox and ambitious
overhaul, say, in the shop directly behind that wall.

(Now the P.A. calls E.Z. to his office. He's the
salesman -- his highly apt real first name is Ezekiel,
that is, he of the wheel -- who sold us, yes, our newest
set of wheels. He's also the only human being on earth
who sent me a birthday card this year. In fact he's
never forgotten me or D at birthday time or the two of
us together at Christmas.) (Oops, wagon's ready.) ---

36

A busy eighter. Agonizing. Now -- download some
jyze. As the skanky dudes working the bar take turns
circling the pool table in the raised back section, cues
at the ready. Loud music playing, maybe "acid jazz" and
maybe not but not too bad. (One dude's wondering aloud
why they've got two people on duty tonight when it's
been known for days -- though not by me -- there would
be no live music this evening. -- "Or maybe one of us
is supposed to be cleaning up," sez the other, because
tomorrow they're shooting in here. A scene for a movie.
"I'll tell ya something," retorts the first, pausing for
dramatic effect: "Movie personnel suck." Then bends
over and nails a bank shot with a resounding clunk and a
triumphant "Yes!")

Sunday night. Technically this is the right day to
be jyzin'. I'd been running a day behind my official
schedule, but much better to go at it here and now than
to wait a day and do it at home. Home is not where the
heart is at the moment (and likely to remain the place
where it's not for a multitude of moments to come --
until I'm finally outta there for good).

But -- yes, I'm eager to get on with "Ghosts" too,
and well fortified now for the task. Slash out
something fresh and shocking and howlingly funny. (Did
I write this exact line sometime before? Suddenly I'm
all but certain I did.)

Green walls crowded with big four-by-four (that's
feet) canvases. More likable ones this time, although
perhaps overly influenced by a certain popular Russian
fabulist best known for his flying brides and rabbis and

farm critters. Black wrought-iron chairs with red
crushed-velvet upholstery. Plenty of light back in this
area owing to the spotlights for the paintings and the
kinky aluminum fixture hanging above the pool table.
Funky atmosphere. Some fine shabby elegance. And for
young true-blue punks these bartenders are all right.

Only one other customer in the joint at the moment,
and he's an Asian-looking fellow who appears to be doing
pretty much what I'm doing: scribbling in a blank book.
Japanese heritage maybe, though I'm really just guessing.
His buzzcut, however, is about as close to brute fact as
anything tonsorial could ever be.

And it's early. I hit town one boat ahead of my
usual vessel because I needed to get to the only real
bookstore (ORB) before its six p.m. Sunday closing time.
How come? Well, because I'm losing it. Left my
checkbook there last week. Wasted a lot of time
searching for it at home before they called yesterday
and said they had it. Got too much on my mind these
days, that's what.

Mainly it's Mom. A second x-ray confirmed Doc B.'s
suspicion: the chemo has stopped working. Immediately
he proposed that she switch to a newly available form of
treatment, taxol. Without it she'd have three to six
months, he estimated, and one sensed (I did; I talked
with him at a later point) it might well be less than
three. With taxol, if it worked, she'd have an
additional six to eight months. The odds of it working?
Very similar to those for the first course of chemo:
somewhere around one chance in three. (To me he said
thirty to forty percent; to her the next day he said
twenty to thirty and denied he'd told me thirty to forty.
But I know he did; I even wrote it down at the time.
We've noticed his shakiness with numbers before. But
I'm not worrying about it. Basically I trust the guy.
And even if I didn't, where else to turn?)

Also as before, Mother wasn't at all sure she
wanted to go ahead with the taxol, and this time she has
better cause, I'd say, because her health is
deteriorating. Nonetheless I favored her trying it.

Barb was again refusing to say what her position was
(she wouldn't want to open herself to criticism later --
this was her sorry excuse). Jim Q. was in favor. Rob
was in favor. Jeff was more ambivalent than I'd been
expecting -- probably because he'd spoken by phone with
Barb. I determined all this through a series of phone
talks of my own over a couple of frantic days. Mother
wasn't feeling up to making the calls, so I did it for
her. I also contacted Jim Q.'s niece, Beth, whose
mother underwent taxol therapy several years ago when it
was still experimental. Beth was in favor of it.

     By the time I got back to Mother she'd already
reversed her position, mostly owing to a second talk
with the doc, who after our conversation had called her
to clarify his prognosis.

     She goes in next Tuesday for the first treatment.
It will be harder to take than the first chemo was
(taxol in a sense is also a form of chemo). She'll be
hospitalized overnight and has been told to expect some
pain in the "area of administration" (not specified).
The side effects afterwards may or may not be worse (for
Beth's mother they weren't). It'll be three weeks
before we know whether the treatment's working.

     And she's in a lot of pain anyway. Coughing
frequently. Chest pain. Problems with incontinence (a
direct result of giving birth four times). Really
dispiriting stuff. I ache for her, what she's going
through; I can barely slog through the days myself just
thinking of what she's facing. But during our second
talk her spirits were much higher; she was fighting
again. And as long as hope remains that she can have
lengthy pain-free periods while also keeping a clear
mind -- and the doc says, as does Beth, this is a real
possibility if the taxol works -- then I think it's
good she can keep fighting and I hope she will. I know
she's glad she's had the additional six to eight months
the first chemo gave her. And I know the rest of us
are glad too, except possibly Barb, whose awful behavior
can still be forgiven, when all's said and done, because
she's had to put up with so much.

[Jyzemelt]

     (Barb's view of the successful first chemo regime:
how do we know things wouldn't have gone just as well
without it? And of course we can't know with certainty.
We can either accept the medical interpretation of the
probabilities involved or we can reject it. Barb
rejects it. Way too cavalierly, in my view, not to say
hypocritically since she routinely accepts the
interpretations of the medical establishment when they
involve her own health.)
     So that's it. Another period of waiting begins.
Because of her success in beating the one-in-four odds
in the first round it's harder to accept the similar
high likelihood of failure this time. Again, one
chance in three, as the doc now confirms, it works.
                              *
     Back from the head. Wildly loud organ music
playing, recorded kind. Excellent sound system. The
legend on one of several types of bar T-shirts for sale
boldly declares "Ars longa vita brevis" and beneath
these words a silkscreened print shows a scrum of crazed
seventeenth-century English roadhouse partiers. (But
that was the B.J. era, Before Jyze. -- Which glumly
points out, jyze does, that in truth nearly all art, and
eventually all art, is short also.)
     While wandering around up front I kept an eye out
for that picturesque tabletop readymade from last time,
the hoover. Is it still locked up in a closet somewhere
raring to go? If I stick around long enough maybe
someone will roll it out. One of the punk bartenders,
after all, did mention the possibility of cleaning up,
and the carpeted area near the entrance could use a
hoovering for sure (not that I'm being critical).
     Earlier I was browsing at the ORB. An hysterical
and flagrantly wrongheaded book-length attack on my
favorite contemporary neoprag antiphilosopher. A street
kid's diary. A newly translated volume of Chinese
poetry that's so far beaten the longevity odds by a mile
(it's older than any thousand-year-old egg!). A
collection of essays on the last credible (barely)
analytic philosopher's bogglingly tangled views on

religion. Two pretty good contemporary novels on the
remainder table for a buck ninety-eight apiece. -- And
I bought all of these except the first four, which were
full-price hardcovers. Got out of there for a little
over four bucks including tax.

But the real down-to-earth point here is, I'm back
into book-buying, even if only in a small way. The
grisly period of abstinence is over. Or will be soon,
anyway, though for a while I'll have to be choosy about
what I lay out money for -- more so than I'd like to be,
I mean. This week, for example, I was called in to work
only one night, which was a boon in most ways, but it
means for the week I'll clear no more than sixty bucks.
-- And at no point will I be back in the green to the
extent I was before. But with two incomes at home I
won't have to be.

And how long will I be at home? On that crucial
question all I can say is things are still holding. In
the same wretched state as before, true, and it gets a
little bit more crushingly unbearable each week, but --
holding. And I'll do everything I can to keep it that
way. Even if I grind my teeth to dust in the effort.

-- No more pool players. In fact no one, period,
in this whole huge place, or at least what's visible of
it, because now I can hear someone talking up in front.
The other scribbler took off with nary a nod even though
I cracked a mildly complicitous smile at him when I
thought for a second, apparently wrongly, that he was
doing the same to me. And in place of the purported
"acid jazz" some pulsing/pounding industrial music, I
guess it's called. Nothing particularly new about it.
Reminds me of some tracks I once used for a promotional
film back in my more versatile period artistically
speaking: electronic music as it was called then.
Always good for keeping things moving right along in an
unobtrusively upbeat and sometimes even sprightly way.

Meanwhile the baseballers' "miracle run" has run
out. Refusing to lose proved futile, finally, but (as
the headline said) "THANKS FOR THE GREAT RIDE." Myself,
I really did enjoy it, having become a fair-weather fan

of sorts, but also recalling what the old days of true
baseball fanaticism were like. My own, I mean, as a
green and raw young dude. (In "Jyzer" I decided just
yesterday I would cut out the sections in which narrator
G plays for a city-league hoops team. I want this guy
to be serious. Of course I was serious myself that
first year of grad school, very serious indeed, although
I still didn't succeed in going cold turkey on sports.
I played intramural ball and reffed. Even narrator G
will be allowed to play pickup three-on-three a couple
of times a week. But he's smart enough to know he
shouldn't get caught up in any leagues. He knows he's
too competitive and too perfectionistic to be able to
limit his participation as he'd like once he gets
started. Which sounds as if he's maybe a little too
wise. -- So maybe I should rethink all this yet again.)
     -- But I overhear someone saying they'll be closing
in a few minutes. So -- pack it in. (But note first:
still no hoover.) (Maybe it got hoovered up itself by a
bigger, badder, technologically more advanced hoover?
If so its story would be exemplary for our era.)
                    *   *
     -- Night streets to the broiler for a little grub.
Shortly after my arrival one of the huge spiders
currently terrorizing the region came racing in the door
and everyone jumped up on a stool as in a cartoon. I'm
not exaggerating, or only a little (not everyone jumped
up on a stool; just two people did, and likely for comic
effect. Others, however, edged behind tables or headed
for the back room).
     These spiders look like miniature intergalactic
space machines on stilts, except miniature is not how
they look. They're about three inches long, maybe four.
European imports, it's rumored. Invaders. Colonizers.
Settler colonizers even. And they can move. As yet we
haven't seen any in our isolated corner of the outback
but the city media have been going wild over them. And
now for the first time I can see why.
     Then up at the office I discover a new
communications snafu between me and reporter Naomi, the

second in a week. Not too serious, I hope. But I'm
starting to worry. We don't want her thinking this
agreement we've struck is more trouble than it's worth.

And my new clock's ticking away. The old one
became too unreliable. This new one is a cheapo travel
model from a dreary mini-mall five miles along an
alternate "Third Way" route to the camera factory. I
made a special trip down there to pick it up (turns out
it's the closest mini-mall to our house, but we never
knew of its existence until last week). I must be
able to get some sleep when I come into the city and
it's just about impossible to do so without the aid of
a working alarm clock. Even with such a device fully
deployed it's difficult, but without one, forget it.

Eight bucks for the thing, about as cheap as they
come these days. Yet it's right on the button with the
time thus far and for three trial runs in a row the
alarm's gone off just when it should've. The old-
fashioned kind, it boasts hands of different lengths and
they go round and round like the wheels on the bus.
Reminds me a lot of the travel clock Cindy L. gave me as
a high-school graduation present. Was that the same
brand? Might've been. But that one at least had a
spiffy simulated-leather case. This one has a brown
plastic case that doesn't even try to look like leather
except for the brown color -- or no, take that back.
Closer inspection (right now) reveals an almost
invisible leatherlike grain pressed into the plastic.
So we're talking about a quality item here. In
admirably subtle fashion it upholds an important
tradition, yes it does, just in case some antiquarian
nitpicker, myself for instance, wants confirmation of
his outmoded aesthetic values.

1:17 a.m. it says. Or no, it doesn't say the
"a.m." part or indicate it in any way. This is one of
the drawbacks of the old-fashioned kind of clock. But
not to worry, because I happen to know it's a.m. and can
confirm this if I want by looking out the window (and
with my confidence still shattered from misplacing my
checkbook I think I'd better). -- Dark out there.

[Jyzemelt]

Scattered lights smeared on the bay, some twinkling
because of the wind action, which is strong and gusty
tonight. And it's chilly. Not a good night to be
crashing in downtown doorways, though on the way over
here I passed by at least a dozen unfortunates who were
doing just that. And with the former out-party
promising to demolish the welfare state will we soon see
far greater evidence of poverty and homelessness? Or
will that party also arrange to keep most of it hidden
from public view? (Of course they'll try to do that.
But will they succeed?) (Their leader, the ultimate
ultra-rightist of our era, is a true grinch. Every time
I see his photo I'm possessed by the urge to strangle.
It may be he inspires this reaction in more of his
countrypersons than any USAn politician ever has,
possibly excepting a certain virulent anticommunist
senator from the Mentoka zone. And yet the man knows
what he's doing. He won't be easy to bring down.)

     But what arrives in the mail? Of a personal
nature? A postcard from the irrepressible Tom T. --
from his new home only sixteen hundred miles to the
southeast. He's moved! His recently merged railroad
company transferred him to the other mergee's main
office down there. (Actually I knew the transfer was
coming but I had no idea it would be so soon.)

     I'll miss the guy for sure. But I still talk with
him anyway because he hangs out in the depot at Mentoka
Falls -- in fact he's the night ticketmaster there. One
of my favorite "Jyzer" characters, and based entirely on
Tom T. But by the time I'm done, most of the
ticketmaster's best lines will probably be cut, or at
least should be, because in truth they have little to do
with the story. He and Jyzer G just like to talk
trains: "dark territory" and "consist" (as a noun) and
the like. A little gorky, no question, but then that's
exactly the point. And it's whistle-tootin' fun!

     And the big news can now be released: I've gotten a
raise. A nickel a page, which should work out to maybe
a buck and a half an hour on average. And D too has
been granted a raise and also a promotion, but she

starts from such a low base that she adds only two bits
to her wage, which goes up to $5.25 an hour. She still
likes the job, that's the important thing. And several
guys out at the factory are still panting after her and
she's still getting a big charge from this, almost as if
she were twenty-two again (at which point -- that is,
when she was that age -- I was myself one of several
guys panting after her, so I know what it's like and
what she's like when it's happening). But the hours she
puts in on making herself up and doing body-beautiful
exercises -- incredible. Always, now, with neo-punkish
alt rock playing, and usually the same stuff over and
over, and especially the band called -- but no, I'll
resist the urge to utter its name. Meanwhile I've
observed that the red tones in her hair are becoming
quite noticeable under bright light. A sign of aging,
she told me once, long ago. And so I ask again: is that
what's driving her in the current era?
      Is she loving someone else? Sleeping with him or
possibly even her? I don't know. At the moment I tend
to think not. Maybe it's cooled off, whatever and
whoever it was, if it was. Maybe it never got quite
that far. Saying no is extremely difficult for her but
she also has a terror of STDs, most of all HIV/AIDS.
(As do I. Now I have to be thinking about this sort of
thing again for myself as well. Welcome back to the
real world.) (But I do know one person I won't get it
from: her. Sex between us is finished.)
      Will there ever be another lover in my life? At
this point I really do wonder. Once in a while I can
still go weak in the knees at the sight of an
exceptionally attractive woman (or nubile girl for that
matter). But I have no illusions that any of them are
doing the same at the sight of me. Or put it this way:
I may still have a few illusions but they're harder than
hell to justify or maintain. And so -- or no, not "and
so." Just: face it.
      How it is then. I'll probably prefer a loner's
life, at least for a while. Later on if I could find
someone suitable for the likes of me, terrific; and yes,

[Jyzemelt]

I'm sure I could love again. I like loving. I like
being loved too. I get off on both, especially when
they're simultaneous. I'm not burned out on loving and
doubt I ever will be. I have no problems envisaging
myself as Mr. Decrepit snuggling up with Ms. Decrepit
just so long as there's a strong mutual interest there.
And just so long as it doesn't begin happening for a
good long while -- a jyze age, let's say.
     Wow, tonight I'm suddenly forward-looking, hopeful,
optimistic, free of bile. Quick, I'd better stop so I
can leave things on this wholly unexpected high note.
                            *
     Twenty seconds later I tack on a kwikjyze PS. I
almost forgot to mention that today is our "meet
anniversary." It's the only anniversary we've ever
celebrated except for the first year or two after the
"zen marriage," which went down on July 22nd, as it
happens, nine months to the day after we met (but no, it
wasn't a shotgun zen marriage, or at least not in the
sense she was pregnant; in the sense that her parents
were about to arrive on the scene, well, maybe it was --
but in that same sense she was the one wielding the
shotgun, not them, and I was the one happily yielding).
     Anyway: we met eighteen years ago today. "The
Emerson Street Dancer" touched down before the bugged-
out eyes of the former "Blue Dragonfly" shortly after
the end of a modern-dance program in which she performed
spectacularly (got bravos, whistles, and a standing O
which included me) -- this alightment occurring in the
lobby of a certain college auditorium about a thousand
miles down the route of one of the three continental
trains that serve our city here, and the only one I've
never been aboard. But in my lifetime city No. 11, yes.
     This year neither of us has mentioned the
anniversary. I've wrestled with the question of
bringing it up -- just dropping a couple of caustic
words about it maybe -- but decided not to. Why give
her trouble? Why try to make her feel bad? Did she
want the big love of her life to sputter out? I'm
sure she didn't, or at least not until it was well

along toward doing so. Did she give that love her
very best shot? I'm sure she did.
     -- Well, but suddenly I'm stumped. What do I say
next? In truth I'm not sure of anything, but I'm
willing to grant her the benefit of the doubt. Right
now I am. And I know I'd be better off if this were to
continue to be the case. -- But will it? Who knows.
(And who needs to know? Not me. Not at this moment.)

37

     Burnin' thighs. Burnin' eyes. Fried goddamn
nostalgia synapses.
     It's an old hangout from more than six years back.
And what a night for it. Goblins and ghosts floating
about in the early evening. Jack-o'-lanterns grinning
gap-toothed on front stoops, real carved pumpkins with
real flickering candles inside. On no other day of the
year can you see so many folks out walking the streets
in the residential districts. Reminded me of my time in
Japan, the robed villagers clip-clopping in wooden geta
to the communal bath in the evening. Caused me to laugh
aloud with delight on the way over here tonight -- two,
three, many times. And the eyes to mistify as well.
     Maroon-hooded death in its cloak behind the bar, an
impressive Grim Reaper. The Mad Hatter perched a couple
of seats in front of me on the bus. Sherlock Holmes
operating the cash register at the U bookstore. (Of
course only one out of maybe every five or six people
you see is in costume. But you focus on that one and
the nature of life around you changes.)
     I picked a great day to track down the last missing
piece for "Jyzer." But did succeed. The Special

Collections Room at the U coughed it up: a rare first
edition, in English translation, of the first European
explorer's protojyze-like account of his expedition to
Mentoka and environs, including his apocryphal discovery
of the (nonexistent) Longue River. Lahontan himself,
yes! -- More chortles of delight to have a copy of his
masterpiece laid out on the table before me. Complete
with infamous phony map drawn up by the master's own
hand. As I suspected all along, this map shows the
bogus Longue branching to the west at almost exactly the
spot where the fictively renamed Mentoka branches to the
northeast. I ordered fotocopies of the apposite pages
and they'll be mailed to me and then I can read all the
words. Time was too short today for anything but a
quick skim.

For the nocturnal creature pushing this J-stick
it's been a topsy-turvy day. Up at ten-thirty in the
morning like an almost normal person. A lift to the
county bus stop, bus ride, foot ferry, then running into
a new gaggle of old cronies (several of whose names I'd
forgotten) on the one-ten auto ferry, then a hike up the
downtown hill to catch a city bus, the ride out to the
U, a quick march up and down nearby main avenues to
check for changes (to be incorporated into "Ghosts"),
then the campus on a sunny brisk autumn afternoon, trees
still colorful and fallen leaves fluffed up calf-deep in
places on the footpaths. And then after the library and
visits to several local book shops (to pick up a
quarterly available nowhere else in the city along with
a recent novel in the original German for Mother's kind
neighbor Rikki) -- then a crowded bus ride five or six
miles farther northeast at rush hour to scope out
another setting for "Ghosts," a stop for a fast-food
burger (which I had to gobble on the move because the
joint has no seating, a fact which I'd spaced out) and
then finally a long uphill hike to the old hood.

First time I've been back here since we moved out
of town. Six and a half years. My first glimpse of the
three-story apartment house which went up where our tiny
bungalow used to stand. Very nice. Gray. Balconies in

front. An electronically powered green-skinned witch
stirring a steaming cauldron (dry ice likely producing
the steam) on one of the second-floor balconies, the
scene dramatically spotlit. Most of the big old firs
still standing. The lot still boasting the same thickly
bushy and abundantly flowery borders and all the
neighboring homes looking about the same. For a moment
when I approached the rear of the property via the
private drive to "the Chinese place" I thought my old
hand-built shed was still standing too, but up close
this turned out to be a mirage -- as well it should've
since I tore down that shed myself. But in pretty much
its exact former spot stood a prefab plywood garden shed
of roughly the same size and shape. (And the backyard
is now only about a third the size it was. And the wild
roses, the tangled patch a dozen feet square with
offshoots that overgrew a large portion of my old shed,
have vanished, as has the nearby blackberry patch, which
I always viewed as indestructible.)

Weep weep. My time on this particular set, and for
that matter all sets -- but later for moaning about
those others -- is slip-slip-slipping away. Our five
years living out here: neither our best period nor our
worst. Maybe it was the last time some genuine hope
glowed for us -- or at least I had some. I mean for the
full hundred-percent heart-to-heart forever kind of
deal. (Retrospectively it's easy to see this, but at
the time I had only occasional glimpses, eminently
suppressible and therefore duly, even vigorously,
suppressed.)

A long-running gradual disconnect, wire by wire,
while keeping the facade lit up. That's what. No doubt
we're both guilty of it. "Guilty." -- No, I won't
accept my own term "guilty." No crime was involved on
either side. It happened and that's it. -- Not that
this makes the loss any easier to take.

*

Meanwhile the old watering hole here languishes on.
"Proud to be a smoking establishment." Three pool
tables on one side of the rectangular central bar, three

dartboard lanes on the other side. A big-screen TV and
a couple of smaller ones. Mostly oldies and country on
the box. Mostly retirees and vintage working people
hanging out here now, it appears, along with a
sprinkling of oddball younger folks. Not even a hint of
hipness or punkness or grungeness or altness. (But the
contrarian Jyzer G of "Ghosts" might take a perverse
liking to a place like this just because it's so
blatantly orthodox and old-school.)
     Otherwise it's been another tough week. I mean
real tough. Mother's still hanging on but only just
barely. The first taxol treatment almost did her in all
by itself, and afterwards the doc put her on a portable
home oxygen unit. The company that provided the machine
tried to scam her into buying it for an outrageous sum
with her own money -- but even on her last legs she
still could put up a ferocious squawk and succeeded in
keeping it a rental paid for by her insurance. The
second day after the treatment her temperature hit 102.
Yet by the time I talked with her again on Saturday
night (four days post-treatment) she was starting to
feel better. (Though she had no idea what day it was
when she answered the phone, her mind soon cleared and
she sounded almost normal -- except for the surflike
hissing of the oxygen machine in the background. During
the first call she seemed frightened -- "You don't think
I might go tonight, do you?" I've had to find it in me
to become the voice of calm reassurance and hope.)
-- And the hospice is starting to make twice-weekly
visits. But the insurance won't pay for them until the
docs say she has less than six months to live, and they
won't say that until it's clear the taxol's not working.
And we won't know about the taxol for two more weeks.
So she's toughing it out, her lung capacity down to a
fraction, and I mean a small one, of what it was.
     Grim.
     (But here come a couple of human-size fuzzy pink
rabbits limping through the unfrozen grass of the
parking lot. Suddenly this place is filling up more
than I want -- I'll probably have to move on soon. Back

ends of pool cues looming into my near field of vision
and stirring fears my brow'll get bonked. A big black
steel safe squats behind me, incongruously enough, file-
cabinet size (two drawers) much like my fire safe at
home, a box of used chalks resting atop it "cueing," for
me, a flood of high-school and college pool-shooting
memories. The wall to my right is papered entirely with
sports schedules up to eye level where the picture
window begins, and right outside the window stands --
the old bus shelter! Something like -- pausing to
figure -- something like, yes, twelve or thirteen
hundred times I caught a bus out there.)

Which could explain why it all feels so familiar
here, yes it could. Feels comfortable, even, though in
a wholly unexciting and for that matter increasingly
disquieting way. I could never love this place (and
never did) but it's all right, I suppose, in a pinch
(and always was). (And how many times have Lady U and I
performed the old copulative act over these eighteen
years and one week? Just thinking. And I'll say I
don't know, but for sure a lot more times than I hopped
on the bus out there. Maybe even double or triple that
number. Which could also go a long way toward
explaining why I'm seeing things as I am these days.
But enough said on that. Too much.)

*   *

More than ever embarrassed. But you gotta laff.
(Haven't I been doing that?) Because I've now shifted
to my old No. 1 dive in this town, the funky back room
thereof. On Halloween night. With a big cold crescent
moon hanging in the sky directly above the joint just
like the one the floozy clings to on the sign jutting
out over the entrance (if I remember right). And back
here these aren't autumn leaves we're up to our calves
in, they're peanut shells. And many still enclose
peanuts.

One turf and one turf bar deeper into personal
history. To go any deeper than this I'd have to head
down to the train depot and climb aboard that third
continental to city No. -- what was it again? Have to

check, as almost always. (I have the list written out
on a notecard now, taped inside the back cover of the J-
book along with several others containing similar
reminders.)
     Eleven. City No. 11. This one right here is 12.
     Hard rock playing, the traditional kind. But a
moment ago it was grunge. The scruffy and the raunchy,
the weathered longhairs, the new punks and the old
punks, the nasty and the spacy, the moony and the loony,
the raucous and the -- what? -- the rocked out? -- Lots
of smoke, dim light, beer in the air, pool balls flying
(and a youngish mixed couple set up in a secluded booth,
both scrawling away at sketchbooks: might almost be me
and Lady U in our early days in this hood -- though the
mix here is Afrusan male/Eurusan female).
     By appearance I still fit in just fine. And this
place, unlike the one where I was holing up an hour ago,
I still love. And it's still a foolish love, just as
back in that distant era -- no denying.
     What I'm really up to today, it seems, I'm trying
on the old life for size. Do I want to attempt to slip
back into it full time? Would it beat a more isolated
existence in the home port? And: I'm already tilting
back toward thinking it would. Oddly enough I suspect a
second round in the city would work better for the
simple reason that I now know much better what I'm doing
with my writing. I wouldn't be thrashing around quite
so blindly as before. Maybe I wouldn't even have to be
too lonely. (Boo-hoo, that's right. Let's hear it!)
     One other guy in this back room at the moment, and
he's giving me plenty of space. A drifter dude, I'd
say, roughly my age; he's munching on peanuts plucked
from the floor and noisily cracked open karate style.
Meanwhile I'm gazing at a wall plastered with yellowing
picture postcards -- most sent back to the old prime
hangout by its legions of friends, a number of whom are
now big names around here and elsewhere, in one or two
cases around the world. (Here's a bloke in a threadbare
pea jacket and plaid cloth cap tentatively plunking away
at a battered old upright piano whose existence I'd

forgotten about. -- But it's still a basic no-nonsense
back room through which one must pass to get to the
women's head and could pass -- it's one of two access
routes -- to the men's head. A long bench built into
the west wall, two thoroughly carved-up and thickly
revarnished picnic tables, movable benches, a vintage
cigarette machine big as a fridge. And the blue neon
beer sign glowing up high on the back wall. Posters
tacked onto the ceiling next to a ten-foot banner with
the bar's name writ large on it. A pay phone hanging by
the entrance -- and out there in the main room the U-
shaped bar, the silhouetted patrons, the picture windows
throbbing in various beer-sign colors, and beyond that
the reds and yellows of four lanes of heavy traffic
crawling along outside, both directions, and shadowy
student-dominated foot traffic trudging by as well.)

I do recognize the place. I most definitely do.
In fact I can't detect a single way it differs from the
place I used to know. Even the piano is coming back
now.

And all during this singular day I've been
devouring a book by my favorite neoprag antiphilosopher.
There's never been any other thinker with whom I've
chimed so -- harmoniously? Is that the way to put it?
It's no barrier at all that his politics aren't quite as
radic-prog, say, as mine -- that he's more a postwar or
even prewar kind of liberal. Or in a way it does matter
because I become uneasy -- but never mind. Who cares,
uneasy! The main thing is gratitude. I even think of
writing fan letters to him as Barb's previous boyfriend
Lawrence used to do to a completely different kind of
thinker -- in fact Lawrence and I once sat in this very
bar until closing hour every night for a week arguing
about this very same pair (Lawrence was a go-down-with-
the-ship analytic type). -- But fan letters, I suppose
I'm getting a little long in the tooth for those.)

A matched set of orange and black balloons, their
ribbons loosely entwined, floats by. A party goin' on
here! Stories being told! Echolalia! Laughter! On
the other side of the doorway every bar stool occupied.

[Jyzemelt]

Shadowy faces. Cigarettes. Lovers. Halloween masks.
Sparring on-the-makes. Sports chatter. Drug talk.
-- Flare of a cigarette lighter right now as I glance
up. Sneers. People who know each other. Some serious
poetry talk. Clinking glasses and knocking knuckles
(knocking on wood, followed by splashing dice).
     So far a slight aura of novelty in all this for me.
You forget. Just as you forget about the existence of
whole blocks of houses in a hood where you lived for
five years. You forget on which cross street the tavern
stands which you visited several times a week for five
years (a different five years). You forget how it is to
have all those faces peering at you as you lurch down
the aisle on a moving city bus just like the ones you
rode for a decade. The little dramas of, say, will this
person or that person sit in the empty seat next to you?
Or would they rather take their chances with the nasty-
looking dude slouching across the aisle? Can you
predict the order in which the empty seats will be
taken? (And can you unclumsily pile all your bags and
your coat on your lap to make room for someone -- and
should you try to do so anyway even if you suspect it
would be for naught?)
     The big excitement back home: Goat mounting the
doghouse in B&B's kennel, then propping his splayed-out
legs atop the fence so he could nibble on the tempting
nearby sapling with its bare tender limbs, many of which
were soon history. (And D shrieking at me when I
sarcastically thanked her for helping me put up the
groceries, which of course she hadn't done. And again
something snapped. -- My newly evolved feeling being
it's best, however, to pretend to myself, and therefore
if at all possible to actually believe, that at least a
faint hope still flickers that she'll see the error of
her ways over the next four or five months and decide to
mend them. To get away with this she'd have to go a
long, long, long way, but I'm still better off thinking
it could happen. Otherwise I can't stand being there.)
     (Likewise I'm better off acknowledging that things
between us basically came to an end in the Marco time.

In the thirteen years since then there's been no real
reciprocity, or little. I decided I'd love her anyway,
and I did, and for reasons of her own which I don't
pretend to understand she decided to let me do so. For
this I'm better off if I can feel grateful. She did the
best she could to love me back. Alas, as a bogglingly
spoiled only child of relatively aged parents she's not
so good at loving, though she is very good indeed at
getting along with a lover if she decides she wants to
do so -- and especially if the lover is relatively aged
himself and carrying lots of baggage as well, like, say,
me. And for a long time she did decide to do that. But
now it would appear she's decided it's time for a change.
And rather than raise a stink, I think I should just
accept this.)

    Why sure. The Halloween Declaration! Just do it!
(And I'm working on it, here in my corner, though the
smoke is starting to bother my eyes. Luckily no job
awaits me at the office tonight. My intent is simply
to stop in down there for a little magic-carpet shut-
eye.)

    -- I came very close to saying to her we ought to
face the facts, we're done, but how about if we go easy
on each other, how about if she lets me hang on at U
Acres until my mother dies (this is the brute reality)
and we close the place up and sell it, as we're supposed
to be doing anyway late next summer (though neither of
us has made reference to this fact in a couple of
months). I wouldn't bother her, I would only ask that
if she's seeing someone else in a sexual and/or romantic
way that she not bring that person home (and I'd be just
as circumspect for her) -- but I'm afraid this approach
would backfire. New furies (revenge, say) might be
conjured on either side. I'm rejecting it for now.

    -- And thinking I'll roll along. Don't know what
time it is -- which means I'll have to stand down at the
corner in the thirty-degree cold for up to thirty
minutes since that's how often the buses there run at
this hour, meaning by the law of averages I'm likely to
wait fifteen minutes -- and that's assuming they're

running on time. In the real world the likely wait
would be closer to twenty minutes, and that's
eliminating from consideration the ultra-long "outlier"
waits owing to collisions, breakdowns, on-board
violence, and much, much more.

(Saying this is all right, this life at the old
No. 1 dive which I re-sample every five years or so, I
could tolerate it and maybe even enjoy it once in a
while. True, I'd much prefer the loving mostly-stay-at-
home coupled-up life, but I suspect the possibility of
coaxing a new one of those into being has drifted beyond
my reach. Eighteen years ago I already thought that
might've happened and that's why I believe now I
primarily ought to be grateful for the reprieve D
accorded me, weird and one-sided though it was for much
of its course.)

These folks sitting next to me now are about to
move on to some big party, "not too lame from what I
hear." Parties everywhere tonight. Tricks and treats
in the old urban zone. -- Could I live in some sort of
privacy-respecting commune? Find some decent people to
share a house with? Hit upon a bearable artists' co-op?
Oh but the packing and moving will be a colossal pain.
How much can I cut back on my possessions -- which means
basically my books? Could I come up with some sort of
workable storage arrangement? (That is, one that's not
too expensive and which offers fairly easy access to a
renter lacking wheels.)

Yeah, and it could be pathetic. I could be. But I
want to discard all thought of that very real
possibility. Just go at my work with all the force and
focus I can muster and hope for the best. (Sure!) If I
go down, go down fighting. (Beautiful!)

(Here's a scrawny beagle nosing about in the peanut
husks. A guy in stage-quality graybeard makeup featuring
a horrific augmented Neanderthal brow. A red-eyed blond
woman flaunting more curves than we the scuzzed-out
vintage denizens of the back room could ever hope to
properly adore. A male professorial type of, one might
guess, deconstructionist bent, amusingly pristine black

leather motorcycle gear and all, who gives me a curious,
faintly dismissive glance as if he's worried I just
possibly might (or worse, might not) recall him from
the old days (as I guess I too am worrying he might or
might not recall me, even though the truth is I'm
pretty sure we've never set eyes on each other before
tonight). -- And I won't continue.)

*   *

Or then again, why not? Because I didn't really
mean I would cease continuing for all time. I just
meant for that particular venue on Halloween night in
the year jyze two.

Had to wait only thirteen minutes for the bus
according to the familiar bank time/temp flasher a block
east of the stop, but the flasher perhaps shouldn't be
trusted since it's still running an hour, more or less,
ahead of real time, that is, Standard Time, which we
"fell back" to Saturday night. Several of those minutes
I passed, after checking the schedule at the bus shelter,
nibbling on an apple fritter in the nearby twenty-four-
hour doughnut shop (this the same greasily funky
downscale student hangout where I waited for Mother and
Barb at the end of their last joint visit here together
seven years ago this month).

The bus driver on the double-length bendable coach
slowly wending its way downtown wore a black witch's
hat. A man. Definitely witches have dominated the all-
genders costume ball tonight, at least by my jaundiced
estimation.

But what a miserable stormy week it's been. Back
at jyze central five or six days ago I finally had to
give in and turn on a heater. Lawn whacking is finished
for the season (and a good thing too because my right
elbow is taking its time healing). Out with the quilts
and the winter overcoats and the heavy henleys. Once
again I'm piling coats and sweatshirts atop the single
thin blanket beneath which I nap every night on the
study couch. (My self-imposed banishment from the
bedroom when D's in there is complete and, I'm all but
certain, permanent.)

[Jyzemelt]

     The smashingly successful first annual city book
festival, staged at a pier just a notch or two down from
the ferry dock and featuring a number of literary heavy
lifters, I was not able to attend. I wanted to. It
sounded like lots of fun. The very saloon I was
visiting earlier tonight (the second of the two) was
granted the cafe concession! But alas, though not
surprisingly for one who maintains the hours I do, the
timing was bad. (And a few days earlier the United
Nations celebrated its golden anniversary. And just
yesterday a Canadian province voted, by a whisker, to
remain part of Canada. And in between the King of
Norway visited our city. He even paid a brief visit to
a Norwegian theme town out in the woods not too far from
U Acres. But the timing -- again, terrible.) (This
king is the son of the one whose hand fictive narrator G
shakes as a young lad in Gramps S.'s presence back in
the Mentoka JIFT zone. What's more, the Norwegian theme
town near us here stands in fictively for the small
touristy town eight hundred miles down the coast where
the real Gram and Gramps S. retired.)
     A barren life at home. But I decided it might be
good for me. It might help me create a new life in the
world of "Ghosts." That's my new pitch-to-self anyway.
     And just yesterday the "Memorials" proof finally
arrived. Most of the next week will have to go for
correcting that and then it'll be out of the way and the
decks will be clear. Because otherwise I'm ready.
     -- All this sworn to here in the office conference
room before a brand-new gigantic-screen monitor and
video camera. Their controls are very fancy and I have
no idea how to operate them. Technology is moving
beyond me. And I could care less. (But I did buy
several new rubber stamps today and this form of
technology I can still handle. Here's one: "SHRED"
(red). And it's self-inking! Just like Jyzer G when
he fills his J-stick!)

38

Stormy election day, November type. The microphone
works and the speaker's voice is powerful. The rain is
like sandblasting. Such fine maritime grayness was
sliding by the weepy windows of the ferry as we plowed
across the bay coming in, huge shadowy freighters
bucking in slow motion on tethers. (Now I'm switching
tables because soon the folks sitting in the other room
will be lining up for autographs right here, it turns
out; the clerk has just arrived carrying a cashbox and a
stack of freshly shellacked, so it appears, copies of
the speaker's book. The speaker himself is a recently
retired public TV news commentator whose elaborate
hairdo looks only slightly less shellacked.)
                                 *
Now hunkered down in a somewhat more sheltered
spot. The voice drones on, queasily familiar and
authoritative, at the moment responding to questions.
("Today we're so much more informal," the voice
observes, "than we were a generation ago.") (But he's
right; and he's not despairing over the change and he
says just that. This is a man not without a certain
winning, if opportunistic, flexibility.)
     Concentration. The attempt.
     It was the four o'clock, the workingman's boat.
The workers are from the shipyard and almost all male
and nearly all grab a booth bench and are stretched out
and snoring sometimes even before the boat pulls out.
Piles of mingled and mangled newspaper sections litter
the tabletops. (Also in the gray out there on the other
side, riding at anchor and looking invigorated by the

storm, was the infamous destroyer that started the
Vietnam War under false pretenses, the pride of the
transit port -- not to mention of my fellow denizens at
the bar across the inlet in "jingo heaven." In which
town, by the way, I've decided I definitely will not be
living. "Whatever could you have been thinking?" as ol'
Mom might've inquired.)

Now the authoritative voice goes silent and chairs
scrape and the autograph line starts forming. Upscale
types mostly, older, earnestly concerned liberals --
public TV viewers -- and why is it one suspects they
have no clue as to how most of the world sees their
country? Could it be because so much of what they know
comes from the TV commentary of this or some other fully
authorized and utterly anodyne observer: the shellacked
anchorperson?

Let's see. Jyze. The news. My life. Hum a few
bars of the dirge.

Tonight Mother's supposed to call with the news on
whether the taxol treatment is taking (she calls it what
sounds like "tax-law" and chuckles over her inability,
so uncharacteristic of her, to keep the name straight).
After nine bad days she was finally feeling pretty good,
and her care situation had improved markedly because the
hospice had begun sending someone over for two hours
every afternoon to help with chores and Mother's
insurance was picking up the tab. Of course this also
meant the docs had officially given her less than six
months to live (or so she believed, from something
someone had told her some time ago about how the
insurance works), but we all knew her time was short so
there was no shock (and if the taxol takes she might
have closer to a year).

So she totters about on a tether of her own: fifty
feet of transparent oxygen tubing. She says she may
even risk attending the theater (using a portable oxygen
unit, as one of her elderly second cousins does). She
lets me know she's well aware the family's split on
whether she should go on "being a fighter" (Rob and I
for, Barb and Jeff against), and she'll make her

decision about the taxol (that is, if it's taking) based on how she reacts to the second round. If it hits her as hard as the first round did and for as long a period she'll probably stop it. (She's counseled with cousin Lars, the law professor, about this, and he's reminded her the decision is entirely her own to make. Having the hospice services means she would feel less guilty about imposing on Barb -- whose daily help is no longer so urgently needed -- and thus the odds favoring a decision to fight on appear to have improved.)

In any event Doc B. has told her she has at least two or three months left. And she's decided she shouldn't be embarrassed by her deteriorating appearance, or rather shouldn't let her embarrassment override other kinds of emotions, and so she's invited me to come down for Christmas (when Rikki and Mischa will be away and I can again crash in their apartment). And of course I'll go -- unless her health takes another unexpected sudden bad turn and I need to go before then.

Meanwhile today I'm carrying around the corrected proof of "Memorials." Tomorrow I'll mail it down to her so she can check to make sure all the captions match the pictures -- and also to be sure she'll at least get a glimpse of the final product. On the phone she turned all weepy about how Popeye would've been so proud of the work done by "his eldest grandchild" on "what he always thought of as his most important project." After a while I nearly broke down myself over the way she was talking, "the last wishes of the dying."

It's been a labor of love, I assured her, and I wasn't lying. But a lot of work, yes. Just as predicted, most of the past week went to it (what didn't go to scoping 340 tough pages at the office). And more labor lies ahead: next, hammering out a promotional press release. Not at all my idea of a good time.

But what the hell. (The entire autograph line for the commentator has now filed by and they're out of here, himself included.) So jyze on you crazy bastard. Your life, make it squeal. Goose it. (Har har, honk honk -- as if I've got it in me today. But I can always

fake it, I suppose -- or at least try. Well sure, and
doing so is just fine because what else is jyze but
faking it? Artificing it. Even more than other kinds
of writing. The only relevant question is: how
interesting is the fake? Or some variation thereupon:
how entertaining, say, or how enlightening or inspiring.
-- Just as long as it all checks out, that is, of
course. Fact-checkers rule!)

A right-wing fanatic assassinates the Israeli prime
minister. His country in mourning. A blow to the cause
of the good guys, no question. These days seems like
more than ever it's one such blow after another. Of
course it's entirely possible it's always and everywhere
seemed so, excepting brief interludes when mostly
hormonal surges of hope prevailed.

-- But I did have a short chat with Lady U today
(after a number of dismaying actions on her part in the
past week) and it took a load off my mind. She didn't
react badly to my observations about the slimness of our
chances of remaining together and the hope that we can
be civil about the parting if we do break up and the
further hope that we can stay on together in the same
house so long as my mother's still alive ("because it
would just crush her to see us break up now"). She's
amenable. We'd be more like housemates who're basically
strangers and just tolerating each other's presence --
this is how I interpreted her comments (none of which
were anything like straightforward).

Why the big change in her feelings toward me? She
can't say. She claims not to know why. Apparently she
doesn't even care enough to explore the issue. Amazing.
I can say something like "I have the very strong
impression you really don't want to have me around here
anymore" and she doesn't react at all. "Is there
anything about what I've said that you want to correct?
Am I misreading you in any way?" No, there's nothing.

Her story is she's too busy to think or care about
anything but her "work." By this she doesn't mean her
personal work, her art -- which she appears to have
dropped pretty much completely -- but simply her

moneymaking job. Yet she's putting in only eight or so
hours a day on that, usually five days a week, just like
most people, and her commute is less than twenty minutes
each way. Most of her free time continues to go to
exercising and applying makeup while avidly listening to
the music she used to despise. She's just -- gone.
Gone where, I don't really know and probably never will.
     But I'm relieved to learn she's willing to say
she'll be civil and she won't show me the door
immediately -- the other shoe won't fall this week or
next. I can't be sure she'll hold to this, of course,
and so my relief is only partial and provisional. But
it's an improvement. I think I can obsess less on the
subject. I can avoid confronting her about matters
which make her uptight. Maybe I can even get some
fictojyzing done.
     (What triggered most of the bad scenes with her
this week was a phone call from her old high-school
buddy Marissa. D was off at work and I had to answer
because of the possibility it was Mother calling. Would
I mind, Marissa wanted to know, if she paid us a visit
shortly after Thanksgiving? She was calling
specifically to ask me because the U's had advised her
to do this, to get my okay. Sure, fine, come, said I,
because what else could I say, especially since Marissa
and her filthy-rich husband Curtis are the people to
whom the U's hope to sell the house. But when D heard
about this she hit the roof. She wouldn't have time to
entertain Marissa! So D called her parents and urged
them to beg off with Marissa -- basically blaming the
whole incident on me ("You try to get him to clean up,"
I heard D say to them, even though I've done all the
cleanup for months and I'd already told her I would do
it for Marissa's visit) -- but this is standard
operating procedure with D. So now Marissa's visit has
been postponed until "January or February" when D will
also, she's suddenly saying, be returning home to renew
her driver's license. Who knows what's actually going
on. Today D was even denying -- to me -- it's a sure
thing her parents will be selling the house. "My

mother's starting to talk about moving here again."
     What rot. I just hope I won't be around next
summer to have to deal with another installment of it.
     -- Only half past seven. A women's book club, six
strong, chattering away at the next table. Me, I've got
scoping to do. At this point I'm still unaccustomed to
the new routine. To avoid hiking to and from the county
bus stop in this miserable weather I'm catching a ride
there with D on her way to work. This means I leave
home at two p.m., dawdle for an hour at cafes or saloons
near the ferry docks, dawdle a couple more hours here at
the only real bookstore or some other downtown watering
hole, then try to get three hours' sleep on the carpet
at the office and have D pick me up at the same county
bus stop at ten a.m. (after I've dawdled some more in
the morning at ferry-dock cafes and elsewhere) and then
aim for three more hours' sleep at home if I have to go
in again later the same day.
     Am I imposing on D with this routine? Only a
little. The county bus stop is right on her way to the
camera factory. And if she's not working that day, the
four-mile round trip to the stop takes ten minutes tops
(and I ask her to drive me there no more than twice a
week). Meanwhile she's the one who gets to use the
wagon every day for any and all purposes, including her
own commute, even though she could take a county bus to
the factory just as easily as I take mine to the home
port, and she wouldn't have additional ferry rides and
walks and in-transit layovers and delays awaiting her
after the bus journey. And I'm the one who paid for the
wagon! (That is, the half that's paid.)
     I'm also still doing all the cleaning, dish-washing,
bed-making, etc., and I'm rustling up my own meals,
coffee, whatnot. Thank god the grass has stopped
growing. I also burn the trash and take what can't or
shouldn't be burned to the recycling center and the dump.
And yet: am I complaining? Hell no! Much better to do
all this basic upkeep stuff myself rather than try to
deal with D in apportioning it. True, the setup as it
stands is grossly unfair to me, but fairness no longer

matters a whit with the relationship hitting the rocks.
As long as I have a certain minimal amount of time for
my personal work (the JIFT) I don't care about the
rest. Feed the cats, water the plants, mop up the
septic overflow, you name it. I'd start breaking rocks
with a sledgehammer and selling them as gravel if I
thought it would help.

   -- One day on the front page of all the newspapers
a spectacular photo appeared of a star being born
somewhere in deep space. Another day an alarming report
about world foodstocks resuming their downward course
(per capita) and the expectation that this trajectory
will now continue indefinitely -- that is, the so-called
Green Revolution is over and so is the putative respite
from that aspect of the larger ecological/climate crisis.
According to this same article world population has
grown almost half a billion just in the first half of
this decade. Eye-opening, even for one who likes to
think he's pretty well informed on most of this.

   And so. What fakery! Splendid, riveting
adhockery! Good enough that now I can say I've advanced
this jyze thing another ten pages without provoking a
single complaint. So far! And after this won't matter
because I'll be hightailing it through the rain
somewhere else. (And we'll see later about tomorrow.)
                *   *

   Tomorrow is here and the news is bad. The fix is
in, the worst kind: meaning the taxol isn't working.
Mother said I shouldn't take it too hard, "It's all
right," I guess implying (trying to) she's ready to go,
but you could tell from the overtone of forced and
almost hysterical cheeriness -- giving way to long
aching pauses -- it's just not so. But it will happen
anyway, regardless of any and all attitudes about it,
and possibly quite soon. The proximate cause of death
can't be known in advance, other than to say it will
likely be one of half a dozen, and all of them ugly:
bone cancer, rupture of a blood vessel in a lung, heart
attack, stroke, and -- two others. I've lost them.

   Most of the time we talked about possible items for

inclusion in the press release for "Memorials." She's
working up a letter for me about this. And just
yesterday she mailed off a number of boxes containing
prized possessions she's bequeathing to her
grandchildren. (Any number of times she's made me
promise to inform son -- grandson to her -- Elgie of how
much she's always loved him, should I ever get the
opportunity.) Probably right up until the last second
she'll be plugging away on a dozen different projects.
     Will I still be going down there for Christmas?
She might be able to hang on that long. Or should I try
to go earlier? But there will be no place for me to
stay except for her apartment, and she let me know
that's out of the question now because so much medical
equipment has been brought in. And she doesn't want to
spend money on hotel rooms, and of course I have very
little money. And even if I had more -- enough -- it's
not at all clear she would want me to be there; and if
she doesn't want me to be there, I don't think I should
be. But is this what she really wants? Will there be a
deathbed conversion or reversal on the matter?
     Grim times ahead.
     Barb was taking the news well, Mother said. She'd
just called, Barb had, asking if we children had ever
been baptized. Yes we had, Mother told her; she'd
gotten around to it a little later than she should've,
but the Reverend John A. had done the deed on all three
of us in a single group dunking, as it were, at the
Gatewood Community Church (Rob wasn't born yet). And
why, I asked, did Barb want to know about this? "I'm
not quite sure. She said something about 'remission of
sins.'" Sounds ominous to me. Sounds like Barb has
gone all the way over to the legions of, as the current
preferred appellation on the antitheistic side has it,
the Sky God. The Supernatural with a capital S. The
biggest baddest warlord of them all. (Though it's not
to be denied: in certain quarters this deity is reputed
to have some, even many, redeeming qualities as well.)
     -- This going down in a booth at the home-port bar,
the ever notorious "jingo lounge." Candles still stand

on the bar itself, not lit at the moment but ready for
duty. Apparently power was out most of the night on
this side of the drink. The TV's talking about floods
"inundating the western half of the state" (making it
all a kind of drink, could say). A particularly nasty
series of gusts nearly blew me off the dock a short
while ago as I hurried out to make the foot ferry.

On the big ferry plowing over against the wind I
wrote a card to Rikki, Mother's downstairs neighbor.
Rikki I like. A good person. Would she, could she
appreciate someone like me? Even, say, in the absence
of major sparks? Suddenly I find myself thinking about
such things. And I don't want to be doing so. It's
that same old hormonal programming (not, of course,
without a strong cultural overlay and frequent media
booster shots) that makes me do it.

"Goddamn it's cold. It's raining, it's blowing.
Sheez, what a day!" (And that wasn't me. A guy at the
bar. Same guy who rails pretty much nonstop at the TV
-- wants the asshole president drawn and quartered and
his asshole wife thrown to the sharks and says what we
really need is more bombings like the heartland
blockbuster -- I've heard his disgusting reactionary
spiel dozens of times. And he's by no means the most
fanatical one around here.)

-- There is this to crow about: my nickle-a-page
raise is now confirmed. Which means for last night's
four hours of scoping I made an additional 185 nickles,
or nine bucks and change. Admittedly degree of
difficulty on the job was about as low as they go. And
I'll still be well below subsistence level if I have to
be my own sole support. Nonetheless things are looking
up. Not all sectors in the life of the jyzer are down.

The lights flicker. Eep. This is too bizarre,
the timing of all this stormy stuff. How pathetic can
a fallacy get? (And yet taken as a whole the election
results don't look too bad. Maybe people are waking up.
Yay! -- But don't count on it.)

[Jyzemelt]

39

    Booth at a transit-port saloon. An hour to vamp in
an unexpected place because I lost track of time and
missed the three-thirty foot ferry and therefore the
four o'clock auto ferry. But no problem, no big rush to
get to the city. And that's why I wasn't watching the
clock very closely in the first place.
    Looking out on the inlet, the dock -- and now the
big passenger ferry as it glides up. (Roars or glides?
Chugs? Putt-putts up.) Just getting to sundown. Blue
sky overhead but menacing black clouds to the southeast.
Long lines of shipyard workers waiting to board. Four
more such workers in the next booth arguing politics
over a pitcher of beer. As of yesterday the federal
government is shut down in a budgetary impasse between
the legislative and executive branches and I'm assuming
many or most of the guys in here and outside -- and
everyone in sight's a guy except for a couple of servers
-- may soon be feeling the pinch. Though they hate to
think of themselves this way, they're virtually all
government employees or military pensioners or both.
    A huge stuffed swordfish swims in smoky air
currents directly over my booth, suspended on nearly
invisible wires sort of like Peter Pan. An antiquated
Brit rock star is crooning and I'm not ashamed to say I
recognize the voice: same one that was belting out some
apropos jukebox lyrics around the time D and I met:
"Hold me closer tiny dancer." Pool balls are clicking.
A TV is flashing silently high above the bar, muted
pregame talk for this evening's pro-hoops match,
starting early because it's being played two time zones

to the east. A row of six neon beer signs of widely
varying hues is glowing brighter by the minute as dusk
deepens. (The sixth isn't a beer sign, I see belatedly,
as if this could matter: it's shilling a soft drink.)
   As if any of this could matter! As if the whole
idea here weren't to be reaching for the quotidian and
the trivial just to help keep myself propped upright
(and yet also hoping to make it all glow -- the whole
schmear, yes -- just as bright as any neon sign).
   With these four next-booth guys, at least, it
sounds like the "revolution" proclaimed by the hardcore
right-wingers of the former congressional out-party is
in deep doo-doo. I wonder, though: is this a majority
view? A decade ago I'd've been sure it was. Today
that's doubtful. These are union guys and this town is
not the burbs, to say nothing of the backwoods or the
bible belt or (lord help us) the old Confederacy.
   To heck with it. (As the passenger ferry backs out
and then roars off, sounding and looking just like a
grossly overgrown cabin cruiser.) Now we can stare at
the skeletal structure of the new passenger shelter
going up on the dock, halfway out, green steel, cone-
shaped, its design appearing at least at this stage to
have been inspired by some sort of Mayan pyramid. And
on the sidewalk outside a gull is vigorously shaking a
live fish in its beak. Savagely. Quite possibly it's
the same gull that was peering at me so intently from
point-blank range a few months ago at the terminal just
across the street. Meanwhile all four workers, much
like me, are pausing to gawk at the Darwinian spectacle.
   A luscious dream today. Front-seat canoodling in
Dad's old commuting car with Karen A., her wonderful
warm full crinkly-nippled breasts, and no sooner do I
get back home than a tearful Lady V shows up and
declares she's discovered she loves me after all. This
poses a dilemma for me -- for all three of us -- but in
the end there's no doubt which one I'll go on with. A
fine dream, for it reminded me that if Lady U's about to
zap herself from the lists I can always fall back on
loving Lady V -- by JIFTing about her. And the same's

true for Lady S or Lady K or even Karen A. (dead thirty
years next spring -- and four years before Lady V
popped into my life). Somehow I'd forgotten about
such possibilities for a while.

On Monday night a miserable call from Mom. That
morning she'd thought the end had come -- had a terrible
time breathing, and this with the oxygen tube in place,
its twin "claws" jammed up her nostrils. More and more
I'm fearing she won't make it to Christmas. I hinted I
could come down for Thanksgiving but she wouldn't go for
it. She's back to insisting she doesn't want to be
remembered in the condition she's in now. At times
during our recent phone conversations she's turned
panicky and appeared to be losing her grip, but then
she's pulled herself back together. The "Memorials"
proof had just arrived that day and we talked about her
disappointment with several of the photos and what she'd
like me to highlight in the prepublication release I'll
soon be working up.

Any of these talks could be our last. The chances
I'll see her alive again are worsening by the day. I
think about her a great deal and slip into absentminded
funks which go on for what seem like hours. I face up
to the sad fact of -- what? (Even now I'm losing it.
-- As the big ferry, all lit up in the deep dusk, floats
into my left peripheral view and relieves me of the need
to go on with this -- for a few minutes anyway.)

*   *

So aboard and just a trace of deep purple lingers
in the sky to the west. Lots of bright shipyard lights
shining out there. And lots of folks going about their
lives right here on the main deck. Excited kids. Bored
shipyard workers sitting sideways on the booth benches,
backs braced against the internal bulkheads (or let's
just call them walls), skimming newspapers before
sliding down out of sight, except for their feet in most
cases, to their fifty winks (meaning minutes of sleep).
We've got students, we've got lovers, we've got drunks,
we've got pompous execs, we've got garrulous salespeople,
we've got a picnicking family (Dad's a tyrant), we've

got a teacher grading papers and an architect pecking
away at his laptop and some other guy barking self-
importantly into his cellphone -- in short we've got
the usual motley boatload.

The charge up the "No Entry" ramp and the dash to
claim favorite seats -- it's always a pick-me-upper.
(Except when someone cuts rudely in front of you or,
perish the thought, grabs your accustomed spot.)

-- It was facing up to pain I was trying to get at
back there at the saloon. Not my pain, except
secondarily. Hers. The extreme shortness of breath is
itself a form of pain, although it doesn't actually
hurt, or at least not yet, or so she says. They're
already preparing to administer morphine. How
"comfortable" they can make her last days I don't know.
To what extent she'll remain herself when under the sway
of even more powerful drugs I don't know either.

Essentially I'm trying to accustom myself to the
idea it's all over now. It may be better for everyone
concerned if I don't try to put in one last appearance.
(And in truth I'm content with the two visits we've had
and willing to accept them as our -- what? -- our swan
song, I guess. Let things stand as they are. Because
our relationship is on a good footing now. And I'm
confident she feels this way about it too.)

It's like a carryover from sports. Without
conscious intent I find myself trying to "image" what
every aspect of her dying will be like, from the final
few days (and then hours and minutes) to the immediate
aftermath, the funeral, the divvying-up of possessions,
the months and years of grief and mourning.

Eeeep. How do I prevent this gloomy stuff from --
eating me alive? For matters at home are equally
dispiriting. I'm losing the two most important (there's
that word again!) women of my life -- simultaneously.
And not a damn thing I can do about either one.

-- So quick, change the subject. "Ghosts"?
"Dreams"? "Jyzer"? The going's still tough with all
three. I've resolved a few thorny questions and I've
been inspired by a second reading of the irrepressibly

hokey Lahontan travel journal (admittedly in the real
world no one ever would've named a burgeoning capital
city, even a provincial one, after this man, as I've
done -- and it's the city of my own birth!) -- inspired,
yes, but as a matter of hard fact I'm doing very little
new JIFTing or even revising. Mostly I'm just spinning
my wheels. Losing myself in one after another of the
aforementioned funks. Even when doing light reading I
often find I have to go over lines twice or three times
before I can grasp their meaning, and sometimes I can't
then either.
     This will have to stop at some point. So -- when?
     I've now worked my way a second time through the
entire corpus of my favorite neoprag antiphilosopher's
published work (that is, the stuff that's made it into
book form in books authored solely by him). That's the
one positive point that comes to mind at this moment.
(But now, suddenly, it's a madhouse as we arrive at the
dock, so I'll pack it in and head myself on out.)
                    *   *
     Quite a sunrise this morning as seen from the
ferry. Some of the regulars are actually noticing it.
Gazing at it, even, a few of them. Patches of rosy pink
along the horizon, gray clouds, mist, golden rays, dark
mountain silhouettes, evergreens, a wide expanse of
mirror-still water in which much of this same vista is
reflected upside-down. But so long has it taken me to
eat my boxed dinner and skim the newspapers that we're
now almost ready to dock on the other side.
     While passing through the downtown post office this
morning I dashed off a postcard to Mom -- the picture
side a shamelessly kitschy painting of an antic state
ferry festooned with Christmas decorations, the whiskery
old secularized winter spirit himself at the helm
wearing a red stocking cap -- and looking a lot like Jim
Q., as my note on the card didn't fail to mention.
     Scads of leaves plastering the plaza bricks around
the main federal building (because the government
shutdown includes the leaf-sweepers). The usual five or
six recently chowed-down drifters hanging around outside

the mission across from the bookstore -- the one place
in that area where you're rarely panhandled. An
education writer in the basement at the bookstore
drawing a surprisingly large crowd, including a number
of men in my general age group who struck me just from
their looks as likely to have something interesting to
say (this is unusual). A flashing-eyed Asian beauty in
a long tight black skirt and red top: I was stunned by
her resemblance to Briana T. A couple of free papers
from the bins in the basement, including an extra "alt
weekly" for Lady U. Live trad jazz blazing out from one
of the clubs as I hurried by: a sobbing trombone with a
plunger mute (I call it) and a goofy gamboling tuba --
sounded like good times were rolling in there.

*   *

Now back at the home-port cafe, Vi a little slow in
getting around with the key to open the iron gate
separating restaurant and jingo lounge. I stand
chatting with Tina, the petite, prematurely gray-haired
bus driver (she's almost a full decade Lady U's junior)
who drops me off at my hole in the fence most mornings.
Next to us a boothful of those same yahoo U.S. Navy
retirees is hooting up the budget standoff. "We gotta
balance this goldang thing, we just gotta!" What they
really mean is: We gotta stick it to the goldang
liberals and people of color and if the whole goldang
country has to go down the goldang tubes to do it, fine,
because the goldang Apocalypse is due soon anyway. And
the very thought of this cataclysm is nearly enough to
rapture these fools up all by itself.

Aboard the new foot ferry (which skitters across so
fast) I read a little about ---

*

(That was Tina. Did I mind if she joined me for a
minute? I didn't. Some human company! To hell with
jyze! And it's a good thing she's married -- with three
kids -- or I might've done something rash. Like: "Tina,
you mind if I move in with you tonight?")

*   *

Quick now, while I'm feeling good. Just a whole

323

lot better. And this with vinegar in my nostrils from
the big guy's fish'n'chips in the next booth -- scores
the scales right off my eyeballs, it does.

     Same boat as yesterday but it's a later run, the
six-twenty (which means the two boats flipped
schedules). Pitch black outside, much less crowded
inside. And me, I'm still sweaty from my hike to the
county bus stop -- first time I've had to make it
entirely in the dark. The glare of oncoming headlights
is irritating but what's much worse is the invisibility
of the holes and puddles along the unpaved shoulder.
Thus my squishy left shoe and throbbing left ankle.

     The old back-and-forth. This is how it is now two
or three days a week. Rush like mad for a couple of
days, take a day to recover, then a day or, if I'm
lucky, a couple of days for my own work at home, then
back to the mad rush for a day or two. It's far from
ideal, true, but I'll take it. While I can.

     Old bus-riding pal Haskell, super-cheerful Afrusan
junkyard supervisor: we crossed paths for the first time
in months. And perky Eurusan Wanda in the canteen,
finally hitched now after "dating" the guy (as she likes
to euphemize with a sly little smile) for fifteen years.
Wish I had more friends like these two, a place I could
drop in after work and they'd all be there. Laffs,
sparks, soul and funk dancing: the whole enchilada
including lots of good yadda yadda ying ying ying.

     A chapter on the "supreme fiction" of the red-
wheelbarrow poet also has a hand in my mood flip-flop.
He's a lot more my kind of guy (just as the one who can
see only wasteland and Semitic plots wherever he looks
is Barb's kind).

     And then -- I guess I'm getting used to the idea of
splitting with Lady U. It's starting to hurt less. I'm
seeing the positive side. I'd prefer for love to have
lasted forever, but better to move on than to chain
myself up in a failed relationship.

     Did she betray me? Is she betraying me now? Yes
to both. But I want to make a distinction and I want to
keep it firmly in mind. Relationships don't fail

because of betrayals; rather betrayals happen because
relationships have failed. And the failure is always
the "fault," if that's the word, of both parties. In
the past I've been quick to apply this kind of thinking,
bromidic though it obviously is, to other couples in
trouble; I see no reason not to apply it to us too.

D's betrayal comes solely in the way she's bringing
things to an end with me. It's plenty cruel. She's
turned her back on me abruptly, without explanation, at
a horrible time. She refuses to talk about it -- indeed
is probably incapable of doing so. About all I can say
is she hasn't been as cruel as she might've been. She
could've told me to hit the road right now. Or had a
gang of her jailbird pals from the camera factory do it
for her.

Often I think of the way Lady S reacted when I was
breaking things off with her. On the one hand I see
better why she reacted as she did. On the other hand I
do my best not to show D the same kind of petty
vengefulness and bitterness Lady S laid on me. (In my
own defense I'll say at least I did all I could to
understand why the relationship with Lady S was failing
and to try to salvage it by thrashing things out with
her and, that failing also, to explain why I was doing
what I was doing, or at least why I thought I was doing
what I was doing. With D there's none of this: open
discussion of emotions is something she'll engage in
only with extreme reluctance, if at all. But again,
though this has become more and more the case as the
years have gone by, it's been there from the start, a
matter of culture and family mores as well as
personality. It's not as if I didn't know.)

Truth is, I've never believed in the kind of
relationship she and I have had. That's exactly why it
always seemed downright miraculous that it could prosper
as it did -- despite its many flaws! -- and survive so
long. And it's also why I can be so shocked and at the
same time not surprised at all by the way she's ending
it now.

I could make this ending every bit as painful for

her as it's been for me. And yet: I don't want to.
(Except when I do. But somehow I manage to keep those
nasty urges under control.) I know her limitations
about as well as I know my own and I know she's reached
the point where she'll likely be happier with someone
else. I want her to have that chance. Smarmy as it
sounds, it's the truth. Or maybe it's just a matter of
being self-serving: for once I want to see myself as
having been loving to the max from beginning to end.

    I dunno. Who cares. Later for the postmortems.
This isn't the first time and I'm sure it won't be the
last, but I say I'm over the hump on this thing.

    (Is this the new pattern for jyze entries, a gloomy
first half and then a pep talk about the breakup? He's
back upright again? You can't keep a good Daruma doll
down forever? -- Nah. I'm figuring jyze will rescue me
no matter what and that's the sum and substance of it,
the true jyst.)

40

    Oh the hurt. The hurt she put on me. Yes she did.
    So now I try to fight back. In my own way. (But
here she is now, and this time I have something to ask
her. So break the rules -- this once. Or rather --
this once more.) (How I know, creak of the back door.)
                          *

    So it's settled real quick. She gets tomorrow off
(it's Thanksgiving), so I'll take the wagon in the
evening since I have a back-order rush job to scope at
the office (they called this afternoon). She also
showed me the contents of the mail-order box that came
in today from an animation outfit, including a hat, a

mug, a pin, and a bag, all bearing the company's cartoon
logo. She's an official member of their club now! And
I asked if I could see the movie-poster catalog which
arrived a couple of days ago, but she said she's already
given it to Zach, who's also a member of the same club.
"That's how he gets ideas, looking through catalogs."

Cartoonist Zach -- is he the one I'm being thrown
over for? She spent all day with him Saturday, in the
city, until three in the morning. To my eye the dude
looks about sixteen, but she insists he's twenty-six.
Which is to say: if that's true, the gap in age between
her and him is the same as the one between her and me.

A real tough week -- tougher even than the previous
week, which had seemed about as tough as they get. And
I think I said the same thing that week too, about the
previous one. Or if not, should've.

Barb called Monday night. Things are much worse
down there. Mother had to be put on morphine and she
didn't react well to it. One of the ill-paid hospice
workers may have accidentally overdosed her somewhat --
but at this point no one can do much for her and
regardless it's just about impossible to know exactly
what should be done, if anything. So now she's
bedridden, in diapers, unable to talk on the phone,
often incoherent, sometimes raving but also sometimes
"almost clairvoyant." When Aunt Shar telephoned, Mother
called out, "Tell her I'm not afraid to die."

So now Barb takes over. (Her chance to play the
martyr again? No doubt. But I'm grateful she's there
to do it.) She's moved in and she's taking family-leave
time off from work so she can be with her as much as
possible. She's feeding her (mostly tiny portions by
eyedropper), changing her diapers, keeping the oxygen
machine charged. Sleeping on the couch. Her primary aim
is to enable Mother to die at home among people she knows
and loves, in her ancestral bed, in a room filled with
ancestral items. But she can't do it all, Barb can't,
and although the hospice sends someone over every day,
it's for a total of only fourteen hours a week, and of
course Barb can't stay away from her job forever without

losing that job (which she says she may decide to allow
to happen), and she has to sleep sometime, so when I
talked with her she was planning to hire a full-time
nurse (that is, forty hours a week of nursing help, over
and above the fourteen hospice hours).

The deterioration was more sudden and more extreme
than anyone expected, doctors included. Yet this is how
it often happens, the hospice nurses have told Barb:
abrupt catastrophic decline rather than a gradual steady
fade. But it's also possible Mother will seem to
improve for a while as she learns to tolerate the
morphine. Though she appears to be much closer to the
end than she did just a week ago, no one can say for
sure how long she's got -- whether it's hours, days,
weeks, or possibly even months.

I'm guessing weeks. She's always loved Christmas
and she'll probably try to hang on so she can experience
one more. She may be able to do this by sheer
determination, so strong is her will. Or then again she
may decide she doesn't want to continue placing such a
burden on Barb or to continue eating up the funds she
wants so much for her kids to inherit -- she may even
contrive to find some way to bring the ordeal to an end
sooner rather than later.

Everything's on a day-to-day basis now. Barb will
call if a major change occurs or if it appears the end
is near. (Or will she? She may very well want to have
Mother "to herself" at the end. There's nothing I or
anyone else could do to prevent this from happening, and
I guess in some sense it's Barb's "right" to decide to
do it. For the past year or two she's devoted herself
to Mother in a way the rest of us haven't -- couldn't,
really -- and so I feel I should let her decide, with no
input from me, the way things will go. It's sad but...
this is how things are now.)

So the deathwatch is ratcheted up to a higher level.
There's only one level higher than this, and that's "the
end is here."

*

-- And in the realm of love and romance it's

328

something similar. After the blatant insult of Lady U's
trip into the city Saturday with Zach (not to mention
the cascade of day-to-day humiliations) I decided I had
to act. This deathwatch too, in short, is ratcheted up
to its next-to-highest level. I've started taking
concrete steps to prepare for the breakup.

Of course I'm still trapped in this house for the
(un)foreseeable future. And I'm hoping I'll be able to
bear living here three more months, maybe four. To make
this psychologically possible for both of us I'm trying
to keep contact with D to an absolute minimum. Nor is
this particularly hard to do since she also appears to
be going to extreme lengths to avoid me. (Tonight's
brief conversation was the most extensive we've had in a
week.) Nonetheless I've moved my center of operations
into the guest room in the basement -- a/k/a the library,
a/k/a jyze central -- and when she's home and up and
about I try to stay down here with the door closed. If
I need sleep and she's home I crash on the couch here.
I eat and read here. I slip out the utility room door
and piss into the bushes. As much as I can I stay out
of her sight. (Should it ever become necessary, for
some bizarre reason, to justify any of this to her, I
would simply say I thought this was what she wanted and
I also believed this would be the best way for us to be
able to stay on, as we must, in the same house over the
winter.)

The other concrete step, I've started packing.
This will be an immense job in itself and the actual
move even worse. At this point I'm trying to do a
couple of boxes a day, limiting myself to the shed and
the barn and inconspicuous items down here in the house
so that the lady won't be alerted too early to what's
going on. I don't want a crisis to arise in which
she'll try to kick me out before I'm ready to go.

My plan is to rent a storage unit as close as
possible to the home-port ferry dock and start moving my
stuff -- these boxes -- over there piecemeal, one
wagonload at a time. Just when I'll do the actual
renting I don't know, but I'm hoping I can put that off

for a while -- possibly even until February. It's a
matter of bucks. Even assuming I'll soon have access to
a small income as a result of Mother's death (and I have
no choice but to think in this crass way), and also that
the Jyzer Ink proceeds will remain about the same as at
present (by no means a sure thing), it'll still be touch
and go whether I'll be able to afford anything beyond
the most basic kind of subsistence living. The working
idea is to put as many of my things as I can into
storage, find a place where I can live short-term, then
start the search for a long-term place.

By delaying my departure from this house as long as
possible I should be able to build up the funds to pay
for the storage unit and the initial expenses for a room
(deposit, first and last month's rent, miscellaneous
others). If possible I want to avoid using any of the
principal from the inheritance.

-- This does not do jyze proud. None of these
words here. It's the most basic kind of subsistence
jyze, that's what. I'll try for something better in the
morning.

*   *

Sweep back the curtain -- Thanksgiving Day is just
dawning. Gray and wet. Patter of rain, trickles, drip-
drops. And in here I lean into a pool of warm light
beneath the desk lamp. Twice during the night as I read
on the couch immediately behind me the power went out
briefly, the two lamps flickered, the radio fell silent.
During one of those outages the digital clock on the
microwave in the kitchen (as I just discovered) crashed
to triple zeroes.

Warm night. In my sweatclothes with the green-and-
white blanket and the old tan unzipped sleeping bag
drawn over me I was way too warm. Head and back propped
on four pillows and the davenport arm, working my way
through the current reading stack. Narcotizing myself,
knowing I wouldn't be able to sleep anyway, not after
caving in at five p.m. yesterday (just after the office
called) and returning to bed for an extra three hours'
rest. My sleep routine is totally screwed up right now.

The same could be said for just about all my routines.
     But I have a plan. Yes I do.
     This rain, it reminds me of last week's monster
storm. That one, packing winds this one doesn't even
approach, roared in with exquisite timing late one
afternoon just as I was setting off on foot for the bus
stop. A mere two blocks up the road I was thoroughly
soaked but the only option was to keep going. Along the
way I nearly got picked off at a bend in the road by a
car whose driver evidently lost sight of the edge of the
pavement in the downpour -- perhaps because he'd been
shocked by the nightmare vision of a lone human figure
lurching into his headlights -- me.
     My heart was thumping over that near miss the rest
of the hike and then I was shivering all the way in on
the bus. Didn't get warm again until I stood directly
beneath the high-powered ceiling heat vent in the corner
seat cluster on the auto ferry. The dock scene at the
transit port was downright purgatorial with its huddled,
trudging, cursing masses, swarms of cars idling, winds
gusting across the inlet at sixty miles an hour and
more, high waves exploding against the dock and heavy
rain blowing sideways like airborne whitecaps. For sure
I wasn't the only one who was soaked that day -- but I
doubt anyone was more soaked. You just can't get any
wetter than that and not drown.
     But even then things were starting to look up.
True, they'd soon be falling apart again what with Lady
U's trip to the city with Zach and then, just as I was
starting to recover from learning about that, Barb's
call to report Mother's turn for the worse. But still a
solid basis for further improvement existed, and it was
simply this: a check for Jyzer Ink finally came in from
the office. Not just any old kind of check but one big
enough to give me a little room to maneuver. No longer
do I have to beg and plead with the lady for every penny.
     (That stormy night, I meant to say, what made it
especially memorable was the arrival earlier that same
afternoon of "No. 72," as all us savvy local nautical
types call it, an attack aircraft carrier which is now

331

being homebased here as a result of the post-Cold War
military shake-up. Hundreds of sailors changed into
civvies were lined up at the ferry dock eager to get
their first look at the area, and what they were seeing
was that notorious weather they'd heard so much about.
"Holy shit, can you believe this!" -- and these guys
had all just crossed the North Pacific in mid November!)

But the money. Mentioning it I'm reminded of a
fine little irony. Because a big chunk of the sum I'm
about to inherit is invested in a so-called rapid-growth
mutual fund of some sort, I have to start worrying about
the stock market, the business climate, all that
claptrap. Do I dare risk leaving those bucks where they
are? (And this week the Dow Jones average topped five
thousand for the first time -- and for the year to date
the value of Mother's investments has increased by
almost a quarter, which is preposterously high and to my
way of thinking means a fall must come soon.) Would I
be better off putting the bundle in the safest available
investment, as I've always recommended that Mother
herself do? (Because even at a very low rate of return
her principal has always been large enough that, with
the income supplemented by Social Security, she'd've had
plenty to live on.)

I hate to be worrying about this kind of stuff.
But already I'm doing it. And just as I'm locking into
the descent pattern myself on Social Security and
Medicare/Medicaid we've got the market-maniacal former
congressional out-party whittling away at both.

The inheritance. My one shot. Do I bet the bundle
on the Mentoka trilogy? I still may decide to do it.
Depends on how much I like the current draft of "Ghosts"
when it's finished. If I see some real commercial hope
in it I may cast aside all caution (an irresistible
phrase, that) and go for broke (that too).

Meanwhile it's unfortunate but what I must do is
think of Lady U as a dud. There's no way around it. I
know it's not true, but I go all wishywashy if I try to
keep both sides of the story in mind simultaneously.
And I can't afford to be anything but tough-minded

toward her now. -- I don't mean a bolt of lightning
just turned her into a dud, say along about this past
March or April. I mean she's been one all along. Back
at the start I let myself be dazzled by certain very
attractive superficial qualities. Because at that time
I badly needed to be swept off my feet. And I was.
It's that simple. (Of course it isn't at all -- I
already said that. But it's still better to be thinking
this way, at least for a while. Probably a couple of
years at the very least. That's how it was in the Lady
V aftermath, the only real comparison.)
     Thanksgiving. Neither of us has mentioned it. And
we won't, because we're basically not speaking. After
five p.m. or so I won't even be here.
     I was recalling that along about this time last
year I was wondering if our relationship could survive
D's going to work full time. And now the answer is in.
And this may well be the last serious hitch-up of my
life! I look back and I don't see a lot of success in
my various romantic "affairs" -- my loves. And love has
always mattered so much to me! Too much, no doubt.
First comment anyone would make in assessing my life.
     And yet....
     No, no, let's not get into the "and yet"s just yet.
     Brighter out there now and also rainier. All by
themselves the drops from the eaves make a nearly
impenetrable curtain like a waterfall -- or no, they are
in fact a waterfall. Of course they are! And the grass
as seen from this very pleasant heated and lighted cave
behind the waterfall looks a mite long but very, very
healthy. Few leaves remain anywhere except in the
blackberry patch and at least half of those are yellow.
(Blackberries are so tough, if they could be converted
into football players they'd go undefeated.) (Haw!
Where'd that one come from? How can I arrange to send
it back so no one will ever know of its brief escape?
-- But I refuse to scratch anything out. Instead simply
scratch onward. Scratch and scratch and scratch until
you have to be scratched yourself -- as in, scratch that
jyzer! All in favor of a jyzer-free world say aye!)

[Jyzemelt]

    Whooing wind now. A couple of dark yellow leaves
dart straight across the yard left to right at chest
level like muddied-up canaries. I guess this is turning
into the Thanksgiving Day Storm of the year jyze two.
(Kirstie, the jovial granny I sometimes encounter on the
ferries, told me that one of the old-time almanacs has
predicted this November and December will be the worst
in a hundred years. But I'd say November hasn't been
all that bad so far, here or anywhere else I know of.
Even last week's monster storm was pretty much standard
late-fall fare in these parts. -- Nonetheless I'm still
betting on a continuation and worsening of the pattern
of extreme weather brought on by global roasting. Among
other things it plays a big role in "Ghosts" so I guess
I'd better.)
    Groan. I did my best, coach. Some days you just
don't have it. (Seems like I've been dishing out this
excuse a little too often lately. I'm wearing it out.
-- But no, I don't think so, or rather I don't think it
matters. For excuse or no excuse, it's always better to
have jyzed something rather than nothing. A jyze truth.
If it's jyzetime, you jyze. And having jyzed, move on.)
                *   *
    This coda on hull No. 348 chugging in -- the one
I've shipped myself in and/or out on more than any other
over the past six, almost seven years. Today it's the
Thanksgiving boat -- mostly carrying folks coming back
from gramma's house out in the sticks. But old albino
Neil ("Sombrero Slim") is zonked out in the booth behind
me, in my usual spot. This is his normal boat and not
mine, so he gets first dibs. And he was ahead of me in
line and got there first anyway. (He has unusually long
legs and is an extremely fast walker, belying his death-
warmed-over look. And because he works at the federal
reserve bank downtown, he started wearing a ridiculous
bulletproof vest to work after the heartland bombing, as
if it would protect him from a massive explosion; and
even that heavy ungainly thing hasn't slowed down his
footspeed, no more than his eponymous weatherproofed
Mexican headgear does. And the sombrero he's never

without, because to him the sun blasting into his face
-- the ultimate in pale faces -- is far more dangerous
than any terrorist bomber, actuarially speaking.)

-- Do not dread! I'm trying to jolt myself alive
again. Death, however, is right now much livelier, not
just warmed over but spectacularly asizzle -- and
obviously this is no longer describing the death aspect
or the dread in Sombrero Slim. I mean in me.

When I called Mother's number about five p.m. no
one answered. Half a dozen more attempts over the next
hour, same result. It was the one eventuality I hadn't
thought of (or more accurately put, one of an infinite
number of eventualities I hadn't thought of, but of all
those probably the most likely to occur, though I
realized this only in retrospect). I had thought the
answerer might be the new full-time nurse, might be a
hospice worker, might be Keith, might be Jim Q., might
be Rikki from downstairs, might even by some miracle be
Mother herself, but most likely, of course, would be
Barb.

No answer -- what does it mean? Maybe Barb was
exhausted and turned the ringer off and didn't want to
be bothered with hooking up the answering machine.
Maybe she'd fallen deeply asleep and Mother herself
heard the ringing but was helpless to pick up. Maybe
(truly by some miracle) they both had gone out somewhere
for dinner, as they'd once been talking about doing for
Thanksgiving (and this as recently as a week ago).

Or maybe -- and the odds would certainly point
here -- Mother's condition has worsened again and she's
been shunted to a hospital and Barb hasn't gotten around
to letting the rest of us know, or simply hasn't had a
chance to.

So I'm here to say goodbye to my mother in the
only way I can. Is that it? It must be.

Just got to -- shrug. Howl. With pain, with
rueful laughter, with perplexity. With a bow to
inevitability. With watery eyes. With unclear vision.
With unhearing ears. With all due respect and a whole
lot more besides -- just call it dumb gratitude.

[Jyzemelt]

     A jyze tribute to Mom -- with here a jot, there a
jot, everywhere a jot-jot -- and only a tiny portion of
the jots can make it onto this or any other page. Or
simply call it (fear not sappiness and corn -- as if this
J-book be a turkey and of course on this day it must be
stuffed) simply call it, I say, the jyze of Thanksgiving.
Slightly delayed, it's true, but with homemade cranberry
sauce and pumpkin pie and real whipped cream and real
fruit salad and all the other fixings old Mom herself
used to prepare and serve. Giving soul-deep thanks.
Sentimental slob is what I am, yeah -- but if ever there
were a time for it, now's it. And I'm feeling it. Maybe
even had to get out of the house to be able to do so.
     Dread not! (Dread not the dread not, nor the
dreadnought, the mighty mo, the big momentum, the
excruciating emotion, the connectingest connection of
them all, and its severing, with old Mo herself.)
     And now we float in on a high tide and I have to --
have no choice but to, thank god -- stop.
                    *   *

(Next evening.)
She died this morning, Friday 11/24, age seventy-
five and four days short of nine months.

                       41

     Now sixty hours later at the airport and I've got
some time to burn. A cafe, a deep-corner table still
rocking like crazy despite the two matchbooks inserted
under the legs (by someone else) and the pad of folded
napkin I've added. "Ding-dong, ding-dong, Christmas
bells are ringing" -- the carol on the P.A. As outside
the long row of picture windows jets roar skyward in the

dark at short intervals and once in a while a huge tail
assembly like a giant shark's fin glides by seemingly
almost within arm's reach.

So it's finally over. Everything's postmortem now.
And after a couple days of wrestling with the anguish --
or actually more often just going blank for long
stretches -- I'm starting to rematerialize. Where was
I? But I know. I was in a place you're in only once in
a lifetime and from which no knowledge is allowed to
escape. Except maybe a few stray rays at odd and
unpredictable and sometimes frightening moments.

(But here are flashing red lights. And "O Little
Town of Bethlehem" -- reminding me of my departure from
the office on Friday morning, a couple of hours before
Mother breathed her last, when I was startled by the
appearance overnight of a fifteen-foot-tall Christmas
tree in the ground-floor lobby -- which is a glass cube
several stories high and brightly lit up at all times --
and parked near the tree several large cartloads of
ornaments and fancy gift-wrapped boxes stacked so high I
stopped to gape at them and I thought: now this is gonna
make for a mound of presents that beats even the old
Christmases at home -- except here the boxes are all, of
course, empty. Yup, I thought that.)
                          *
-- Back from scoring another coffee refill. This
will be a very long day and I'm operating on only a few
hours' sleep since Friday. You just can't sleep at a
time like this. Huge changes coming down in my life.
Grief, anger, despair, perplexity, anxiety, excitement
-- all at once. In constantly and wildly fluctuating
proportions.

It was Rob who called with the death news. This
was about half past four Friday afternoon and I'd just
gotten up and hadn't yet started brewing my coffee; as
usual at such times I was groggy and loggy. And
probably it's just as well I was. "Glen, I'm afraid I
have some bad news. Mother passed away this morning."
(When I first picked up the phone he was on the floor at
work -- on this famously busy "Black Friday" prime

shopping day -- and he told me to hold on, he would go
to the extension in the back room. So I had time to
think about what the message might be. But I don't
think I actually did think anything, other than dully
expecting it to be bad.)

Barb had called Jeff in Lahontan, Jeff had called
Rob here (and also tried to reach me, he told me later,
but I must've been asleep and D must've already left for
work or wherever it was she left for). And only last
night when Jeff called again, this time from Mother's
apartment, did I begin to get some details beyond these.

She died in her own bed at about eleven Friday
morning (probably when I was winding down in my parlor
armchair shortly after arriving home from work and again
failing to get an answer at Mother's number, as had been
the case all night). The deterioration was rapid, Jeff
told me, so much so on Thanksgiving Day that Barb felt
she couldn't both tend to her and deal with our phone
calls -- so she disconnected the phone. Friday morning
Mother "was moaning in the other room" -- meaning Barb
was elsewhere in the apartment, presumably -- "and then
she wasn't moaning and Barb noticed the silence."

This is just about the full extent of the details
as I know them. I expect -- but I'm not at all sure --
I'll soon be learning more.

Privately I'll say here (and only here) I'm not
pleased with the way Barb handled these last days. She
never did call in the full-time nurse. I guess she
couldn't bear to let a stranger horn in on the scene and
I don't doubt she also feared the nurse would
inadvertently do something to worsen the situation or at
least tarnish Barb's last hours with Mother. But a
nurse's presence also would've made it possible for the
rest of us to have a last moment with Mother, if only
largely symbolic: Barb could've been more rested, less
caught up in moment-to-moment nursing concerns, and she
could've answered our Thanksgiving calls. (Rob and Jeff
also tried to get through and failed and I don't doubt
are just as dismayed about this as I am.) -- But this
is Barb. At the end she held true to form: she kept

Mother to herself and tended to her own moral purity and
the ramifications for others didn't trouble her, or if
they did, no one's heard anything about it yet from her
and no one's expecting to.

However. You have to forgive her. You have to try
to forget all this. You must keep in mind the difficult
nature of her relationship with Mother (and the world)
and the excruciating pressure she was under, the
sleeplessness, the uncertainties, her own pain.

-- Turning gray out there. And I'm already feeling
better for having gotten all this grousing off my chest
right at the top. I think I can carry on all right.
(And I've publicly vowed to do my best to prevent any
bad scenes from developing. I volunteered this. "Ol'
Mom wouldn't want things to get too gloomy -- she might
even have preferred Uncle Hank's Irish-wake approach."
Jeff agreed.) (Barb had gone off to get some rest when
Jeff and I talked. Rob was there too and he came on the
line for a while. Our phone talk Friday had left me
with the impression that he wanted us to transport our
"bequeathals" up here by truck as soon as Thursday so he
could be at work Friday morning -- but that's off now,
if it ever was on. Maybe I just misunderstood in my
grogginess and shock during that earlier call.)

Barb and Keith are moving into the apartment
immediately. Mother made us all promise to clear out
the stuff she's left to us within a month after her
death, but it's tough to just go in there and start
stripping the place. We each have our own list we
worked out with her, and she went to such great pains in
hopes of helping us avoid the sort of nasty scene that
followed upon her own mother's death when the three
sisters had to divide up the property at 4202 with few
clues (and those conflicting) as to Nana's intentions
for them.

Barb stayed alone with the body for a full eight
hours before calling in the medics.

And the word is that Barb does not regard it as a
blessing that the final deterioration was sudden and the
end came quickly. Despite Mother's pain and incoherence

                    [Jyzemelt]

Barb was still "getting something of value for our
relationship" right up to the end, as Jeff quoted her
saying, meaning in essence, in my view, that even on her
deathbed Mother was likely being subjected to Barb's
sermonizing.
     So be it.
     -- I've said my farewells a thousand times. And a
whole lot more lie ahead. (I keep getting up, meanwhile,
to check the time. About ten more minutes. I don't want
to be left behind and I'm not sure how far away the gate
is.) (An odd coincidence, by the way: the fancy
restaurant next door is called The Carvery. That's also
what I'm calling the premier restaurant in downtown
Mentoka Falls (seat of Carver County, near the heart of
the old Carver Grant territory which makes up a major
part of the state of Mentoka) -- except I'm spelling the
word with an i-e at the end instead of a y. Or I was.
Now I think it reads better with the y -- and I guess I
think this just because the spelling here has taken on
the authority of being real, i.e. (another kind of i-e --
aiee!) -- i.e., it's in print and it's drawing in
passersby. Or I could say: it's JIFT being informed by
JIRT -- fictive time by real time.)
     As for the love of my life, Lady U, forget it --
I'm so disgusted with her I'm speechless. On this
infinitely long weekend when my mother died Lady U not
only didn't have a single kind word to say to me, she
couldn't even come up with an expression of condolence
or a warm look, a touch -- anything. So she's succeeded
in her aim of driving me away. I've already rented the
storage unit. The severance process ("disaffiliation")
is irreversible now, period. (But I'll try to slash my
way back to a better attitude toward her -- later.)
               *   *

     I'm shocked myself by this abrupt transition but --
lying now in Mother's bed where she died just six and a
half days ago. Nana and Popeye's bed it once was, an
antique four-poster. During visits to their house in
Lahontan as a kid I used to love lounging about in this
very spot on this very bed in their upstairs bedroom.

                        340

Foghorns sounding periodically -- a little past
midnight. Barb asleep on the living-room couch, Jeff
just laying himself down on the air mattress between
stacks of packing boxes in the hallway. He and Rob have
already had their nights in here, as of course Barb has
also (on the last night Mother was alive -- and then for
those eight hours when she wasn't).

Hard to keep my eyes open -- I mean what I could
really use right now (and shall soon consign myself to)
is some sleep. Right. For all these six days and
thirteen hours I've been going on virtually none.

Today the four of us walked five or six blocks up
to the hilltop park and scattered the ashes. A perfect
day for it: windless blue skies, temperature close to
seventy, yet because of the lateness of the season not
too many people were present in the tower area. The
actual spot was about fifteen steps down from the summit
via the new brick staircase, steep and zigzaggy, in a
wooded zone on the east side of the hill. We took turns
carrying the box of her "cremains" as we spiraled up the
hill on the access road (the box hidden inside my black
backpack which we passed from sib to sib). (And now
that backpack, along with the dark blue velvet
drawstring bag in which the crematorium box arrived and
the inner plastic bag, still dusty with her ashes, rests
next to me on the bed.) (Feels a little ghoulish, true,
but really not all that much so. I'm trying to think of
this as the closest I'll get to having a last moment
with Mom.)

The tears flowed freely. Few words were spoken.
The green ground cover slowly whitened as in a light,
gritty snowfall as all four of us tossed out handfuls of
ashes and tiny scraps of bone.

Walking back down the hill Rob and I both became
fascinated by the sight of a monarch butterfly quivering
atop an acacia flower. Earlier on the way up all four
of us filed silently past a medical team rushing a
patient on a gurney out of an apartment and into a
waiting ambulance parked on the sidewalk with emergency
lights flashing. (I don't know what the others were

thinking but my own reaction was something like:
Couldn't death have given us just a moment's respite
before going after the next victim in the hood?)

(Such a familiar creak now as I shift positions on
the bed. I'm sure I've heard that sound hundreds of
times, possibly thousands, many of them well before I
had anything but "goo-goo" and "Mama" and "Dada" and
maybe "Gunnah" (as I pronounced my own name early on)
for language. -- The way the death actually happened, I
should note, was that Barb stepped out of the room for a
moment to answer the phone -- she'd turned it back on
just minutes before -- Rikki from downstairs was calling
-- and when she returned Mother was essentially gone,
into the death convulsions.)

And the gory business of breaking up the apartment,
distributing the possessions, packing. Nonstop almost.
Filling up boxes, crating paintings and valuable pieces
of furniture that must be shipped long distances. Goods
piled everywhere. Playing "bequeathal poker" with
Mother's albums and CDs. Gazing at the framed and
amusingly altered "Georgie Girl" movie poster Rob gave
her at age fifteen which has stood watch over us from
the kitchen counter at all times for the past few days.
Lots of emotional moments and at times giddy hilarity,
even perversely so, none of us able to stop ourselves.

Before tonight I stayed downstairs at Rikki's
place. Last night I took her out for a drink. She's
within a few months of D's age, it turns out, and
wonderfully thoughtful and good-hearted. I was quite
touched to see how well she'd gotten to know Mother in
the short time they'd been neighbors.

-- But...this bed. This time to say goodbye --
thinking the odds are probably against the four of us
ever being together again in this apartment or for that
matter anywhere else. (Though we like to think
otherwise.) So far tensions have been manageable, only
a single brief flare-up between Barb and me, and that
over something inconsequential.

But I can't continue. Simply too tired.

*   *

[Jyze to the End of the Night]

    Deathbed jyze part two. Seven hours later, the
morning entry. More sleep than I've racked up all the
other nights of the week combined. White curtains. Low
murmuring voices of Jeff and Barb coming from the
kitchen. A grandfather clock ticktocking quite loudly
out in the hall. Antique furniture in here, most of
which I recognize from my childhood and all originally
from Kaskieki and the far southeast provinces. Only
picture hooks remaining on the walls (and almost
undetectably faint pale rectangles where the pictures
were hanging). Large bundles of clothes in black
plastic trash bags piled on the floor awaiting the
Salvation Army's visit later today. A plug-in radio
shaped like an old-fashioned mantel clock on the bedside
table (the hands stopped at 1:40 -- probably because the
outlet down below was needed for the oxygen machine).
    A dream of flying using just my arms, a march along
a riverbank. Wish I could remember more. Dream of a
very special night, once in a lifetime -- at the end of
a very special lifetime. Simple sappy mournful truth.
    "Beneath thy deep and dreamless sleep" -- the words
just popping up like a dream themselves. For sure I've
heard them a few times this week as the Christmas season
continues its relentless rollout.
    (Better get up. They're afraid to make noise
thinking I'm still asleep and many noise-making things
remain to be done -- by me too -- and time's short.)
    (But warm, clean, dreamy, yes, at peace with her
here in her sheets -- thinking of myself as an infant in
diapers sprawled out on her chest as she lay on her back
more than half a century ago, on an antique bed very
much like this one and just a half-dozen steps away from
the room where this one stood at 4202 in Lahontan -- no
doubt a lot of what I felt toward her and coming from
her back then being just about the same now.)
                    *   *
    Gate 6, forty minutes until departure time. It was
a fine ride over here -- talking hoops with the shuttle
driver -- and I got all the packing done I'd hoped to do
and left on good terms with Jeff (whose shuttle came a

343

couple of hours earlier) and Rob (who had to take off
last night) but with Barb the final hour was a disaster.
Now it looks unlikely she and I will be able to maintain
much of a relationship, if any at all, in the months and
years ahead.

There was that slight flare-up between us last
night, mentioned earlier, when I disagreed with
something she said about a condolence note sent by
Jeff's ex, Volly. It wasn't even an unfriendly
disagreement, I would say (and later Jeff concurred),
but for an unknown reason or reasons it set her off, and
a moment later when Jeff said he read Volly's note the
same way I did -- Jeff too speaking in nonprovocative
fashion, at least to my mind -- Barb lit into him and I
was soon entirely out of the picture as they quarreled.
Eventually they struck some sort of truce and then Jim
Q. arrived for the evening and I assumed the whole
incident (minor as it seemed) had been forgotten.

Today I found out different. Barb was cool toward
me all morning. Finally with only an hour remaining
before my scheduled departure time I decided to say
something. I worried over exactly what words to use and
approached her with some apprehension. What I finally
said was, in essence, this: As the tensions of the past
year ease off over the coming months, Barb, I hope we'll
do better at getting along and be able to put our
relationship back on a good footing.

Her reply was snooty and nasty at once, shocking
me. Having me around had been a "liability," she said,
and until I could stop "attacking" her, my presence was
something she could do without. Of course she loves me
and respects me, she lamely added.

Outrageous. I was too stunned to say much in reply
-- just babbled something about things working both ways
and the need to exercise extreme care if we want the
relationship to recover and the necessity of stopping
her own "attacks." She declared she never attacks; I'm
the only one who ever does. So I said I can't accept
being defined as the bad guy; either it works both ways
(insisting now) and we both accept some responsibility

for the shortcomings of our relationship or the
relationship will stay as it is or deteriorate further.
     And that's where we left it. I went back to the
bedroom and did my final packing. The shuttle arrived
a little early and Barb and I had time for only a brief
hug. "I really do wish you well, Barb," I said. And
she: "I wish the same for you, Glen."
                              *

     Now aboard. Just a few more words on this topic.
Barb's gambit (or just call it the way her mind works)
is to claim the moral high ground for herself, then to
make condescending remarks about those who disagree with
her (and sometimes very sharp-edged, even brutal
remarks), and then to describe herself as being
"attacked" when the person she's consigning to second-
class personhood objects to the consignment.
     For long periods I bite my tongue or manage to find
a way to disagree which doesn't ruffle her further. But
sooner or later something I say does that anyway,
usually something I'd consider utterly harmless, and she
goes on the warpath, flying off into righteous
indignation, hurling all kinds of nasty accusations,
threatening to storm out or actually doing so.
     Can this dynamic between us ever change? I'm still
a little hopeful -- for the very reason I mentioned to
her: the prospect of lessening tensions -- but I'm also
plenty disturbed to be treated this way. I guess I'm
honorbound to make at least one more attempt at
rapprochement (for Mother's sake). Maybe I can think up
some new strategy in the next couple of weeks before I
fly back into the dragon's lair one more (one last?)
time.
                    *   *

     Whoosh. Fog over Mother's and Barb's city, cottony
clouds down below and a fiery orange rim of sunset, then
pure night, then light rain in my city. So I report
from the baggage-claim area -- as just now the Flight
471 load already begins spilling onto the carousel.
                              *
     Done, luggage retrieved. Next the wait for the

shuttle, about fifteen minutes. The past two days we
were reading front-page stories in the papers down there
about continuing heavy rains and floods up here. Now
the floods are the main topic of just about every
conversation I overhear. "Bad as '70, maybe worse." In
our brief and sadly unloving phone talk on Tuesday night
Lady U told me the ceiling in her closet had sprung a
nasty leak; it was hard to get new empty buckets under
it quickly enough. (Sounds like our relationship, I
can't resist saying. And Barb's and mine as well.)

   And so ends the funeral trip -- with the deluge.
As I sit next to my black backpack which is riding atop
my small brown suitcase and watch cars endlessly
circling in the liquid night. No doubt I've failed to
note many important details about the past five days.
If any truly crucial ones come to mind I'll try to
mention them next time. For sure I'd like to find some
way to prevent that sorry last scene with Barb from
spoiling our memories, hers and mine both, of the
previous days. But now -- onward to the office and
what's certain to be a hard night of catchup scoping.

42

   Ritualistically crazy no doubt. To start I haul
out the dark blue velvet bag, dip my fingers into the
plastic bag inside until they're coated with dust. And
then take up the J-stick.
   An odd feeling, but only a little odd. Try licking
my fingers.
   The only taste is my own finger taste.
   Nonetheless I like having this reminder of her
here.

[Jyze to the End of the Night]

-- On a Saturday night. At jyze central. With a
woodstove fire burning in the next room and old blues
playing on the radio in this one.

Two weeks and a day since her death. And how am I
doing? Just barely functioning. Using this time in
which I can do nothing to do a nothing kind of thing
which will soon count for a lot: to pack. So far I've
moved about thirty fully loaded boxes to the new storage
unit. Mostly books. And I'm doing it, just as before,
when Lady U's asleep or not around so as to avoid
alarming her prematurely.

I'm still hoping to be able to hang on here through
the end of February or even the end of March. But I
also want to be able to make a fast getaway should that
prove necessary or advisable. Therefore I'm aiming to
have most of my belongings in storage by the end of this
month -- everything that won't be conspicuous by its
absence from the house. Since I've always kept at least
half my books and papers up in the shed and barn (both
of which D rarely visits this time of year), and since
she pays little attention to such things anyway, this is
a lot. Enough to fill at least a hundred medium-size
storage cartons, I figure.

The storage place is across from a mall where we
occasionally shop on the outskirts of the home port,
about nine miles from here. My unit, No. 161, is ten by
fifteen feet with a slanted ceiling eight feet high at
the entrance -- which is a roll-up garage door -- and
almost twice that at the back wall. Plenty of space.
Eighty-one bucks a month, and the owners happen to be
recent migrants from the Mentoka zone, a small town near
Wachute (which of course they know by its real, meaning
nonfictive, name). And the unit will be accessible from
the city when I no longer have wheels: just two ferry
rides and then a short bus ride or a one-mile walk away.

Which is to say: there's been no change in the
impasse (call it) with D. And there won't be one either,
unless it's a worsening.

Meanwhile I'm all set to return to Mother's
apartment a week from Monday to pick up Rob's and my

347

inherited stuff. Airline flight reserved, rental truck
for hauling the stuff back also reserved. (And at what
incredible cost on the truck: twelve hundred bucks for a
fifteen-footer!) The only remaining question is whether
Jim Q. will be riding with me on the way back up.
According to Rob he's volunteered his services. But he
was also supposed to be calling me about this and I
still haven't heard from him.

As for Barb, I did talk with her once and neither
of us mentioned her "you're a liability" ultimatum.
Hopefully this bodes well for our ability to maintain a
civil relationship. It won't be more than that, though,
unless she changes her stance and is willing to look
equally to herself, and not just to me, for the sources
of the discord between us.

It's not likely she'll be able to do that. Jeff
helped me see this. As he summed it up: "Compromise
just isn't in her nature." (He and I talked on the
phone a couple of times, though only briefly about Barb:
mostly about rental trucks and financial matters.) My
consulting four or five books by and about her favorite
religious thinker of the current era also helped. All
offer lengthy introductions describing the extreme
difficulty of personal relations with this Jewish woman
who converted to mystical Christianity, and in all cases
those relations sound a whole lot like mine (and those
of many other people over the years) with Barb. Nor had
I realized before now that the age gap between this
woman and her older brother (a prominent mathematician)
was about the same as that between Barb and me: three
years. And it's quite clear to me Barb is becoming more
and more like her. I see a similar spirit of martyrdom,
a similar moral absolutism and pursuit of mystical
purity, a similar almost manic mixture of pitying
condescension and wrathful indignation directed toward
those whose notion of "the truth" differs from her own.

In short, what's happened is I've been banished.
Excommunicated from the Church of St. Barbara. It seems
she's now reached a point where she can tolerate no
criticism at all. To disagree with any moral view of

hers -- and in essence they're all moral -- is to
"attack" her.

Or with Mother gone will she perhaps find herself
less inclined to pursue sainthood? Will the more
practical, if also somewhat dreamy and geeky as well as
testy, Keith perhaps be able to nudge her in another
direction?

Can always hope. And will. But won't be trying to
add any nudges of my own. Better to remove myself from
the line of fire. In fact this might be the best kind
of non-nudge I can offer: to stop expressing views
against which she can rebel by denouncing their, and my,
heresy. In any event that's what I intend to do.

-- And so here I am, all alone in the world. This
is the nitty-gritty of the new reality. Jeff and Rob
are still around, of course, but my relations with them
are limited and will likely remain so. Neither of them
wants to be truly close, beyond a certain basic warm and
friendly brotherliness, and quite possibly neither is
capable of being significantly closer than we are now,
and for that matter maybe I'm not either (that is, with
a man, even if he's a blood brother). I do have several
cousins, both male and female, with whom I could attempt
to build stronger bonds, but I've seen no evidence any
of them would want me to do that or that much could
develop from such bonds even if we did miraculously
manage to achieve them.

What's happened here, over the past few months I've
been dropped flat by the three most important women in
my life -- in the one instance unintentionally, to be
sure, but in the other two all too willfully.

So what does it mean? It means my life moves into
a whole new phase, that's what. The third major phase
of my adult years, as I'm seeing it. A rising phase, a
high phase, and now a declining phase (but not a goddamn
trace of self-pity in saying this). A searching phase,
a stable phase, and now -- what? An astoundingly
productive phase, could it be? Yes! -- That is, if it
goes as I want it to.

The theme for next year is already clear, and it

too is trifold. It will be a year of mourning, a year
of new beginnings, and a year of getting a whole lot of
my own work done.

And I have a pretty good notion about the
particulars of the new life. It'll be unlike anything
I've tried before. I'll be living somewhere in the
city, preferably downtown or close to it, hopefully in a
loft of some sort, probably sharing it with two or three
others to keep costs down. I'll also have my own
cubbyhole office in the "historic quarter" near the city
ferry dock, where they can be rented for as little as
$115 a month, I've learned, and that's where I'll do
most of my JIFTing. And I'll have the storage unit in
the home port, easily accessible, where I'll keep most
of my books and papers and any other items not needed in
the other two places (where space will surely be at a
premium). I'll be able to walk from my living quarters
to my place of work and use public transportation to get
around in the city and I'll ride the ferries (also
public) to get to the storage unit.

-- I had hit on all this (or rather realized it was
what I wanted) just a few days before Mother died. I
was even excited about it. To hell with the Divine Ms.
U! And now that excitement is beginning to build again,
at least a little.

Can I really pull it off? It'll take some luck.
Will I be able to find acceptable roommates? Will the
cubbyhole-office idea really pan out? Will the decently
paid part-time scoping job performed for reporter Naomi
(through the Jyzer Ink contract) hold up? -- For the
moment anyway I'd say the chances look pretty good on
all of these.

And for this, Mom, I owe you a heap of gratitude.
Without your help I could never do it -- not even a
chance.

(I never mentioned the visit we paid to the offices
of Mother's financial advisor. All four of us trooping
up there in our funky informality, top floor of a spiffy
apartment building. Gorgeous water view. Robinetta, or
Robbie as everyone calls her, gently explaining, in her

southern accent so much like Nana's, the state of
Mother's holdings and her own, Robbie's, willingness to
have the four of us stay on as clients if we wished,
even though after the distribution of the estate we'd
individually fall far short of her normal minimum
threshold. What she'd do, she said, she'd keep us on as
a loosely affiliated group, much in the same fashion she
handles gay couples. -- And we could all hear Mother
screaming from the site of her "cremains" on that one.)
(Jeff, with his long history of dealing with banks --
though usually in his own bankruptcy proceedings, sad to
say -- asked the tough questions. I played the ingenue,
the "financial virgin." Barb was apparently too
overwhelmed to say much of anything, and Rob also chose
to remain quiet for the most part. Nonetheless Robbie
seemed charmed by us. "Family dynamics!" she marveled
with a kind of Tolstoyan wink to her assistant, Lynn,
who'll be handling our accounts on a day-to-day basis.
"Isn't it fascinating how each family is so different?")
     My chunk of the estate I've decided to leave with
Robbie for the time being. Thanks to this year's hot
stock market it's about a fifth larger than I'd
expected, but the quarterly income will be slightly less
than what direct investment in T-bills or something
similar would provide. Roughly a thousand bucks a
quarter, it would be, or about forty percent of what a
minimum-wage job would pay for the same period. To
Robbie this is a laughable pittance. To me it will be
enough to make the difference. Or so I'm hoping anyway.
(And if it's not, I may go for T-bills after all, or
even an outright cash-in. But first I'll see if I can
leave the money in a place where it has a chance to grow
and eventually supplement my Social Security benefits.)
     It was Mother's hope I'd use this money to buy
myself the opportunity to get the Mentoka books written.
(And I'm thinking now of the way we talked about it
during that wonderful conversation last spring. Of all
our talks -- ever -- that's the one I'd most like to
remember her by.) And so now that's what I'll do, one
way or another, or at least know I've given it the old

college try. Or old Mezzu try, call it.
*   *
     -- Miserable night. As I slosh by the outdoor pay
phone I hear a guy moaning about the freeway being
closed down -- "It's sheer ice" -- and the possibility
of several bridges going out. In the nearby parking lot
more puddle surface than asphalt is visible and some of
the individual puddles are so big they claim half a
dozen parking slots and so deep the slot numbers are
unreadable. (But I do like the concept of secretly
numbered parking puddles.)
     The old train depot. Dim lights but heat and a
reflection of the holiday season: crowds. Relatively
speaking, that is, which is to say we're a few dozen
strong. Wreaths and evergreen boughs adorn the walls
and still you'd have to say holiday cheer is in short
supply here. Or is it me? No doubt it is, at least in
part. Though it's true, just fifteen or twenty minutes
ago I was moved by the sight of a Christmas tree whose
glowing all-red lights were glinting off the rain-wet
cobblestones of the historic quarter at night -- the
tree hauntingly alone and isolated at the middle of the
large empty central triangle with century-old brick and
stone buildings looming on all three sides (the same
triangle where jyze did its thing as a racial brouhaha
raged a few feet away some fifteen months ago).
     Is this my new hood? I can hope. As I passed by
the basement stairs leading to the jazz record shop
(closed like most other commercial establishments in the
quarter, saloons excepted, on this Sunday evening) I was
studying the upper floors of the former industrial
buildings on the other side of the street. Lights up
there, lots of them. Lofts and studios. Music.
Silhouettes moving behind shades. A block farther on,
an arty-looking young woman in torn jeans and a hand-
decorated yellow poncho was shouting up to someone
hanging halfway out of a third-story window; then she
trotted across the street and disappeared inside a
doorway. When I passed the same doorway moments later I
saw her inside talking intensely with a slim grayhaired

man in a raggedy black trenchcoat, surely some kind of
artist himself and possibly even older and scuzzier than
me. "Right here is where I wanna live!" I cried aloud.
Wailed! Declaimed! (For the sidewalk was empty now.)
Then around the corner and across the street I entered
the puddly parking lot. Chain o' puddles. Roaring
gutter cataracts but only a few portages necessary.

    -- Whew, this spot is almost unbearably hot. A
glance overhead reveals I'm sitting directly beneath
some sort of radiant heater. But it's about twenty feet
up! (No doubt those heaters were goosed to the max
during this week's cold snap and no one has thought to
dial them back down even though the weather's changed
again. All week long we were fearing a major "Arctic
Express" snowstorm -- our driveway puddles froze solid
on Tuesday and didn't unfreeze until last night -- but
the snow never arrived, and now it appears a drenching
"Pineapple Express" may be hitting us instead.)

    A week from tomorrow morning I catch my flight back
to the city of my mother's last years and certainly I
won't be catching it here, but regardless I'm thinking
of this as a departure entry. Jyzin' at the train
station beats jyzin' at the airport any old day. Next
time I pop up in these pages I expect to be perched on
the zigzag steps in the hilltop park paying my last
respects at Mother's ash-bestrewal site.

    (The P.A. tells us one of the continentals is now
arriving and I do hear the rumble, I do feel it, I do
hear a diesel "whistle" blaring -- whatcha call that
sound again, like an elephant trumpeting? -- I do hear
excited kids' voices and running footsteps and the loud
splatter of rainwater cascading from eaves as doors open
-- and cool damp air arrives suddenly here at my seat
like a roiling stormfront, a "Winter Depot Express.")

    Cards and letters. Your mother dies and you get a
few. Down at her place they were pouring in, but I've
also received some up here: from D's parents and another
from her Gramma Kiku and Auntie Alice (who's recovering
well from her own health emergency), from Naomi, and
today a nice note from my Aunt Shar (in which she quotes

her daughter Georgie, Mother's namesake: "Today the colors have gone out of all the flowers"). And I still have a letter of my own to write, a self-appointed task: to Eddie, Mother's main heartthrob before she met Dad and the only other man she slept with in her life before Dad's death, as she told me for the first time this past spring. Last fall they renewed acquaintance by mail and phone, she and Eddie did, and if he hadn't recently remarried I don't doubt they'd've gotten together again, or at least mounted a serious reconciliation effort. From my extensive talks with Mother about her college days and even more from reading her college diary and scrapbooks (which focus on her relationship with Eddie) I feel I know the man well -- in fact as a former college newspaper editor he reminds me a lot of myself in certain respects, albeit (albeit!) as I was long ago.

(The crowd from the continental surges through. Bundled up -- and bearing bundles too, holiday type. Even a couple of Santa hats bobbing along. Double-decker silver cars still standing so close outside the depot doors you can see only their bottom halves. Are they faintly quivering or is that also a miragelike effect of the radiant heat in here? When I look around inside it appears everything's trembly and blurry, though not, I'd still say, as much so as those coaches. They're doing the shimmy in two directions at once, as if about to dematerialize: beam themselves up to another realm and be done forever with those pesky constrictive rails. -- Cavorting track-free in railroad heaven!)

Thinking of Mom at odd moments. She sneaks up on me. Sad Christmas carols especially will call her forth ("...who mourns in lonely eh-eh-exile here....") and of course so will the official anthem of a certain USAn state named after a certain English king, just as she was, though indirectly ("Still in peaceful dreams I see / the road leads back to you..."), as well as a professional basketball team's fight song as altered and sung to her on long-ago birthdays and other celebratory occasions by the Sandefjord siblings plus one, "Sweet Georgie Mom" ("No mom made has got a shade on...") (the

"plus one" being Dad, I maybe don't need to note) --
but in truth she's likely to appear at just about any
old time. Lively jazz will do it quite often, especially
tunes from the bop and swing eras which she listened to
virtually nonstop at her apartment (and some of the same
radio shows are syndicated here). All over our house
items whisper to me of her -- dishes, paintings, towels,
shirts, books, records -- she's just about everywhere.
And the same's true internally. Sometimes it seems half
the words and phrases I use, instead of doing what
they're supposed to do, serve only to trigger memories of
Memere. Such sentimentality I could gorge on! And do
sometimes -- but then other matters rear up. These days,
after all, I've got some serious distractions. And maybe
it's better I do, I don't know. I go back and forth on
this, uncontrollably, reverbing, but then I'm able to
duck out of the freefall cacophony (I'll call it) by
focusing on the practical. So it's all right again for a
while.

     -- We're down to three lobby sitters. Where are
the carols now? Even the restrooms are closed, I see.
The fancy black wrought-iron gate over there, I'd just
like to mention, is surely worthy of being one where
lilacs last bloom, at least for purposes of this jyze
entry right here. One more memorial popping up in what
I expect to be a lengthy procession of them.

*

     This morning out in the shed I packed eight more
boxes. Autobiographies, diaries and journals, Korea
books (stumbling upon an old note to me from Lady S in
one). Kerosene heater glowing, cold rain falling, early
light seeping in aqueous gray. I marveled at those
finely built custom bookshelves -- fashioned by myself
and none other! -- which I'll soon have to abandon. I
ached some and fumed some and exulted some. Then I
hiked back down to the house and went to bed. No words
with my former beloved, who no doubt still is my beloved
if I could let her be (not talking about whether I'm
still her beloved). -- But I can't let her be and I
won't.

355

[Jyzemelt]

43

   Pushing hard -- and mainly so I can be doing this.
But here? Has to be, I guess, for fuel. Burger kind.
Once again under the sign of the clown. Up his alley.
Halfway between the subway station and the hill with the
glorified headstone on top. Hill of the ashes.
   Meanwhile the airline's lost my suitcase. I hung
around for two more flights but it still hadn't shown
up. Nothing much in there aside from Christmas gifts
for Mischa and Rikki and my usual rags, toilet kit, a
few books. The bag itself is the thing: the antique
boxey leather beauty -- so splendidly travel-worn. The
airline promises they'll deliver it to Mother's place
the moment it arrives. But in fewer than forty hours
I'll be leaving town again and if it hasn't appeared by
then, what'll I do? Truck myself eight hundred miles up
the coast in funky squalor, I guess. In the rental
fifteen-footer, and with Jim Q. along for company,
barring some new disaster or change of mind.
   Drab and dismal industrial wasteland and then
clattering through the tube under the bay and out into
glitzy lunch-hour crowds in the financial district and
then straight north, my chucks well knowing the way.
   And all this time moving along in a cloud of
strictly literary anxiety to go with all the other real-
world anxieties of the day. Ferrying, busing, flying,
the whole journey enveloped in same. "Anxiety of
influence." I'm impressed, a whole lot more so than
when I first sampled this critic's stuff a decade or two
back. But how impressed? How anxious? Or is it mostly
"been there, done that" -- mere exultation over a nice

356

fit with "Jyzer" needs -- mere "repetition" -- or is
such high-level repetition really ever only mere?

But anyway I want to keep reading what I'm reading.

Up there, the home port, I pulled off a big coup
shortly after dawn yesterday when I delivered my large
wooden cabinet to the storage unit. The thing's been
traveling with me ever since my time as an uncertified
adult-literacy "reading specialist" (and I originally
noticed it, like so many of the current appurtenances of
my material existence, in the musty basement storeroom
of the branch library where I worked; and later I nabbed
it on its way to the dump and redirected it to the first
apartment, unfurnished at the start, in which Lady U and
I lived together). -- And already I've hit the midpoint
target of fifty cartons transferred. So neatly stacked
they are against the three walls of the storage unit,
with so much yet to be packed and delivered and plenty
of space for all of it.

Stormy week. Long power outages. Candles.
Brooding in the dark and the cold of the early December
deeps, though fortunately the cold was actually quite
mild by normal winter standards in other parts of the
country at or near our same latitude (northern Mentoka
for example). And then another milepost on the roadway
to oblivion with Lady U. She equivocates on her plans
for various weekend days, finally announces she'll be
"playing poker" all night Saturday night; won't be back
until "noonish" Sunday. When she says this I let it
echo a moment or two. I'm not about to ask where, with
whom, for what kind of stakes. I'm not about to inquire
into the nature of any other unexplained long absences,
of which the number only keeps growing. I'm not about
to delve into the causes of her coldness, nastiness,
utter lack of caring contact which have become pretty
much the norm over the past four or five months.
Instead I ask, trying to be as nonchalant as I know how,
"You have any objections if I also stay out overnight
when I'm not working?" Sez she unperturbed: "I don't
have any objections." Tone saying: are you kidding?
Objections? Almost as if restraining herself from

clucking at the absurdity of the notion. And out from
the kitchen she sails with microwaved lasagna dish in
hand, bound for her room, in which, when she's not
locked in the bathroom or the bedroom, formerly ours and
now essentially hers, or gone from the house, she's
almost always closed up -- perhaps even barricaded in.

Breaking up shouldn't be too hard. The main
question at this point: will we still recognize each
other when we say our last goodbyes? That's how fast
the changes are coming down as we whirl apart.

More anxieties. Oh what a fine year it's been for
anxieties! Oh am I terrifically toughening up my
character this year!

-- And now...toughen up some more. March on up
that hill. (In the mist. In the midafternoon. Monday
exactly a week before Christmas. "I'll be home for" --
and am! But...is any part of my home still here in my
old city No. 2/7? No no no, I know that's not something
to ask. Not now. Sparklike thoughts flying randomly
off into the mist and feebly sputtering out.)

*   *

So here I am. Actually it's thirty-nine steps down
from the hilltop plaza, not thirteen as I wrote last
month (or fifteen?). (Feet now trudging by.) At the
first small landing past the bend. And I sit here on a
low angled uphill brick staircase sidewall (the steps,
also brick, reddish, "brick red" I guess, are only about
thirty inches wide, and an iron railing is anchored in
the downhill sidewall, which is to my right) and a
moment ago when I leaned over that railing I could see
some of her ashes still lingering there beneath the ivy
ground cover. Or little chips of bone rather.
"Cremains," right. Or who knows, they could be someone
else's -- but I feel sure they're not. They're my
mother's, they just have to be. Or: they are my mother,
period, the physiological, the material human creature.
Somehow I can't seriously think otherwise -- though it's
also true I can't seriously think they are. Not with
the kind of acceptance that goes all the way down.

But yes, a good spot for her spirit to dwell. Tree

canopy overhead, birds chirping, the city and the bay
and a span of the nearer of the two great bridges
revealing themselves in spectacular leaf-filtered views
down below and outward. Brick pathway zigzagging
attractively down the steep hillside with here and there
a landing at which to pause and catch your breath if
you're coming up -- except then you glimpse the views
and go breathless all over again.

Acacia still in bloom, hundreds of tiny droplets
suspended on pink spikes -- glittering like shiny silver
Christmas-tree balls, or so goes my dim thought. (And
these bricks I'm sitting on are damp too -- and uphill
ivy brushes my left elbow as I jyze away using my left
thigh as a platform -- in good ol' Mom's beyond-death
presence!) Luminous clouds visible to the west as you
circle the hilltop plaza -- the bronze statue of the
leader of this hemisphere's first known band of Cawk
invaders (a band of even more barbaric Scandis excepted)
reaching skyward with outstretched arms and hands from
his pedestal at the center, almost as if to put an angel
atop a (nonexistent) Christmas tree -- and the more
distant of the two great bridges just spectrally visible
(faintly orange) through the mist four or five miles to
the west. And pigeons clinging to the ledges high up on
the tower here, presumably keeping a wary eye out for
the hawks who like to snack on them.

I trudged eight or nine blocks straight north from
the clown joint, then a block east past Mother's former
flat where I stayed during previous visits before this
year, then up the cement hillside steps (a drug deal
blatantly going down a few feet below in the cul-de-sac
shadows but I guess I looked too harmless or preoccupied
or simply too drugged-out myself to spook them) and onto
the same upward-spiraling park access road the four of
us walked three weeks ago carrying the ashes. Liked
glancing through gaps in the greenery at the city
arrayed below, mostly, except for certain downtown and
farther-west skyscrapers at the level of whose upper
floors I plodded along, spiraling ever higher, the whiff
of eucalyptus especially strong after the heavy

[Jyzemelt]

rainstorms of recent weeks. A few small mudslides were
in evidence along the uphill edge of the road. Fallen
leaves and wind-torn branches snagged in unexpected
places. Only a dozen cars parked in the plaza circle at
the top with its spaces for a hundred or more. Scattered
sightseers gazing out through coin-operated binoculars at
the bridges and the notorious prison island and points
beyond. Posing for photos, talking in foreign languages
which didn't sound so foreign to me (because all I heard
happened to be the only ones I know at all, even a
smattering: Japanese, Korean, German).

     -- A few isolated raindrops falling now. I hear
them but so far none have hit these pages. I'm hunched
over. A living jyze shelter!

     -- But here come more drops. No doubt about it:
soon I'll hafta split. A good thing too, most likely,
because I'm worn out -- in this condition it's hard to
be as receptive to ol' Mom's spirit as I'd like to be.
Though I'm feeling it anyway. And will elsewhere as
well. But will recall this moment as long as I live --
"tears of the sky" -- and mine. (No lack here of the
lachrymose, the lachrymope -- whoopee! And now we
hightail it before we drown -- here we go drowning again
-- as a few more chips of bone wash down the hill -- or
into the hill. Yike! Deluge! Scram!)

                    *   *

     Seven sleepless hours farther down the road but
also just down the hill -- the other side of the hill,
that is, western instead of eastern. Holding forth in
the armchair beside the kitchen table in the second-
story bay-window nook at 517. Barb and Keith have just
gone off to bed. Rikki's working on her German paper in
the kitchen directly below this one (a couple of hours
ago she came up for a break and sat sipping brandy in
this very chair). Yellow half curtains half open. Warm
glow of a floor lamp. Foghorns. (Last night Keith was
startled to hear sea lions barking as he lay in bed.)

     So far so good -- or at least not so bad. No
quarrels. We've gone through all the lists and
segregated all the items to be loaded onto the truck

360

tomorrow. We've gone out for a Chinese dinner. Barb
and I have negotiated our way through all six file
drawers of old family papers and photos and the like and
we've agreed it's best if I take virtually all of them
with me, thus keeping them together in one spot (that
being No. 161, my storage unit -- which I've already
told Barb and the others about, though in the guise of
normality: D and I "will be moving soon") (don't want to
complicate matters too much at this delicate juncture by
spilling all the beans about our looming breakup).

And my lost suitcase finally arrived here about
seven-thirty p.m., delivered by an enormous but
strangely meek grayhaired Russian-accented man -- no
explanation, no apology, no facial expression to speak
of. And no promised fare-discount coupons either.

So here it is, my mother's final home. Five months
ago she sat in this chair and gazed at me across the
table as I labored away at proofing "Memorials" -- her
persnickety eldest looking as close as he ever would or
could to being the scholar she always wanted him to be,
like her father. Mom in the last of her kitchens --
what a collection of images of her near-final self she's
left me with. Doing her exercises, saying goodbye to
relatives and old friends on the phone, working at her
files, searching for dishes in the cabinets, rustling
up meals at the stove, gamely dancing solo to the jazz
station with a drink held at shoulder level in her hand.
Feels as though she could appear at the door any second
now. Look up and it almost seems to happen. Is not the
air vibrating with readiness for a visitation of the
"beam me down from the hilltop, children" kind?

After I leave here Wednesday morning (with Jim Q.;
it's all set, much to everyone else's horror because of
his poor driving record and deteriorating health) --
after that, I say, it's not too likely I'll ever be
back. But it's still possible, I suppose. -- Back to
this apartment, I mean. That I'll return to almost any
other spot I've visited or where I've resided in this
dazzlingly beautiful and, for me, memory-packed city, of
course including the hilltop site where Mother's spirit

surely does dwell and always will, is much more likely.

Even as I'm moving things out Keith and Barb are moving in. Continuity, yes, and I'm glad of it, but it's still not of a very reassuring kind. And unless I see some strong signs that I'm wanted -- not looked upon as a "liability" -- I don't think I'll be trying to partake of it. Which is a shame and a pity but I doubt I can do anything about it.

Goods piled everywhere in the small living room -- we've left just barely enough space for me to catch a few winks on the floor, probably having to lie on my side, folded in several places to fit the narrow zigzaggy open area, maybe holding my breath.

The strange jyze of exhaustion. So lifeless is it, it might even be picturesque, like a desert landscape, say, during an eclipse. Or if not that, a lonely USAn realist painting -- second-story window viewed from across a steeply slanted nighttime city side street, pool of light up there, oddly disorderly kitchen, a guy just inside the yellow half curtains gazing blankly at the far wall, a pen poised motionless in his hand for long periods above an open composition book as if he's wondering whether there's anything more to write or it's worth trying to write it and apparently failing to come up with any answers.

Sleep. Sleep. (But maybe another chance like this tomorrow night, and that one truly the probable 517 finale.)

*   *

-- Yup, tomorrow night it is, Tuesday night, and I'm in the very same seat as last night at just about the same time (what was the time last night?) (okay, so having checked, it's now an hour before midnight rather than an hour after) and under pretty much the same circumstances except more so. Exhaustion squared. And here's a big bottle of blended whiskey. Not ordinarily my drink, but tonight anything handy could be my drink. And this, from an otherwise well-stocked liquor cabinet Mother won't be needing again (and no one else around here ever touches the stuff) -- this, I say, is handy.

[Jyze to the End of the Night]

      But actually -- is anything really bad right now?
Nah. Not at all! Things are moving along quite well.
(I'm hearing Rikki's footsteps downstairs directly below
where I sit and thinking once again how starved I am for
a little loving female companionship. And just how is
Lady U up there in our backwoods brier patch selling me
even farther down the river tonight? But no, I won't go
off on that sorry subject again, and neither will I be
seeking any female companionship, loving or otherwise,
tonight or anytime soon. Not until I'm good and ready
for it, and that probably won't be for a long, long
time, or maybe never -- though I still have my hopes,
sure, and regardless -- but to hell with all this
squishy nonsense.)
      So at eight a.m. off we went to rent the truck. A
few minor snafus, but we succeeded. And what a stickup
they pulled on us! Yes, twelve hundred bucks, plus
another two hundred in tax and "incidentals," insurance
and whatnot. For a boxy yellow truck with cab-over and
fifteen-foot bed (just as expected). Not really a big
truck at all -- but then how formidable it suddenly
seemed when we were about to climb into the cab. And
yet I managed to drive it over here, following Keith and
Barb as they ran interference for us in Keith's car, and
park it at an angle across the driveway, and later
parallel-park it in a double space that miraculously
appeared just a few yards up the hill (of this quick
parking job without a single false move on a serious
grade in a vehicle exceedingly strange to me and tough
to maneuver I was especially proud); and now I look down
from this window, through the sparsely leafed late-
autumn crowns of sidewalk trees, and thar she blows,
shadowy, steeply angled, flush to the curb, streetlight
reflections glinting oddly from her -- okay, its --
roof, but unmistakable, a real honest-to-god truck.
      All day we packed. Keith helped a lot (his
knowledge of knots proving invaluable) and seven-year-
old Mischa, Rikki's kid, was my superanimated companion
throughout (and I his superannuated companion). Tonight
at our celebratory dinner at this table right here Rikki

confided to me that Mischa had told her this was "the
best day of my whole life." For that reason all by
itself I can say it was as well one of the better days
of my own whole life. (But the kid is a hyperactive
handful and I definitely couldn't take too many more
days like this one cumulatively no matter how good each
might be individually.) (And yet I sure did enjoy,
especially, running that late-afternoon errand with him
that took us to the hardware store and the bank, just
the two of us, with bonus stops afterward at an ice-
cream shop and a used-book store. For one thing this
kid looks a lot like me, as everyone says, and you can
see that strangers in the street take us for father and
son. For another, we can goof together real well. For
a third, he was still wearing the railroad cap I gave
him last summer. All of which of course makes me think
about what I've lost in having to give up Elgie. And
strangely enough I don't mind being reminded of this
from time to time.)

Another piece of good news, Barb offered to handle
the cost of the truck through the estate, with the sum
to be subtracted later from my share when it's
officially apportioned. For me this is a lucky break
because it means financially I'll be much less behind
the eightball than expected over the crucial months
ahead. I'll have greater freedom of movement if I need
it. And it's a pretty damn good bet I'll be needing it.

Then Jim Q. dropped by toward the end of dinner and
somehow Keith lost it for a moment (as he's notorious
for occasionally doing), tempers flared, suddenly Jim
was calling him a "smart-ass jerk" and muttering that he
was just asking for a punch in the nose. I had to step
in as a peacemaker -- and somehow managed to cool the
combatants out just enough to let Jim slip away a few
minutes later. Shortly after that Keith and I were
working closely together down in the truck doing a few
last-minute tie-downs (using flashlights) and it was
almost as if nothing had happened. Keith obviously felt
bad about the incident, however, and I pretended I
hadn't seen what started it (although I had) and we were

soon back to normal relations (he and I hit it off quite
well too, just as Jim and I do; in this crew it's only
with my own sister that I have big problems) (ah the
mysteries). I did mention privately to Keith that I
hoped the current troubles between Barb and me could be
blamed largely on the tensions of the past year and that
our relations would soon be improving. He said he hoped
so too, "because I know she really wants to be on good
terms with her family."

Can it happen? Maybe. The "you're a liability"
remark hasn't come up again, but neither have Barb and I
had much of a chance -- almost none, really -- to talk
casually, much less intimately or seriously. So I'll
say just this: at least a shred of hope remains.
Possibly even two shreds. But then again when I put
those words down on paper they look way too optimistic.
One shred is it.

Condolence letters keep pouring in. Mother's local
friends, of whom there are scores, will be holding a
memorial for her in January ("they say they want
closure," Barb explained). A short obituary appeared in
all three northern cities where she lived as an adult,
as well as the two southern cities of her childhood and
of her family roots on both sides, and all were written
by -- Keith. None of us could bear to do it.

A letter from the last of her municipalities --
this one right here -- arrived today calling her for
jury duty. Independently we all came up with the same
quip when first hearing of this summons: so strongly did
she take her civic duties, she'll probably show up at
the courthouse. Even cremation won't keep her down.

-- And now a decent, relatively, night's sleep.
Maybe five hours? No doubt I need a bath real bad after
all this physical work but I need sleep even more. At
nine a.m. I'll be picking up Jim in the truck at his
place and then we'll hit the interstate. He may need to
hold his nose for the first four hundred miles or
however far we have to go until we can find us a motel
with a shower. But oh what a lovely ride it'll be....

And so, local spirit of Mom-of-mine, I bid you

adieu. (We did burn an extra-large candle for you
tonight, along with several of the small votive type,
one for each of the rest of us.) But I'll be back,
one way or another. And won't be away at all in yet
another, more important sense. And will be meeting up
with other spirit incarnations of you (as it were!)
where I live now and wherever else I may be living
starting before much longer. So don't despair. We're
going on and for the two of us, I insist, I'd even say
it's crystal-clear: all's well.

44

     Nine candles burning on Christmas Eve, four of them
gathered around this book as the only source of jyzin'
light -- here where it all began. Lots of flickering, a
good deal of gentle shimmering from the kiri ribbons,
whose numbers down here have tripled in recent days. A
three-foot-tall Christmas tree, a familiar potted live
one, standing atop the low bookcase in front of the
radio. A string of medium-size lights glowing on it, a
few candy canes and shiny colored balls dangling. The
blues show playing, special holiday edition.
     (Hack hack, honk, snuffle -- I picked up a nasty
cold on the trip back. No doubt the severe shortage of
sleep set me up for it.)
     As it happens, it was a month ago today that ol'
Mom ascended to angel status, I'll say (and her own
mother, I learned while at 517 this last time, died on
not the same date but the same day -- was it thirteen
years ago now? -- on "Black Friday," the day after
Thanksgiving). And tonight I'm aching for ol' Mom, and
also for myself in my solitude -- but determined to make

merry anyway in proper all-blues fashion, with funk,
grit, soul, and a whole lot of upside-down, inside-out
yuletide melancholy -- transformed! Celebration!

Or am I just jivin' myself again?

No way to know at this point. So let the jyze --
but maybe not so much the jive -- speak for itself.

-- In any case we made it, Jim Q. and I. An
excellent trip, switching off behind the wheel every
eighty or ninety miles much like the drivers on last
summer's hippie bus. Not a drop of rain did we see all
the way. Mostly blue skies and spectacular snow-covered
volcanoes, the famous five. An overnight stop at a
motel-cum-shower in that same college town where D and I
once thought we might reside, a riverside walk there to
a restaurant recommended by the desk clerk for a very
good late dinner (dominated by loudly quacking ducks,
this walk, and silently bicycling students). "Your
mother must've interceded with a higher power," Jim
opined, "to make conditions for this trip so perfect."
Agreed. And she was a constant presence in spirit, both
of us (Jim and I) relishing this chance to talk about
her in a relaxed way. "I've known some fine women in my
time," Jim sighed, "but she was the special one." And I
knew he wasn't just jivin' -- himself or me.

A bonding of sorts, no question. Then in my mail
when I finally got back here after that first full
night's scoping I found a Christmas card from Jim Q.
containing a hundred-dollar check and a touching note
requesting that the money somehow be used to "celebrate
the life of Georgianna Chandler Hutchison Sandefjord"
(her maiden family name misspelled, as is only
appropriate -- on the way up Jim acknowledged he'd
regularly sought Mother's orthographic help -- "She was
just a phenomenal speller").

They'd both be pleased, then, to witness this scene
right here, right now. Except for one aspect of it, the
absence of my eighteen-year mate. She ain't interested.
She's upstairs closed inside her room as usual (when
she's home at all). She's scarcely had a civil word to
say to me since my return. For all practical, and for

that matter impractical, purposes we're already exes.
Evidently she's feeling so uptight and guilt-ridden
about what she's doing she can't let her guard down for
a moment to utter a consoling word. Not a single one!

Just how it is. One more ache to apply some blues-
judo to. (So how about this tune coming on right now:
one of the greats wishing someone -- and it might as
well be Lady U herself, on my behalf -- if she were
listening to this same show up there, which I'm sure
she's not -- "merry merry Christmas, baby.")

(But yes, of course I still want to throttle her.
I hurl numberless imprecations at her -- though never
when she's around. Because I'm determined to end this
alliance, I'll call it, in what I consider the right
way. And I suspect the more intent I show myself to be
on doing this, the more outrageous she'll become in
trying to provoke a showdown. Not suspect -- expect.
I'm all but certain of it. What's more, it's equally
likely she'll succeed sooner or later. That's why I'm
trying to do as much of my moving as possible in
advance. Minimize the strife later on.)

Candles. Smiling spirits. I do insist. Why the
hell not? And thinking along about now, some eight
hundred miles to the south, Barb, Keith, Mischa, and
Rikki are leaving for midnight mass. In the old days
(some two thousand miles to the east, and as to be
portrayed soon in the Gatewood section of "Jyzer") we
Sandefjords might be leaving Gil and Marj K.'s annual
party at this hour, one faction bound for church and
another (including me most likely) for home to work on
the usual zany last-minute Christmas-gift schemes. (And
throughout the latter half of this paragraph, I just
can't resist mentioning, an all-time rocker favorite of
mine from that era has been urging "run run Rudolph.")

-- And will say this: ol' Mom sure did succeed in
putting the love of Christmas in me. She knew what it
took and she did it, and for many others too. Of all
nights of the year this is the one I associate most with
her.

"A blue, blue Christmas without you." Another tune

that keeps grabbing me. Sneaking up unexpectedly. (And
just now I sneezed. And I'm starting to sweat heavily,
mainly owing to all these candles, I think, their
surprisingly large heat production -- and the smoke
maybe having something to do with the sneezes. But them
chills! Drafty room, the candle flames flickering like
crazy and making for some intriguingly complex shadow
dances, especially those involving old J-stick No. 5
right here as it races scratchily along about twelve
inches in front of my nonstop-snuffling schnozz.)
      Driving up the coast Jim Q. and I saw literally
thousands of houses decorated with elaborate outdoor
Christmas lighting, some of them phantasmagorically so.
It seems the homeowners just can't resist the urge to
entertain, if not proselytize, the unending captive
freeway audience. And we enjoyed the show. -- And then
our darkened house (the lady was out somewhere,
supposedly at work). Before leaving for the airport and
the flight south I'd set out a few Christmas items in
the kitchen and living room, expecting even then that
Jim might be accompanying me on the trip back and
possibly coming inside at least briefly as we unloaded.
Then when we actually arrived the first thing he said
was, "I see you've got your Christmas tree all ready for
trimming," pointing to the small potted pine that's been
standing by the stacked logs in the open area at the
back of the carport for the past several years -- in
fact since well before there even was a carport. "It's
raring to go," I agreed, hugely grateful for the tree's
existence, which I'd totally forgotten about. "G.A.,"
as he often calls Mother (as Dad did also) (both of her
sisters, being younger, usually called her "Big") --
"G.A. would be happy to know you have a live tree," he
said. "She was a fanatic on the subject of having a
live tree at Christmas, or at the very least a fresh-cut
one. 'No artificial trees in my house!'"
      So here it is, that same potted pine. I brought it
down to jyze central just for tonight and decorated it
with the string of lights, the balls, the candy canes.
Looks good too. And I'll note it's played a similar

role before -- at least twice that I can recall.
Nonetheless I'm sure the sudden transition from
subfreezing temperatures to this cozily warm room is
shocking it. "To save the ceremony we had to destroy
the symbol." But no, I'll strip off the decorations and
return the tree to its accustomed spot outdoors as soon
as jyzetime's over. The flickering candles, the
twisting fluttering kiri -- they're plenty all by
themselves.

I even have a present. The annual Christmas shirt
from the U's -- it's sitting in a red box on the director
chair ("Mowjo Queen") where D unceremoniously dumped it.
I also have two paper plates of Christmas cookies baked
by Naomi. But that's it. As is only right for a
Christmas like this one. And yet it's disappointing
regardless, I can't deny. "Still a kid at Christmas."
Every year that line pops up again no matter how hard I
try to stomp it down. Oh the aches. The tree. The
glowing lights. The music. The suspense. The giving,
the receiving. The goofy "to" and "from" labels. The
elves. The Santa sightings. The enraptured younger
siblings. The exhaustedly beaming Mom and Dad. The
whole eye-rollingly cliched and sentimental celebratory
ritual right there, year after year, and what's more each
one with bells on it! (Thick frost this morning, by the
way: it looked like about an inch of snow and hung around
for hours.)

Christmas in Korea also comes to mind. A lot of
similarities between this one here and the one there.
At least for this one here no third person is involved
-- no kid suffering. (Except me, sure. But Lady U as
well, I imagine, in her own way.) (But then back in
Korea I was a "kid at Christmas" too. Lady S, however,
I would say wasn't. Couldn't be, maybe. She was a
mother fighting a traditional mother's battle and many
of the traditions involved were all but otherworldly to
me, just as Christmas itself was to her.)

Maybe another couple of pages in the morning.
Can't go on now. (It's getting to me again just like I
knew it would.)

[Jyze to the End of the Night]

                    *   *

     And here we are, Christmas morning in the woods.
That is, in the shed, looking out toward the woods,
starting about three feet away. And if I swivel my head
a hundred and eighty degrees (which sounds rather
owlish, even with a twist of my neck and back included),
it's a white, white Christmas I see out that way, a
dense frost just like yesterday's covering the lawn and
the shrubs while a thick fog, also white, embraces the
nearby evergreens and obscures the ones on the far side
nearly to the vanishing point (as my vaporish breath is
doing to a lesser degree to the words on this page, in
pulses, almost like puffy white clouds rolling across
the face of the moon -- but a rectangular moon that
folds in the middle and is inscribed with black-on-
white selenoglyphics -- my fancy new stocking present
of a word for jyzic moon-writing).
     Already this morning I've carted six big boxes of
books down to the house. These are Mentoka books,
loosely stacked inside the boxes, destined to replace
half a dozen shelves of China and Korea books in the
house. Those in turn I'll pack more tightly into the
same boxes after they're emptied and then I'll haul them
over to the storage unit, perhaps as soon as tomorrow
morning. In another week or two this shed will be
completely stripped of papers and books. And, for a
while anyway, no one will know this except me. Fun and
games!
     Puff after puff, like a steam engine. And this
even though the large kerosene heater is cranking out
the therms just a few feet away, silently except for an
occasional self-satisfied gurgle as the fuel depletes.
     I read a while and then slept on the couch right
behind the desk chair where I was celebrating last
night's J-fest. And snuffled and hacked and honked, and
I mean mightily on all of those (and am still doing so),
and produced some impressive hot and cold sweats. I
mean this boy is one sick puppy and still he churns out
the jyze! Wotta kid! A kid at -- yeah.
     Seasonal colors up here too, including several more

kiri (undulating so prettily) and the large framed red
print (with broken glass) that Mother sent me a decade
ago. Dozens of watercolors and reproductions hung or
tacked up, mostly the work of writers I like, including
the picture-poems of Kenneth P., but also a number
(nine, in fact) of Lady U's. Two of these are eight-
and-a-half-by-eleven "photo-realism" paintings she did
some years ago of kitschy half-century-old magazine
covers, one of Diary Secrets ("I Loved Not Wisely But
Too Well") and the other of My Private Life ("Men Didn't
Respect Me"), with a not-so-photo-realistic mug looking
something like mine featured on both.

    Such a fine shed this has been for me. I'm pleased
to have this chance to shut it down gradually, relishing
each piece as I pack it away possibly never to see it
again. (Eventually will the property of the deceased
owner of storage unit 161, where all this stuff will be
going sooner or later, be auctioned off? That is, am I
about to establish a way of living that will serve me
the rest of my days? I'd say the chances of that, for
better or for worse, are looking pretty good, yes.)

    Midmorning. Back in the figurative mists of
childhood Christmases the gift-opening frenzy would be
at its peak right about now. Individual gift stacks
mounting fast and the huge pile of discarded wrappings
and boxes even faster -- roughly five or six times
faster. Meanwhile here in the literal mist of a
backwoods Christmas we've got the first dim intimations
of sun fading in and out up there. Behind the scenes
it's chomping voraciously at this fragile angel's-hair
stuff and in another half hour or so its work will be
done and everything will be back to its normal muddy
wintry browns and greens and it'll be hard to believe
what this Christmas morning looked like just a short
time earlier, as with a fast-fading dream fragment.

    Me, I've got work to do. Lots of thank-you cards
to write, not for gifts this year, for the most part,
but for condolence notes. And then I've got a last week
to devote to preparation for moving and also to getting
my act together for the big push on "Jyzer" which I'm

planning to mount right after the first of the year.
(Yes, "Jyzer." "Jyzer" lives and so does the rest of
the trilogy. It's just from an excess of holiday good
will that I'm allotting most of the ink to these other
matters this time around.)

45

    Grueling year. Just about over at last, only two
and a half hours to go. Mercy. Mercy, mercy, mercy.
I'm begging for it.
    Again locked into jyze central (for long spells,
weeks on end, even months, I forget the door between
this room and the "pantry" can be locked; but this week
I haven't been forgetting, and I'm not tonight either).
Live celebration from the opposite coast on the jyze
station (as I might as well call it, especially now
having written it, even if accidentally). Big names,
big voices, big sounds, big whooping and whistling
applause. I for one am convinced they're all having a
grand time back there, just as I was similarly convinced
last year when I, along with the lady of the house,
listened to this same show at this same time -- but
under, no question, far different circumstances.
(Though now the broadcast's about to jump westward for
the next stop in the stage-party festivities.)
    A single candle burning here for my good departed
mother. A steady flame, well-shielded from the drafts
coursing through the room.
    (They're cheering now -- and this year the middle
stage will be going down in a club I know well. City of
our origins as a couple, D's and mine, my own personal
city No. 11, yes, toward which I can feel nothing right

now but grim shudders.)

I'm still coughing and running a fever. Even worse, I've been stuck all week in a catatonia of dispirit. Can't get a damn thing done. If I'm not reading something for distraction I'm obsessing about my sorry plight.

How sorry is it really? Guess I'll soon be finding out.

As on with a roar switches the wall heater. Action! The candle flame starts undulating a bit. This is a draft I neglected to shelter it from.

Even if I were feeling physically better I'd be holding forth right here tonight and feeling otherwise just as bad or even worse (since then I'd lack the excuse of physical illness). This is the way the year must close out and this is the place.

Among other sadnesses and disappointments of the week I didn't hear from Rikki and Mischa. So much for my admittedly feeble efforts to woo them. I have to wonder aloud (maybe not for the first time): just how unappealing have I become as a prospective mate? It must be pretty bad. And this when I'm about to regain my eligibility. Or in fact already have, though the fact is not yet widely known.

One jazz/jyze celebration after another pulsing from the radio. "Happy New Year, Central Time, Happy New Year!" (That would be Mentoka they're addressing, would it not? It would! Not to mention Gatewood and Centropolis, et al.: the whole dang JIFTy kaboodle.)

-- In theory, or in design anyway, tonight should be for looking back. "The Year in Jyze." But here in real time I'm finding any such effort would be too painful. Unendurable. Same's true just for plain old looking inward. And looking outward I see nothing. This candle, that kiri. Windows covered by curtains. The familiar jyze central setting. Wall of Japan books. Fluorescent light in the utility room shining through the cracks in the folding doors (which can't be locked, I'll note, so if the lady really wanted to slip into this room she could still do it, and I'm sure she's well

aware of the possibility and of course so am I -- not
that any of this means a whole lot).

Endure. How long can I hang on in this house? If
I had the money for it I'd move out immediately -- I
mean drop everything else (except scoping work, which I
can't afford to give up) and pack/move until I myself
dropped (at which point the plummet would hopefully be
into a whole new setting).

As a matter of fact I do have the money. In
theory. I could cash in the investment fund more or
less immediately (technically it's not mine until the
estate closes, but I could perhaps use it as a kind of
collateral), and I could live in a motel or hotel
temporarily while looking for a more permanent place.
It would be stupid but I could do it.

Oh how I'd love to do the stupid thing. Oh how
tempting it is.

(In a moment they'll be talking with bandleader X
-- whose name I didn't catch, nor did I want to catch it
-- talking about "the universal language of jazz." Or
of jyze, of course, as I'll now and forever more be
liable, and what's more pleased, to transpose it.)

Down to the real basics. The fundamentals. The
hard choices. The grim realities. The vicious truths.

-- And should I keep going with this? It's still
more than an hour and a half until our own midnight
ball-drop here in the jyzone. Maybe I should gnaw on
the question for a few minutes.

*   *

So I'm back. Thirty minutes of pacing and watering
the plants. Pleading with the patron and matron spirits
of jyze for help. Frank? (Relaxing those same rules.)
Walt? Jack? Sei? Henry? Herman? Leo? Virginia?
Shikibu? "Just" -- or no. Orphic silence is better.
("Just do as you must," I was about to have them groan,
the jyze spirits, Greek chorus like, but come to think
of it they didn't do that out there in the real world or
for that matter here in the world of supplicating jyzer
self, or at least not that I heard.) (Marina? Norman?
Fernando? Ralph? Junichiro? Yasunari? John? Samuel?

375

[Jyzemelt]

William? Richard? Brothers G? Chu-i? James? D.H.?
Fyodor? -- Same unpuzzling vatic opacity.)
     "The lad's beyond help" appears to be the verdict.
(Even Charles maintains a stone face. Mr. Banana Plant
too. Mr. Ten Foot Square Hut. Mr. Scribbler Kafu. Mr.
Kusamakura. Mr. Tsurezuregusa. All of them.)
     The city of our origins. I'm thinking. Go back
and start where I left off, but do it in the city here.
An eighteen-year detour -- "Try this kind of love." So
I tried it. Shrug. Fell asleep at the switch. The
years passed. Their number exactly matched the number
of years the young soon-to-be urjyzer lived at home in
Lahontan and city No. 2/7 and Gatewood, sequentially and
in that order, while being raised up. Now ol' Rip Van
Jyzer awakens to find the world vastly changed and his
own beard graying.
     Eek. Eking and eeking and eching and echting it
out, every last jot. And I'd just as soon not. None of
those ways. Lay this damnable year to rest. So long,
Mom -- year of your "chanson du swan." That I won't
forget and certainly wouldn't want to, its courage and
splendor as well as its heartbreak supreme. As for the
rest of the year -- be gone! And you, Lady U, love of
my life -- stay outta my sight! And you, jyzer self --
slide on around that corner into the year jyze three and
don't look back! -- Or at least not for a long, long
time.

                         END